He Drank, and Saw the Spider

ALEX BLEDSOE

He Drank, and Saw the Spider

AN EDDIE LaCROSSE NOVEL

TOR®

A Tom Doherty Associates Book
New York

This is a work of fiction. All of the characters, organizations, and events portrayed in this novel are either products of the author's imagination or are used fictitiously.

HE DRANK, AND SAW THE SPIDER

Copyright © 2013 by Alex Bledsoe

Map by Jon Lansberg

A Tor Book
Published by Tom Doherty Associates, LLC
175 Fifth Avenue
New York, NY 10010

www.tor-forge.com

Tor® is a registered trademark of Tom Doherty Associates, LLC.

Library of Congress Cataloging-in-Publication Data

Bledsoe, Alex.
    He Drank, and Saw the Spider: an Eddie LaCrosse novel / Alex
Bledsoe.
        p. cm.
    ISBN 978-0-7653-3414-5 (hardcover)
    ISBN 978-1-4668-0827-0 (e-book)
    I. Title.
PS3602.L456H4 2014
813'.6—dc23

                                                        2013025455

Tor books may be purchased for educational, business, or promotional use. For information on bulk purchases, please contact Macmillan Corporate and Premium Sales Department at 1-800-221-7945, extension 5442, or write specialmarkets@macmillan.com.

First Edition: January 2014

Printed in the United States of America

0 9 8 7 6 5 4 3 2 1

For Amelia
Welcome to your new kingdom.

SPECIAL THANKS

Joolz Denby
Tom Doherty
Paul Stevens
Marlene Stringer

and the members of Team Bardolator:

Deborah Blake
Emily Carding
Maya Chhabra
Kevin Coleman
Leslie Currier
Liz Gorinsky
Rachel Graves
Anthony F. Isbell
Melissa Olson
Elizabeth Russell Miller
Sarah Monette
Virginia Mason Vaughan
Miriam Weinberg

And as always,
Jake and Charlie

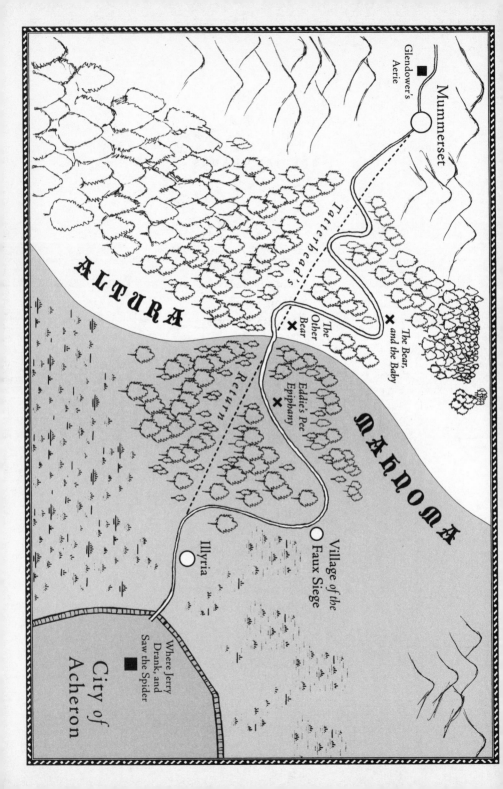

Part I Isidore

chapter
O N E

The battles had been hard, the gold had been scarce, and the company—other mercenaries like me, most of them older, all of them unsophisticated as bricks—had gotten on my nerves. So I deserted. Or, as we called it in the trade, "chose to pursue other opportunities." That was the whole point of hiring out your sword arm instead of actually joining an army, wasn't it?

I was a young man that summer: long-haired, beardless, and still hiding behind a mercenary's blade from the truth about myself and my past. There wasn't a tavern wench I hadn't known, a farm girl I hadn't tried to know, or a noble lady I hadn't considered getting to know. I drank often, ate whatever came my way, and took what I needed when no one was looking. I was Eddie LaCrosse, no longer Edward, the heir to the LaCrosse barony in Arentia, and I went where the wars were. Unless, of course, the war turned out to be boring.

And that's how I ended up in an Alturan forest just below the mountain foothills, minding my own business and pissing on a tree, when a man entered the clearing screaming and running for his life. A moment later he exited, pursued by a bear.

I fastened my pants and took off after him on foot, knowing my horse was useless in the undergrowth. Over the past sixteen years, I've often wondered why I did that. I was all business in those days, and business meant gold. I wanted to sign up with the Alturan army, then about to go to war with its neighbor Mahnoma and its paranoid king, Gerald. But instead of sticking to my plan, I ran to help a stranger without even a second thought. I suppose I believed there might be a reward for rescuing him. Yeah, that must've been it.

The man's screams and the bear's roars made them easy to find, but by the time I reached the top of a ridge and looked down into the little gully, it was too late: the bear had him. He lay beneath the beast, curled into a ball facedown on the ground, screaming as the great claws sliced into his unprotected back. The animal bellowed and snapped, trying to get a clean bite on the man's head.

No thought went into my next decision, either. I drew my sword, held it like a dagger, and jumped down onto the bear's back. I put all my weight and momentum behind the weapon, which struck the animal's shoulder blade, slid off the bone, and buried itself to the hilt in the furry body.

The bear was a monster, easily six hundred pounds and, when it reared up in response to my stab, twice as tall as me. It smelled of musk, mud, and bear shit, and its hair was slick and oily. I clamped my heels against its sides and clung on to the sword hilt with all the strength my terror suddenly gave me. The great claws swiped the air overheard, splattering me with blood and bits of the man's flesh.

"Run!" I yelled to the man on the ground, but he remained curled up, protecting his belly at the expense of his flayed-open back.

The bear stumbled backwards, still upright, and slammed

me into the nearest tree. Six hundred pounds in motion can do some serious slamming, and my lungs emptied under the pressure. Little flashes sparkled at the edge of my vision. My legs slipped free and flailed in the air. I knew if I lost my grip on my sword, I was done for, so I held on despite everything, twisting the hilt and wrenching the blade as much as possible in search of some vital organ.

"Run, will you?" I yelled again.

Finally I hit something essential, because with a combination roar and wheeze the bear fell forward and hit the ground. The impact tossed me over its shoulders into the leaves beside its victim. I lay there and waited for my lungs to refill. The bear did not move, which was good, because I was out of juice.

At last I could breathe, and got to my knees. "Dude, you need to—"

The man I'd failed to save was still alive, his eyes wide and staring, but the bubble of blood between his lips told me he wasn't good for long. I said, "Don't move. You're really hurt."

He rolled himself over onto his ragged back. I winced at how much of his insides fell out through wide gaps as he did so. I wasn't squeamish—I'd gutted my share of people—but there was something grotesque about it, and it made my stomach knot.

Faster than I would've thought possible in his condition, he grabbed my tunic and slapped the edge of a dagger against my neck. "Take . . . her . . . ," he said.

I looked down at the bundle now resting on his chest: the bundle that he'd given his liver and big loops of his intestines to protect. A bundle that was *moving*.

A tiny pink fist emerged.

A baby.

From inside the bundle came an annoyed, wailing cry.

The man's eyes met mine as he finished. ". . . somewhere safe!"

I knew I should at least pick up the child from his bloody chest, but I hesitated. Man-killing bears were one thing, but a baby was something far outside my experience. I had no brothers or sisters, and my friends back in Arentia were all about my own age. If they had infant siblings, we never had to deal with them. "Uhm, look, pal—," I started.

"Take her," he said, half-spoken and half-gurgled. He dropped the knife and tried to hand her to me, but he lacked the strength.

"Let's just get you patched up, okay?" I said quickly, knowing it was futile.

He shook his head. Now he was bleeding from his nostrils. Overhead, an opportunistic crow announced the man's imminent death to its murder-mates. "Please, save her, she's—" He sucked in a deep breath and his whole body went rigid from the waves of pain hitting all at once.

There was no escaping it, so I took the bundle with all the grace of a man fondling his worst enemy's testicles. I pulled back one corner of the blood-spattered blanket, revealing tiny pink feet. Then I reversed the bundle, opened that end, and saw the baby's small, rubbery features.

The man slapped another bundle into my hand. This one was smaller, with the distinctive metallic sound of coins. Then he gestured me close.

"Her name . . . is Isidore. Please save her."

"I will," I said; what else could I say?

"Take this," he said, and fumbled in the bloody folds of his clothes. "It proves . . . who she . . ."

He produced a small glass ball that glowed icy blue from inside. I'd never seen anything like it or, at that point in my life, anything I would accept as real, genuine magic. Because I was so startled, I didn't reach for it, and then the man's whole body spasmed with pain. The ball fell from his hand to the forest floor, where it burst like a soap bubble and turned into a fine, grayish powder that disappeared into the ground.

"Shit!" the man hissed between his teeth, blood spraying forth.

"Don't worry," I said quickly. "Your daughter will be safe."

"Not my . . . not mine . . . she belongs to . . ." Then he died.

I sat there beside him for a long time holding the tiny girl, who seemed quite content for the moment. She had wispy blond hair, big blue eyes, and fat cheeks. When I tickled her under her chin, she laughed, but I knew she'd need something to eat soon, and I was no wet nurse. How had her guardian managed? I checked and found a small ale-skin bag on his belt, and when I sniffed it it had the distinctive odor of milk.

I hated to leave him to the mercy of the forest scavengers, but I was sure he'd understand. The living took precedence over the dead, and the flies were already thick in the air. "There's a good girl, Isidore. Let's go get my horse, and then find you a home."

She cooed. And damn it, I fell in love a little.

SHE suckled eagerly at the ale-skin, which had a makeshift nipple affixed to the cap. Her little hands pushed on the sides, which told me she was used to being fed this way. There wasn't much left, though, and I didn't know how long I had before it went sour. I climbed onto my horse—not easy to do holding a baby—and headed for the road I'd crossed earlier. A road, after all, must lead to a town, and there I could dispose of my unwanted bundle of joy, even if I just left her on the doorstep of a moon priestess chapter house.

Her little face scrunched up in annoyance at the uneven ride, and my horse tossed his head angrily when I kept him from going very fast. "So, Isidore," I said to her as we moved along, "I take it you're from this area. What does a young lady do for fun around here?"

She looked at me seriously and farted.

I laughed. "Sometimes I do that, too, just to see what will happen."

She giggled and kicked her feet as if she understood.

The road was narrow, with barely room for a wagon to pass without scraping the tree trunks on either side. It told me there wasn't much regular traffic, probably only one-way travelers going and coming based on the farming cycles.

Finally we emerged into the clear area of the mountain foothills, and the road began a meandering climb. Here we were out in the open, and the fighter in me cringed at the vulnerability. Ahead I saw a small village nestled between two hills, and on the slopes shepherds drove herds toward the town. Like most people who spent time around horses, I had an instinctive aversion to mutton on the hoof. But since I had an absolute hatred for horses, I actually ended up not minding the sheep. So to speak.

"You belong to any of these people?" I asked Isidore. She refused to reply, being far more interested in chewing one blood-free corner of her blanket.

I heard music as I got closer to the village. Multiple pipers trilled in a cacophony of tunes, and Isidore began to cry at the noise. I awkwardly put her on my shoulder, stuck my reins in my teeth, and patted her on the back the way I'd seen nurses do when I was a child in Arentia. A moment too late I also remembered what I'd often seen as the result, as she threw up milk down my back.

I sighed. "You're not the first girl to puke on me, Isidore. But let's not make it a habit, okay?" I wiped her chin with my sleeve.

A circular stone wall surrounded the town. Eight feet high, it was a remnant from the days when the village needed protection from rampaging hordes very much like the one I'd just deserted. I say "remnant," because in places it had crumbled with age and never been repaired, meaning that large-scale violence was no longer an immediate danger. The wall sported four gates, one at each cardinal point, that could be closed, I assumed, but looked like they never were: the wood was old, rotted, and overgrown with the same vines that laced the stonework.

The town announced its name on a faded sign by the southern gate: *Mummerset*. The second *m* was arrowed in from above after the *u*. If this was the central town for a bunch of shepherds, I knew it would consist of mostly the various services needed by the mutton industry. People wouldn't live here; they'd have small farms out in the hills. I'd find a farrier, maybe a couple of weavers, a trading post for sundries, and most important of all, a tavern. If I was lucky, there'd also be a moon priestess chapter house, where those mysterious women who've taken a vow to answer need would take Isidore off my hands.

When I passed through the gate, I saw a considerable crowd ahead of me, jammed into the town's central courtyard.

Of course, I thought. It was close to the spring equinox, and therefore time for their festival. This was a standard celebration to mark the return of warm weather, the birth of babies, both human and animal, conceived during the long winter months, and to encourage the fertility of the land over the coming growing season with pageants, games, sacrifices, and other activities.

I smiled. "Other activities" to encourage fertility could mean a lot of fun for someone like me. If I could ditch my current minuscule girlfriend, of course.

I stopped at the first hitching post I found, outside a small building that displayed elaborate wool tapestries. Dismounting while holding a baby was more difficult than I expected, and I nearly dropped her. She began to cry, and an old lady in the shop shook her head at my ineptitude.

"She's not mine," I said defensively.

"That's what men always say."

Isidore was still fussing as I walked toward the town center. The crowd had gathered for a mass shearing competition, and the snip of cutters as they removed the wool was loud enough to compete with the pipers.

One man threw up his arms and shouted, "Sheared!" A cheer erupted. He was shirtless, soaked with sweat, and white bits of wool stuck to his torso so that he looked like some sort of were-sheep. The denuded animal before him was pulled aside, and another fully wooled one took its place. He bent to his task.

I stayed at the back of crowd, bouncing Isidore on my shoulder and taking in the scene. In addition to the musicians and competitors, there were many young ladies dressed in loose clothes, with ribbons in their hair and bells on their wrists and ankles. Some were also a little tipsy from whatever home brew they drank here. *Now, that's more like it,* I thought, as one saw me, smiled, and winked. Things were looking up.

Then Isidore cut loose with some truly epic cries. "Green isn't your color, short stuff," I said to her. I found a leaning spot out of the sun, took out the milk, and tried to feed her, but she wouldn't take it. I jostled her, none too gently, but that didn't help, either. I began to get annoyed.

Then a girl with bright red lips and blue smears over her eyelids stopped and said, a bit woozily, "You need to change her."

She was lovely, in a farm-stock sort of way, and one of her shoulder straps would not stay in place. "Into what?" I said.

She giggled. "Her diaper, silly. Don't you smell that?"

"I don't smell anything but sheep."

"Well, if you undo that blanket, I'll bet you find she's left you a gift."

I felt the same instinctive revulsion all men feel at the thought of handling dirty nappies. "Really?"

"Really. Don't you know how to change a diaper?"

"She's not actually mine."

"Oh, silly man, just accept it. A child is a miracle."

Before I could ask for actual help, she swirled off in a cloud of drunken lace and jingles. I looked down at Isidore, still crying, her face scrunched up like an angry red monkey. "All right, goddammit," I sighed. "Just give me time to find some help, will you?"

No one at the festival seemed the least bit interested in a strange blood-spattered man toting a fussy baby, a sight that I'm sure would've raised at least a few eyebrows any other day. I wandered through the crowd and tried to ignore the many young women while I sought an older one who might have some practical advice about my dilemma.

At last I spotted a tavern called the Head Boar. A middle-aged woman stood behind the bar wiping glasses, although there were no other patrons at the moment. I cleared my throat. "Excuse me."

She winced at a particularly loud squeal from Isidore. "That baby ain't happy."

"That makes two of us," I said.

"Where's her mama?"

"I have no idea. She's not mine."

"Denial is a coward's way out, son."

"No, seriously. I found her in the woods. There was a man with her, but a bear killed him. He died protecting her. This is the closest town, so I figured she was from here."

She looked me over. "Is that where the blood came from?"

"Yeah. I killed the bear."

Her skepticism returned. She looked me up and down. Even back then, I wasn't automatically intimidating. "*You* killed the bear?"

"Yes."

"Single-handedly?"

"No, I used both hands." Isidore shrieked again.

She thought it over. "Well, good on you, sir. Bears eat sheep, and sheep feed us, so we're always glad for fewer bears. My name's Audrey."

"Eddie. Pleasure to meet you."

She nodded at the baby. "Are you planning to just let her keep squalling?"

"A girl out there said she needs a diaper change."

"And?"

I held Isidore out to the woman and said, only half-joking, "Help?"

She laughed. "Give her here, then. Six kids and ten grand-kids out of me, I should know how to do this. Come here and I'll show you."

"No, I meant, you take her. Keep her yourself, or find her a home, I don't care."

"Oh, I'm too old to raise another baby," she said as she gathered Isidore into her arms. And damned if I didn't feel a jolt of mixed jealousy and possessiveness at the sight. She put the baby on the counter and began unwrapping the blanket.

"Where is everyone?" I asked, gesturing at the empty room.

"Outside, where the drinks are free. When the complemen-tary stuff runs out about nightfall, they'll come wandering in here willing to put down gold for even the worst stuff I've got." She held up her hand, which was now stained red from the bloody blanket. "Is this more bear blood?"

"That's probably from the man who died." I realized with a start that I hadn't checked *Isidore* for injuries. "Is she all right?"

"She's marinating in her own pee, but otherwise, yeah." She stopped as she was about the throw the blanket aside. "This is silk. This is *expensive*. No one from here would have a blanket like this. It's a bearing cloth for a squire's child, at least. What was this man like that you say you found her with? Did he look rich?"

"Hard to tell by the time the bear got through with him." I felt the weight of the gold bag on my belt, but didn't men-tion it.

She put the blanket aside, then sharply sucked in her breath.

"What?" I said, concerned.

"Who would do this to a *baby*?" she said, appalled.

She held her so I could see. Across her tiny back, someone had tattooed—on a baby!—an elaborate circular design. I didn't recognize it.

"Damn," I said.

"It must've been done right after she was born."

"That's . . ."

"'Awful' is the word you're looking for."

I knew a lot of organizations and societies used tattoos to mark alliances, relationships, even social castes. All of them, though, waited until youngsters reached puberty, or at least were walking around on their own. I knew of no group that marked its members this way from birth.

"Well, at least she doesn't seem to be suffering from it," Audrey said, and began work on the more pressing problem of the baby's wet bottom. "And she's definitely not a local girl. If anyone tried this on their children around here, they'd end up on the business end of a burdizzo."

"What's a burdizzo?"

"Keeps the male sheep under control. Works just as well on male shepherds."

"Ah. Well, she's a local girl now. See ya." I started for the door.

"You just wait right there, young man," she ordered. She'd already wiped Isidore clean and was fastening what looked like a dishrag around her. "This child may not have sprung from your loins, but that doesn't mean she's not your responsibility."

"Yes, it does," I insisted.

"*Look* at her. You want her to go back to the people who used her like a sheet of vellum? Who the hell's going to take care of her if you don't?"

"You?"

"I'm too old, I told you."

"Well . . . where's the nearest moon priestess?"

"Two weeks to the south," she said.

I raised my hands. "Look, this is not my problem. I've done my good deed, okay? Do whatever you want with her."

And that might've been it. That *should've* been it, and it would've been, if four grim men on horseback hadn't appeared outside the tavern and dismounted.

Experience told me they were trouble. Instinct told me they were trouble for *me*.

Two of them came into the tavern, while two stayed on guard outside. They all had the same haircut, which marked them as military despite their attempt at civilian disguise. But whose army? Not Altura; all their soldiers were gathered at the king's castle preparing for war, which was where I wanted to be, too. I'd hate it if they started without me.

Despite the noise from the festivities, the tavern seemed to grow silent, and the air thickened. I eased into a shadowy corner and stayed very still, waiting to see what would develop. It seemed unlikely they were Otsegan soldiers sent to retrieve me after I deserted, but you could never tell. Old Colonel Dunson didn't care for quitters at all.

The second man looked at me. The light was dim enough that he couldn't make out the blood splattered on my clothes or, more important, that I was armed. He nodded once to say, *I know you're there,* then resumed staring at whatever his boss looked at.

"Hey, barmaid," the first man snapped at Audrey. His attitude told me he was used to being obeyed, and having his questions immediately answered.

Audrey was equally used to not putting up with such nonsense. "When you talk to me like that, smile. Who are you?"

"I'm Arcite. *Mr.* Arcite. Remember that, if you know what's good for you. We're looking for a man carrying a baby."

"Men don't carry babies," she said. "They're not tough enough. Get your father to explain it to you."

The second man laughed. It was high and loud, like a donkey.

This was going to escalate fast, I realized. Arcite said, "Look, bitch, I've been here for five minutes and I'm already sick of the stink of sheep. So answer my goddamned question. Have you seen a man with a baby?"

"I dare you to say 'sick of the stink of sheep' three times fast," Audrey shot back.

I couldn't figure out why she was deliberately antagonizing this guy, until I suddenly noticed that Isidore had vanished from the bar. Where the hell had she gone? It's not like she could've gotten up and run off. Could she? I'd had so little experience with babies that I wasn't totally sure.

Arcite strode to the bar and slammed his hand on it. It sounded like the snap of a gallows trapdoor. "I don't like bitches who don't know their place. You're a fucking barmaid, and I'm a goddamned soldier. You better learn to respect that."

"And I don't like goddamned soldiers," she fired back without flinching. "You all act like serving your country gives you an asshole license."

"Well, tell you what, maybe I'll drag you out back and show you my battle lance, see if I can't change your mind." He turned to his henchman. "Strato, grab her."

I didn't want to get involved. Really, I didn't. I was still kicking myself for trying to save the guy from the bear. Nothing good ever came of sticking your nose—or whatever—in where it wasn't invited. But before I'd even made the conscious decision, I heard myself say, "Ease up there, pal. You're in the lady's bar, after all. Show some manners."

Arcite slowly turned to me, his eyebrows going up in a slow burn that would be hysterically funny if I lived to tell this story. "Look, sheep dip, if you don't want your insides handed to you, run back to your farm and stay out of what don't concern you."

" 'Doesn't,' " I corrected. "What *doesn't* concern me."

Now he gave me a look that said he was amazed I was so stupid. "Farm boy, I will end you so fast, your shadow will wonder where you've gone."

"That's a good one," I said. I realized he still couldn't see my sword belt in the shadows. "I'll have to remember that."

He strode toward me, intending to slap around the local boy, the soldier–civilian dynamic at work.

I calmly kicked him right in the balls. Much harder than I needed to, just because he pissed me off.

He folded like a battlefield observation chair.

Instantly I whirled to face Strato. I didn't go for my sword, and neither did he. His expression told me that Arcite had deserved this for a long time, and could get himself out of it.

I looked down at Arcite. He'd landed in a shaft of sun that came through the door, and his face was bright red. "My balls!" he squeaked.

I said, "You're not as tough as you think you are, and you're a terrible judge of people. It's probably better that you can't pass those traits along." Again I looked at Strato. "You got anything to say?"

"He holds a grudge," he said, but showed no inclination to continue the fight.

Arcite's eyes were watering now, but his hatred was unmistakable. I said, "Then maybe I should just gut him where he lays so I don't have to waste my time looking over my shoulder."

"Not in my tavern, you don't," Audrey said. There was still no sign, or sound, of Isidore.

"Your lucky day," I told Arcite. "Our hostess doesn't favor cleaning up a bloody mess." To Strato I said, "Who is this baby you're looking for? Why is she so important?"

"We don't know. Our commander told us to go find a man who'd run off with a baby. We picked up the trail and followed it to a dead man and a bear. Another trail led us here." He could see the blood on my clothes now, but didn't mention it.

"Looks like you made a wrong turn somewhere," I said.

"That's true." He put his fingers in his mouth and whistled. His two friends came in from outside.

Every muscle from my brain down to my fingertips strained to reach for my sword, but I held back. They didn't know how good I was, but I knew just as little about them.

"Arcite here opened his big mouth again," Strato said. "This time somebody closed it for him. Get him out of here and back on his horse."

Arcite whimpered as his compatriots grabbed him under the arms. They dragged him out with less care than I'd show a bag of potatoes. Guess they didn't like him any better than I did.

Strato casually saluted. "Enjoy the rest of your festival," he said, then followed the others outside.

When they were gone, I turned to the bar. "That was close. Where did you—?"

Audrey was gone.

I rushed behind the bar. There was no sign of Isidore, either. There was, however, a pile of dishrags on the floor with a baby-shaped indention, and beside it, another rag whose corner had been dipped in ale. It explained why Isidore kept quiet.

I couldn't explain the panic I felt. After all, getting rid of her was exactly what I wanted to do. But I ran out the back door into the street, looking around wildly for them, as if I'd lost some great treasure.

I slid in the mud created by years of tossed kitchen slop and slammed into the stone perimeter wall. To either side were the backs of other buildings, and all I could hear was the sound of the festival. She couldn't have gotten over the wall, so she must've gone into the crowd.

I ran around the corner toward the noise, smack-dab into a man painted entirely green down to his navel. He was also naked below the waist, trying to pull on a pair of green pantaloons.

"Whoa, there, youngster!" he said. He wore a kind of headgear made of bright green leaves and vines through which only his face peeked out. His beard was also stained green, and decorated with twigs and flowers. The odor of ale engulfed me as he said, "Take a deep breath and smell the flowers. The festival's just getting started; I haven't even yet made my grand entrance."

I tried to disentangle myself from his clumsy embrace. "Thanks, I appreciate that. Have you seen a lady with a baby?"

"Sure, she's right around the corner. But you shouldn't chase after her, there's plenty of young ladies just waiting to blossom tonight. Try one of them, why don't you?"

I didn't want to hurt him, but his grip was stronger than I expected. "I don't have time to—"

"Behold!" he bellowed in a full-throated theatrical way that made me jump. "I am the Green Man, I bring the coming of life after the dead time of winter! The time for sad tales is over!" Then he grinned. He'd even painted his teeth green. "'Coming of life,' get it? 'Coming'? And you, young man, let whatever drives you melt away with the winter's snow. This is the time for love, and frolicking, and frolicsome love!"

I wrenched loose and ran into the crowded central court. I hopped up on a wagon to get a better look, but saw no sign of

Audrey. When I climbed down, I grabbed the arm of the next person to pass me. "Excuse me," I said, "but have you seen a lady with a baby?"

It was a beautiful young woman holding a baby of her own. I guessed she was about seventeen or eighteen. She had soft blond hair in a braid down her back, and a gown that left her shoulders bare. Good shoulders were a particular weakness of mine. She looked me up and down, made a skeptical face, and asked, "Is this a trick question?"

"I'm sorry, not you. Another woman with a another baby."

"Your wife ran away, eh?" She touched a spot of blood on my tunic. "I don't blame her. You seem to be nasty."

I took her by the arms, careful not to jostle her grip on her infant, and said very deliberately, "Please, I'm looking for a woman from the tavern over there. Her name is Audrey. She has a baby with her. Have you seen her in the last few minutes?"

"Get your blood-nasty hands off me if you don't want to draw back two nubs," she snapped. "You might be able to bully your wife, but you damn sure can't handle me."

I was getting desperate. "This isn't her blood, it's from a bear. *Please,* can you help me?"

"Aren't you a little young for Audrey, anyway?"

I started to reply, but suddenly I felt a rush of what I could only call perspective. Not only was I too young for Audrey, I was too young to be running around like a headless chicken in search of a baby who was no doubt better off wherever she was than she'd be with me. Audrey had saved her from the bad guys and spirited her away; my job was done. It was like a weight came off, my misplaced idealism melting away just like the green man said. "You know what? Yeah, I am. Way too young. My name's Eddie. What's yours?"

"Beatrice."

"Beatrice, are you married?" Experience taught me that in

these isolated little towns, the presence of a baby did not always mean there was a husband, or even a boyfriend.

"I beg your pardon?"

I nodded at the baby. "If you are married, I apologize, but I'm new to town. If you're not with anyone, I'd really like your company."

"You're kidding, right?"

"No, not at all. For the rest of the day, and for however long you can put up with me tonight, I'd be honored to escort you." I smiled my best winning, totally harmless smile.

A teenage boy nearly knocked me into her as he ran past, pursued by a girl who seemed determined to hit him with a handful of flower petals from the basket on her arm. Another young man, far more sensible, stood nearby and let his girl shower the petals down on him. As they settled, he leaned in and kissed her.

Beatrice and I were very close now, looking into each other's eyes. Her annoyance began to crumble, but she wasn't an idiot. "How dumb do you think I am? You're covered in blood. You say it's bear blood, and I almost believe you. But it's still *blood*. And you think you can just swap one woman with a baby for another?"

It did sound a bit loopy, so as calmly as I could, I said, "I found a baby abandoned in the woods. I saved her from a bear. I gave her to Audrey to keep safe until somebody comes to claim her." That last bit was a stretch, but not a total lie. The next thing I said, though, surprised even me with its truthfulness. "I just wanted one last look at her before I left town."

"At Audrey?"

"At Isidore."

"Is that the baby's name?"

"Yeah."

"That's a boy's name around here."

"Well, it's her name, and she's definitely a girl."

She shifted her own baby to the other shoulder and continued to look at me, measuring me with the same level of scrutiny a commander might use in selecting someone for a suicide mission. She had a gorgeous way of thinking, and the way she pursed her lips while doing it implied that kissing her would be worth the wait.

One of the basket-bearing girls paused beside us, and Beatrice grabbed a handful of petals. She raised her hand over my head and showered them slowly down.

"Looks like I caught you," she said. "You're supposed to kiss me now."

So I did, leaning forward so we wouldn't pin the baby between us. And it *was* worth the wait. I decided that if she wanted to catch me again, I would not be hard to snare.

She said, "All right, then. One drink, and enough time for you to convince me you're not a dangerous lunatic. Let me get rid of my baby sister here."

"Oh! So this is—she's not—"

She laughed. "No, she's not my daughter. This is my sister Cassandra. One of four younger siblings, I should warn you. Follow me."

I did, admiring the way her skirt swayed with her walk. And everything would've been fine if I hadn't, completely accidentally, glanced at the face of the baby peeking over her shoulder, gazing back at me with that blank, pudgy baby look. Suddenly all I could see was Isidore's scrunched-up little face, looking at me with the open trust of someone helpless but safe under the protection of someone strong.

Then movement across the courtyard caught my eye. I gently stopped her and pointed. "Uh-oh. I should get out of sight."

Beatrice looked at the four soldiers, whose grim demeanor was in such contrast to the joviality around them. "Oh," she said. "They do look like trouble. Except for the one who's walking funny."

"No, he's trouble, too. I made him walk like that."

"Really? Good grief, how long have you been here?"

"I don't know. Maybe an hour?"

"If you stayed for a whole day, there wouldn't be a building left standing, would there?" She took my hand and said, "Come on."

She pulled me around the fringe of the crowd. I stayed low and tried to avoid attracting Arcite's attention. I guess my blow to the groin had not done as much damage as I thought; well, either that, or his target was a lot smaller than most, which also explained his attitude.

Flies and dust danced in the sunlight, stirred up by all the frolicking, stumbling folk cutting loose after a winter locked indoors with each other. Bits of clothing had been trampled underfoot; by nightfall, it would be crazed.

We reached a woman seated on an overturned basket, keeping a close eye on the containers of raw wool for sale in front of her. The family resemblance was clear even before Beatrice handed her the baby.

"Eddie, this is my mother, Bianca Glendower." Beatrice passed her the baby. "Here, Mom. She's fussing again."

Her mother, who had the same general look as Beatrice but with the signs of her difficult life, took the baby. As she undid her dress and let the child begin to nurse, she said, "And where are you from, young Eddie? I don't recognize you."

"He's some traveling ruffian who wants to pull me into a dark corner and do unspeakable things to me," Beatrice deadpanned.

"The man that gets *you* in a dark corner better be well armed and well rested," her mother said.

"Mom!" Beatrice cried in outrage.

"My daughter's strong-willed," Bianca said to me. "That's

spinster-bait around here. If she has any sense at all, she's looking for a husband while the men aren't thinking clearly."

"Don't pay any attention to her," Beatrice said dryly. "She's content with a view of sheep, rocks, and grass. She doesn't care that there's a world out there."

"I've seen the ocean, young lady," Bianca fired back. "And the great houses of Boscobel. I'm just content with my lot." To me she added, "And that's what drives her crazy."

Beatrice took my arm. "Come on, if we keep this up, I'll end up being sent to my room. Oh, that's if I *had* my own room," she added in annoyance.

I nodded to her mother, who grinned. "Get married if you want your own room!" she called after us.

When we were safely away, I stopped Beatrice and began, "Listen, before we—"

She kissed me the way I'd always wanted to be kissed, only I hadn't realized it until that moment. She smiled up at me, knowing exactly how good she was.

I waited for my head to stop spinning. "Wow. Okay, look, that was great and everything, but—"

"But?" she repeated in disbelief. "There's a 'but'?"

"I really want to find out what happened to Isidore. Look, everything I told you is true, it's just . . . I just want to make sure she's okay."

"You said she was with Audrey."

"I know."

"Then she's safe."

"But with those guys around—"

Beatrice rolled her eyes. "All right, come on. I'm pretty sure I know where Audrey took her."

We reached a barn with small flocks of sheep crammed into corrals around it. Beatrice knocked on the door.

A young boy opened it. "Hey, Beebee," he said.

"They call you, 'Beebee?' " I said.

"Yes, they do. You, however, may call me Beatrice. Or

'Miss Glendower' if you're nasty." We went inside. Beatrice asked, "Angus, did Audrey Fencinger bring a baby in here a few minutes ago?"

"Yeah," he said, and sneezed. "Man, I hate crib duty."

It was dark, and my eyes took a moment to adjust. Sunlight found every crack in the roof and western wall, making bright shafts outlined by dust and pollen. It was warm, and the smell of wool, manure, milk, and hay was overwhelming.

Beatrice squinted and said, "Audrey? Are you in here?"

"Nah, she just dropped off the baby and left. Said not to tell anyone."

"I see you listen as well as always. Which baby is it?"

"Hell if I know. She put it in a crib and vamoosed."

By then my eyes had adjusted enough to comprehend what was in the barn. The stalls were filled with cribs, and most of them held babies. To me they all looked identical. "Shit," I muttered.

"I'm just watching them until my sister gets back," Angus said defensively. "She had to go make out with Cletus Snow."

"Do you farm babies here?" I asked.

Beatrice said, "No, but a lot of the mothers are young, and the festival is their one chance to pretend they're still girls. So which one is she?"

I looked at enough of them to confirm that I couldn't tell them apart any better than Angus. Audrey understood the basic strategy of hiding in plain sight. "I don't know."

"Men," Beatrice said in annoyance.

I was about to mention the tattoo when someone pounded on the barn entrance. Arcite bellowed, "Open this goddamned door right now!"

I started to draw my sword, but felt a hand on my arm. Beatrice said, "You will *not* pull a weapon around all these babies."

I scowled at her, but she was right. Arcite's voice had already stirred up a few of them.

"Who is that?" Angus asked, scared.

"The big bad wolf," I said, "or as close as you ever want to get. Find somewhere to hide, and keep quiet."

Beatrice went to the door and opened it slightly. Through the gap I saw Arcite's grim, hateful face. She said in a whisper, "You do know we have sleeping children in here."

Arcite pushed her back and strode in like he owned the place. Just as in the tavern, I slid back into the shadows before his eyes adjusted. I looked around for Angus, but he had either hidden himself very well, or escaped through some unseen exit. For folks who lived and worked on wide-open hillsides, they were great at disappearing.

One of the babies began to cry in earnest. "That's good, tough guy," Beatrice said. "You scared a baby."

He grabbed her by the face, crushing her cheeks. "You better be scared, too, bitch. I'm tired of you country whores getting smart with me. I'm looking for a particular baby, one someone found outside of town and brought here to you dumb fucks. She has a tattoo on her back. If she's in here, give her to me now and I won't fuck you up any more."

I could tell Arcite enjoyed this, but Strato and his two compatriots looked uncomfortable as they filed in after him. Whatever their mission, they didn't like pushing women around and threatening children.

Strato closed the door and said, "Miss, I'm sorry about my friend. He got kicked in the balls and it put him in a bad mood."

She wrenched free of Arcite's grasp and glared at him with an intensity that could melt rock. "Don't you *dare* touch any of these children," she hissed.

Arcite laughed. "Bitch, you're just a bad judge of people. If you won't tell me which one she is, I'll kill *all* the little fuckers. After I deal with you." He went for his sword.

The thing about reflexes is that you don't know they've kicked in until they've moved you from one place to another. I had no memory of drawing my sword or jumping from the shadows, but Arcite's blade clanged against mine on its way to strike Beatrice. He looked as surprised as I did.

"There's a lot of things I'll stand by and let happen," I said, "but not killing nice girls or babies."

"You," he said softly; venom dripped from the word. "Oh, do I owe you some payback."

"Then let's take it outside," I said. Our blades quivered in the air, neither of us willing to admit the other's sword arm was stronger. Shivering sunlight reflected from them onto Beatrice's face. She did a good job hiding that she was scared to death.

"My friends are in the same outfit, farm boy. You know any-thing about military loyalty? That means if you take on one, you take on all. You think you can handle all four of us?"

He suddenly pushed his sword against mine, expecting the weak and inexperienced arm of a sheep farmer. My blade didn't move.

"I don't think I'll have to," I said, hoping to all the various gods that I'd read Strato right.

"Cut the heads off all the little bastards," Arcite ordered. "Now! Then we'll finish this fuck and his whore!"

None of his men moved.

"Did you hear me?" he yelled. He wanted to glare back at them, but knew better than to take his eyes off me.

"Sir," one of them said, "this is—"

"Wrong," Strato finished. "I didn't sign up to massacre babies in their cribs."

"You signed up to take orders, and I gave you one!" Arcite yelled.

"Do it yourself," Strato said. "We'll be outside. Guarding the perimeter."

They left without looking back. I kept my sword hard against Arcite's. There was the slight sound of metal rubbing against metal as neither of us committed to a move.

"You should leave, too," I said through the gap above our crossed blades. My arm was getting tired, so I knew his was as well. "I'm not one of these people. I'm more like you. This won't end well."

"I have a job from the king," he spat through his clenched teeth.

"King *Ellis*?" Beatrice said in outrage.

"No," Arcite said. "A *real* king."

"A king who wants a baby killed?" I said. "Sounds like something Crazy Jerry from Mahnoma would do."

Arcite laughed, but I couldn't tell if it was in confirmation or mockery at how wrong I was. "Now, get the fuck out of my way, or I'll make you watch while I add your girlfriend's head to the pile of baby skulls I'm about to make."

There was nothing for it. He was a soldier to the core, and he'd been given an order. I prepared to feint, then cut him down as fast and thoroughly as I could.

At that moment, the barn door slammed open. Audrey and a half dozen other women, along with Angus, burst through. In contrast to their festive clothes, ribbons and flowers, they simmered with maternal fury and carried farming implements that might not be actual weapons, but would still make a thorough mess of you. They leveled them at Arcite and me.

"You two scum just stay where you are," Audrey said. More babies began to cry. "Are the children okay?"

"They're fine," Beatrice said. "Just scared of all the noise."

I started to point out that I was one of the good guys, but at the moment it seemed prudent to remain silent. So prudent, in fact, that I knew Arcite couldn't possibly do it.

He laughed: cocky, mocking, and stupid. "Look at this, a whole herd of bleating, sheepherding whores. You think I'm afraid of pitchforks and scythes?"

You should be, I thought but didn't say. *You should be more afraid of the look in their eyes.*

Abruptly he drew up one knee, put his foot against my midsection, and kicked me away. I stumbled back into a bale of hay, and it took every bit of self-control not to jump up and attack again.

He yelled, a cry that would freeze the blood on the battle-field.

The women didn't flinch. One threw a pitchfork, javelin style, at him. He tried to knock it away, and did divert it a little, but one tine impaled his sword arm.

He shrieked in pain and dropped his weapon. The weight of the pitchfork pulled him off balance, and he fell. He let out another shriek, but not before the women surrounded him and began hacking. His cry was cut off in the middle.

Each of the women struck no more than twice. But it was enough. When they stepped back, he looked like a child's doll ground between millstones.

Then they all turned to me.

I put down my own sword and raised my hands. "I'm on your side," I said. "Audrey, Beatrice, I could use some kind words here."

"He is," Beatrice said, and stepped in front of me. "He brought the little girl here so she'd be safe."

"That's true," Audrey said, Arcite's blood dripping from her sharp-edged hoe.

I really worried they wouldn't listen. The sunlight through the cracks sparkled on eyes maddened by righteous anger. They were amateurs, I could take most of them down, but I knew I wouldn't strike a blow. If this was my time, I could accept it.

Fortunately they lowered their implements. I retrieved my sword and put it back in its scabbard. My heart continued to test the tensile strength of my ribs.

"Which one is she?" Beatrice asked.

"Right here," Audrey said, and picked up one of the squalling babies.

My heart pounded in a whole different way when I saw her tiny mouth expressing her disapproval at the top of her lungs. Audrey handed her to Beatrice, who shushed her expertly. The other women put down their weapons and went to calm the rest of the children.

I looked at Angus. "Smart to go get reinforcements. Why didn't you get men, though?"

"They're all drunk. Besides, nothing's meaner than an angry mom."

"Good point. Did you see where those other soldiers went?"

"To the tavern," he said. "I guess they're waiting for their general to come back."

I turned to Beatrice. Over the top of Isidore's head, I said,

"You should probably do something about the body and all the blood. I'm going to deal with his friends."

"But why? They didn't—"

"No, they didn't. But they're still highly trained enemy soldiers in a foreign country on a mission. I'm going to make sure they don't complete it."

"You'll kill them?" Audrey said. She carried two more babies, one in each arm, and jostled them gently to calm them down. "In my tavern?"

"If I have to. I'll try not to," I added defensively. "I'm not the one who killed *him*, you know."

"I know," Beatrice said, then stepped close to kiss me. It was the kind of kiss I felt in my scabbard. She said, "Come find me when you're done," and nipped my lip.

Outside the sun was sliding low in the west. I found Strato leaning against a post outside the tavern, watching his two fellow soldiers dance in a complicated line with several attractive young women.

He saw me as I approached, and moved nothing but his eyes. When I was within earshot he asked, "If you're here with all your limbs and manly parts, I assume you killed Colonel Arcite?"

"Yeah," I said. I wasn't stealing the credit for myself; I wanted to minimize the chance of a reprisal raid against the town. "Where does that leave us?"

"We didn't exactly volunteer for this job," he said. "We were in prison for desertion, and they gave us the choice of this or the gallows."

"And what happens when you go back and say you couldn't find her?"

He smiled, very slightly. "Who says we didn't find her? That bear was pretty thorough. Not only killed the child and the man with her, but Colonel Arcite as well. Gave his life to save the rest of us. He'll get a banner in Warriors' Hall."

I didn't want to trust him. I didn't even know him. But I

had little choice. I wasn't yet the judge of character I'd become later, but I was pretty good. I nodded and said, "So you'll be heading back to . . . ?"

"Our unit," he said, ignoring my lead. His origin would remain a secret. "Once my friends get a little rambunctiousness out of their systems. Not a lot of pretty girls in prison."

I watched the other two men dance. They looked happy as children, as did the girls they danced with. This was as safe a resolution as I was likely to get without killing them and disposing of the bodies, which truthfully I lacked the resolve to do without more provocation. So I gave him the same half salute he gave me earlier, and left them to their gambols.

When I got back to the barn, most of the babies had been taken away, along with Arcite's body. Fresh hay covered the bloody ground where he died. Angus and a teenage girl, whom I took to be his AWOL sister, whisper-argued in the corner about who was going to get in the most trouble.

Audrey fed one baby from a wineskin, and Beatrice sat on a hay bale with Isidore asleep in her arms. She put a finger to her lip as I approached.

"How is she?" I whispered.

"See for yourself," she said, and before I could react, she put Isidore in my arms. I lay her on my shoulder, but she began to fuss. "Shhh," I said, trying to lightly bounce her.

"She likes singing," Beatrice said, amused.

"Then sing," I said.

She shook her head and gestured that it was up to me. Her smile was mischievous, and irresistible.

I tried to remember any of the dignified songs I'd learned as a child, songs of courtly love and noble deeds. They all fled my memory. At that moment I could, in fact, remember only one song, so I sang it as softly as I could.

She fell upon her back with her feet up in the air,
I knelt between her thighs and admired all her hair,

You're quite the fuzzy lass, I told her as I dove
Into the furry gate and along her soft pink road. . . .

The afternoon sun blazing through the slats in the wall was
tinted a bright amber, which hopefully hid my blush. Beatrice
snickered and tried very hard not to laugh out loud. But Isidore
contentedly cooed.

Then Audrey, with the baby she'd just fed on her shoulder,
softly chimed in:

She said, "I like the furry gate between my lovely thighs,
It keeps me warm in winter when winds begin to rise
Soft as gray goose down it is, a comfort for your head
And none who have embraced it have ever fled my bed."

She winked at me. Her baby burped, on beat. We all laughed
as quietly as we could. Isidore wriggled close to me.

chapter

FOUR

I t was dark by the time the last baby had been taken home. The music from outside had grown more rambunctious, and some of the lyrics were so raunchy, they put my own lullaby to shame. But I had no desire to join them: I was content staying in the barn with Beatrice, cuddling Isidore while she slept and stealing kisses like the young courtier I'd once been.

Strato and his men kept their word and left town. I wondered how their story would play with their superiors. I hoped they didn't end up back in prison, but so often in the military, no good deed went unpunished.

Audrey returned to close down the nursery and prepare it for the next day. She folded blankets and arranged the cribs in neat rows. "Nice to see a happy family," she said to us.

"The baby's not mine," I reminded her.

She laughed and indicated the way Isidore slept in my arms. "Maybe not by birth, maybe not by blood. But a parent claims a child by love, nothing else."

I looked at Beatrice. "Seriously, I can't take care of her. I'm a mercenary, for God's sake."

"You could change," she said, and the invitation in her eyes was grown-up and serious. "You might find living here more adventurous than you think."

I remembered Janet, the girl I'd loved and lost far too young, and shook my head. "No. I can't. I need you to help me find someone to take her in."

Beatrice continued to look at me, as if hoping her steady gaze would batter down my defenses. She got closer than anyone had, but the blood on my hands, both metaphorical and, at that moment, literal, was too thick and too dear for even the cleanest love to wash away. At last she looked down in defeat and said, "All right. I know someone. They have so many kids, one more won't make a difference. Bring her along."

"Have a good evening, you two," Audrey called after us. She seemed totally unaffected by the violence she'd earlier helped mete out.

We emerged from the barn just as the crowd in the courtyard filed out through one of the wall gates, making a singing, chanting line up the hill toward a huge pile of wood. It must've taken a while to gather all that from the forest and lug it up here. I remembered one town where, at just this time of year, a human sacrifice was placed inside a big wooden idol and burned alive, to ensure the coming year's fertility. Fortunately this group seemed far more laid back.

"Want to go to the bonfire?" Beatrice asked. "There'll be dancing. Sometimes clothes come off."

"No, Beebee," I said seriously. "I want to make sure Isidore is okay."

"You're the first person who called me that, that I haven't wanted to punch. Come on, then."

"I have a horse. We could ride."

"On a night like this?" She laughed and took my free hand.

We went out a different gate and followed the narrow road across the hills. The sky was magnificent, a wide umbrella of stars with a bright moon in the east. Its light, now that my eyes had adjusted, was brighter than some overcast days. The breeze was just cool enough to be comfortable, and once we left town, the sheep corrals were thankfully downwind.

A cheer went up from the distant hill as the bonfire blazed to life. Shadowy forms danced around it, and their songs faintly reached us. It had a powerful tug, all right: the lure of a home always did to the deliberately homeless. And the woman beside me certainly added to the allure.

Beatrice took my arm, careful not to jostle Isidore. "It's like this a lot, you know. We work hard, but we always remember to play. And pretty much no one ever dies violently. You sure that doesn't appeal to you?"

I guess she didn't know about the impending war. I saw no reason to mention it; its effects might never reach Mummerset. "You just met me."

"Yeah, but I'm a good judge of people."

"I hope I am someday."

"Just trust people to be who they are. If you pick up a viper and it bites you, it's not the viper's fault, is it?"

"I'll remember that."

"Remember this, too." She moved in front of me and, when I stopped, leaned up to kiss me. This was totally different from the fun, almost joking kisses we'd exchanged in the barn. This was a solemn promise kiss, an offering of far more than soft lips on a warm night. She slid one hand along my cheek, her palm warm and soft against my stubble. When she stepped back to look at me, it was with the serious expression of a woman quite aware of what she was pledging.

I was speechless. In her sleep, Isidore let out a sigh of contentment.

"Well, at least *she* liked it," Beatrice said wryly.

"Oh, I liked it, too," I said.

"But not enough?"

"That's asking a lot of a kiss." .

"There's more, don't worry. But first let's get this little girl to her new home."

We continued on across the hills. The windows of several isolated cottages were visible, lit by lamps and hearth fires within, and it was quickly clear which one was our destination. One small corral held three ponies, another a flock of recently shorn sheep. A dog barked and ran to meet us.

The dog jumped up and began licking Beatrice's face. "Get down, Varro," she said, but didn't mean it. "Behave, or you'll sleep outside."

Suddenly I understood where we were. "This is your place, then?"

"My family's. I still live here because, as my mother likes to advertise, I'm not married. And my mom just had a baby three months ago, about the same time this little angel entered the world, if I'm any judge of such things. So Mom can wet-nurse her."

"How will she take it?"

"Isidore? She'll be fine with it. Wait and see."

"I meant your mom."

"I'm not giving her to my mom."

"Well, then who—?" Suddenly I got it. "You?"

"Just come on."

She opened the door without knocking. It was a small dwelling, but there were sleeping lofts overhead and a separate bedroom for the parents, which made it practically a manor house for this area. The stone floor was swept clean, and something truly savory simmered on the hearth. I realized I hadn't eaten since breakfast.

Beatrice's mother sat by the fireplace, mending someone's clothes. The amber firelight took years off her demeanor, and she looked more like Beatrice's sister than like her mother. "You're not at the bonfire," she said.

"Nothing gets past you, does it, Mom?" Beatrice said as she closed the door behind us.

Bianca turned to me. "And that, good sir, is the mouth that's kept her unmarried." She looked me up and down. "We don't allow swords in this house, young man."

"For God's sake, Mom," Beatrice sighed.

"No, that's fine," I said. With my baby-free hand, I unbuckled my sword belt and propped it against the wall outside the door. I felt surprisingly okay without it, a sensation that I hadn't experienced in a long time. Then I bowed as much as I could holding Isidore. "Pleasure to see you again, ma'am."

"Good grief, this one has manners," Bianca said. "I knew you'd be running about with some lad or other tonight, but I'd assumed it would be that nice Kellington boy."

"That nice Kellington boy isn't as nice as you think," Beatrice said. "Especially when he gets you alone down in a dark gully. Besides, this was an emergency."

Bianca looked at Isidore. "So is this the little one who caused all the commotion today?"

"This is her. Isidore." I added, "She's not mine."

"Imagine a man saying *that*," she said with a laugh.

"She's mine," Beatrice said.

Bianca's eyes opened wide. "Really? Your baby sister Cassandra is no older than this one."

"I know. You can nurse them both. I'll handle everything else. Just like you'll have me doing with Cassandra, anyway."

Bianca put aside her sewing, stood, and reached out for Isidore. I handed her over. She fussed a little at the change of hands, but Bianca quickly shushed her. "How will you explain this to everyone?" Bianca asked. "Especially to Kurt Kellington?"

"It's nobody's damn business, especially Kurt Kellington's," Beatrice said. "And if it comes down to it, I'll simply tell the truth: She was abandoned at the festival, and I took her in."

Bianca looked at me. "Is that how you want it?"

"I want her to have a good home," I said.

"And if she's not yours, then what is it to you whether she does or not?"

I explained where and how I'd found her, but did not mention the bag of gold or the strange, glowing blue ball. I also told about the men hunting her. When I finished, Bianca said, "And you expecting me to risk my family for this girl? What if more soldiers come looking for her?"

"Mama," Beatrice said sharply. "She's a baby. None of this is her fault."

"And that'll be small comfort when we're all skeletons on the floor of this burned-down cottage. You think it's fair to put your brothers and sister in this kind of danger?"

"There's no danger," I said. "Word will get back to whoever sent the soldiers that Isidore died in the bear attack."

"Isidore?" Bianca repeated. "I thought you said this was a girl."

"You can name her whatever you want," I said.

"And so you think you can trust a soldier to keep his word? Are you naive or just an idiot?"

I smiled. It was clear where Beatrice got her spunk. "I don't blame you for being skeptical, ma'am. But I know soldiers, and I know when one's telling me the truth. He didn't realize they were being sent to murder a baby, and he didn't like it when he found out."

Before Bianca could reply, the front door opened and a man entered. He had big arms, a barrel chest, and a long beard littered with bits of hay and wool. He said, "Both those worthless sons of mine are off chasing girls at the bonfire, not a one left to help tend the animals. I swear I'll—" He stopped, blinked at me, and said, "You're not one of mine."

"No, sir," I agreed.

"Is that your sword propped by the door?"

"Yes, sir."

"This is Eddie," Beatrice said. "He's with me."

Her father's eyes slowly opened wide. With genuine, delighted surprise, he said, "You have a boyfriend?"

Beatrice closed her eyes and blushed a little. "Dad, you're embarrassing me."

"As if having a grown daughter still living at home isn't embarrassing to me," he said. He kissed Bianca's cheek and started to tickle Isidore beneath her chin. "Hey, wait," he said. "This isn't Cassandra."

"She's mine," Beatrice said, and put her hands on her hips.

He looked at her. "Daughter, I may miss a lot, but I *know* I haven't missed that."

To save time, I gave her father the quick version of events. He took it all in without changing expression. When I finished he said, "Well, that's quite the tale."

"It's the truth, sir."

"I hate to say that a man with such manners is a liar, but you'll admit it strains belief."

"I can take you to the dead man and the bear if you want."

"No, I'll not be traipsing through the Harm's Wood at night, even with a man with a sword. I'll take your word for it. But I can't take on another mouth to—"

"Yes, we can," Beatrice said. "I want this. She'll grow up as one of us, never knowing any of this, unless one of us tells her. And we won't, will we?"

Bianca and her husband exchanged a look. I sensed that whatever else they might think, they did love their spirited oldest daughter and hated to deny her anything. At last the man said, "Well, I suppose one more girl underfoot won't matter. Give Cassandra someone to play with. She'll have to do her part around the farm, you know."

"I know," Beatrice said.

Isidore began to fuss, and Bianca said, "Let's see if she takes to my milk. If she doesn't, this is all for nothing." But the baby nursed contentedly, cooing and sighing as she filled her little tummy.

I suddenly felt claustrophobic, as if the cottage was shrinking around me. It was nothing physical, of course; it was just that Isidore had been taken into the family, and I was now on the outside looking in.

Bianca stood, Isidore on her shoulder. "Come along, Beebee, let's fix up a crib for her. We have to change that name, though. Might as well name her David or Robert. . . ."

They went into the bedroom and closed the door.

The father put out his hand. "Owen Glendower."

"Eddie LaCrosse."

"Pleasure to meet you. Why don't we step outside while the womenfolk tend to women's business?"

"I heard that," Beatrice called from the bedroom. Isidore began to cry. "It's only women's business because you men don't have the balls to do it."

Glendower rolled his eyes. "That girl," he said, as if it explained everything.

I followed him out, retrieving my sword on the way. He steered me far enough away from the house that we wouldn't be overheard. In the distance we could just make out the tunes around the bonfire.

We stood together silently for a long time. It might've made other men nervous, but even then, I was very good at waiting. I knew he was deciding whether or not to kill me, and I seriously hoped he didn't try, though not from fear. I liked him, I liked his daughter and his wife, and I didn't want to spill his blood.

At last he said, "You got the eyes of a killer, lad. You earn your keep with that blade. I'm not often mistaken about such things."

"You're not this time, either," I agreed. "I'll be leaving soon, though, so don't worry."

"And yet you come bearing a child."

"I haven't always been a hired sword. Once I was a human being."

He laughed at that. "Well, young sir, I think you did the right thing. Bianca may holler and fuss, but truly, the young lass will be no real burden. We'll raise her as we have our others."

"Based on Beatrice, I'd say you'd done a good job."

"I don't know. Might have been better if that one had been born a man."

"Well, *I* don't think so."

He laughed again.

And then, for no good reason that I've ever been able to determine, I held out the bag of gold. "Isidore also had this with her."

He felt the weight and whistled. "Lad, that's the feel of a fortune."

"If it is, it's hers, not mine."

"I may have been too hasty in my judgment of you."

"No, you weren't. You had me pegged. Just make sure she never knows this isn't her home."

"Take it to my grave."

"Thanks." I turned to walk away, back toward Mummerset and my horse. The war I came to join was still waiting for me.

"I think Beatrice expects to see you," Glendower said.

"It's probably better if she doesn't. She's more persuasive than you think, and I'm not made of iron."

"She also has a temper."

"I bet. But I have to get somewhere where people aren't as nice as you folks before I forget who I am."

"Best of luck to you, then. Will you ever pass this way again?"

"Seems unlikely." And with that, I walked away into the night. And what I said about returning was true . . . for sixteen years.

Part II Isadora

chapter

FIVE

Sixteen years later . . .

You've met a lot of kings, haven't you?" my girlfriend, Liz, said as she drove her delivery wagon toward Acheron, the capital of Mahnoma. She was about my age, mature but in no way old, and had grown her short red hair out to her shoulders over the winter. Now, in spring, it made her look positively girlish, especially when the wind tickled the loose strands around her face.

"I've met a few," I agreed. My boyhood friend Phil, also known as Crown Prince Philip, now ruled Arentia. I'd known the legendary King Marcus Drake in the days before his legend collapsed around him. And I'd crossed paths with others, often in my capacity as a private sword jockey. Even the most powerful, it seemed, had dirty laundry and closeted skeletons.

"I've never met one," Liz said. "What's it like?"

"They're just people. The good ones know there's no real difference between them and us."

"And the bad ones?"

"They believe there is."

I sat in the passenger seat of Liz's biggest delivery wagon, the one with the high sides and the wooden top that could be bolted down and secured with locks. Fully assembled as it was now, it was like hauling a big wooden box down the road, and inside could be anything from a hay bale to a five-man death squad. In this case, though, it was something in the middle, a package sent up the Gusay River from the ocean and now delivered overland by Dumont Delivery and Courier Service, Liz Dumont head cook and tankard washer.

We reached the gate into Acheron. The arch itself had collapsed and gone unrepaired, while the stones lay beside the road, overgrown with weeds. The three guards seemed very unconcerned with us at first, content to continue whatever game they were playing on one of the fallen rocks. We were almost through, in fact, before one of them called, "Whoa, hold it, you two."

He got up from the card game, spit at the ground, and walked over to our wagon. Other people, on foot and horseback, passed us in both directions without comment. The guard's uniform was dirty and didn't fit; it occurred to me it might not even belong to him. He scratched under his chin and said, "In Mahnoma, you want to go for a stroll, you have to pay the toll."

"There's nothing on the sign about a toll," Liz said.

The guard smiled. It was one of those vicious little smiles petty men enjoy when they think they're about to bully someone. "I don't care what the *sign* says, Little Red, *I* say you have to pay."

"What about them?" she said, indicating the passing traffic.

"They're not your concern," he said. He glared at me, the kind of tough-guy look that was supposed to terrify me into silence. I let him think it had. He said, "What's in the wagon?"

"Delivery for the palace," Liz said.

"Really?" he said with a laugh. "A little number like you has something for Crazy Jerry? What is it?"

She smiled. "Nunya."

"What's 'nunya'?" the guard asked.

She smiled even wider. "Nunya business. That's as much of an answer as you're going to get. And as much of a toll."

The other two guards stood up now. I was absolutely certain they weren't official Mahnoman troops, just petty criminals who'd found an easy scam. Apparently the chaos I'd heard about was true, because no one else even looked our way.

"Sweetheart, you don't want to make us mad," the guard beside us said. "We can hurt you more ways than you know."

"Aw, you called me 'sweetheart.'" Then she slashed him across the face with the ends up the reins. He yelled in pain, but before he could respond, she kicked him under the jaw with the point of her boot. She'd taken a hint from me and put metal caps in the toes, and I heard the man's jawbone crack from the impact.

I stood up and leveled a crossbow at the other two. They'd been so busy watching Liz, they hadn't seen me get it ready. Morons.

"You can only shoot one of us," the nearest of the two said.

"You're right," I said. "Who's it going to be?"

That stopped them. Grinning boy writhed on the ground, his hands to his shattered jaw. Liz calmly gathered the reins, sat down, and urged the horses forward. I kept the crossbow on the other two until we were far enough down the street, we were lost in the crowd. If anyone else noticed, or cared about, what had happened, they gave no indication.

"A free-for-all kind of place," Liz said at last.

"Those can be the most fun," I said. "If you know how to handle yourself."

"I'll watch out for you," she said with a wink. "Don't worry your pretty little head about it."

The castle of King Gerald in Acheron wasn't as big as the one I knew best, Phil's palace in Arentia City. For that matter, nothing about Mahnoma was as big, or as elaborate, as Arentia. But it provided a central location for all the kingdom's power brokers, as well as any outside interests hoping to gather influence. That kept them off the streets, if nothing else.

The day's market was set up at the castle's main drawbridge, and highborn nobles mixed with the common folk to peruse food, jewelry, and assorted other acquirables. They didn't actually buy anything, of course; that task was for servants sent back later. An elaborate language of verbal cues and hand gestures assured that whatever Lord and Lady Whozits selected would be there when their lackey returned, and if the price had mysteriously risen, well, that was the cost of doing business.

"Have you ever met Crazy Jerry?" Liz asked.

"King Gerald? No. I almost joined the army over in Altura to fight him once, back in my mercenary days. But the war got averted at the last minute." I snorted in mock contempt. "Imagine stopping a perfectly good armed conflict just in the nick of time to save thousands of civilian casualties."

"I'm sorry for your loss," Liz teased with a straight face.

"And I don't think we'll meet him today. From the stories I hear, he doesn't have much contact with anyone. He even sits in his throne room behind a screen and issues his edicts."

"Then how do people know it's really him?"

I grinned. "Now you sound like me. I don't know, and unless someone wants to drop twenty-five gold pieces a day plus expenses into my money bag, I don't really care."

We showed our paperwork to one of the drawbridge guards, and he indicated a service drive that went around one huge, featureless defensive wall. A farmer's cart approached us on it, empty of whatever produce the castle chef had ordered.

"You ever been here before?" the guard asked Liz. He was

an older man, with cropped military hair and a worn but well-maintained uniform.

"No," Liz said. "Why?"

His concern sounded genuine. "Mahnoma has a lot of problems right now. Just do your job and get back on the road, okay? You're safe enough this close to the palace, but out in the city, well . . . you're a pretty girl and you might not be."

"Not be pretty?" she deadpanned.

"Not be safe," he said, ignoring her humor. He looked me up and down with disdain. "Even with your hired muscle over there. It's one thing to just *look* tough, it's a whole other when you're surrounded by bandits."

"A whole other what?" she asked.

"Thing." At last he caught on that she making light of him, and smiled wryly. "Ah. Well, forewarned is forearmed, right?"

We drove past him, and Liz said, "You're supposed to look so scary that people don't start trouble. I don't think you're doing it right."

"I'm not the sharpest sword in the scabbard," I agreed.

"Is that how you get out of things? By just agreeing instead of arguing?"

"I just assume you're always right. You're my compass, baby, always pointing to true north."

"But it's so much more fun when *you* point north," she said. We both laughed.

The empty wagon passed us, and we let the horses walk down the road beside the wall. "Wow," Liz said, looking up at the featureless stone, now marred with elaborate graffiti up to a height of about eight feet. If anyone cared to clean it off, they hadn't made much progress. Most of the designs were gang symbols, part of the criminal underworld that flourished under the lackadaisical rule of Crazy Jerry. "You really grew up in one of these?"

"No, my best friend grew up in one. I only played in it. We had a manor house a couple of miles away." And acres of land,

and tenant farmers, and a whole lot of other things my father considered essential, and that kept him simmering in annoyance from morning to night. He never mastered the idea of trusting people to do their jobs.

"But you did have free run of the palace, right?"

"Pretty much. Phil was the crown prince, and he could always pull rank on the servants or guards. There were a few people we had to avoid, but for the most part we could do what we wanted." Truthfully, our only nemesis was Emerson Wentrobe, the king's chamberlain, but after I grew up I realized he'd looked on it as a game the same way we did. When he did catch us dead to rights, he usually kept silent after extracting our promise not to do it again. And we didn't—we moved on to some brand-new mischief.

"I just can't imagine," Liz said. She shielded her eyes and looked up at the spires behind the wall, where the actual castle rose. We were too close to see more than the very tops, but we'd had a good look on the drive in. It made me smile; Phil and I always said you could tell the country folks in Arentia City because they kept rubbing their necks, which were sore from looking up. Apparently that was true everywhere.

"Your house wasn't this big, I take it?" I said.

"Ha. Hardly. Five rooms, and two of those were in the cellar. Stone floors, floppy shutters on the windows, and in the winter we shared space with the milk cow."

"But you were happy there?"

"Most of the time, yeah. Were you?"

I thought, *Up until that horrible day when Janet died and I should have, yes.* "Most of the time," I agreed.

By now Liz knew me well enough to understand the distance in my voice. She put her hand on mine and said, "Sorry, Eddie. Didn't mean to bring her up."

I lifted her hand and kissed the back of it. "No problem," I said, and smiled. "Just a passing cloud, not a storm."

We reached the service entrance. Two guards in fancy livery stood at the warehouse gate, which was big enough to drive wagons through. They held extra-long lances in their velvet-gloved hands. Unless the men were very good, those lances were too unwieldy to be anything more than expensive decorations. But it was important to put on a show, too. If there was a gap in the castle's security, it wasn't likely to be so obvious.

They also checked our paperwork. "Clean up after your horses," one admonished before letting us inside. "The warehouse steward will take care of you."

The door opened into part of a big central warehouse where the castle's supplies were kept on carefully labeled floor-to-ceiling shelves. I idly wondered what they stocked on the top shelves, reachable only by ladder.

The two horses' steps echoed off the stone walls until Liz gently pulled the reins and murmured, "Whoa." The door closed behind us.

The steward approached, one of those efficient little toads that liked to rule over his petty kingdom of spare tables and curtains. He reached us just as we climbed down from the wagon's seat.

"And what do we have in here, hm?" he asked in a tight, superior voice.

"Liz Dumont, Dumont Delivery and Courier Service," she said.

"I did not say *whom*, I said *what*," he said down his nose.

Liz's eyebrows rose at his tone, but she stayed professional. "A set of Benvolian dining dishes."

"Is that right? I suppose you've taken them out and inspected them, then? You're an expert on Benvolian tableware?" He turned his attention to me. "And who are you?"

"I'm security," I said with a genial grin. "Oh, wait, you asked who, not what. My name's Eddie."

"You could use a haircut," he said dismissively, "and a shave, especially if you plan to make this a career. Couriers often meet their betters, and should dress and groom accordingly."

I just continued to smile. Liz did not need my help with middle men like this one.

"Hey," Liz said, and snapped her fingers in his face. "You don't deal with him. You deal with me. I'm the courier."

"Oh, a redheaded spitfire, how original," he said disdainfully. "Open up, then, and let me peruse these wonders."

Liz unlocked the back of the wagon and dropped the tailgate, which also served as a loading ramp. It made a loud, echoey *thud* against the warehouse floor. In the bed were three wooden boxes, each filled with dishes padded by silk. Around the boxes, protecting them from damage, was a thick carpet of packed hay. The steward pulled one of the boxes roughly toward him, scowling at both the effort and the puff of hay dust.

"Whoa, be careful," Liz said. "Those things are fragile."

"I'm certain they are," he said. He opened the lid and pulled out one of the plates.

"See?" Liz said. "Benvolian place settings."

He looked it over with apparent expertise. Then he said, "This is not genuine."

"That's not my problem," Liz said. "My job is to deliver them. I have. Your job now is to pay me for it." She held out the vellum sheet containing her invoice.

He snatched it contemptuously with his free hand and looked down his nose at it. "Hm. I don't suppose you even *thought* about selling the originals and trying to pawn off these cheap imitations as the genuine article?" He crumpled the vellum in one hand and smashed the plate against the loading ramp with the other to make his point. "I think I'll teach you a lesson in manners, peasant."

I stepped in front of her. "I think you won't."

Liz pulled me back. "No, Eddie, I can handle this." She got right in his face. They were about the same height, but he shrank as she emphasized her words with repeated pokes to his chest. "I was hired by the royal office of Benvolia to deliver these boxes. Their reps loaded them in the wagon right off the boat, and I brought them straight here. They're the exact same boxes, pal, and the very same contents as the Benvolians gave me. Now, if you intend to start a commotion—"

"Who's starting a commotion?" a new voice said. It was strong and carried the conviction of someone used to being obeyed.

We all turned. A middle-aged man in a cloak strode down the aisle, followed by six serious-looking guards.

The steward gasped and dropped to one knee. "Your Majesty!" he cried.

Liz and I exchanged an *uh-oh* look, then did likewise. An annoyance had just become much more serious.

King Gerald, also known as Crazy Jerry, stopped before us and made an impatient gesture. "No, not the damn bowing and scraping. On your feet, all of you."

We did as he commanded. His guards spread out in a practiced formation, unobtrusively blocking us in.

I had my Gadshill Marauder sword at my waist, my trusty knife in my boot, and two other swords hidden on the wagon. Liz was no trained swordswoman, but she had a seldom-indulged vicious streak that had claimed more than one would-be bandit. We could make a good fight of it, but that's all. If it came to blows against professional guards, we were screwed.

And if the steward were any more intimidated, he'd melt into a puddle. Even I felt sweat on my neck. The presence of royalty didn't bother me, but unlimited power in the hands of the unbalanced did. He didn't seem crazy standing there in front of me, but once you got a reputation as a lunatic, it was hard to shake. King Gerald never had. And Crazy Jerry might do anything.

He looked at the open box of dishes. "Is this the delivery from Benvolia?"

The steward nodded so hard, his uniform cap almost flew off. "Yes, Your Majesty. But these brigands have—"

"Who broke this?" he said, bending to pick up one of the pieces. He saw the piece still in the steward's hand. "You?"

"Your Majesty, these aren't real Benvolian table settings, they're—"

"The table settings my grandmother used in the Siege of Bolingbroke," one of the guards finished.

We all turned in surprise. The guard was tall and rail thin but possessed the energy of a much younger man. He stepped in front of King Gerald and glared at the steward.

The steward looked from the king to the guard, trying to interpret what was happening. "I don't, I mean, I didn't—"

The guard undid his cloak. Beneath it, he wore expensive, tailored clothes and a tunic with the royal seal of Mahnoma. "You want to talk to me," the guard told the steward with a nod toward the king, "not him. You're excused, Hector."

The steward suddenly realized that *this* was King Gerald, hiding in plain sight in the guise of one of his own bodyguards. His stand-in gracefully backed away to let the true king have the floor, and put the guardsman's cloak around his own shoulders.

"My grandmother painted these dishes by hand to look like Benvolian porcelain," the real king said. "They're a gift from King Dorset and Queen Johanna of Benvolia, who are also my distant cousins. They're family heirlooms. They may not be genuine, but to me, they're priceless, and they're crucial in maintaining strong ties with Benvolia. Particularly when Dorset and Johanna come to visit next month."

The steward turned white.

"And you broke one," the king finished.

"I-I-I didn't—"

"Think?" Gerald roared. He had a perfect voice for shouting, rich and full like a herald's, and all of us, even the guards

and Gerald's stand-in, jumped. "I'm not surprised. If you could think, you wouldn't be stuck clerking in my warehouse." He turned to us. "Has he paid you yet?"

Liz, not accustomed to royalty, let alone ostensibly insane ones, barely squeaked out, "No, Your Majesty."

Gerald smiled at her nervousness. Very reasonably, he said, "Don't be afraid, young lady. I'm sorry about the theatrics. They may call me Crazy Jerry, but I promise, I'm not. I'm just careful." He turned back to the steward. "Pay them. Give them a ten percent bonus for dealing with you. And then expect that very soon your duties, responsibilities, and pay will significantly change."

"Y-yes, Your Majesty," the steward said, quickly counting out gold coins from his purse. Liz took them, recounted them, and put them in her own money bag.

Gerald turned and walked away. His guards fell into formation, and his double followed outside the little knot of security, still dressed as a king. That, I reflected, must be the most nerve-racking job ever.

Then suddenly Gerald stopped, turned back in our direction, and pushed past his guards. "Miss—?"

Liz's mouth moved, but no sound came out. I whispered to her, "Dumont."

"Dumont," she blurted. "And this is my associate, Mr. La-Crosse."

"A pleasure," Gerald said with a nod to me. Then to Liz he continued, "Would you do me the honor of having a drink with me? I feel the least I can do is try to convince you that my representative here—" He glared at the cowering steward. "—doesn't accurately reflect Mahnoman hospitality."

"Oh, Your Majesty, we couldn't bother—," Liz began.

"Miss Dumont, it's a bother if *you* ask. When *I* ask, it's no bother at all." He offered her his arm.

"A moment, Your Majesty," one of the guards said. I didn't

recognize his rank insignia, but it was different from anyone else's, which usually indicated an officer in charge. "We need to check them with Opulora's stone."

"Of course," Gerald said wearily. To us he added, "I apologize for this. Security, you know."

The officer took a small metal box from his belt, opened it, and withdrew a stone. He held it close to Liz. Nothing happened.

Then he held it in front of me. It began to glow red.

"Take off your sword, please, and place it in your vehicle," he said by rote.

I did as he ordered. The glow dimmed, but still shone.

"Please place any other weapons in the vehicle," he said.

The only weapon left was the knife in my boot. I thought it over, then took it out and placed it on the wagon's seat beside my sword.

The stone's glow faded. The officer said, "Thank you. No unauthorized weapons are allowed within the castle's private chambers."

I nodded at the stone. "That's a handy thing to have."

"Yes," he said, without any inclination to tell me more about it.

Gerald again offered Liz his arm. "Now that we're all officially friends, shall we?"

She was sweating with nervousness, and I desperately wanted to laugh; Liz was usually so cool, and totally in control. Instead I dropped into step behind her and the king, the guards behind me, and followed him into the castle.

I was nervous at being in the presence of Crazy Jerry, too, but I'd always assumed the stories about him had been exaggerated. I'd tried very hard to become a good judge of people; he seemed a bit paranoid, but that's not unusual in royalty. Still, the thud of the inner door as we left the warehouse had a disturbing finality, like the sealing of a tomb. Hopefully that was just *my* paranoia.

chapter
SIX

The passageway was narrow, which meant it was designed only for discreet travel by highly placed members of Mahnoman society. Gerald, with Liz still on his arm, led the way, I came behind, and the guards brought up the rear. Somewhere along the route, the decoy king slipped away down a side passage. The air was warm and stifling, thanks to the frequent oil lamps on little sconce ledges, and the total lack of any circulation.

I tried mightily to reserve judgment. This was no sign of Gerald's paranoia; every castle had secret passages. Not every king used them for normal conduits, but perhaps it was simply the shortest route between the warehouse and wherever we were being taken. Or, of course, we could be walking right into an insane ruler's diabolical trap, but I could only watch for signs and hope I'd be able to handle it unarmed.

Gerald kept up a murmuring monologue that I couldn't quite overhear. Liz nodded along, but I knew by her body language that she was no closer to being relaxed. How would I handle it if Gerald made a move on her? He had no queen, and in that situation he wouldn't be the first monarch to sample whatever feminine morsel crossed his path.

Then I smiled to myself. I wouldn't have to handle anything. Liz could take care of herself at least as well as I could defend her.

We passed arched doorways that led into branching tunnels, and in one I caught a glimpse of movement. At first I thought it was a trick of the light, because the shape seemed too large to be a man, and was hunched over to fit through the passage. It was quick, though, whatever it was, because even though I spotted it twice and was ready the third time, I never really got a good look at it. And it made no noise at all.

It did, however, carry an odor. It smelled like sweat and urine, human smells but tainted with something lower down the food chain.

No one else noticed, or thought it odd. I glanced back at the nearest guard. "Big rats down here."

"Just keep moving," he said dryly.

"You know, you cut some vents in the rock, it would really improve the air quality."

"I'll bring it up at the next staff meeting."

We emerged into a comfortable royal lounge. There were sumptuous couches, top-notch tapestries, and a well-stocked bar. A young, very attractive woman in the kind of outfit you wouldn't wear outside on a windy day said cheerfully, "Welcome, Your Majesty!" She curtsied, revealing an awful lot of exquisite female flesh. "What would you and your guests like?"

"Hello, Adele," Gerald said. "Something light, these folks are traveling."

"Certainly. May I recommend the Rasmillian ale? We have the winter stock, fresh off the wagon."

"That's fine."

The girl poured our drinks and delivered them with a

deep bow that displayed her, uhm, assets to great advantage. I made certain not to smile.

A painting dominated the room. Larger than life size, it depicted a beautiful woman wearing a crown, with a boy of about eight standing beside her. Neither smiled. The boy held the woman's hand and leaned toward her, as if frightened by whatever they both looked at. I was vaguely aware that Gerald had lost both a wife and son, but knew none of the particulars and, given his erratic reputation, wasn't about to ask.

"My queen and my only child," Gerald said when he saw me looking. "They both died quite some time ago."

"I'm sorry for your loss," I said.

"Yes," he agreed. "As am I."

As I took a drink, I also took note of the exits. One led into the network of corridors we'd traversed to reach the room; the other led, probably, directly to the throne room. Both were guarded on the inside, and likely on the outside. There was bound to be at least one secret passage, but it wouldn't be obvious and I had no graceful way to search for it, other than assuming it would be behind a tapestry. In this room, that didn't really narrow it down.

Gerald touched goblets with Liz and said, "So, do you often make deliveries of this sort?"

Liz tried to speak, but nothing came out except her quick, nervous breathing. I said, "Yes, Miss Dumont runs a courier business. I decided to come along with her on this trip as a little vacation from my regular job."

Gerald's gaze flicked to me. His eyes were guarded but clear, with none of the haze of madness. But the thing about crazy was that you could never tell when it would show itself. He said, "Really? And what job is that?"

"I'm what's called a sword jockey, if you're familiar with the term."

"Oooh, I love sword jockeys," Adele said from behind the

bar. "They always have such great stories. Much more interesting than soldiers," she said with a knowing scowl at one of
the guards.

"Adele," Gerald said warningly.

"I know, I know, no flirting," Adele said, and started vigor-
ously wiping a mug.

"I gave her permission to always be herself around me,"
Gerald said. "On some days it's a bit tiresome. So—you're a
sword jockey."

"I am."

"My high chancellor has employed several of your kind
over the years. That's how Adele has heard all those stories.
I'll admit I've not been too impressed with them, but I won't
hold that against you."

"Why did your chancellor employ them, if I may ask?"

"Different things." Then he seemed struck by a new thought.
"Although, now that I think about it, I have never known exactly—"

"Yes," Liz suddenly blurted, finally answering Gerald's
initial question. Her voice was a tight, choked gasp. "I'm a
courier."

Gerald laughed. "Miss Dumont, please, I promise you the
stories about me are exaggerated. I don't lurk in a darkened
room talking to myself. I hold court just like every other king,
and if I resort to subterfuge, I assure you it's neither extreme
nor unwarranted." He took her hand and formally kissed it.
"If you're this nervous, my dear, perhaps I should just let you
be on your way."

She relaxed a little. "I'm sorry, Your Majesty, I just didn't
expect to be dealing with royalty today. I'm not properly dressed
for it."

"You are properly dressed for your job, as am I." He turned
back to me. "And where will you two be going next?"

I saw no reason to be secretive, but I could still be vague.
"We're going to meander through some of the spring festivals.

Here, Altura, Leonatia. Take our time, enjoy the drinks and the dancing."

He nodded. "The sheep-shearing festivals are quite enjoyable, so I've heard. Certainly they make sure we have plenty of wool for the next winter." He kept looking back at me, deciding whether or not to add me to the list of sword jockeys who hadn't impressed him. Mostly I hoped he didn't, because I was enjoying being unemployed.

Before he could continue, a tall woman with short gray hair appeared in the room. And by "appeared," I mean just that. One moment she wasn't there, and the next she was. No door had opened, no tapestry rippled to reveal a hidden passage. And I was almost positive she hadn't been there when we'd all entered.

"Bloody hell!" Gerald yelped, which actually startled me more than the woman's sudden appearance. "Don't *do* that!"

"My apologies, Your Majesty," she said with a deferential curtsy. "I heard you had unexpected guests. I apologize for my late arrival." She nodded to us. "I am Opulora, high chancellor to King Gerald."

"Eddie LaCrosse," I said, "and my associate, Liz Dumont."

Gerald watched Opulora as if she might bite at any moment. "No one summoned you. Why are you here?"

"I merely wanted to see if I could do anything to make your guests' stay more pleasant."

"Opulora's a sorceress by trade," Gerald said. "Popping into a room with no warning is one of her favorite tricks. Don't worry, she won't turn you into anything small and slimy, despite her reputation. Her skills lie in more . . . subtle transformations."

The sorceress scowled very slightly at the implied insult, but I was more fascinated by the change in the unspoken power dynamic. Gerald might be king, but Opulora was definitely in charge.

I was instantly on my guard. Magic—or at least the science

so subtle and advanced, it was accepted as magic—was an un-common thing. The best-known practitioners, the moon priest-esses, carefully screened applicants and preferred to raise new priestesses from girlhood, the better to inculcate them in the rules of their order. It wasn't a foolproof method, because sometimes a priestess did go rogue on them. I'd met one, who single-handedly managed to bring down the Kingdom of Grand Bruan over a perceived slight to her mother.

But the true freelance magic practitioner was a lot like a sword jockey: answerable to no one, and available for a price. Of course, you also had no quality control, and someone could call themselves either a sword jockey or a sorcerer with no one to dispute it. Well, until it came time to put up or shut up.

Many royal courts had magical counselors who hovered in the background and made vague predictions that carried weight only because royals desperately wanted to believe. Luck made some guess right often enough that they amassed power. More often, they perfected the art of the elaborate excuse for their errors.

And then there were the special cases, like Opulora.

She said to us, "I hope your visit to Mahnoma has been a pleasant one."

That meant that our visit was, in fact, over. I bowed slightly, making sure it wasn't as far as I'd bowed to Gerald. "The king's been very generous. But we really must be going."

"Yes," Liz agreed quickly. "Thank you so much for the drinks."

"Before you go, may I see your hand?" Opulora said.

"Why?" I asked.

"Oh, it's her idea of security," Gerald said dismissively. "She thinks she can sense harmful intent in people. Go ahead, it won't take a second and then she'll be satisfied. Right?" he added in annoyance.

"Don't," Adele blurted from behind the bar. She stood very

still, and the cockiness was entirely gone from her voice, replaced by a pleading desperation.

Opulora turned to her. "Adele," she said gently, "be quiet."

Adele started to say something else, then thought better of it. Or, if you were so inclined to believe in such things, she couldn't speak because Opulora had magically silenced her. Either way, she quickly resumed wiping down the counter with so much force, I worried she'd wipe off the wood grain. I wasn't sure if she'd been warning me, or the sorceress.

"I give you my word," Opulora said to me, "I mean you no harm, and I will only look."

I let her take my right hand, palm up. I knew the basics of palmistry: how the way the lines in them could tell a skilled reader all sorts of things, from your trade to your age, and from them he or she could extrapolate a future. I also knew most of the time they were completely inaccurate. Lots of people trusted them, though, including people like kings, who really should know better.

Her own hands were soft and dry, and she ran her index fingernail lightly over the lines on my palm. I wondered if she could pick out the two old scars from the normal folds and creases. She was about to say something noncommittal when she suddenly tightened her grip and stared. I was on the verge of pulling my hand away when she looked up at me and said softly, "You get around, Mr. LaCrosse."

"Yeah? What was your first clue?" Liz said a bit possessively. That made me smile.

Opulora said, "I'm sorry, that was needlessly cryptic. I meant simply that I sense a great deal of traveling in your past, including through this very region."

There was an urgency in her eyes that betrayed her casual tone. What was she after here?

"May I get a second opinion?" she asked. Before I could reply, she produced a small glass ball from somewhere in her gown. With one finger and thumb, she held it daintily over my palm. The faintest of blue glows appeared inside it.

(Okay, I know what you're thinking: I should have immediately realized that this glass ball was identical to the one the man tried to give me when I rescued Isidore. You have to remember, though, that was sixteen very eventful years prior to this. Actually, the blue glow reminded me most of the flickering light I'd once seen in a dragon's mouth, which was more recent and, ultimately, made a great deal more of an impression on me. So cut me some damn slack.)

She looked from the ball up to me. Her brow furrowed, then she turned to the king. "When were you last here, Mr. LaCrosse?"

"Never," I said. "This is my first time in Mahnoma."

"What about Mazeppa? Or Altura?"

Both those countries bordered Mahnoma; in fact, we'd traveled through the boot heel of Mazeppa on our way here. And the name Altura rang a bell, but I couldn't dredge up the memory. Besides, I didn't know what made her so interested, and that made me suspicious. "I'm not sure," I said, deliberately vague. "It was a long time ago, that's all I can say."

"Do you remember anything unusual happening when you were here?"

"Like I said, I've never been here."

Her eyes narrowed. She knew that I knew that she was fishing. Then she released my hand and smiled, all trace of suspicion gone. "They're perfectly safe, Your Majesty."

"I knew that," Gerald snapped.

"But I do understand your need to be going," she finished with a slight bow. "Safe travels. And please—don't add to the gossip about King Gerald. He's been a gracious host, remember that."

"We'll say nothing but good things about him," I said, and took Liz's hand. I bowed, and Liz curtsied. "Thank you for the drinks."

"Thank you for delivering my heirlooms with such care," Gerald said.

"I'll show you the way," Opulora said. She gestured at the door, and the guard made a smooth lateral move. "If you'll follow me?"

Now I was worried again. Like I said, Opulora was a special case. If Crazy Jerry had a dubious reputation, she, as the ostensible power behind the throne, was considered rock-scorpion dangerous. Stories circulated as far as Neceda about how the king's enemies often vanished after encountering her, or went as mad as Gerald himself supposedly did. The consensus was that she had been the one who drove Gerald crazy all those years ago and arranged the deaths of the queen and crown prince, and now kept him on a very short leash. I couldn't speak to the former, but the latter didn't seem far off the mark. She was the white crow, the one real sorceress who disproved the rule that all magicians were frauds. At least, according to her reputation.

I glanced at Adele. She watched us, still silent, still with an expression like we were about to fall off the edge of the earth. But what else could we do but follow Opulora?

When we were in the tunnel leading to the warehouse, Opulora stopped and faced us. The guards dropped back to give us privacy. I made sure to position myself between her and Liz.

She said, "Thank you for not making a scene with the king."

"Why would we?" I asked.

"Come now, you know his reputation. 'Crazy Jerry'? I can't tell you how many people have tried little digs and taunts, just trying set him off."

"Has it worked?"

She continued to look at me strongly. "I don't feel it's my place to answer that."

"He seemed fine to me."

"In small situations, he *is* fine. In moments where nothing crucial is at stake. But he's still the same lunatic who nearly destroyed the kingdom sixteen years ago. I was able to contain the damage then, and I've worked very hard to keep it under control ever since. Do you ever wonder why there's no queen or crown prince? There once were."

"Why are you telling us this?" I asked.

The mannered pose left her demeanor, replaced by the urgency of truthfulness, or a very good facsimile of it. "Because I'm tired of being vilified. I did not curse Gerald; he did that all by himself. He drove his queen, and their young son, to their deaths. Have you any children, Mr. LaCrosse?"

"No."

"Then you can't imagine the loss. And not just to the family: the kingdom lost its heir."

"Why hasn't he remarried, then?"

"Because I won't *let* him," she snarled, then drew back. I could tell she hadn't meant for that to slip out. The wounds might be old, but they were still unhealed. "I apologize. You're very good at asking things so that people want to answer. The king, of course, is free to do as he wishes, but he has asked my opinion, and has been content to be guided by it."

"Is that what he'd tell me, too?" She started to reply, but I held up my hand. "Look, I'm sorry, it's none of my business. We're just delivering some plates and cups, you know? It doesn't matter to us. You want me to say nice things about you, then I will. You've been nothing but kind and polite to us anyway, so I won't have to lie. But I think it'll take more than a sword jockey and a delivery driver to rehabilitate his reputation."

"You're a sword jockey?" she said. She hadn't been in the room when I'd discussed it with Gerland, and a whole new sort of interest showed in her eyes. "Have you always been?"

"No one starts out as a sword jockey. You just end up as one when no other work suits you."

"Then I'll not delay you any further."

Opulora led us down more hallways, but different from the way we'd come. I caught Liz's eye and saw that she realized it, too. I said nothing, but kept my eyes open.

I realized two things almost simultaneously. First, the guards were gone. I don't know when they vanished, but we were alone with Opulora. Then I caught a whiff of that earlier rank smell, and within moments it was strong enough to make my eyes water.

Something leaped from a side tunnel into the hallway ahead. I say some "thing," because although it had a vaguely human outline, it was also distorted and twisted: massive arms hanging past its knees; a mouth too wide and filled with yellowed, ragged teeth; and a skull ringed by twisted plaits of dirty hair that fell to its shoulders. It wore simple trousers and a sleeveless tunic, all cut to its gargantuan proportions. When its feet hit the tunnel's stone floor, I felt the vibration.

I assumed it was male from the scraggly beard that started just below his eyes and seemed to spring from the skin all the way down to his chest. If there had been room for him to stand upright, he might have been seven feet tall. As it was, he blocked our way as effectively as a cave-in.

I backed up a step. I didn't want to provoke this . . . guy . . . until I knew who or what he was.

I found out the first right away. "Tatterhead!" Opulora scolded. "What are you doing?"

"You let me out," he said in the deepest voice I'd ever heard. "You summoned me."

"I did," she said. "But not to harm our guests."

He lumbered toward her. His big bare feet slid on the stone, never entirely lifting from the floor. She did not back away.

His huge face was right in hers. His voice was a whisper, but because of his size, it still rumbled through the air. "When you first brought me here, you gave me water with berries in it. You taught me to name the light of the day, and the one of night. You stroked me, and made much of me."

"And I will again," she said calmly, "when you prove to me you can be trusted. You have frightened these friends of the king."

He turned and stared directly at Liz.

"Hi," she said with a little wave.

A grotesque approximation of a smile spread across his face. It was not the kind of smile you wanted directed at your girlfriend. "Pretty," he said.

I stepped in front of her. "And taken."

He cocked his head and looked puzzled. I bet not many people stood up to him, and truthfully I wasn't real happy with myself for doing it so reflexively. I swear I heard the muscles and tendons in his arms creak as he slowly curled his fingers into fists.

"Tatterhead!" Opulora snapped. "That is unacceptable. It's why you must stay in your room. I'm taking these friends of the king back to their horses, so stand aside, and mark them as we pass so next time you'll know to behave. I'll be back to deal with you later."

I knew how dogs "marked" things, but all Tatterhead did was lean that huge head toward me and sniff, long and deep, again like a dog taking the scent. He did the same to Liz, a bit too lasciviously for my liking, then skulked backwards into a darkened room. He chuckled—so deep, I felt the air buzzing in my ear.

Opulora closed the connecting door, then said, "I'm sorry."

"What bridge did you find him under?" I asked.

"Tatterhead is a—" She sought the word. "—project of mine."

"You made him yourself?" Liz asked dryly.

"He was kept in a cage for years by the peasants who first found him. They thought he was a monster."

"I can see why," I said.

She scowled at me. "Yes, for the simple and superstitious,

he would be hard to explain. But he's not a simpleton. He can comprehend language, art, and literature."

"But not hygiene?" Liz asked.

Opulora ignored the comment. "I'd hoped to civilize him, to show that appearances didn't always truly represent the soul. It hasn't gone quite according to plan, though."

"I don't know, he's as civilized as most of my old boyfriends," Liz said, and we all laughed. But I wondered if the monstrous foundling had anything to do with the death of Gerald's wife and son.

"This way, please," Opulora said. "And again, I apologize. Tatterhead is entirely my responsibility, he has nothing to do with King Gerald, so please, when you tell of this, leave the king out of it."

I nodded, but wasn't fooled for a moment. She'd ditched the guards and brought us down this hallway because she *wanted* us to meet this Tatterhead; I couldn't imagine why, but then again, this was Crazy Jerry's castle. Hopefully our rapid exit would remove any reason for further concern.

AS we left the castle in our now-empty wagon, Liz said, "I need a drink. A real one. Possibly several. In fact, we may not make it out of the tavern tonight."

I laughed. "Why were you so nervous?"

"Why weren't *you*? That was Crazy Jerry. He could've gone off at any moment. We could've ended up locked in his dungeon for the rest of our lives, with no one the wiser. And what *was* that Tattletale thing?"

"Tatterhead. I don't know. I've never seen anything like him."

"I didn't know trolls really existed. Then again, I never thought dragons did, either, so I shouldn't be that surprised, I guess. God, that smell is all over me. Did you see how he looked at me?"

"That's how *I* look at you, too," I said lightly, but it was entirely for her benefit. I still wondered what little drama we'd accidentally walked into the middle of.

"*You* don't look like you want to have me for dinner when you do it. And I'm not being metaphorical. Was he even human?"

I shrugged. "That's covered under my previous answer. But he must be at least partly human. He could talk." I gazed thoughtfully back at the castle. "There's something going on underneath everything, that's for sure. Gerald may be tense, but he didn't strike me as crazy."

"What about Opulora? With everything you've seen and told me about, all those ghosts and goddesses and shape-changers, are you saying you aren't afraid she might have real powers? Maybe she does control Gerald. Maybe he doesn't even know it."

"I didn't see sorcery. I saw a loyal member of the court trying to hold down the fort—well, the castle—because no one else was doing it." And that was true, I got no real sense of menace from either monarch or sorceress. But if I was right, then how did her relationship with Tatterhead fit in?

Liz shook her head. "You're usually a good judge of people, so I won't argue with you. But I'm still glad we're out of there."

A voice I hadn't heard in my head for a long time suddenly rang out: *If you pick up a viper and it bites you, it's not the viper's fault, is it?* Who had said that to me, and when? I could almost tease up the memory, but it stayed just out of reach. I said to Liz, "I just trust them to be who they are."

"That's good. Because you can trust me to be drunk as fast as I can get there. I'm on vacation now, too."

chapter

SEVEN

At the Hearth and Road Inn, we found a table, ordered drinks, and asked to see the menu. Liz downed two tankards before our food arrived. The room was crowded, and the mix of voices, clanking silverware, and sloshing mugs combined in a buzz that let my mind easily wander while we ate.

I'd known only one king well: Dominic of Arentia, Phil's father. Phil was a king now, too, but when I'd run around with him, he'd been merely the crown prince. Dominic was a big man with hard muscles, a short beard that turned gray before his hair did, and eyes that could damn near make you wet your pants if he looked at you when he was mad. As a monarch he was ruthless, hewing to the constitution implemented by his grandfather even when common sense dictated otherwise. But he was not a cruel man; he saw consistency as a king's greatest virtue, whether he was disciplining his son or an errant province. He also maintained the peace, avoiding war even when other kings tried directly to provoke him. He once famously told another king's regent, "When your lord and master decides he's an adult, tell him to pick up his room, make his bed, and then contact me with his demands. Until then, he can just rage in his own playpen."

I'd met other kings since then, of course. If nothing else, wars let you rub elbows with your betters. Some were tyrants, some were jokes. The greatest of them, King Marcus Drake of Grand Bruan, was, of course, tragically killed, sparking a civil war that still raged. Neceda's King Archibald was ruled by counselors and courtiers, whose often contradictory advice he never questioned. Luckily Neceda was such a small and insignificant country, it caused no larger conflicts. And young, ice-veined Princess Veronica waited patiently in the wings, to seize the throne from her wastrel brother when Archibald finally kicked off.

And now there was King Gerald, Crazy Jerry, who didn't seem crazy but who *did* seem unduly influenced by his court sorceress. I couldn't get his look of deeply hidden but nonetheless present horror and despair out of my mind, because it reminded me of my own. I'd carried that look for years, until some cathartic violence in Boscobel and the arrival of Liz in my life finally drove it out. In my case it was due to the guilt I felt for having indirectly caused the death of Janet, my first love, when we were both teenagers. Did Gerald feel it because of what he'd done to his family?

"What are you thinking about?" Liz said, her words blurring together from the mix of food and alcohol.

"Dead kings and live ones," I said.

"You're on vacation. *We're* on vacation. You shouldn't be thinking at all, let alone about serious stuff like that."

I took a long drink of my own ale. After King Gerald's, this stuff tasted like varnish, but it still did the trick, as Liz amply illustrated. I said, "Hard to keep from thinking sometimes."

Before Liz could reply, a loud voice from the corner said, "Part of me says I can't keep drinking like this. The other part says, 'Don't listen to that gentleman, he's drunk!'"

It came from a large, round, scruffy-looking man seated at a small table. He had his bulk wedged into the corner and clearly lorded it over his two equally scruffy companions, who laughed uproariously at his joke.

"Why don't you try drinking water instead?" one of his companions suggested.

"Oh, I do sometimes, just to surprise my liver!"

The two men laughed again. The mistress of the tavern came over to him and said something I couldn't hear.

"What?" the fat man exclaimed. "He's here? Send that old swaggerer to my table!"

The tavern mistress stepped back and wagged a finger at him. "Oh, no, if he swaggers, he's not coming in here! I have my good name to consider, and I'll put up with no swaggerers!" She put her fists on her hips, rocked back on her heels, and glared at the fat man.

The fat man, either oblivious of or used to this sort of thing, smiled and patted her on the rump. "He's no swaggerer, my dear, I promise. He's totally tame, you can pet him as you would a puppy."

She did not look convinced, but huffed off to attend to another table. The fat man laughed, and I saw a tall, slender, very rough-looking man peek in the front door and quickly skulk, no swagger in evidence, over to join him.

"Hey," Liz said. I turned back to her. "You're looking for clues again, aren't you?"

She'd caught me. "I have to stay in practice."

"They have nothing to do with us, sword jockey." She leaned close. Under the table, she put her hand on my thigh. "*I* think it's time to practice some interrogation. Secrets need to be divulged."

There was no mistaking her implication. "Interrogation can be pretty . . . ruthless, you know."

"It sure can. If it's done right."

"Want to get a room upstairs for the night?"

She grinned. "One with a bolt on the door? I'll take care of it. You go get some rope from the wagon."

On my way out the door, I noticed that the alleged swaggerer was conveying urgent information of some sort. The fat man's expression turned serious, and he heaved his bulk from the chair. He followed me out the door but went the opposite way, in the general direction of the castle.

BY the time I got back with the rope, I had to carry Liz up to our room above the tavern, not out of romantic intent but because she was too intoxicated to manage the steps. "There's only one thing I can't stand when I'm drunk," she said as I hoisted her off her feet.

"What's that?" I asked.

She giggled. "Up."

This was precisely the third time I'd seen her this drunk; only the hangover I knew she'd have in the morning kept me from teasing her.

I put her on the bed. She snort-laughed and kicked her feet in the air. I managed to get her boots off and stored under the bed before she said, "It's time to get to the secrets, Mr. Sword Jockey. Where's the rope?"

"It's right here. Go get that chair by the wall. And bolt the door."

Ten minutes later she stood before me, dressed entirely in my clothes, complete with my sword. It accented the confident cock of her hip. My garments were big on her, but they were also very, very sexy. She'd cinched my belt tight at her waist, and my tunic hung off one bare shoulder. Her hair fell loose around her face, and the ale-shine in her eyes matched the playful scowl she gave me. I could see her breasts sway beneath the fabric as she sauntered across the room toward me, my boots sounding loud on the wooden floor. She did a fair imitation of my look-how-tough-I-am swagger as she paced in front of me; I was pretty sure the tavern mistress would disapprove of it, too.

At last Liz said, "All right, you son of a bitch. You have something I want."

I sat naked in the room's lone chair, my hands tied behind my back. My part of the game was to keep from responding to her sexiness as long as I could. Certainly, undressed as I was, I couldn't hide it if she brought me to, ahem, attention. "You think you're strong enough to get it out of me?" I said. "I've resisted a lot worse than you."

She walked around me, inspecting me closely, almost falling over her feet in my too-big boots. The ale made her face glow with the same look it had during particularly intense lovemaking. The room was also warm now, and I felt sweat run down my chest.

She took out my sword, which seemed huge in the small room, and put the tip against the scar over my heart. I got a little frisson of fear from this; if she tripped again and fell forward, the weapon would go right through me, just like the one that originally left the scar. I doubted I'd be lucky enough to survive such a wound a second time. But under the circumstances, the fear just added to the arousal I fought.

"You've got quite a few scars," she said, still in character. "You must think you're tough."

"Tougher than you," I said, my voice hoarse. I bit the inside of my cheek to keep from responding to her.

"Is that right," she said, and lifted the sword until the tip lifted my chin.

Her nipples raised bumps on the tunic's fabric. I said, "You think you can make me talk, do your best. Or your worst."

She smiled slightly. Her breathing was rapid now, and she pulled the sword away. "You might survive my best, sword jockey. But my worst will burn you alive."

She tossed the sword onto the bed and put one foot on the edge of the chair between my legs. My boots had metal caps in the toes, and I winced a little even though she didn't actually touch me. She leaned down, grabbed a handful of my hair, and pulled my head back. "How are you holding out now?" she snarled.

I could smell her ale-scented breath. Her lips had gotten that slightly puffy look that meant she was thoroughly aroused, and my tunic gapped on her enough to show the soft, firm tops of her breasts. I felt the tingles that meant I was about to lose the game. The nice thing was, even if I lost, I still won. But I didn't want to give in without a real fight. "You can't get anything out of me, even if you had a battalion to do the dragging."

She drew the knife from my boot and put it against the side of my neck. "I can get sweet red blood. Maybe I'll just cut you and watch you bleed for a while."

The blade was cold against my skin. "You'll never get what you want then." I fully lost the battle then, and if she'd glanced down, she would've seen it.

"Maybe that *is* what I want," she said. Her lips were so close to mine, I could sense their movement with the words. "Maybe I want to know I've killed you, slowly enough that I can enjoy it. Maybe I want to see the life run out of you." She flicked her tongue against my upper lip for emphasis.

By now I'd slipped my hands from her knots and slid them under the tunic, touching the silky skin of her waist. "Okay, you win," I said quietly as I moved my hands higher. "You'll get everything."

She closed her eyes and sighed. The knife clattered to the floor. "Ohhhh, yes. I know I will." She fell slowly to her knees and moved into my arms, her kiss wanton and open as my trousers slid down her legs.

★ ★ ★

IF you pick up a viper and it bites you, it's not the viper's fault, is it?

I stared at the ceiling. Noise from the tavern downstairs filtered through. This late, I bet swaggering was inevitable.

Liz lay on her stomach, one bare leg outside the covers, snoring in a drunken, most unladylike way. I smiled. She'd pay for it tomorrow, and it would likely be years before it happened again. Not that she had to be drunk to play our little games.

I turned my head and kissed her shoulder, tasting sweat. The contact made her shift a little and murmur something. Beneath the tangled hair fallen over her face, she smiled.

Who had told me about the viper? And why did it seem to be related to this part of the world? The last time I'd been through here was in the hazy years between first leaving Arentia in disgrace and waking up the only survivor of a massacre, with no memory of *how* I'd survived. That had sobered me, both literally and emotionally. I abandoned my job as a mercenary and tried several other trades before discovering that, as a sword jockey, I actually had a use for all those skills I'd accumulated that might actually help people.

I tended to only remember my near-death experiences from back then. Cheap ale, the blur of constant battle, and the simple fact that nothing really mattered to me made the years a fog out of which only a few names, faces, and events emerged with any clarity. There was Colonel Dunson, who began as a fine battle leader but whose pride eventually drove me, and all the other good hired swords, out of his employ. The first few deserters had been tracked down and executed, as examples. That just made the rest of us do a better job covering our tracks.

When I left Dunson, I heard about the brewing war between Mahnoma and Altura. Crazy Jerry had . . . well, gone crazy. Relations with Altura, peaceful for just under a century, had turned toxic almost overnight, though no one knew quite why. I'd flipped a coin to decide which country deserved my sword, and Altura won. So I'd gone there . . .

. . . and couldn't remember anything else. Except that the hostilities never materialized. What defused them was a mystery to me now, and probably was then, too.

But that bit of advice, *If you pick up a viper and it bites you, it's not the viper's fault, is it?* was tied to that time, and this approximate place. Who had told it to me, and why? Because it had become a guiding principle of my life.

My eyes began to close. It had been a long day, and a fairly active evening. As my brain shifted to sleep mode, two faces drifted before it. One was a beautiful girl, golden-haired and smiling. The other was a baby, scrunch-faced with infant annoyance.

I couldn't put names to either of them. I had no children that I knew of, certainly none I'd ever seen. And the girl could've been anyone from that time.

At least I didn't get an overwhelming sense of guilt from these half memories. That was always nice. Whoever they were, I hadn't done anything to deliberately screw them over. Maybe I'd even helped them. But before I could think about it any deeper, I was asleep.

USUALLY I'm better at picking lodging, making sure the windows face north or south, not west, and *definitely* not east. But I guess I was distracted the previous night, because now I found that the room faced directly into the sunrise, flooding us with blinding light and rising heat. Those are two things I really don't enjoy waking up to, especially on vacation.

I opened my eyes, squinting until they adjusted. Liz stood beside the table, a water basin before her. Naked to the waist, she was washing off with a rag, and the backlighting made it something worthy of a painter. I watched sparkling rivulets find their way along her skin, dripping from assorted points that held my attention. By the time I looked back at her face, she smiled in a wry, knowing way.

"Morning," I croaked. "How's your head?"

"You've never complained," she said with a wink. "And I feel fine."

I sat up. "Even after all that ale?"

"We sweated a lot of it out, I guess," she said as she squeezed out the rag. "How do you feel?"

"Okay," I said, waiting for the sore points in my back and legs to loosen up. "Hungry and thirsty, though."

"You put in a solid night's work," she said as she turned and sauntered over, still topless, and straddled my lap, facing me. "Ready for the day shift?"

I kissed her, then nuzzled some of those same points still wet from her washing. She sighed and ran her fingers through my tangled hair.

I drew back and said, "What time do they stop serving breakfast downstairs?"

"I'll make sure you get fed."

"I bet you will." And then we went back to bed for what turned out to be a fairly long time. No ropes or cross-dressing was involved, but I felt sorry for anyone in the room next to us. Unless they enjoyed eavesdropping.

At last we got up for real, washed, dressed, and went downstairs to the tavern. Over lunch and ale, we discussed where to go next.

"Altura," I said.

"Where's that?"

I gestured vaguely. "There's a shared border. Shouldn't take too long."

"Why there?"

I wanted to tell her about the half-remembered faces, the vague sense of something significant, and the advice that had stuck with me for so long. This, however, didn't seem to be the time. I wiped a tiny spot of gravy from her chin, licked it off my own finger, and said, "No reason. I just seem to remember going through there once, and the scenery was beautiful."

Liz shrugged. "Okay. Altura it is. There's probably dozens of little spring festivals we can visit."

WE took our time after leaving Acheron, staying overnight in the first little town we came to. They had a festival going as well, but after checking it out for an hour or so, we returned to our room and used the music from outside as accompaniment for some more intimate activities. I'm happy to say we did a better job improvising than the musicians. When we left the next day, someone told us about a mock tournament held at another village. They had an elaborate faux siege set up around a fake castle, and participants got to join in and pretend to be warriors and knights. At Liz's urging, I took up a wooden sword with a blade padded by leather and down feathers, and led a charge that was just barely repelled by the defenders. I "died," cut down by more padded swords, on the fake drawbridge, mere steps from victory. Liz thought this was hysterical.

We resumed our journey the next morning. It was a beautiful day, and the breeze was cool enough to balance the blazing sun. The road gradually rose as we passed through the forest; eventually we'd emerge from the trees onto the rolling, grass-covered hills, where shepherds replaced farmers and huntsmen.

I stopped to relieve myself, and walked a short way into the forest. As I stood behind a tree, my eye fell on a patch of ground where the leaves had been pushed aside by something with a large, broad foot. Five claw marks indicated the front edge. I fastened my pants, frowning as something tried to come to the front of my brain.

And like a hammer dropped on a cold toe, the events of sixteen years earlier came roaring back. Audrey. Arcite and Strato. Beatrice. *Isidore.*

"Oh, shit," I said, louder than I intended.

"What's wrong?" Liz called from the wagon.

"Ah . . . nothing," I said.

I wasn't keeping a secret, exactly. I just wanted time to sort through the memories and get the story in the right order. Besides, the chances that we'd end up in the exact same town, or that any of those people would still be there, or that they'd remember me if they were, were all pretty slim.

Right?

Right.

The original sign had been replaced. This one announced *Mummerset* in real calligraphy, and with no misspellings. The ivy-covered wall around the town looked in better shape, too, although that could just be the vagaries of memory. I recalled it as more crumbling and pitiful-looking.

"Cute little town," Liz said. "Very quiet-looking."

"Most people live out on their farms and sheep ranches. They don't come to town unless they need something."

"Looks like everyone needed something today," she observed.

A group of young girls approached over the closest hill. They wore bright white kerchiefs and dresses with red skirts that fluttered in the breeze. Most of them carried distaffs, and as they talked and giggled, one arm was extended to spin off the yarn, which was in a variety of colors.

A dozen wagons were stopped along the road, and their horses were either tied loosely or simply let go into the open fields, where they milled about munching grass with the sheep.

Many of these wagons were uniquely designed so that the sides looked like ladders. I'd seen wagons like them in other hilly places, and knew they were especially good for traveling down uneven roads and across rugged terrain, since they were far more flexible than rigid wagons like the one we drove.

A few people also milled about, mostly men dressed in snow-white sheepskin capes or embroidered white leather coats lined with black fur. The wind wasn't bad now, but I could imagine it got rather chilly after the sun went down. I might have to buy one of those coats myself.

It seemed that most people were inside the town wall. A faint murmur of crowd noise reached us, growing in intensity as we neared.

I'd told Liz the story of my previous visit, as best I remembered it. And I was honest, even about the girl. She reacted exactly as I knew she would, too: by mercilessly teasing me the rest of the way. How could I not love her?

"Seems like a happy place," Liz said. "So this is where you left your baby?"

"No, I did not leave *my* baby here. I left *a* baby, that I *found,* with someone who could take care of her. I was a kid myself back then."

She leaned over and kissed my cheek above my beard. "Sorry, Eddie. I just think it's funny to imagine you saddled with a baby."

"Hey, I like babies," I said defensively.

"I've never seen you interact with a child younger than ten."

"That's because they don't get my jokes until then," I said with more genuine annoyance that I should've felt. Why did this bug me so much? The fact that Liz teased me was one of the things I normally liked best about her.

I drove the wagon off the road, slotting it in between two others. Compared to those battered and oft-repaired vehicles, our well-worn wagon was right out of the wainwright's shop.

A cheer rose from the town as we stepped to the ground. "They know we're here," Liz said dryly.

"I always get a welcome like that," I said.

We undid the horses and walked them to a long trough set against the wall. Liz noticed some flowers planted along it and said, "Oh, those are pretty, aren't they? Wonder what they are?"

"Striped vorrygills," I said.

She narrowed her eyes playfully at me. "Did your rich family teach you gardening, too?"

"Yes, but they called it horticulture."

She took my nose and playfully tweaked it. "You know what they say: You can lead a horticulture, but you can't make her think."

As we stood there watching the horses drink, I heard a man's voice—harsh, arrogant, and mocking—from behind another wagon. "She was crazy," he said. "It was like going to bed with a rabid sheepdog. She was all thrashing and snapping, even barked like a dog a couple of times." Other male voices laughed at this.

"Eddie," Liz said very softly. I followed her nod, and saw a young woman huddled near a wagon's wheel, hidden from the group of men but clearly listening. She was also silently sobbing, and I realized she must be the girl they were discussing.

I looked at Liz. She nodded and went to comfort the girl. I made sure the horses were okay, then went to see the young men.

They were three tall, sturdy farm boys, tanned and muscular, none of them over twenty. The one who'd been talking had a mop of unruly blond hair streaked from the sun. He said, "Ah, I have to get back home."

"Your wife got your balls in a basket?" one of his friends taunted.

He didn't look old enough to have a wife, but out here in the country, what else are you going to do? He said, "On a scale of one to ten, my wife is a two, and that's only because I've never seen a one. She better keep her mouth shut, if she knows what's good for her. She's already popped out two kids, and neither one was a son. I'm only giving her one more chance."

"Wow, man, that's . . . harsh," his other friend said.

He ignored the implied disapproval. "Besides, the banquet's tomorrow, and they can't find a damn onion in an onion field without me." Then he noticed me, and when I said nothing challenged, "So what do you want, old man?"

"I think the girl you've been talking about can hear you," I said.

"So?" he shot back, and his two friends laughed.

"You're being kind of mean. You made her cry."

"Listen, old man, get on out of here before we make *you* cry, okay?"

I smiled. "I think you should apologize."

All three laughed.

I took two steps into the middle of the group, grabbed the blond kid by the face and bonked his head against the stone wall hard enough to daze him and get his attention.

I had my sword out and up against his nearest friend's throat before any of them moved. I wanted them to be scared, so I wouldn't have to hurt them. "Put your goddamn hands up where I can see them," I snarled. To the third boy, I said, "You, too." They did as they were told.

"Do you know who I am?" the blond kid said, his voice growing whiny. "My father's the biggest—"

I held him by the front of his tunic and put the sword's point against his belly. "You got a mouth that really needs to stop moving. You don't speak again until I say you can. Nod if you understand me."

He nodded. Then I pushed him ahead of me around the wagons until we found Liz and the crying girl.

"Eddie," Liz said, "this is Rachel. Rachel, this is my boyfriend, Eddie."

"Hello," she said, her voice raw from crying. She turned red when she saw the boy, but kept her chin high, retaining as much dignity as she could. I knew that in a small town, stories like this could ruin the girl's life, and fought mightily to keep my temper down.

By now a few people had emerged to see what the commotion was about. They watched in apparent great interest. One man had a tankard of ale, and sat down on a rock as if we were putting on a show just for him. I got the definite sense that this boy had had this coming for a while.

"Nice to meet you, Rachel," I said. "Liz, this is . . . What's your name, punk?"

"Gordon," he said sullenly.

"You're a very rude and thoughtless young man, Gordy," Liz said. "The world has enough of those. You're really not needed."

He said nothing, and wouldn't meet her eyes.

I shook him. "Apologize to Rachel, Gordon."

"What the fuck for?" he muttered.

Liz whistled through her teeth, sharp and loud. "Over here."

He looked up at her, contempt blazing from his eyes. "Don't whistle at me. I'm not your fucking dog. You look more like a dog than I do."

"Now you're talking to *my* girlfriend," I said. "How smart do you think that is?"

"Yeah, you're real tough with a sword in your hand, old man," he said, not meeting my eyes. He knew he had an audience, and was caught between the sensible idea of doing as he was told, and performing for his crowd. Moron.

I tossed my sword to Liz, who caught it by the hilt. I released Gordon and stood in front of him. "I'm going to slap you. With my right hand. And you are not going to be fast enough to stop this old man from doing it."

He wasn't.

I grabbed him by the hair. "Call me 'old man' again, and I'll knock out your front teeth. You couldn't stop me on your best day, and this is far from that." I pushed him over to Rachel and forced him to his knees. "Apologize to this girl."

"I'm sorry!" Gordon snarled through clenched jaws.

"Say it like you mean it," Liz said. "No—say it like your life depends on it."

"I'm sorry!" he repeated, with a hair's more sincerity. The audience, now at least a dozen people, clapped in approval.

Rachel looked down at him, her humiliation mixed with contempt. "I thought I loved you, you know that? I really did. Even though you're married. But you're just . . . just . . . ."

"An asshole," Liz said helpfully.

"An asshole!" Rachel cried, finding her voice. "Yes, that's it, you're an asshole. Fuck you! Fuck you, and you two?" She indicated his friends. "Fuck you, too! Fuck all of three of you! And . . . and . . . fuck you!" she ended, back at Gordon.

I released Gordon with a shove that sent him sprawling. Our watchers applauded. Liz gave Rachel a hug, then strode over to me and took my arm. "Shall we visit the festival now?"

I watched Gordon and his two friends, to see if they were at least smart enough to stay down and quiet. They were. "Sure," I said. "I'll buy you a drink."

"I'll take it," she said, and kissed me. We strode out of the wagons, through the gate, and into Mummerset.

As we passed, I scanned their faces of this little crowd, looking for some sign of recognition, either in them or for my-self. *This is supposed to be fun*, I told myself yet again. *Stop thinking about it like a case.*

The whole street down to the central courtyard was arched over with decorative boughs covered in flowers, no doubt brought from the forest downslope. The fallen petals, crushed into the street's dry dirt, gave the ground spots of pastel color. Music, played on pipes and drums and barely audible over the sound of people rhythmically clapping, reached us from the courtyard. Liz squeezed my hand in anticipation.

We hadn't gone far when three teenage girls stepped out into the street. They were beautiful, although I doubted they were older than sixteen: Isidore's age, I realized. That counted as a grown woman in the countryside, I knew, and certainly the parts of them that I could see were definitely full-grown. But their faces were still those of children.

They wore solid color dresses in green, yellow, and blue, and carried baskets of flower petals that matched their clothes. They threw them in the air over us.

"The warmth of spring brings life to all," they sang in unison, "and here we answer to its call."

They moved aside, and a fourth girl stepped out. Her straight brown hair was woven through with ribbons, braids, and flowers.

"Welcome, new friends," she said with a smile. "I'm standing in for Ancillay."

"So you are," I said. "Is Ancillay out sick?"

All the girls laughed. "No," the new one said, "Ancillay is the handmaiden of Eolomea, our goddess of the spring and fertility. She greets new souls as they arrive in this world, as I greet new souls who arrive for our festival."

I bowed, and Liz curtsied. I said, "It's a pleasure to meet you, Ancillay. I'm Mr. LaCrosse, and this is Miss Dumont. We're traveling through and hoped we might join you in celebrating the spring."

"All are welcome," she said. "What was the commotion outside?"

"A boy was picking on a girl," Liz said. "Someone made him apologize."

"That was probably your brother," one of the girls said to Ancillay.

"If it was, he's had it coming for a long time," Ancillay said, and reached into her basket. She produced two flowers on long stems, each with a ribbon tied around it near the blossom. "I present you with monea, miss, and bachelor buckles for you, sir. May they bring beauty and grace to you both."

Liz said, "I saw some flowers outside, growing in a bed by the wall. They were beautiful: red petals with blue streaks. What are they?"

"Some say the most beautiful flowers of the season," Ancillay said. "Striped vorrygills."

"Told you," I whispered, and got an elbow in the ribs for it.

"But we also call them spring's bastards," the girl added with distaste.

"Why?" Liz asked.

Ancillay's face creased as she sought the right words. "Because they're not real," she said at last. "Someone combined two flowers to produce this one. It's not natural."

I thought about some of nature's little jokes I'd encountered, like the Grand Bruan half sisters so identical that they switched places and no one, not even one's husband, noticed. "Oh, I don't know," I said. "You can combine things all you want, but they won't grow if nature doesn't want them to."

"I suppose," Ancillay said. "But I still prefer things as they are, rather than what they're changed into, no matter how they're changed. Besides, it's like putting on makeup." She turned to Liz. "Would you like it if he—" She nodded at me. "—only wanted to be with you when you wore lipstick?"

Liz laughed. "If that was true, we'd never have gotten past, 'hello.'"

Ancillay curtsied to us, and her ladies-in-waiting did likewise. Then, whispering and giggling, they retreated back to await the next arrival.

Liz looked at me with mock-narrowed eyes. "You have boots older than her, you know."

"I have no idea what you mean."

"You're lucky I trust you, Mr. Sword Jockey."

"I'm lucky for a lot of things," I said, and kissed her. The girls, still watching, giggled some more.

The town smelled like flowers, which almost covered the ever-present odor of sheep. Thankfully the ground was dry and hard, except for a few small puddles where someone had either spilled something or relieved themselves. The shops were closed and the one tavern we passed was empty, just like the one I'd visited the last time I was here.

I opened the door, stuck in my head, and looked around the dim interior. It was called the Head Boar; had that been its name sixteen years ago? It looked, and smelled, like every other rural tavern. I just couldn't tell if this was the same one, though; the details of that memory were lost.

When I closed the door and turned back to Liz, she lightly smacked me with her flower. "Stop thinking. It was a long time ago, you said so yourself."

"I can't help it. Do you think Ancillay was the girl?"

"You wish. Then you could seduce her with the old 'I saved your life once' ploy."

"I only seduce you."

"You don't have to seduce me. That's what makes us such a good couple."

I flicked my own flower at her in response.

We reached the back of the crowd packed into the courtyard and began working our way through it. A group of men ran past us and almost knocked us down. They wore long, multicolored togas and screamed at the top of their lungs. The ones at the front of the line tossed handfuls of colored powder, and those at the end splashed cupfuls of water from big buckets. This made the powder turn to ink and leave smears of bright color on all those they passed, none of whom seemed to mind.

They missed me, but got Liz. She wiped at the wet green

stripe across her tunic, then laughed. Her hair fell over her face and she tucked it behind her ears.

"You're staring at my hair again," she said.

"It's beautiful. *You're* beautiful."

"It's a pain. I'm cutting it as soon as we get back to Neceda."

A young man, no older than Ancillay, suddenly stopped in front of us. He was naked except for a loincloth, and there wasn't much of that. His muscular torso gleamed with sweat and painted symbols, and he wore a pair of wooden ram's-horns on his head. He knelt before Liz and offered her a pink cloth circle, like a bracelet. "Beautiful stranger," he said, "I give you this as a symbol of my devotion."

She took it with a big grin. "Thank you, young man. *Very* young man," she added with a sly glance at me.

He continued, "At this time of year, the fertility of men and women helps the land provide for us. What happens in Mummerset stays in Mummerset, so if you'd like . . ."

Liz laughed. "I might, at that. But I try to keep my word, and I've given it to this guy. So I'll have to decline."

He smiled. "If you change your mind, beautiful stranger, just put this serficon in your hair!" And then he was off into the crowd.

Liz looked at the cloth loop. "What does 'serficon' mean?"

"Foreskin," I said. "That's the symbolic tip of his manhood."

She held it up. "Think it's life size?"

"If it was, he'd need a bigger loincloth."

She laughed. I could listen to her laugh all day. The wind blew her hair down into her face, and as she gathered it, she said, "If *you* want to buy me a romantic gift, you can get me a nice hair ribbon. I'm not using anyone's foreskin, symbolic or not."

We edged through the press of rural folk to an artisan's cart, where a middle-aged woman sold bright ribbons. Many of the girls in the crowd had several tied in their hair, and when they spun during their dances they resembled unraveling Maypoles. Liz finally found a vivid blue one she liked, and turned so I could tie it for her.

I gathered her hair and kissed her on the neck. "What's that mean?" she asked.

"It means 'I love you,' and a few more implied things that we need the cover of darkness to fully express."

"No, goof, *that*."

I followed her gaze. The livery barn had a banner stretched across it that read, babies here.

"It's where they keep the babies so the moms can have some fun," I said as I finished tying the ribbon.

"In a barn?"

"Seemed like a good place before." I fought the urge to go into the barn and see if Angus was still there tending the infants. He'd be old enough to have his own now, of course.

Nothing got past Liz. "We can go in, if you want. Say hi. Pretend we're shopping."

"No," I said. "It was a long time ago."

"Yeah, but I know that sword jockey brain of yours. If you don't go in, you'll brood about it for the next five years, wondering 'what if.'"

I mock-glared at her. "Stop doing a better job of knowing me than I do."

"I will, when you get better at it."

We went to the barn door and I pushed it open. As before, it was dim inside and it took a moment for our eyes to adjust. Light came through the slats in the wall, illuminating the rows of cradles in the stalls. The outside noise was muted once the door swung shut behind us, allowing us to hear the soft, chaotic chorus of contented infants.

A teenage girl sat in a rocker, feeding a milk-skin to a baby. She looked at us with the universal annoyance of someone left out of the party. "Dropping off or picking up?"

"Neither," Liz said. "Just browsing."

"This is the nursery," she said with a tired sigh. She pulled the milk-skin away and put the baby on her shoulder. She patted the tiny back until she was rewarded with an adult-sized burp.

Could *this* be Isidore? Would I be disappointed if it were? Could a baby who endured such a strange and wondrous survival have grown up to be a totally typical farm girl? She tenderly placed the baby in a cradle, making shushing noises as she did so.

It could be worse, I suppose. I extended my flower to her. "Here. This is for you."

She took it, then looked up at me with a mix of wonder and suspicion. "Why?"

"This is a thankless job. Someone should show you you're appreciated for doing it."

"I'm doing it because my dad caught me with Alonso last week," she said. "He didn't believe me when I said it wasn't my idea."

"The reason's not important. You've got a job to do, and you're doing it well. On behalf of everyone, I thank you."

She tucked the flower behind one ear and fought valiantly to hide her smile behind the blasé seen-it-all of a young woman. "You're welcome."

Outside the barn, Liz kissed me. "Thank *you*. Just when I think I know you, you do something that surprises me."

"Hey, I'm a ruthless killing machine, and all who hear my name piss themselves."

"Uh-huh." She kissed me again.

Arm in arm, we passed one of the other open gates out of the town. This was the one I'd gone out with Beatrice when we walked to her home. On the hill, a group of men prepared this year's bonfire. Several flocks of sheep were being driven toward town, bells and barking dogs providing the accompaniment.

"Care to take a walk?" I asked.

"Where?"

"The family I left Isidore with lived out that way."

Liz squeezed my hand. "Probably faster if we ride."

"Probably. You're taking this all fairly well, considering."

"Considering what? That my boyfriend is the kind of man who both saves innocent babies and then wants to check up on them when he's back in the area? That's all good stuff, you know. It's a sign that you're good in here."

She lightly poked my chest, over my scar. I felt a tingle along the path that long-ago sword had taken through my body and out my back.

chapter

NINE

The scenery was breathtaking. We lived in Neceda, a town on a muddy river, and so were used to things in shades of brown. Here it was all individual solid colors: blue sky, green grass, gray rocks, and white sheep. The bright red of a kerchief or tunic popped out as well. The air carried the sharp sounds of sheep bells and shepherd horns, punctuated by the barks of herding dogs. Behind us, the occasional cheer reminded us that we were missing the fun to indulge my personal (not even professional) curiosity.

Shortly we saw a small hovel set back off the road that matched the one in my vague memory. Certainly it was old enough, although the mud chinking between the stones was fresh and the roof had been regularly rethatched. Smoke rose from the chimney, and a maned dog rushed up to bark at our horses, alerting anyone inside that they had company.

"Is this it?" Liz asked.

"I think so," I said. I qualified it out of habit rather than uncertainty. There was the spot I'd stood with Glendower and given him Isidore's gold before I slunk away into the night.

"What's that smell?" Liz said, wrinkling her nose.

"Manure."

"Yeah, but where's it coming from?"

"Sheep butts."

She stuck out her tongue at me, then said, "Too bad your friends don't live in that." She pointed at the top of a large manor house just visible over the hills. Three chimneys rose from the gabled roof. It was all we could see from our position, but the mere fact that we *could* see it said a lot about its size. I hadn't noticed it back in the day, but then again, it had been dark and I'd been preoccupied.

When I got down, the dog jumped up on me, wagging its bushy tail. The hut's door opened and a gray-haired woman stepped out. "Greetings," she said. "Looking for the festival?"

"Not exactly," I said. I tried to imagine her as she'd have been back then, but she didn't look like my memory of Bianca, Beatrice's mother. "I came through this area about sixteen years ago and knew the people who lived here."

"In this house?"

"Yes. There was a farmer—"

"That'd be Owen Glendower."

"That's him."

"Well, they moved. This is the Gwingle farm now."

"Where'd they go?"

"Up. And over." She pointed at the chimney tops. "Glendower's Aerie."

My eyebrows rose. "Really?"

"Yep. He came into some money and moved the whole family up there, including his spinster daughter and granddaughter."

"His granddaughter? What's her name?"

"Isadora." Her eyes narrowed. "You're not coming along

claiming to be her father, are you? We get men like that at festival time. It doesn't end well for them."

"And it won't for him, if he tries that," Liz said.

"I just wanted to visit the Glendowers and say hi," I said.

"Well, there they be. Isadora's standing for Eolomea at the festival this year, so she'll be in a tizzy. The rest of them should be home, getting ready for their big party."

I got back onto my horse, the dog still barking. The horse chuffed and stamped in response.

"Hotspur!" Mrs. Gwingle scolded. "If he chased sheep as much as he does horses, he'd actually be useful. Get back here and leave them alone!" The dog rushed back to the house and sat at her feet.

I waved to Mrs. Gwingle, and we headed over the hill toward the chimneys. "Looks like you get your wish," I said to Liz. "We get to visit the mansion."

"Think he used the girl's gold to build that?" she asked.

"Don't know."

"A man who's come so far in the world might do a lot of bad things to stay there."

"We don't have to go."

She gave me that sideways grin that meant she knew better. "Yes, we do. Just remember that you don't really have any say in what's happened. You're not the guardian, or the avenger."

"I know that," I said. But truthfully, I also knew it wouldn't take much to make me step into either role.

"Or, she added slyly, "the proud papa. Right?"

"Right."

THE mansion stayed no more than a roof in the distance until at last we topped one particularly high, rolling hill and finally saw it in its full glory. It was definitely impressive, and just as definitely not the sort of thing you got from raising sheep, no matter how good you were at it.

"That's a step up, all right," Liz said. "Does it bother you?"

"I gave him the gold with no strings. I don't really have a say-so."

"But does it?"

"It might," I allowed. I needed to know more before I could say for sure.

It was built of stone, like the smaller houses. Around here, it would pretty much have to be. It was two stories high in a landscape where most houses were often partially buried in a hillside. There was a big turnaround drive like the one at my family's estate, and a garden walk that led from the drive to the front door. *That* you wouldn't see in Arentia: gardens were for the back of the house. You invited people to see it, you didn't put it out there where just anyone could walk through it. Of course, no one in Arentia would also have barns, corrals, and sheep pens this close to such a grand edifice.

"Good grief," Liz said. "How much gold did you give him?"

"I didn't count it," I said.

We rode down the hill, turned onto the road, and followed it up the drive. No livery boys appeared to take our horses, just the same type of hitching post you'd find outside any home in the area. The garden was more elaborate than it looked from the hill, with neat benches and gravel paths among the blossoms. Statues peeked out from them, and one central goddess stood on a pedestal. We tied our horses to the post.

"I don't know Alturan etiquette," Liz said. "Are we being rude if we just go up and knock?"

Before I could answer, a young man appeared from the house. As he got closer, we heard him repeating, "Three pounds of sugar, five pounds of currants, saffron to color the pies—" He saw us and stopped. "Hello."

"Hi," I said. "I assume this is the Glendower residence?"

"Yes, sir. I'm Clancy Glendower."

"Are you one of Owen's sons?"

He grinned. "Yes, indeed. I—" He frowned. "Dammit!"

"What?"

"I forgot what I was supposed to get at the market!"

"Three pounds of sugar," Liz said helpfully, "five pounds of currants, and saffron to color the pies."

Clancy's eyes opened wide. "How did you *know*?"

"Ah . . . I heard you talking to yourself when you came out."

"But I was going over the list *in my mind*," Clancy said, still astonished.

Liz smiled and laughed nervously. I said, "Is your father here?"

"Oh, yes, he's helping get ready for the festival dinner tomorrow night. He always hosts the neighboring farmers. That's why I have to go to the market."

"Can we see him?"

"Of course! He's not invisible or anything."

I looked at Liz. Her cheeks trembled with the effort not to laugh.

"Is he in the house?" I asked slowly, keeping my own face straight with great difficulty.

"Yes. Oh! You meant 'see' like 'visit.' Yes, wait here and I'll go find him. You are Mr.—?"

"LaCrosse. We met sixteen years ago."

"We did? I would've only been about five. I'm sorry I don't remember you."

"Your father and I met."

"Oh! Okay, just . . . wait here." He scurried off back into the house.

"Living with him must be exhausting," Liz said.

We milled about in the garden. The plethora of freshly cut stems and carefully shaped branches told me it had been recently spruced up, no doubt for the festival. Liz wandered about admiring the flowers, while I picked a bench in the shade of a small blossom-covered tree. I looked up at the windows, wondering if one of the rooms was Isidore's, or rather Isadora's.

I also wondered about Beatrice. Did she still live here? It was possible; the place was big enough for multiple families, especially if they had ties to the business. Would she still be mad about the way I'd left without saying good-bye? Or had she come to understand it was the right decision?

"Eddie, look at this," Liz said.

I joined her at the monument she'd found. It was a woman's statue, draped in cloth with her head down in sorrow. Beneath it was chiseled the name *Bianca Glendower* and a pair of dates barely fifty years apart.

I remembered the fierce, strong-willed maternity I'd sensed in her, and how I'd been glad to know she'd be there to help Beatrice raise Isidore. It looked like she only got to do it for a few years.

We turned when a door opened. A man with white hair and beard, dressed in well-cut clothes just a hair too ostentatious for good taste, strode out ahead of Clancy. My memory of Owen Glendower was hazy, since I'd spent only a few moments with him, but this man seemed a reasonable image of how he'd look sixteen years later.

He offered his hand as he approached. "Hello, Mr. Large Hoss," he said. "I'm Owen Glendower."

"LaCrosse," I corrected. "Eddie LaCrosse."

"Ah. My son has trouble with details."

"I don't have trouble with the tales," Clancy protested. "I can tell a story with the best of them. Once there was this hummingbird—"

"Clancy!" Glendower barked. More calmly he added, "Shouldn't you be on your way to the market?"

"I can't remember what to—"

Glendower held up a piece of vellum with a list on it. Clancy snatched it and strode away toward the house, then caught himself and rushed the opposite direction, toward the drive. "Don't take one of the guest's horses!" Glendower called. To us he added, "He's a good soul, but his mind tends to wander.

Now, Mr. LaCrosse, was it? What can I do for you?" He realized where we stood. "My late wife," he said sadly. "She died of fever less than a year after we built this place. She was a remarkable woman."

"I know. I met her once. At this same festival."

He still looked blank.

"Sixteen years ago."

The blank look stayed there for a moment; then he turned whiter than his beard. "You," he said with a whisper.

"Me," I agreed, and gave what I hoped was a friendly smile.

He looked around to make sure no one overheard. "Why are you here?" he whispered urgently.

"We're on vacation," I said. "Mr. Glendower, this is Liz Dumont."

"Charmed," Liz said.

His words spilled out in a panicky rush. "You're wondering about the house, aren't you? You think I used up all of Isadora's gold building it?"

I held up my hands. "I'm not here to—"

"Yes, I used her gold as seed money to expand my farm, but I promise you, I paid it back and more. She's got a dowry only a king could rival!"

"That's fine, I just—"

He grabbed my tunic in desperation. "Please, don't kill me! I did the best I could for her! I love her, I've helped raise her as one of our family! She has no idea where she really came from!"

I pried off his hands. "Stop and listen, will you? I just wanted to visit, say hello, see how she was doing. I don't want to give away any secrets, and I don't want anything from you."

He stared at me, then at Liz for confirmation. She nodded. He stood back, straightened his clothes, and said, "Well, then . . . I, uhm . . . it's nice to see you again, Mr. LaCrosse. And to meet you, Miss Dumont. It appears time has been good to you, sir."

"Better than I deserve," I said with no irony.

"You and your friend must be hungry and thirsty after your long ride. May I offer you some refreshment?"

"That would be great," I said. "Thank you." Liz took my arm as we walked into the mansion.

The foyer was stone as well, decorated with tapestries and lit, when needed, by a large iron chandelier. Many voices came from somewhere else in the house. "The kitchen staff is getting ready for our banquet," Glendower said. "You'll have to excuse the commotion." He picked up a large bell from a table and rang it three times.

A pretty young maid came running out of somewhere and skidded breathlessly to a stop in front of us. She said, "Yes, sir?"

"Tea and cakes for our friends, please, Mopsa."

"I'm Dorcas."

Glendower waved his hand at her. "Whatever." After she scurried off, he said, "Never hire twins. Sometimes I think they switch names just to confuse me."

"Could be worse," I said, again recalling Grand Bruan's two Jennifers. "They could have the same name." Then I remembered that Liz, too, was a twin, although her sister, Cathy, was dead. I wished I'd kept silent.

The tapestries that decorated the foyer's stone walls depicted pastoral scenes that could've occurred a hundred yards from the house in any direction: shepherds dressed in incongruous furs reclined on hillsides, their sheep contentedly grazing before them, a dog keeping a far more watchful eye than his daydreaming master. "Who did your decorating?" I asked.

"My daughter," he said. "She's quite the weaver. I'm sure you remember her."

"Oh, he does," Liz said, winking at me. "Her name is Beatrice, I believe?"

Before I could respond, a woman said, "Who's talking about me?"

chapter

TEN

She entered the foyer in full stride, followed by another, younger woman carrying a basket. "So who's this?" she said as she joined us, oblivious of the fact that the woman behind her was about to spill tomatoes all over the foyer.

Beatrice's hair was still golden, although it was combed loose around her shoulders instead of braided. Her gown fitted well enough to verify that she hadn't gone matronly, either. And that sauciness remained, the sense that the world had better look out. But it was shadowed by a weariness that comes only from bitter experience.

Glendower said, "Beatrice, this is an old friend, Mr. La-Crosse. Do you remember him?"

She looked me over. "I'm afraid not." She turned to the girl with the tomatoes. "Do you think we're handing those out at the door? Go take them to the kitchen before my brother starts throwing things again." As the girl scurried away with her produce, Beatrice said to me, "When did we meet?"

"Sixteen years ago," Glendower said carefully, trying to

convey the date's significance. He narrowed his eyes and gritted his teeth, pre-wincing against the anticipated explosion.

"I didn't have a beard then," I said. "And my hair was longer."

Beatrice still shook her head. "I'm sorry."

"He brought us a gift back then," Glendower hinted.

She cocked her head a little. "Really? And what was that?" Then it hit her.

"You," she said, sounding exactly like her father.

"Me," I said again.

Her face shifted through an eloquent symphony of expressions: recognition, relief, rage, sadness, yearning, and finally, guarded worry. "Why are you here?"

"Just passing through," I said, trying to sound nonthreatening. "Beatrice, this is Liz Dumont. Liz, Beatrice."

They shook hands quickly, the way women do. Beatrice gave Liz an up-and-down evaluating glance. Liz just smiled and said, "Pleasure to meet you."

"Likewise," Beatrice said. Her lips moved as she almost said several other things, then settled on, "I suppose you want to see Isadora."

"She's working on her gown for tonight," Glendower said. "Isn't she?"

"Yes, and she's way behind."

"Is she still having problems with—?"

"Yes," Beatrice said, the way you say it when you don't want something discussed in front of strangers. To us, she continued, "If you're staying for the festival, it might be better to see her then."

"Okay," I agreed. The terror coming off both of them made me feel very guilty. "Only if it won't cause any trouble."

"But you can't take her," Beatrice blurted, the words bursting out as if they were escaping horses. "I don't care who her real parents might be, I've raised her, I've loved her for sixteen years, and that counts for something. They can't have her back!"

"I don't want to take her," I said. "And I still don't know where she came from. Do you?"

"No. I never tried to find out."

"That's fine, then. She doesn't even need to know who I am."

"Then wh-why are you here?" The fearful tremor in her voice told me all I needed to know about her attachment to her daughter.

"Really, we were just passing through," Liz said. "We made a delivery in Mahnoma and decided to go festival-hopping."

"I didn't realize where we were until we got here," I added. "Then we just thought we'd stop in and see how you were doing." I indicated the house around us. "Pretty well, it seems."

We were all silent. Finally Glendower said, "I apologize for our reactions. I've had sixteen years to dread this moment, and as you know, you only dread the worst. I imagined you coming back in the middle of the night, putting a knife to my throat in my bed, and demanding the gold back. Or worse, taking Isadora away. I'm sure Beatrice had her own worries." He held out his hand. "I shouldn't have thought so little of you. A man who rescues a baby and then turns over a sack of gold he could've easily kept isn't the kind of man who would skulk back to retrieve it."

I shook his hand. "I understand. No grudge here."

Dorcas, the maid, returned bearing a large tray. She scowled and said, "I didn't know Miss Beatrice would be joining you."

"Now you do," Glendower said. "Fetch another cup. Is it that complicated?"

She put the service on the table and scurried off.

Glendower gestured at the tea. "Shall we?"

And as if we did it every day, standing there in the foyer, we took tea with the biggest sheep farmer in Altura.

★ ★ ★

IT was late afternoon by the time we left Glendower's Aerie. We'd discussed the price of wool, the cost of grain storage and, gods help us, the weather. I'd watched my father squirm through social engagements like this, and now I had a whole new sympathy for him. The elephant in the chamber was Isidore, aka Isadora, who neither appeared nor was mentioned again.

"I need a drink," Liz said as we rode back to town.

"You've been saying that a lot lately."

"You've been taking me places that make me say it." She looked back at the house. "Would we be like that if we got rich?"

"I've been rich."

"Well, lah-dee-dah," she said, and mockingly stuck out her tongue.

"At least now I don't have to worry about her. Isidore's in perfectly good hands."

"Isadora."

"Right. Isadora."

"And you can accept just seeing her from afar tonight?"

The Glendowers told us that the ceremony for Eolomea, with Isadora in the title role, would happen in Mummerset just after full dark. "Sure. I mean, what would I say to her, anyway?"

"And you're ready to put all this aside and enjoy our vacation?"

"*Yes,*" I said. "Why wouldn't I be?"

She didn't have to answer. The look in her eye said it all.

The festival was even more rambunctious by the time we got back to town right at dusk. Luckily the tavern had opened, and we found a lone empty space at the bar. I let Liz take the stool, and I stood beside her. The atmosphere was giddy and festive, the way hardworking people often are when they're allowed to cut loose. Later, as the drinking progressed, things might turn ugly. Old grudges could be restoked, new insults not tolerated. But for now, all was well.

The bartender was a stout, round man with a florid mustache that curled up on the ends. I wanted to ask about Audrey, to see if she was still around, but after the weird tea party with the Glendowers, I thought better of it. If she showed up, I'd say hi, but I wouldn't ferret her out.

After her first tankard, Liz motioned me close and said, "I don't know if I ever told you, but I was Queen of the Fair once."

"No. How old were you?"

"Thirteen. They tossed a coin between me and my sister, and I won. Boy, did she get mad." She smiled, but then it faded a little as it always did when she mentioned her late twin. "Anyway, I got to wear a fancy gown, ride on this beautiful horse, and wave to everyone in town."

"Did you enjoy it?"

"Not really. Knowing everyone is watching you isn't my thing."

"Mine, either."

I paused to take a drink of my own. If I hadn't done that, the next few days might have been peaceful and relaxing, and probably the fate of two kingdoms would have been completely different. But I did.

And I heard a voice say, "Boy, when you become king, don't let them call us thieves. Instead call us 'gentlemen of the moon,' because she's the one who watches over us as we steal."

I recognized it as the same man who'd invited a "swaggerer" to join him back in Mahnoma. I spotted him once again with his back in the corner, presiding over the table before him. This time, only one man sat with him. This companion was young, tall, handsome, and clean-shaven. He wore the same sort of rustic clothes as the others, but on him it resembled a costume; he had never sweated in them doing hard work so that they dried to fit.

He responded to the fat man, "That's not a bad idea, since thieves who work at night have to follow the moon's phases, just like the tides do. Maybe I should call you 'moon-calves.'"

They both laughed, and the fat man touched mugs with his young friend. The younger man drank, then said, "Are you paying for this round, then?"

"Ah, sweet Jack, a thief broke into my room last night while I slept, searching for gold."

"What did you do?" the younger man asked.

"Why, I woke up and searched with him! Neither one of us found a single coin!"

They both laughed.

I looked at the younger man more closely. There were things wealthy, important men taught their sons that were subtle but hard habits to break. Sitting up straight was one of them; resting your forearms and not your elbows on the table was another. This youngster had internalized both. His skin was also considerably paler than everyone else's, indicating he had not spent a lifetime outside doing farm labor. And yet, at the same time, he didn't look uncomfortable or nervous. And I noticed that when another young man, with the bearing and demeanor of a local, said hello as he passed the table, this young man responded in kind, and they exchanged genuine smiles.

I nudged Liz and leaned close to her. "Check out that table in the corner. See the young guy?"

"I sure do. He's yummy."

I mock-glared at her. "I think he's a little above you."

"He could be, if I can ditch my boyfriend."

"Are you done?"

"For now. What's up?"

"I heard the fat guy ask him to do something when he becomes king."

"So he's a prince?" she said quietly, so no one else would overhear.

"I think so."

"Of where?"

Altura had a prince, I knew, but I didn't know his name, age, or personality. Still, if he was in Mummerset, it made sense that he'd be that one. "Here, I suppose. Altura."

Liz turned and tugged on the sleeve next to her. The man's smile diminished a little when he saw me, but he still said, "Hello, lovely lass. What may I do for you?"

"What's the Alturan prince's name?"

"Prince John," he said. "Bonny Prince Jack, we call him."

"Why?"

"Well, he's . . ." He stopped and look puzzled. "I don't rightly know. That's just what we call him."

"Have you ever seen him?"

"He's on the four-bit gold piece."

"But not in person."

He smiled. "Little lady, there would be no reason for Bonny Prince Jack, or Good King Ellis, to ever come to a wide spot in the road like this."

"Not even for your festival?"

"There's festivals all over Altura at this time of year, all over the world, for that matter. I'm sure they could find a better one."

She leaned over and kissed him on the cheek. "Thank you, kind sir."

He nodded, and blushed a little. "My pleasure, lovely lady."

I gestured for the bartender to refill the man's drink on us. Liz smiled smugly at me. "How'd I do?"

"Pretty good," I admitted.

She rested her chin on her palm and studied the young man. "I hate to say this, since we're both showing off our investigative skills, but . . . so what?"

"It's the fat guy with him. I get a certain feeling when trouble's around, and he's trouble."

"He looks harmless."

"Can you think of a better disguise for trouble?"

"Okay, even saying you're right, he's not *our* trouble, is he?"

"I guess not."

"Well, then. Stop trying to impress me and just buy me another drink. And one for yourself, while you're at it. You're going to need several, I suspect."

"Why is that?"

"To bend the rod you've got up your ass tonight," she said, and pinched my nose for emphasis. "I want you to have fun, and I will tolerate no excuses." Then she kissed me and bit lightly at my lower lip.

We resumed drinking, and soon we were drawn into the circle around a bard, who had a seemingly vast repertoire of songs, some so absurd as to be ridiculous. "Here's one that's sung to a very doleful tune," he said, "about a loan shark's wife who gave birth to twenty money bags. And here's another about a fish that appeared and sang this pitiful tune against the hard hearts of women."

"A fish?" someone asked. "A singing fish?"

"Well, not just any regular fish," the bard said. "The man who wrote the tune told me she'd once been a beautiful woman herself, and was turned into a cold fish when she would not, as they say, exchange flesh with her lover."

"Turned by who?" someone else asked.

"Ladies, gentlemen, I don't write the songs, I just sing them." He strummed his lyre. "Now here's one . . ."

The songs were fun, and I joined in the choruses like everyone else. Still, through all this, I kept one eye on the table in the corner, at the young man who might be a prince and the fat guy who might be trouble. They did nothing suspicious, which did nothing to allay my suspicions.

chapter

ELEVEN

A t nightfall, we all went outside to watch the ceremonial Awakening of Eolomea. The central courtyard had been turned into a maze of fire, with blobby homemade candles outlining a spiral path that led to the covered well in the middle of the space. Before that well, on a a faux throne, sat a girl with a white veil over her face. She was completely still, like a statue. Only the slightest ripple caused by her breath revealed she was alive.

I tried to see through the veil to the face beneath it, but of course I couldn't; that was, after all, the point. The girl wore an elaborate gown made up of lots of different-colored cloth, which nevertheless had long slits up the skirt that revealed exquisite, muscular legs, and a low-cut bodice that also showed off the kind of curves men always notice. I admit I felt a little weird noticing them, too.

We got a spot at the front of the crowd. Musicians played somewhere, the kind of simple tunes everyone in this region would know. The only light came from the candles. Anticipation grew around us, and voices quickly turned to whispers. This was more than just a fun event for these people: at some level, they believed that it genuinely *did* ensure their continued ability to survive. Yes, they knew it was just elaborate playacting, that the girl in the chair was just the daughter of a local farmer. But they also believed that the real Eolomea was watching, and judging, and would either grace them or damn them for the coming year based on this evening.

Finally several young men—painted and loinclothed like the one who'd earlier propositioned Liz—emerged into the spiral. They danced slowly, with broad gestures, providing their own percussive accompaniment with small drums. At the end came a final young man dressed all in black, with a veil like the girl in the chair. He also carried a big black basket filled with flowers and what looked like the stalks of weeds.

This was common symbolism in agrarian communities, including some of those in Arentia. It was the spirit of dead winter, represented by the man in black, releasing the spirit of spring, rebirth and growth. My mom took me to a similar festival when I was a boy, and the much more elaborate costumes gave me nightmares for a week. It didn't bother any of the peasant kids, of course. For them, it wasn't scary, but joyous. My elite isolation made it terrifying.

The dancing men reached the veiled girl and knelt in a circle around her. The spirit of winter stood before her and began draping her still form with the contents of his bag.

"These unusual weeds to each part of you do give a life: no mortal woman, but Eolomea, awakening for spring's sweet kiss. This sheep-shearing is a conclave of the petty gods, and you are the queen of it."

As he did this, there was a slight commotion across the way. The fat man from the tavern used his bulk to force his way to the front of the crowd opposite us, then stepped aside to allow his handsome young companion to move up beside him.

Because of the relative silence, I caught most of what they said to each other.

"Stand here by me, Master Jack. I will make the goddess do you grace. You'll see the way she greets me."

Jack, I thought. *Bonny Prince Jack. Ah-hah.*

The man he called Jack chuckled. "I can only hope she'd rather greet me than you, Billy."

"Don't you worry, now. She has eyes only for you, my prince."

Jack scowled at him. "Okay, stop that. Seriously. Here I'm just Jack, got it? Jack. Say it back to me."

The fat man grinned and bowed as much as his bulk and the press of the crowd allowed. "As you say, Jack. As you say."

Jack seemed amused by this, as if his disguise, if it was a disguise, was not truly meant to fool anyone. Was he the prince of Altura, then? Was this all just so he could enjoy the festival? I could accept that, were it not for the dangerous vibe I still got from the fat man called Billy, and the fact that I'd seen him in Mahnoma without Prince Jack in tow.

Even now, as the prince watched the ceremony, Billy watched the prince with tiny, avaricious pig-eyes. What was the relationship between these two? And why did their apparent interest in Isadora set off even more alarms?

At last the black-clad spirit of winter finished draping the young woman with his flowers and stepped back. The previous-immobile form raised its hands and lifted the white veil, exposing this year's face of Eolomea, Isadora Glendower. She opened her eyes and looked up at winter.

She was beautiful. I'd seen a lot of beautiful women and girls over the years, and Isadora ranked near the top. She had big dark eyes, dark hair, and high cheekbones. Her lips were full, and revealed a slight but adorable overbite. She looked, of course, nothing at all like her adopted family. How had they explained that?

She peered up at the Winter King and smiled, very slightly,

the kind of smile that came only from intelligence and self-knowledge. Liz had that kind of smile, too; it struck me without warning that, had things been different, Isadora could very well be our daughter. That realization took me by surprise.

Isadora then let out a trilling shriek, echoed by the throng of other young girls that rushed from the shadows and began dancing with the boys.

Isadora jumped up as well, tossing off the weeds that had covered her. Three men lifted her and carried her around the spiral, somehow avoiding the candles. They placed her on the ground at the edge, and she began skipping and dancing, distributing joyful kisses to those of us in the front of the throng.

She stopped dead in front of Jack, though, frozen in mid-movement as if she'd become the statue she'd pretended to be moments before. I couldn't see her face, but the look on his was plain enough. And even if it hadn't been, Liz said softly, "Uh-oh."

"What?"

"I know that look. He's taken the bait, and she's reeling him in." She shook her head. "And neither of them even knew they were fishing."

"How do you know?"

"That's the way you looked at me that first day in Angelina's Tavern. And if you were really as observant as you thought you were, you'd remember that's how I looked at you."

The kiss Jack and Isadora shared was completely different from the ones she'd been distributing so freely. It was tender and sweetly passionate, the kiss of two people who had not yet experienced the madness love can drive you to. But with Billy nearby, grinning and almost rubbing his hands together in glee, I had a feeling this innocence wouldn't last.

As she pulled away, her legs wobbled and almost collapsed under her. Jack caught her, and they both laughed. Had his kiss been that effective?

★ ★ ★

AFTER the little ceremony, the festival degenerated into random music, dancing, and drinking. I'm not much of a dancer, at least not in a nonformal situation; I can do a fine court waltz, but otherwise I'm pretty lead-footed unless someone's trying to kill me. Liz did not have this problem, though, and after a few drinks I couldn't keep her seated beside me. Not that I minded much, since watching her lithe, supple form move around to music was certainly one of my definitions of a good time.

Once when she returned to take a drink, she said to me breathlessly, "You look miserable."

"No, I don't."

"Yes, you do. If you won't dance with me, why don't you go talk to him and get it out of your system?"

"Talk to who?"

"The fat guy. He's all by himself. His pocket prince is too busy dancing with Eolomea."

She was right: Billy sat on the porch of the packed tavern, a tankard in his hand, watching the people dance in the courtyard. The prince and Isadora were in the center, dancing the way two kids who have recently fallen in love always dance. A low cloud of dust obscured everyone's feet and made the fat man appear to sit in a smoldering cloud.

"Go talk to him, find out who he is and what he wants. You know you want to." She kissed me and returned to her dancing.

I picked up my tankard and sauntered over, playing a man who was looking for a seat and a good drinking partner. I said, "Excuse me, mind if I join you?"

Billy looked up at me. His hair was thin on top but long in the back, and he'd combed little points out of his beard on either side of his chin. There was something fierce and wily in his eyes, an intelligence greater than I'd anticipated finding there. I wondered how many men might have met their end, or at least their detriment, because they missed that. He said,

"Certainly, sir. It's a festival; if you were a pretty girl, you could sit in my lap!"

I sat on the stoop beside him. We touched mugs and drank. Foam and liquid dripped from his facial hair when he lowered his tankard. He said, "Where are you from, sir?"

"Muscodia. What about you?"

"Oh, here and there. No place like home, but no place *is* home, I say. Wherever I lay my lance is my home." He laughed uproariously at his own double entendre.

I smiled as I drank, or rather as I pretended to drink. I sensed I needed to keep my wits about me with this guy. "Is that your son?" I asked, indicating the boy dancing with Isadora.

"Oh, goodness, no, he's a friend. A companion, if you will. Up with the sun, gone with the wind. I met him on the road, and we decided to travel together, enjoying the fruits of spring with these wholesome lads and lasses." He raised his glass to the ones around us. Then he took another drink and said, "By heaven, this rustic ale has a bite to it. I wonder that it doesn't eat away the pit of my stomach."

"Could be worse," I said. "Down where they grow corn and wheat, they draw off this stuff from the bottom of the silos, where the silage has rotted and fermented, sometimes for generations. I've seen it leave a man bald the next day. All over."

"Good heavens," he said, eyes wide in mock horror. "Then I shall be grateful for this libation." He turned up the tankard and drained it in one long swallow.

"That's pretty grateful," I said.

"Oh, the best ale is good for two things. Do you know what those are?"

"Nose painting, sleep, and urine?"

"That's three things. No, good ale, good rum, good *drink*, goes straight to your brain and dries up all your doubts and troubles, then it warms your blood so that even shy persons have the strength to get up and do what needs be done."

He did like the sound of his own voice. I indicated his dancing friend again and said, "Who's the young lady?"

"Why, the queen of curds and cream," he said with a laugh. "She's the prettiest lowborn lass to ever run on these green hills. The daughter of some shepherd, believe it or not. She's far too noble for this place."

"So you know her?"

"My young friend knows her. He made her acquaintance some weeks ago after a falconing incident. That's why he was coming back: he wanted to surprise her, and I'd say he did."

"Coming back from where?" I asked.

"Oh, here and there," he repeated again, and this time he looked at me more closely. I'd have to be craftier if I wanted to get any information out of him without tipping my own hand. "He, like me, moves about following the good food and drink, much like the sheep in these parts. Alas, we have no shepherds to guide us." He laughed again at his own wordplay.

I decided to try something provocative. "I'm in the market for a young, pretty wife myself. Perhaps I'll go ask her to dance."

He put a meaty, stubby-fingered hand on my shoulder. "I wouldn't do that, my friend. I'm as serious as the falling sickness. Crossing paths or swords with that boy will end only in tears and sadness, and all of them will be yours."

"Really? He doesn't look that impressive."

"He has a mighty paternal weight behind him."

I nodded at his belly. "You sure you're not his father, then?"

He laughed. "Oh, heavens, no. Merely a mentor."

"Who *is* his father?"

"A man of power. That's all you need to know." He patted me on the shoulder, then took another drink.

I felt that little knot in my belly that meant a mystery was taking its irrevocable hold. Usually this was a good thing, because usually I got paid for it. But here and now I was on vacation, and the last thing I wanted to do was spend it unraveling the truth of the strange prince, his rotund protector, and the girl I'd once saved from a bear.

But damn it, I knew that's exactly what I was going to do.

chapter

TWELVE

We slept in the wagon, with the lid off to enjoy the stars. The night grew chilly away from the fire and crowd, which made us snuggle close. The festivities in town thinned without entirely stopping, but luckily Liz and I were just drunk and exhausted enough that the songs, drumming, and dancing didn't bother us. We even did some discreet fooling around before we finally fell asleep, inspired by one of the festival songs: *With a trill and a heigh, the thrush and the jay, are summer songs for me and my girl, while we go tumbling in the hay.*

At some point between midnight and dawn, I awoke to a full bladder and climbed down to relieve myself. I pulled on my pants and tunic, in case I encountered anyone. It was cold enough to see my breath, but it helped clear my head so I didn't walk sleepily into something.

A magical view greeted me. Fireflies spread their lazy glow all over the hills, matching the stars in the clear sky. The big bonfire was not yet lit, but smaller ones dotted the landscape, surrounded by tents or groups of people still laughing and singing. Near each one huddled a small herd of sleeping sheep. At least, I assumed they were sleeping. I suddenly wondered if they slept standing up, like horses. I'd have to ask someone.

After I peed, I stayed beside the wagon watching, entranced by the simple beauty of it all. I'd seen so much carnage, so many duplicitous people acting for reasons often they didn't even understand, that this easy community camaraderie really touched me. If I'd taken Beatrice's offer back then, what would have happened? Would I now be a proud father, watching Isadora and her younger siblings grow up? Would I have stood beaming as she played Eolomea in the night's rituals? Without all the years of blade time and skullduggery, would I have been smart enough to spot Jack for what he really was?

The wagon shifted very slightly as Liz rolled over, and her light snoring grew stronger. I smiled. No, I'd made the right decision back then. I couldn't have predicted where I'd end up, but there was no doubt I was where I belonged.

I was about to climb back into the wagon when I heard voices nearby and, out of habit, stood very still to listen. A woman's voice said, "I'm really scared, Jack. What if your father finds out? My God, what if he sees me dressed like this? How could I look him in the eye?"

I had one bare foot on the tailgate. I slowly lowered it, then took my hands off the wagon, careful not to make it shift. Liz continued to snore.

A man's voice responded, calm and kindly. "Shh, people are sleeping in these wagons. And there's nothing to worry about, Izzy. He'd never come around here."

"*You* did."

"Yes, but I was chasing my falcon, remember, not looking for chicks. Ow!" He laughed at her mock blow. "Anyway, my father doesn't indulge. In anything. He sits in his castle and mutters to himself about his subjects. I prefer the personal touch."

They were quiet for a long time. It didn't take a sword

jockey to know what they were up to, or who they were: Bonny Prince Jack and Isadora Glendower.

I knew I should announce myself by a throat-clearing or discreet cough, but habit and curiosity won out. What would two such socially disparate people talk about? Was Liz right about them? Had Billy told me the truth? I silently edged farther into the wagon's shadow.

"Your hands are cold," she said.

"I can put them in my pockets."

"Don't you dare."

Then they were silent again.

"You know I love you, Jack," Isadora said when they came up for air. "I tried not to. I really did."

"And I love you, my sweet Isadora."

"But Jack, you're the crown prince, and I'm a shepherd's daughter. A rich shepherd, I'll grant you, but still a commoner. One day soon you'll have to choose between me and the throne, and there's really no choice, is there?"

"Listen, Izzy. Seriously. I intend to marry you. It's not some idle promise to get under your skirt, you know. Have I ever even tried to do that?"

"No . . ."

"And I won't, not until we're married. 'My desires run not before my honor, nor my lusts burn hotter than my faith.' "

I heard the smile in her voice. "Oh, really? And who said that?"

"A really smart guy. But that's truly how I feel. I can't be anything, let alone the king someday, if I give my word idly and then don't keep it, can I? And if a king can't choose his own queen, what's the point of even *being* king? I'd rather be a shepherd and come home to you every day, than rule a kingdom without you."

They paused, and when she spoke again, Isadora sounded forlorn. "How would I know? I don't know how these things are decided. I only know that I love you, too, and this has been the best spring of my life. But if you marry me, then either I'll become queen, or we'll both be banished, if not publicly executed."

He laughed. "Wow, your tankard is really half empty, isn't it?"

She giggled softly. "I have to get back to the wagon before my family heads back home. I'll see you tomorrow at the banquet, okay? You will come, won't you?"

"Of course I will. Plain Jack Kingson will be there, along with his friend Billy Cudgel."

"Good grief, I don't know if there's enough food in the whole county to fill that mountain." She lightly smacked him. "And 'Kingson'? Really?"

"Best place to hide is in plain sight." His tone grew more serious. "Has your father sent for the moon priestesses?"

"Yes. They'll be here in about a month."

"A month? My father could get them to—"

"No. Absolutely not. They'll be here in a month, and I'll be fine."

"I'm worried about you."

"Don't be. I still have twice your upper body strength, you know."

"Yeah? Prove it."

I heard him go "Oof!" as she slammed him into the wall, and then they both giggled and fell again into that silence that meant a serious kiss.

They made their good-byes, and Isadora slipped back into town to join her family. Jack stayed where he was, apparently lost in thought. He leaned against the stone wall, yawned, and stared up at the stars. I could see his smile in the moonlight. His breath puffed out in happy little plumes as he chuckled in delight.

Here was the crown prince of Altura standing all alone in the middle of the night, with no security retinue in sight. If I'd been his father, I'd be livid, too. One quick knife from the shadows, and Altura was without an heir, a crisis for any country. For one like this, where it was public knowledge that the king had only one child, it would be devastating. Bastard offspring would appear, genuine or not, claiming they should be crowned upon the king's death.

It hit me that I might never get this chance again. So I sidled out of my hiding place, waited until he noticed me, and said, "Good evening, Your Highness."

I didn't catch him off guard. "You've got the wrong guy, pal. My name's Jack Kingson. Not even my sheep call me, 'Your Highness.'"

"No, I don't think I do. Prince John of Altura, only son of King Ellis. That's you."

He pushed himself off the wall and slipped casually into a defensive stance, the kind taught by royal battle masters. His tone was still light. "And that matters to you, why?"

I held up my hands to show I was unarmed. "I just want a couple of minutes of your time."

"That still takes me back to, 'Why?' I should tell you up front, I don't have any money on me, and my influence with my father is . . . negligible. Especially if he finds out I'm here."

"I don't want your money. Without going into a lot of detail, I'm concerned about Isadora. Your attention could destroy her life very easily. You might even get her killed."

"I'd never let that happen," he said seriously.

"Why?"

"Why?" he repeated.

"Yes, why? You can have any well-bred girl in any kingdom around. Why would you dally with a shepherd's daughter? Only reason I can think of is to dip your staff in her flock." I winced at my own metaphor, but to be fair, I was tired and a little hungover.

But it worked; I got the rise I wanted, the one that made him forget who and where he was. "Hey, just wait a goddamn minute, whoever you are. First off, I love that girl. Second, before this festival is over, I'll make it public. And third, it's none of your goddamned business."

"So you really want a shepherdess to be Queen of Altura?"

"Better than some pampered, whiny bitch raised for nothing but sitting in court and spreading gossip!" His voice stayed a whisper, but his outrage was clear. "Ever since I grew old enough to notice girls, my father has been parading these gilded canker-blossoms past me, hoping I'd pick one and be done with it. None of them have any idea what to do with themselves except simper around, gossip, and shop. I don't care how pretty they are, if you can't have a conversation with them, they lose their charm real fast."

He paused, and his whole tone changed. "But Izzy . . . she has a spine. And a brain. She doesn't take anything at face value, including me. And it doesn't hurt that she's the prettiest girl in Altura, either, whether highborn or low. And if my father banishes us for this, I could do a whole lot worse than being a shepherd married to her."

I smiled to myself. If I was any judge of people, this young man was sincere. A bit naive, perhaps, but definitely honest. I said, "All right, calm down, I was just picking at you. Like you said, this is really none of my business."

"Yeah, no kidding. Who are you?"

"Eddie LaCrosse."

"Izzy's never mentioned you."

"Yeah." I deliberated for half a second before saying, "There's a reason for that. If I tell you, you can't tell her."

"Are you her father? Her mother's never told her who—"

"No, I'm not her father." And I told him the story of the bear, the soldiers, and how Isadora ended up with the Glendowers. Even in the dark I could see his eyes widen with disbelief. I finished with, "Three people here know that story now: Owen Glendower, Beatrice Glendower, and you."

"And you."

"I'm leaving. I just wanted to see that she was all right."

Then I paused. "You can tell me one thing: Why are you hanging around with that fat old drunk?"

He laughed. "Billy? He's harmless."

"I wouldn't be so sure."

"You want to know why I'm here, dressed like this, in this sort of company? All right, I'll tell you, then. A secret for a secret." He stepped close, and his voice dropped, low and eager. "Someday I'm going to be the absolute ruler of these people, right? I mean, even if my father banishes me, when he dies, I'll come back. And my decisions will affect them in ways I can't imagine. So how can I be expected to rule over them if I don't *know* them? And there's another reason." He smiled conspiratorially. "Everyone at court knows I've gone rogue like this. They know I'm out carousing, drinking, wenching, probably robbing honest citizens for the sheer fun of it. I'm like the sun, hidden behind the clouds of all these bad habits. But on the day I accept the crown, those clouds will part. After all, a treasure that's been hidden away is a lot more interesting than one that's always been sitting there in plain sight."

I was impressed. "Oh, that's good."

"I know," he said with a conspiratorial chuckle. "I didn't set out to find a commoner queen, but if I had, I couldn't do better than Isadora. And the best part is, I really *do* love her." He patted my arm. "Have a safe journey, Mr. LaCrosse. It's been a pleasure swapping secrets with you."

I watched the young prince saunter back into town, justifiably pleased with himself. I hoped he got to follow through with his plan, because I'd met few princes so concerned with their future status as king. Even Phil, a good prince and a great king, had not been this self-aware.

I felt pretty good myself, not least about Isadora's future. It was too bad I wouldn't be around to see the look on Glendower's face when he found out who his future son-in-law really was, and what his foster granddaughter was about to become. I fought the urge to whistle as I strolled back to the wagon, intending to crawl back in beside Liz and sleep the sleep of the just. Tomorrow I would get up without a care and belatedly dive into my well-deserved vacation.

Instead, I came around the end of a tall-sided cart and froze in my tracks. Liz sat on our wagon's tail gate, wrapped in a blanket and casually kicking her bare feet. And standing beside her was Billy Cudgel.

It takes a lot to totally catch me off guard. I mean, obviously, if it were easy to do, I wouldn't have lived as long as I have. But this little tableau did it.

Billy whispered something that made Liz laugh. When she did so, the blanket slid lower off her bare shoulders, and I saw him stare lasciviously at the newly exposed flesh.

Now, that just wasn't going to fly.

"Well, look at this," I said as I stepped into the open. "What have we got here?"

It was too dark to see if she had that mischievous gleam in her eye that said she knew *exactly* what we had here, but I wouldn't put it past her. She said, "There you are. Eddie, this is Billy. Billy, this is my boyfriend, Eddie."

"The gentleman and I have met," Billy said. "Good to see you again, sir."

"Words fail me," I said as I shook his hand. "You're up awfully late."

"Dear me, this is when I do my best work," he said with a wink at Liz. She giggled, and again the blanket slipped lower. In the moonlight, her bare skin glowed white.

I reached past Billy and tugged the blanket back up. "And just what are you two night owls working on?"

"He was telling me this story about the time he was attacked on the road," she said.

"Really?" I pushed past Billy, not the easiest thing to do, hopped up on the tailgate, and wriggled in between him and Liz. I knew Liz wasn't attracted to this guy, but he was definitely poaching in my forest. "I'd like to hear about this, too. I love a good story."

If I threw him off, he didn't let on. "Very well. Where was I?"

"There were two of them," Liz said helpfully.

"That's right, in leather armor, with scarves to hide their scurrilous faces. The four of them—"

"Wait a minute," I said. "Liz said there were two."

"No, the dear lady is mistaken, I said four. Four of them, all armed with great vicious daggers. The seven of them—"

"Four," I corrected.

"Seven," he said deliberately, glaring at me, then returned his attention to Liz. "They thought I was a simple peddler, with nothing but sheets in my pack. But I showed them the truth, driving the nine of them back with my fierce blade." He unsheathed his sword and shook it for emphasis.

I tensed up, as I always did when someone drew a blade in front of me, but Liz merely giggled.

"Then I disemboweled seven of the eleven, draping their steaming guts around my neck!"

"Oh, gross!" Liz said, still laughing.

"Better to have them about your neck than around your legs, dear lady. You don't need to get your feet tangled when you're up against fifteen ruffians."

"Okay, okay," I said to Billy. "As much as I'm enjoying the story of this ever-expanding battle, it's late and I'm tired. Did you want something in particular?"

"He was looking for you," Liz said.

"Indeed, sir," Billy said. "I'd like a word with you in private."

He put a meaty hand on my shoulder and pulled me down off the tailgate with surprising strength. I glanced back at Liz; she flashed me with the blanket, then winked. I'd get her back for this one.

Billy and I walked away from the wagons until we were out in the open where no one could hear and, more important, no one could come to my aid. The moon made his bulk merge with his shadow, blurring his outline and doubling his considerable size. The wind was considerably colder out here with nothing to block it, and I was barefoot and coatless.

He did not release my shoulder, and the weight of his hand made me lean to one side. He said calmly, "I still have my sword in my hand. I'm not threatening, mind you, just alerting you."

"I'm alert. And unarmed."

"Those are exactly the two qualities I look for in a foe. Well, the latter one, certainly. Now, to the point: I saw you speaking to my friend Jack earlier. Why were you doing that?"

"Why don't ask him? He's your friend."

He got close, his broad furry face right in mine. His breath smelled of ale and cabbage. The charm he'd used on Liz was totally gone, replaced with the seriousness of a man at work. "Because I'm asking you." His stomach growled in the silence. "And I'm as impatient for answers as I am for my next meal."

I was torn between playing along to see what he was about, and annoyance at being bullied. I said at last, "One time, I was in a tavern, and two men were betting over who had the biggest manhood."

"I fail to see the connection."

"Bear with me. The first man pulled his out, and it was impressive. But the second man won. He didn't pull his all the way out, mind you. He just pulled out enough to win the contest." I smiled smugly.

The hand on my shoulder dug stubby fingers painfully into my flesh. He was strong beneath the blubber, and while I was pretty sure I could get away if I really needed to, I also knew I wouldn't learn anything if I did. And I needed to know what his relationship was with slumming Prince Jack, because that affected Isadora.

"When it comes to the truth," Cudgel said, "I expect you

to pull it all out. And make it stand at attention. If not . . . I might have to shave a few inches off it to give you some incentive."

I looked back at the wagon as if ensuring that Liz wasn't listening. I spoke softly and laid on just enough guilt. "Okay, okay. I was talking to him about the girl. You know, the one he was dancing with when you and I were watching? I wanted to see how serious he was about her."

His eyes narrowed. I was telling him the literal truth, but hoped our prior conversation and my performance shaded it so that he believed I was trying to get Isadora for myself. It was easier than outright lying, because I didn't have to keep track of any fabrications. "And what," he rumbled, "did my friend tell you?"

"To mind my own business."

His big head tilted skeptically. "You seemed to part on much friendlier terms than that."

"That's kind of creepy, a grown man like you, sneaking around after a boy."

He didn't take the bait. "I was watching over a naive friend. He's had a very sheltered life. And you also seem to have a perfectly acceptable woman of your own, one with a most delightful laugh. How would she take it, to find that you were sniffing around in search of a younger bitch to bear your next litter? Would she laugh that off?"

I had my way out now. "Well, I wasn't planning to tell her until I worked out the details."

He snorted. The cabbage smell enveloped me. He said, "You're quite the cad, my friend."

"At least I don't get by on the table leavings from a wayward prince."

He was silent for a long moment. I watched the sword in his hand, ready to spring aside if it moved toward me. Surely a man as fat as this couldn't also be quick. At last he said, "And who else knows about that?"

Whew. I had him. "No one. Yet."

"Hm. Then if I stain my sword on your gummed-up excuse for blood—"

"You'll have to do a lot of explaining, because my lady friend will definitely raise a ruckus. And then your prince will have to use his pull to get you out of it . . . or leave you twisting in the wind, however he decides. So why don't we leave it at this: You know something about me, I know something about you. If we both keep our mouths shut, the world keeps spinning just fine."

He considered this, then slowly smiled. He looked as harmless as a kitten. "Well, my friend, it seems you've resolved our issues. I believe you're exactly right, except for one small thing."

"What's that?"

He released my shoulder and patted my cheek. "There's strong evidence the world might be flat." Then he put away the sword and strolled back toward town.

I waited until he was out of sight, then returned to the wagon. Liz was fully dressed, standing with my boots in her hand. "Our stuff's mostly packed, and what isn't won't get hurt bouncing around," she said softly. "Are we leaving?"

"No," I said, and kissed her. "What did he say before I showed up?"

"He was trying to charm my pants off. Or my blanket, as the case may be. As fat as he is, I'm not really sure what could actually happen if he *did* get me in the mood."

"He's bad news. I don't know what he's really after, but whatever it is, it affects Isadora."

She looked at me.

"What?" I added defensively.

"You're going to figure out who she is, aren't you?"

"I don't know," I said rather petulantly. "Maybe."

"Your only clues were eaten by a bear sixteen years ago."

"I found Black Edward Tew after twenty years."

"Yes, but he knew who he was. Isadora doesn't have a clue."

"Then it's an even bigger challenge."

She shook her head, put her arms around my neck, and kissed me. "You are something, Eddie LaCrosse. You do your best work for friends, and never get paid for it. Why in the world do I stay with you?"

I put my hand on the small of her back and pulled her against me. My cold fingers slid up her skin.

"Oh, yes," she said. "Now I remember why. You give me chills."

We climbed back into the wagon.

We intended to sleep late the next morning, but the noises of sheep being herded, children being scolded, and what sounded like a cat being strangled prevented it. This last was due to a piper tuning up on the hillside, and it took him what seemed an interminable amount of time to do it. Even the sheep got annoyed, bleating their disapproval, and I could tell no qualitative difference from when he first started. Still, it got me up and going, so I dressed and went to the well at the center of town for a bucket of water. Some people stirred along the street, cleaning up the debris from the previous night. Some still slept where they'd apparently fallen. The flowered arches were tattered and shredded like a storm had come through.

A portly, bald man with a narrow beard sat on the stoop of a small, closed shop, cradling his head in his hands. At first I thought he was crying, so I said, "You all right there, pal?"

He looked up. His eyes were bloodshot and squinted against the sunrise. "My brain," he said, "is very poor and unhappy this morning."

"I know the feeling," I assured him.

"That fat man in the tavern," he continued. "I don't know where he puts it all. He's been in there all night, and he's still going."

"Fat man?"

"Aye. Billy something-or-other. He's full of stories, and he tells them for drinks. I bought him three times as many as I drank myself, and look at me. Yet there he sits, still rambling on."

"It'll catch up with him eventually. And it'll hurt worse than yours does."

"That," he assured me, "is not possible."

As I passed the Head Boar, I did hear Billy Cudgel's loud voice, just as the bald man said. "There live not three good men unhanged in Altura," he declaimed, "and one of them is fat, and grows old." The laughter told me that he had at least four or five people around him. Did the man never sleep?

As I shuffled back to the gate with the water, two men rode up, tied their horses, and paused to look around. One was very tall, broad-shouldered, with the cocky, rolling gait of a professional soldier who enjoyed intimidating people as much as he did hacking them to pieces.

The other man was older, with a ramrod-straight back and a sense of entitlement that surrounded him like a glow. His clothes were tailored but not ostentatious, and he looked around as if searching for something. Apparently it wasn't the smattering of drunks left from the night before, or the dedicated shepherds up with sunrise.

Three children ran past them, bumping into the older man. "Your pardon, sir!" one of them called back. The bigger of the two looked ready to skewer the youngsters, while the older man seemed peeved but not surprised, as if this were merely the latest annoyance of dozens.

"They're still going at the tavern," I called out. The taller one gave me a narrow-eyed once-over, and I grinned and waved. "Happy spring!"

"Thank you," the older man said, while the big one just scowled.

I looked over their horses when I passed. The tack and saddles showed evidence of much use, but the horses themselves were not farm animals by a long shot. Not even Owen Glendower could afford two such magnificent animals. I considered rifling their saddlebags once the riders were out of sight, but ultimately decided against it. I already had one mystery that no one was paying me for; if I took on another, Liz might marry me just so she could then divorce me.

Back at the wagon, Liz had dressed and combed her hair. She used the same blue ribbon to tie it back, then winced as the practicing piper filled the morning with another series of bleats. "Do you know," she asked sleepily, "why pipers walk around when they play?"

"No, why?"

"To get away from that sound."

I kissed her. "Art demands sacrifice."

Suddenly sheep were all around us, threading through the parked wagons with their woolly chaos. A few more sleepy faces peeked from the other wagons. The animals seemed as confused as the people.

Two boys and an overexcited dog tried to encourage the sheep to move out into the open, but they weren't coordinated and it only confused the animals more. "Sorry, mister!" one of the boys said as he tried to drag a sheep away. "We'll get 'em out as soon as we can."

"The kids here are very polite," I said.

"Yeah, small towns are like that."

"I'm polite, and I wasn't raised in a small town."

She pinched my side. "But you're at your best when you're rude."

"Only with you."

As I bent to kiss her, the dog jumped up and licked her face. A boy whistled sharply, and the animal ran away. Liz looked at me, dog slobber fresh on her cheeks, and said, "Well, come on, what are you waiting for? Kiss me."

Which I did. It takes more than a little dog spit to make me not want to kiss her.

I washed up, got dressed, and then we went into town in search of some breakfast. By then several carts had food for sale, and we wandered as we ate, waiting for the other merchants to get ready for the day.

It did not take long to wander the length and breadth of Mummerset. We passed the Head Boar, but Billy Cudgel's voice no longer rang out. I stuck my head in; except for one man asleep on the floor and another sprawled and snoring on a table, it was empty. Guess even Billy had to sleep sometime.

"So, what's your first move?" Liz asked when I rejoined her in the street.

"I need to talk to Glendower. He can tell me where the gold coins in the money bag came from." Most money was stamped with the seal, crest, or face of the king, queen, or other ruler. Bonny Prince Jack, for example, was on the Alturan four-bit gold piece. That would tell me a bit about the origin of the money paid to her original guardian, the man pursued by the bear. And "follow the money" was a basic sword jockey tenet.

"And then?"

"Depends on what I find out."

The same two men I'd spotted earlier passed us again. Now that I was fully awake, I noticed details I'd missed before. The tall, bulky man wore a sword with a tattered grip and notched guard that spoke of lots of action, and under his rustic clothes seemed to be sporting leather armor. He stayed right behind the other man, his gaze sweeping the path ahead of them. He was unmistakable: strong-arm security, which made me immediately curious about who the other man might be. This isolated festival was suddenly becoming the hottest spot around.

"Hey," Liz said, and nudged me. "What's wrong?"

"Huh? Nothing. Just noticing things."

"Well, stop it. You can't do anything this early in the morning, so just enjoy spending time with me, okay?"

"I always do."

The town came to life around us. More noticeably, men were building several small pens in the courtyard where, the night before, Eolomea had welcomed the spring. A few questions determined that these would be for the sheep-shearing contests coming up shortly.

The two newcomers examined these pens. Well, the older one did. The security man, for I had no doubt about his job now, watched everything else. Including me. If he was good, and I had no reason to doubt it, he'd spotted me as just as out of place here. I'd have to watch it. And them.

The best place to do that, of course, was right under their noses. Liz and I sidled up beside them. Although he was dressed as a shepherd, the older man's fingernails were neat and spotless, and the edges of his hair were nearly trimmed and shaved. *Disguises are more than clothes,* I wanted to tell him, but before I could, he said to me, "Do you believe that?"

"Believe what?"

"They're already selling alcohol to people. It's not even bloody noon."

"It's a festival."

"It's disgraceful."

"If you don't like it, why are you here?"

"I wanted to see for myself."

"See what?"

"Nothing," he said, realizing he'd spoken out of turn. I felt the presence of the bodyguard behind me making the air between us shiver. Who *was* this guy, who needed security when even the crown prince didn't?

And then I knew. *Oh,* I thought. *Of course.*

I had no idea what King Ellis looked like, so I couldn't actually confirm this was him, but it made sense. Sure, your average king would send trusted agents to retrieve a truant prince, but what if said king wanted to see what was up for himself? Not every monarch stayed on his throne all the time. This made me want to like the guy, but that impulse was negated by his one-man security retinue, who I wanted to punch in the face on general principles. He was, I realized, exactly the kind of swaggerer the mistress back in Mahnoma didn't want in her tavern.

If he was King Ellis, and he was here to retrieve Bonny Prince Jack, then this was related to Isadora, and thus fell within the self-defined borders of my "case." Well, nothing would reveal itself if I stayed polite. So I said, "You are an old grouch, aren't you? Denying hardworking folks a little fun?"

The old man looked at me as if unused to hearing such honesty, then laughed. "By heavens, you're right, I *am* an old grouch. I've forgotten what it feels like to be young. Please, enjoy your festival."

He nodded to the bodyguard, and they moved away. Liz looked at me oddly. "What was that about?"

"That," I said quietly, "was the last person you'd expect to find here."

"The king looking for his son?"

"Okay, maybe not *the* last, then."

"It is kind of obvious."

"Yeah. But I wonder why he's here?"

"You just said—"

"I know. I mean, is he here to discreetly drag Junior back to the castle by the ear, or is he planning to make an example of anyone who's helped out with Jack's little masquerade?"

"Is he that kind of king?" she asked seriously.

"I have no idea."

"And what are you going to do?"

"I could introduce you, so you can forget your name again."

She thumped me between my eyes. Then she said, "All right, go to work."

"I don't need to—"

"Yes, you do," she said with the kind of weary forbearance that made me love her even more. "Go see what he's up to. If I can help, let me know." She kissed me. "You're going back to school with the little kids when we return to Neceda, though."

"And why is that?"

"Because you clearly don't know the meaning of a simple word like 'vacation.'"

I thought about this. It didn't hurt that, in the morning sun, Liz looked particularly adorable. "Ah, you're right. They'll keep. Let's have some fun while we can."

Mummerset was way too small for effective shadowing, anyway. If I followed the incognito king directly, his trained ape would try to pound me into the dirt. On the plus side, the town was surrounded by a rock wall, which meant there were only four ways out. So I really only had to stay in the general area. And once the crowd began gathering for the sheep-shearing competition, I only had to keep my eye on the tall man towering above everyone else to follow the king's movements.

A little parade brought the shearing competitors into town. Owen Glendower led his group, a large sheep hook in his hand like a king's staff. He was dressed in an ostentatious robe, again like something you'd see in court, and he passed obliviously by the actual king in disguise. He nodded and smiled to many people, occasionally gesturing with his crook as if it might convey a blessing. I wondered how he'd explained his fairly meteoric rise in status to his neighbors. At least none of them made faces at him when he wasn't looking.

Behind him his son Clancy followed, shirtless and dressed in loose pants, evidently prepared for the competition. I was a bit surprised they trusted him with sharp things like shearing scissors. A younger boy, either a farmhand or another son, brought up the rear, making sure the half dozen sheep stayed together. I saw no sign of Beatrice or Isadora, but Prince Jack and Billy Cudgel now stood near the front of the crowd. Jack couldn't see his disguised father from where he was, and unless the tall bodyguard noticed Billy's bulk displacing the crowd, they couldn't see him. Yet they were barely twenty feet apart.

I shook my head. The once and future kings of Altura, both in disguise as commoners, both in the same microscopic town. This couldn't end well.

"You ever sheared a sheep?" Liz asked.

"Only if that's a metaphor for something else."

"Ha! Didn't think so."

"And you have?"

"We had sheep when I was growing up. Well, two. So yes, I have."

"Want to join the contest?"

"One reason I started my own business and became my own boss was so I'd never have to shear sheep again. Or clean out pigsties. Or milk cows. Or milk goats."

"Or brush horses?"

"No, that I don't mind. I'm not afraid of them like you are."

"I'm not afraid of them. I just don't trust them."

"I've never met anyone else whose 'mistrust' makes them shriek like a little girl whenever a horse backs up toward them."

I played my trump card. "Yeah, well, I saved you from a fire-breathing dragon once."

She jabbed me in the ribs. "You need to find a new clincher for arguments. Really. That one's run its course."

Smugly, I finished, "That's what the dragon said."

The little herdlets were guided into their small pens, where they milled about, sheeping. "How's everybody doing today?" a robust man said as he strode before the contestants. He held a small megaphone decorated with the omnipresent ribbons. "I see a lot of sore heads out there this morning. But honestly, I feel sorry for folks who don't drink. After all, when they wake up in the morning, that's the best they're going to feel all day!"

A cheer mixed with laughter came from the crowd.

"Now, let's meet our first shearing contestants. I remind you, this is a double-elimination tournament, so you'll be seeing both of these shearing masters again. First, from the household of Owen Glendower, winner of second place for seven years in a row, Clancy Glendower!"

There was some polite cheering at this.

"Wow," Liz said softly. "Second place for a third of his life."

"And I bet that percentage will only increase," I said.

"This is the year!" Clancy said, and held up his index finger. "Number one! Wait and see!" Then he put a stool down beside the designated sheep.

"That's the spirit!" the announcer said, and tousled Clancy's hair. "Next up, we have our challenger in her first time on the big stool. Let's hear it for Phoebe York!"

A girl stepped up to her stool. She was young, stocky, and with long blond hair tied up in a knot on her head. Except for a single piece of cloth wrapped around her torso to cover—or control—her breasts, she was as bare chested as the boys.

She raised her fists, and her knot of supporters began to clap and say, "Phoe-*be*! Phoe-*be*! Phoe-*be*!"

"Why do they take off their shirts?" I asked Liz. "Seems like wool on sweaty skin would be irritating."

"Part of the challenge is putting up with the irritation," she said. "It's a lot like dating you."

Phoebe paced in a tight circle before she sat. She settled in, grabbed a handful of the waiting sheep's wool, and shook it as if to ensure it was still attached. Then she looked over at Clancy and winked. He blushed.

"Apparently it's a friendly rivalry," I said.

"Or just good strategy," Liz said.

Before they could start, there was a commotion along the edge of the crowd. Jack Kingson, incognito prince, followed Billy Cudgel as the fat man used his bulk to clear a path. Then the prince stepped up and whispered something to the announcer. The announcer looked puzzled, then motioned for Clancy to join them. Grinning, Jack said something to Clancy, whose eyes opened wide. Then they shook hands, and Clancy stepped back. Jack took off his shirt, to the cheers and catcalls of girls in the crowd, and assumed Clancy's seat beside his sheep.

"What a piece of work!" one girl cried.

"Take him for all in all," another commented.

I surreptitiously checked the king's reaction. He looked as if someone had tapped him hard in the balls. Only his bodyguard kept him from rushing forward, and only the crowd's interest in the contest kept anyone else from noticing. There could be no good end to this family feud.

Jack grinned like this was the most enjoyable thing in the world, testing out the shears' tension and arranging the stool beside the blase' animal. Phoebe glared at him, all business now, and wasted some serious intimidation on an opponent who thought this a lark.

"Shearers, assume your position!" the announcer said. Phoebe and Jack picked up their shears.

The announcer raised a short riding whip over his head and held it there expectantly. He enjoyed the attention.

Suddenly a girl pressed a tankard into my hands, without a word of explanation. She was quite attractive, with long red hair darker than Liz's, and she winked at me and licked her lips suggestively. Then she was gone.

The announcer said, "Ready . . . ready . . ."

Liz nodded at the cup. "What's that?"

Before I could answer, he brought the whip down with a sharp snap. "Go!"

Phoebe jumped up, kicked the stool aside, expertly grabbed her sheep under the front legs, and sat it back on its haunches. The teats revealed it was a female. Phoebe held the animal up with her left hand, while her right clipped expertly in a diagonal line across the sheep's chest.

Jack did the same thing, but with far less certainty. He quickly fell behind, but seemed oblivious.

The birdlike noise of the two blades sliding together rang out in the courtyard. The two sheep seemed thoroughly unconcerned with any of this, and exchanged a look that could rival any veteran courtiers for smug indifference.

The crowd, seeing that Phoebe was going to win, again shouted her name. She began to move with little flourishes, which slowed her down, but not enough for Jack to catch up.

I took a big swallow of my drink. It was mead, thicker and sweeter than ale, and tasted great despite its rather vile odor. I let the first mouthful settle contentedly in my stomach as I drank more.

Jack was only halfway done by the time Phoebe let her the sheep drop to its hooves, raised her clippers overhead, and yelled, "Sheared!" Stray bits of wool stuck to her shoulders and face. Jack finished his sheep and, still grinning, stood and offered his hand. She shook it, and took a victory strut before the crowd. We all chanted "Phoe-*be*!"

Clancy stepped out and kissed her politely on the cheek. She grabbed him and kissed him on the mouth hard enough to curl his toes. The crowd approved.

I hadn't quite drained my tankard, but I did pretty well for this early in the morning. I looked at Liz, who regarded me skeptically.

"You keep telling me I'm on vacation," I said defensively.

"Do you even know what that is?"

"Shum sort of mead," I said.

" 'Shum sort'?" she repeated, amused.

"Some sort," I corrected testily. "I just woke up, you know."

She leaned over and sniffed the mug. "Wow. That's ghastly. How can you stand it?"

I put it to my nose. It was pungent, but I'd smelled worse. "It's not that bad."

"If you're smell-blind."

A heavy hand clapped me on the shoulder, and a man I didn't know said, "Good Lord, man, do I smell Devil's Dew in your cup? Is *that* what you're drinking?"

"I guess. Someone gave it to me."

He laughed as if this were the funniest thing in the world. "I use that stuff on my bull calves before I geld them, it puts them right out! How much did you drink?" He looked in my mostly empty mug and laughed even louder.

Now I was a little annoyed. "Well, I can handle it," I said, but I was also wondering why the strange redhead gave it to me.

A group of girls lifted Phoebe overhead and carried her in triumph around the courtyard. Jack wiped the sweat and wool from his chest. A few girls not involved in celebrating Phoebe's win attempted to console the loser, but he politely rebuffed them. I didn't see Isadora, but it did seem Jack was a man of his word.

Then Billy appeared. The red-haired girl who'd delivered my drink was on his arm, counting coins in her other hand. She jabbed him and said something, which made him give her more money. Then he whispered something that made her laugh.

He looked across at me, nodded knowingly, and winked.

Before my rapidly fuzzying head could process this, the bodyguard and the king moved toward the back of the crowd. The big man parted the way, just as Billy Cudgel had done for Jack. I nudged Liz and said, "I'm going after the kim . . . kiln . . . *king*. Can you keep an eye on Jack?"

"Are you okay to do that?" she asked, nodding at the tankard I still held.

I poured the dregs on the ground and handed her the mug. "I'll be all right. Jush shon't let that guy geld me."

"Wow. Seriously, Eddie, you sound out of it."

My head was a little watery, but I assumed it was no big deal. "I'll be fine."

chapter

FOURTEEN

I once knew a mercenary named Kemp who claimed he'd encountered a fighting technique called the Fist of Despair. Someone with this particular skill could hit you over the heart, and you had three blinks before your heart stopped and you dropped dead. Kemp said he'd personally seen a man struggle valiantly not to blink that last blink, to hang on to as much life as possible, before losing the fight and falling dead where he stood.

That's how the Devil's Dew hit me.

I turned into a sack of wet sand. I could barely walk, my eyes crossed, and I felt saliva drip from my slack mouth. However, I did not do the sensible thing like the man in Kemp's story and fall to the ground. Instead, I obstinately continued, determined to find King Ellis and . . . well, by then my intent was a little blurry even to me.

I passed a horse trough and impulsively ducked my head in it. The muffled sound and pressure of the water against my face felt great, and I actually stayed under so long that someone tapped me on the shoulder. When I rose, I was surrounded by half a dozen people.

"What?" I asked.

"Are you all right?" a thin, older gentleman asked.

"Why wouldn't I be?" I said, tucking my wet hair behind my ears and wishing they'd all stand still.

"You were underwater for a long time," a woman with a cane said.

"You were bubbling," a little boy added.

"I'm fine," I assured them, standing to my full height. That was a bit of a mistake, as I found that the air at that height was rather thin and made me wobble. "Thank you for your concern."

A big hand appeared on my shoulder—so heavy, it almost knocked me to the ground. I turned to find Clancy Glendower's face way too close to mine. "Are you all right, Mr. Lacrosser?" he asked with real concern.

"Just a little tipsy, Clance," I said, and returned his pat. I shook my head, splashing us both with water from my wet hair. Even my beard felt heavy on my face.

"If you need a place to take a bath, I can help you find—"

"No, thank you, I'm fine. Although, have you seen a really tall guy wandering around?"

"Uhm . . . I'm right here in front of you."

"Not you, Clancy. Another tall guy."

"No, it's just me, Mr. Lacrosser. I think you're seeing double." He leaned close and whispered, "That happens sometimes when you drink."

I stared at him. "Wow. Do you dress yourself, Clancy?"

He smiled proudly and adjusted his tunic. "Why, yes, I do. Thanks for noticing. A lot of people think I don't."

"I bet," I said, patted his arm again, and staggered off down the street, deliberately milking my intoxication. What better disguise for a super-intelligent sword jockey than a wet, stumbling drunk?

I still didn't connect my wobbly legs and woolly thoughts with the idea that I should stop what I'd set out to do. Squinting through self-generated fog, I stumbled from building to building, seeking the tall form of the king's bodyguard ahead of me in the crowd. My purposes had narrowed down to this simple task, and although I muttered a lot of "pardon me's," I also just shoved people aside as they impeded my progress.

Abruptly I realized the figure I sought had vanished. I grabbed the next man I saw and said, "Hey, friend, have you seen a really tall guy following an older guy?"

He had the solid build of someone used to managing big, recalcitrant animals; even though I practically used him as a crutch, he didn't bend. He looked at me, then at my hand. "You better let me go, *friend*."

I'd grabbed him much harder than I intended. "Sorry. A few too many ale mugs, too early in the morning."

"You still haven't let me go," he pointed out.

He was right, so I did. He said, "I saw two guys like that head down the street toward the south gate. But are you all right? Is there someone here looking after you?"

"I don't need looking after," I snapped petulantly.

"Hm. You might try sobering up a little; the big one looked pretty tough."

"I'm plenty tough," I insisted, "and plenty sober." I was annoyed that the word came out "shober." I smiled, and as soon as he was gone slapped myself a couple of times, hard. Wow. I used to be able to hold my liquor, I told myself. What was in that Devil's Dew?

The woman with the cane watched me from the porch of the Head Boar. I couldn't quite make out her face, but I was certain it radiated disapproval. Annoyed, I yelled, "I'm . . . fine!"

She said calmly, "You're a fine drunk, if that's what you mean."

Even more annoyed, I said firmly, "Yes!"

I continued past the Head Boar until a firm hand grabbed

the back of my tunic and jerked me into the ridiculously small alley. "Clancy, goddammit—!" I said, before I suddenly realized I faced King Ellis and his bodyguard.

The bodyguard slammed me into a wall, hard enough to make it, and me, rattle. "Why are you following us?" he asked, and shook me for emphasis.

I made myself think deliberately. I couldn't trust my physical reflexes, because they were too numbed and slow. Liz might come to my rescue, but I wouldn't count on that, mostly because it would embarrass me too much. I had no other backup, so I'd have to get out of this myself. To do that, I had to be smart and slick.

So I said, "Fuck you."

Even as I said them, I knew the words were a mistake, and the heavy *thwock* of my skull against the wall underlined that assumption. I battled the nausea threatening to surge up my gullet along with all the Devil's Dew, and added, "And your mama, too."

The bodyguard smiled and drew back a fist as big as a sheep, but the king put his hand on the giant's arm. "Hold on, Ajax. He's sick."

"He's drunk."

"So's your mother," my mouth said, although I was almost certain my brain wasn't involved.

The king grabbed my face and turned it toward him. "Do you know who I am?"

Mess this up, I promised my brain, *and I'll cut you out of my head and leave you on the side of the road.* I said, "You're holding his leash; that makes you the most important guy around." Okay, not my best response, but a definite improvement over "fuck you." Nice going, brain.

The king scrutinized me very closely. Luckily, it's easy to pretend to be a drunken bum when you are, in fact, a drunken bum. I smiled and said, "Hi, pops."

"Let him go," the king said.

"He insulted my mother," Ajax rumbled. "No one does that. That woman is an angel."

"He can barely stand. I think the headache he'll have later will be punishment enough."

"I better not see him later," Ajax said. He shook me once, hard enough that my teeth crushed my tongue, then let me go and stepped back.

I wrestled my tunic back into place, elaborately stroked my hair back from my face, and held out my hand. "No hard feelings, big man?"

Ajax glared at my hand, then my face, then back at my hand.

"Come on, be an adult," the king said impatiently.

He reached for my hand.

I grabbed his wrist with my left hand and his thumb with my right. I bent his thumb back as far as it would go, fully intent on breaking it. He was too strong for that, although he howled in pain and fell to his knees.

He was far from done, though. With his free hand he grabbed *my* right thumb and tried to pry it from his wrist. I did not let go. This instantly became a matter of my masculine pride, one of those immature emotions that seldom surfaced without the aid of alcohol. The Devil's Dew invoked it in spades.

We jointly forced ourselves to our knees, each struggling with the other's thumb. I suppose if I'd been sober, I would've had sense enough to try another move. Evidently Ajax wasn't smart enough even when he *was* sober.

"Stop it!" the king said. "I mean it! Right now! Do you hear me?"

He wasn't *my* king, so I ignored him, and Ajax said nothing. We were now almost nose to nose, grimacing in mutual pain and fury. I felt his spit strike my face as it shot out between his clenched teeth. He said, "After I tear it off, I'm going to shove that thumb up your ass, smart guy!"

"Yeah?" I shot back. "Well, I'm gonna shove yours up mine!" Then I frowned, pondering exactly what I'd said.

In my peripheral vision I saw other people crowd into the little alley. Some of them laughed. Clancy was there, and he looked very disappointed. So did the woman with the cane. "Fight! Fight! Fight!" the other observers shouted, attracting more onlookers.

"Look at yourselves!" the king shouted helplessly. "You're both grown men, and you're *thumb wrestling*!"

Ajax said, "He started it!"

Because I had an audience, I got the brightest idea of all. I'd show them just how tough I was. I drew back and head-butted Ajax as hard as I could, right between the eyes. He didn't see it coming, and his face went slack at once.

Unfortunately, I'd dazed myself so thoroughly that I had no knowledge of anything. I didn't go out, but I definitely went somewhere else. I suppose I hit the ground a moment after he did.

THE obligatory bucket of water splashed over me, dragging me from whatever fantasies my addled brain provided. I opened my eyes and gritted my teeth against my hangover's first agonizing *thud*.

Two women and two men stood over me. One of the women held the bucket. "I guess he's alive," Liz said.

"Might just be death twitches," the woman with the cane said.

"No, I'm alive," I said. "A corpse wouldn't have this headache." A slow look around told me I was still in the alley, leaning against a building. I did not attempt to rise.

"I'm sorry for not getting here sooner," Clancy said. "It took me a while to find your wife."

"I'm not his wife," Liz said dryly. "More like his keeper."

"Like you never get drunk," I muttered.

"When I get drunk, you get lucky," she shot back. "I'm not feeling the luck right now."

"Me, neither," I agreed.

"Billy told me what he did," the other man said. I recognized Bonny Prince Jack's properly apologetic voice. "I'm really sorry."

"Wait till you see how sorry he's going to be," I said, and gingerly braced my feet against the ground. I pushed myself upright with my back against the building. Liz dropped the bucket and rushed to catch me before I fell over.

"How are you?" Liz asked.

"I should be able to think straight in a month or so."

"Who was that man you were fighting?" the other woman asked.

"I'm not sure." I wanted to tell Jack about his father when no one else was around. Then I recognized the woman with the cane and smiled. "Audrey."

She was older, truly old now, but still her eyes still had the fire of the woman who'd stood up to those hooligans in her tavern sixteen years ago. "Do I know you?"

"No," I assured her. I didn't see the need to bring her into this.

"You knew my name."

"Lucky guess."

"He calls everyone Audrey when he first meets them," Liz said, earning my love all over again. Then she added dryly, "It's one of his adorable quirks."

"Sometimes I'm right," I said.

"That's true," Liz said, continuing to back me up. "There's more Audreys out there than you'd think."

I looked around for King Ellis and Ajax the bodyguard. "Where are they? The big guy and his friend."

"They were gone when we got here," Liz said.

"Just as well," I said. The world orbited my head for a moment, then settled back down.

Liz said, "Can you walk?"

"I'll get back to you on that," I said, and closed my eyes.

Liz turned to the others. "Thanks for helping me keep an eye on him. I've got it from here on."

"Will you be at the Glendowers' dinner tonight?" Jack asked. "There might be a significant announcement." I heard the grin in his voice.

"We'll do our best," I assured him. Then I vomited the remaining Devil's Dew in my stomach. When I finished and looked up, everyone but Liz was gone.

I staggered away from Liz just to make sure I could still walk unaided. It was a near thing. "Wow," I said, "if this headache is any indication, that Devil's Dew is something."

"I think smashing skulls with your pal didn't help." A dog rushed past us to get at my vomit. "Oh, look. Now the dogs can get drunk, too. It's a *real* party."

I felt the goose egg just above the bridge of my nose. "I think you're right. I'm going to have some scores to settle, once I can feel my toes again."

She helped me out to our wagon, where I sprawled on the hay and she took off my boots. I draped an arm over my eyes. The thundering in my head was so loud, I had to check to make sure a drummer wasn't actually standing nearby.

Liz stretched out beside me. "Will you be okay? I mean, there's drunk and then there's poisoned."

"I know what poisoned feels like," I assured her, recalling a particularly bad night in a Boscobel casino. "This is just drunk."

" 'Just'?"

"Okay, it's an unjust drunk."

"If you're making jokes like that, you'll be okay. Do you want me to stay with you?"

"Go on, go have fun," I said. She kissed me on the cheek and left me to my misery. And thoughts of sweet, sweet revenge.

chapter

FIFTEEN

Everything, from my attitude to my stomach, was sour when we reached Glendower's Aerie late that afternoon. The sight of so many other horses and wagons did not help. Apparently everyone in town for the festival was also invited to the banquet, and at the moment, I hated crowds. I wanted nothing more than a three-day lie-down somewhere quiet and dark, but I still needed to talk to Glendower about the money I'd given him for Isadora. Its origin would be my first real clue.

People filled the garden drinking, chatting, and laughing about whatever shepherds considered funny. I overheard enough to know that I didn't ever want to be stuck with them somewhere.

"Do you know what you call a sheep with no legs?" one man asked another.

"A cloud," the second man replied, and both laughed.

A third man told a little knot of friends, "So the barbarians come charging over the hill. 'Run!' the head shepherd says.

'What about the sheep?' the apprentice asks. 'Fuck the sheep!' the head shepherd says. The apprentice looks at the approaching barbarians and says, 'Are you sure we have time?'"

A trio played flute, drum, and some sort of stringed instrument. Just as I was relaxing into that, a piper joined in to make it a quartet. It was like fingernails raked across my aching brain.

The afternoon sun blazed overhead, but was just about to slide behind the house and leave the garden in blessed shade. The last thing I wanted to do was talk to anyone, so I kept my head down and let my expression settle into an appropriate scowl. I did check the crowd for Billy Cudgel, but if he was there, he had sense enough to stay out of my sight.

One of the twin maids, Mopsa by my guess, worked her way around refilling goblets. Even though I knew it wasn't possible, I imagined I could smell the ale from across the garden, and it made me freshly nauseated. I stopped to lean on one of the small flowering trees. I hadn't been this hungover since I was a very young man.

"Should I send for the moon priestesses?" Liz asked dryly. "They could probably have your funeral pyre ready by midnight."

I was afraid if I spoke, I'd also vomit, so I concentrated on taking deep breaths. New sweat popped out along my hairline. Finally I managed, "Okay," and stood upright. Liz took my arm and we went inside.

The other twin maid, Dorcas, met us in the foyer. She was dressed formally, which meant in this case bare shoulders and a slit gown similar to the one Isadora wore in the ritual last night. It displayed lots of firmly muscled leg when she curtsied. No reason the servants couldn't look for love at the spring feast, too, I suppose.

"Welcome to our banquet, sir," she said. "Are you Mr. and Mrs. LaCrosse?"

I started to protest, but Liz said, "Yes, we are."

"If you'll wait a moment, Miss Isadora asked to be notici-fied when you arrived." She curtsied again, then rushed off. Noise from the crowd in the main dining hall echoed off the stone walls.

"At least she got our name right," Liz said.

"It's *my* name, Miss Dumont," I said with fake annoyance. "And I wish I could be 'noticified' that there was somewhere to lie down." If I hadn't been so hungover, I'd have wondered why Isadora wanted to see us. But my pounding head kept my uncertainties at bay.

"You can sleep through the festivities if you want," Liz said. "It's not like we have to impress anyone here."

"And leave you alone with all these young farm lads again? Not a chance."

She brushed the tip of her nose against mine. "You're jeal-ous. That's sweet."

"I'm not jealous at all, I just don't want to be responsible for all the fistfights that'll break out over you."

"Oh, and *you'd* be responsible for that? How do you fig-ure?"

"In some kingdoms, a wife is the husband's property," I said with a tired but smug smile.

"And in some kingdoms, the wives poison their husbands at breakfast and give them the antidotes that night. Unless," she added with narrowed eyes, "the husbands step out of line be-fore dinner."

Isadora came down the stairs in a formal gown, one that looped around her neck and left her back and shoulders bare. Her hair was elaborately coiffed and piled high on her head, revealing the elegant sweep of her neck. She was barefoot, and wore a small anklet that jingled when she stepped.

Of course I'd seen her the night before, pretending to be a goddess for the public. But here she was, looking straight at me. I tried mightily to reconnect this face with the hazy, un-formed baby's visage from before, but it just didn't happen.

There was such intelligence and shrewdness in her demeanor that it was, in a strange way, a lot like the first time I saw Liz.

She stopped in front of us. Two little girls no older than five accompanied her, clearly annoyed at also being dressed up. Isadora nodded to Liz, then looked straight at me.

Before she could speak, one of the little girls gave me a once-over and said, "Who's he?"

"He smells bad," the other girl said. She was the younger of the two, and evidently had a child's honesty.

"Helena!" Isadora said, her face reddening. "Haven't you been taught any manners?"

"Manners are for servants," she said with a snort.

"I'm sorry," Isadora said to us. "These are my nieces, Helena and Hero. My uncle is a bit of an elitist."

"No, he's just better than everyone else," Hero said.

"He is *not*," Isadora said. "He's a bully, and one day someone will stand up to him."

"And get a spatula to the skull," Helena said defiantly.

"A spatula?" I asked.

"He fancies himself a cook. He's in charge of the banquet." She turned to the girls. "Go back to my room. And if I hear another snotty comment from either of you, I'll make you stay there. I'm Eolomea, remember, and you have to do what I say."

"Nuh-uh," the girls said in unison. "We'll tell our dad."

Isadora knelt, grabbed each girl by the front of their dresses, and yanked them close. "Listen to me, you little no-neck monsters, I used to beat your daddy from one end of this house to the other, and I can still do it. He knows it, too. So get up to my room before I put one of my dainty little feet against each of your little butts."

While she had her back to us, I noticed faded, blackish marks I first took for old bruises. They crossed her bare shoulders in an arc and formed a circle down to the small of her back. It was the dregs of the tattoo she'd sported as a baby, faded and expanded as she'd grown until now they were mere birthmarks that she clearly didn't fret over. I wished I could remember the tattoo clearly; no doubt the designs would provide a really useful clue.

She released the girls, and they ran screaming up the stairs. Isadora shook her head and smiled. "Sorry about that. Now—would you mind if we talked in private?"

"I'd never turn down a goddess," I said. Which wasn't strictly true, I *had* turned one down once. But it was for her own good.

"Would you follow me?" We entered a small sitting room. She closed the door behind us, then locked it. That sent a little frisson of worry up my spine, but I assumed it was habit. Then she turned and faced us with a small crossbow in her hand.

"Don't make any mistake, I know how to use this," she said. "And I know there's only one bolt, so I can't shoot you both. But I can definitely shoot one of you before either of you can reach me, and I hit what I aim at. So one of you will die."

Normally the sight of a weapon pointed at me and wielded by someone who did, indeed, seem to have the skill to use it, would have made me wide awake and tense. But on this day, I just sighed and said, "Look, you want to shoot me, shoot me. It can't possibly hurt more than my head does."

"I agree," Liz said. "You want to shoot him, shoot him."

"That's a nice act, but I'm not buying tickets," she said. "I heard my mother and grandfather talking last night after you two left. I know you know something about me that I don't know."

I couldn't help myself. "And now we know that you know that we know something about you that you don't know."

"Stop that!" she hissed angrily. "It may be a joke to you, but it's my life. You think I don't know I'm not part of this family? I don't look like any of them, and I'm supposed to believe Clancy and I are from the same family? *You* know where

I came from. So just tell me wh . . . tell me wh . . . tell me wh . . . tell me wh . . ."

She continued to repeat the same two and a half words, with exactly the same inflection each time. Liz and I looked at each other in confusion. I waved a hand, but Isadora's eyes didn't follow it. I stood, and again she did not react. She was like a mechanical toy stuck in the middle of its cycle, repeating the same bit over and over. I walked over and tried to take the crossbow from her hand, but her grip was as strong and solid as rock. I settled for plucking the bolt from the weapon.

"Isadora?" I said cautiously. "Izzy?"

She suddenly collapsed. I barely caught her before she cracked her head on the stone floor. She was completely limp, and for a moment I worried that she was dead.

I carried her to a couch, then sank into my chair again as my own head swirled. Liz said, "What was that all about?"

"I have no idea," I said. I'd seen people have seizures, something known as the "falling sickness" in other parts of the world, but this was completely different.

Liz took the weapon from her now-limp hand and checked her over. "She's breathing. Her heart's beating normally. Isadora? Can you hear me?"

The girl opened her eyes. "What happened?" she gasped. Then she winced. "Oh, man, not again."

"Has this happened before?" Liz asked.

Isadora sat up. "This is really embarrassing. Really. I'm sorry."

"Sorry for passing out?" I said. "Or for pointing a crossbow at us in the first place?"

"Both," she said. "I know you're a professional sword jockey, and I thought I should start out from a position of power."

"Everybody's got more power than me right now, sweetheart," I assured her.

"I heard," she said with a weak smile. "Billy Cudgel slipped you some Devil's Dew this morning. You're lucky you're still walking."

"Keep telling me how lucky I am," I said, and rubbed my temples.

Isadora turned to Liz. "And I'm sorry for frightening you, too. Both with my crossbow, and my . . . illness. It just leaves a hole in you when you don't know who you really are."

"Eddie will find out," Liz said. "He's already on it."

She looked at me. "You are?"

"If no one poisons me or tries to shoot me again, yeah."

"Well . . . what can I do to help?"

"Are you sure we shouldn't call your mother?" Liz said. "You were out. All the way."

"Mom knows all about it," she said. "Grandpa sent word to the moon priestesses down south, and one of them should be visiting soon. There's not much else to do until then."

I'd heard Prince Jack offer to intercede, and her refusal. I didn't feel it was my place to damage her pride. So I said, "I understand there was a blanket with you when you were found. And some coins. I don't suppose you've still got those lying around?"

"I'll ask." She practically ran for the door, then stopped and turned back. "And I'm really sorry. I think Jack might ask me to marry him tonight, and it's got me all in a tizzy. I mean, I'll say yes, of course, but he's . . ." She stopped just before she blurted out his secret.

"What?" I prompted. I wanted to see how she got out of it.

She looked down, organizing her thoughts. Then she said, "He deserves to know who he's marrying. He's never seen me have one of these . . . fits."

"I'm pretty sure it wouldn't change his mind," Liz assured her.

"How do you know?" Isadora asked.

"Because he looks at you the way this mutton head looks at me. And I'm absolutely certain about *him*."

Isadora's eyes grew wet. "Excuse me," she said, and rushed out, leaving us alone.

I looked up at Liz. "Mutton head?"

"It's the best I could come up with. I've been surrounded by sheep for two days, after all."

Someone knocked at the door and opened it without waiting for an answer. Another girl, pretty but no stunner like Isadora, entered. She was dressed in one of the low-cut thigh-showing gowns. "My cousin asked me to—"

She stopped when she saw me, and gave me the standard Glendower greeting, "You."

"Me," I agreed yet again.

"You gave me a flower," she said.

Now I recognized her: the babysitter from the barn. "Yes."

"I heard you were showing off and drinking Devil's Dew."

"Yeah. Didn't realize how strong it was. I do now."

"I'm Cassandra Glendower, by the way."

"Eddie LaCrosse. This is Liz Dumont."

"Pleasure to meet you," she said. "Izzy asked me to show you to a room. She said you might want to lie down before the banquet starts."

"She's a kind girl," I said, and got to my feet.

"Oh, yeah, the sun shines out of her butt," Cassandra said with disdain.

We followed the girl into the hall, where me met Clancy. He smiled and doffed his hat to Liz.

"Clancy, where's Dad?" Cassandra asked.

"Overseeing the decorations, I imagine," Clancy said.

"Oh, God," she said wearily. "Tell him to stop what he's doing and wait for me, I'll be right there." To us, she said, "I don't know why I bother, though, nobody listens to me anyway."

The room she showed us was on the second floor. I worried

that I'd have to crawl up the stairs on my hands and knees, but I made it upright. The room itself was high ceilinged, decorated with the same just-past-tasteful style as the rest of the house, and blessed with a magnificent view of the rolling hills and the mountains beyond.

"There's some clothes in the wardrobe," Cassandra said. "A suit for you, sir, and a dress for your wife. The actual banquet doesn't start for a couple of hours. Right now it's just the preliminary drinking, which I'm assuming you'll want to skip."

"That's a good bet," I agreed.

"Well . . . we'll see you there."

"Thanks."

I settled back onto the bed. I was so stuffed with feathers that I was tempted to check under it for eggs. "It appears the two Glendower girls don't get along."

"They've been raised like sisters," Liz said. "Nobody can hate you like your own blood."

She sat on the bed beside me and brushed my hair back from my face. I groaned and covered my eyes with my arm. "You really are sick, aren't you?" she said with genuine sympathy.

"Yes. So let me sleep off a little more of this headache, so maybe I'll be sharp tonight. Right now my brain is very, very dull."

I got maybe thirty seconds of rest before another knock at the door. Liz said, "Come in."

Beatrice Glendower entered, in the same sort of gown as everyone else. It looked as spectacular on her as it did on her daughter, but at the moment its effect was wasted on me. She said, "Isadora told me you wanted to see this." Her voice was tight with conflicting emotions.

I sat up slowly, having learned my lesson about sudden moves. "Is that the blanket she was wrapped in?"

"Yes, Audrey gave it to us. I've kept it hidden away." She

looked down. "I suppose I should've been honest with Isadora long before this. Of course she'd notice she didn't look like any of us. Maybe I should've invented an imaginary father, one who died some heroic death. Maybe," she said with a wry smile, "a traveling sword jockey."

Liz looked up sharply and cleared her throat.

"Oh, I'm kidding, I apologize. I'm very—" Beatrice stopped and handed me the blanket. "Here. See what you can make of it."

I took it and unfolded it. Dust rose from the fabric. Its rich color had faded somewhat, but wherever she'd kept it, it was still in remarkably good shape. The stain from Isadora's baby pee was still there as well, dried into the cloth. I held it up against the light so I could see the pattern of weaving. My brain, so recently against me, began to again function as part of the team.

"It's expensive," I said. "This kind of weaving takes a while. Look how small the thread is, and how tightly it's woven. And it's still supple after being folded for so long. Someone either rich, important, or both owned this."

I looked close at the satin hem. Several small pulls became visible if I turned it just so, indicating that something once stitched there had been carefully removed. "There was a crest or a symbol here," I said. "Probably the family coat of arms. That would've been useful."

"Does the shape tell you anything?" Liz asked.

"No, all crests are shaped pretty much the same. And I've got nothing to compare it to." I resumed my inspection, until I felt a row of tiny, hard things with the hem, nestled in the tight seam between satin and fabric.

"That's the glowworm," Beatrice said helpfully.

"The what?"

"It used to glow, but only when it was near Izzy. It made her laugh. It stopped working when she was, oh, about three."

"Do you mind if I cut this open? I'd like to see what these are."

She nodded. I took the knife from my boot and carefully cut into the little pocket. It took longer than I expected with the big knife and the small thread. Finally I laid it open and could see what had once made the glowworm shape.

A half dozen oblong clear glass beads.

I tapped them with the tip of my knife. They were solid, not hollow.

I picked one up and held it to the window. (Again, I know what you're thinking: Glowing balls of glass should have rung a bell, right? Well, remember I was hungover, and the glowing glass I'd seen back in Mahnoma looked nothing like these beads.) "Do you mind if I smash one?" I asked Beatrice.

Again she nodded.

I put one on the table, held the butt of my knife hilt over it, and brought it down hard. It shattered.

And screamed.

It was high-pitched and brief, but we all heard it. It sent little shards of agony into my already-throbbing head. No one said anything for a moment.

"What was that?" Beatrice gasped at last.

I leaned close and examined the residue. It was broken glass, and that was all. Whatever cried out hadn't left a corpse. "I don't know."

"You could smash another one," Liz suggested, and I positioned my knife over one, but something in that strange little cry stopped me. There was a level of despair that had nothing to do with physical agony, and I suddenly realized it would be cruel to do it again, when it likely would yield no more clues than the first one. Instead I put away my knife and left the remaining beads on the table. "No, there's no point to that," I said, "and I don't want to destroy any more clues than I have to."

I went over the rest of the blanket but discovered nothing else of note. I handed it back to Beatrice. "What about the coins?"

"Oh, yeah. The gold you forgot to mention to me."

"I mentioned it to your father."

"Yeah. Well, as far as I know, it went into the family business, but you can talk to him about it."

"Can you send him up?"

She gave me a look of mock contempt that took me back sixteen years, to that festival evening when we met. "That's your plan? Just to sit here and have people parade past you? Is that how all sword jockeys work?"

"Sometimes not even this hard," Liz said.

"Okay, if I can get him away from decorating," she said.

"Cassandra went to help him," Liz said.

"Good. That'll keep her away from Izzy."

"They don't get along?" I asked.

"They were raised like twins, like Dorcus and Mopsa," Beatrice said. "It all started when the boys started paying more attention to Cassie than Izzy."

It took a moment for that to register. "Wait, she's jealous because the boys pay *more* attention to her than they do Izzy?"

"Yes. She just wants to go off and be a moon priestess, but Dad won't hear of it. He thinks they're a bunch of whores. He insists that she's going to pick a husband or never leave the house."

"That's tough," I said. I knew better about moon priestesses, but I also knew that self-determining women frightened many rural, small-minded men.

"Yes. I've offered to mediate, but Cassandra won't hear of it. She insists on handling it her way."

"A lot of stubborn women in this family," I said with a little smile.

"A lot of stubborn *people,* period."

I hated to do it, but I said, "And how long has Izzy been having those fainting spells?"

"She told you about that?" Beatrice almost gasped.

"No, she had one in front of us."

"Oh, God," Beatrice sighed. "I guess it's been about a year since they started. They've been gradually getting worse. Now it's like she's a machine that locks up."

"Anyone else in your family have the same condition?"

"No."

I didn't pursue this. Until we knew more about Izzy's real birth family, there was no way to tell if it was hereditary. "Well, thanks again." I watched her leave the room, the gown swirling to reveal her smooth thigh and calf.

Liz slapped me on the back of the head. It made my pickled brain painfully slosh against my skull. "Ow! What was that for!"

"You joust for the lady you came with, hotshot."

I pulled her into my lap. "I'm sorry, you're right. That was rude."

"Yes." She scratched my beard under my chin. "But you made me jealous. Do you like that?"

"What happens if I say, 'a little'?"

"You get a little of this." She kissed me. I began to forget about my headache. Then, of course, there was yet another knock on the door.

"Come in," I said as Liz got back to her feet.

Owen Glendower entered, in the same ornate robe he'd worn for the shearing competition earlier. He carried a small wooden bowl filled with three apples. "I thought you might need these," he said to me.

"Why?" I asked.

"Cassandra said you got dosed with Devil's Dew. We give apples to the rams after we use it on them, to help shake off its effects."

I put the bowl on the table beside the glass beads. "I'll take that under advisement. Thanks."

"I understand you have some questions for me," he said.

"Yeah. Do you have any of the gold I gave you back when I left Isadora?"

"I told you, I put it all back, she's got a dowry—"

"No, I mean the actual coins. I want to see where they came from."

He thought about it, the way you do when you're considering giving away a big secret. Then he said, "Yes, I kept one. For luck."

He reached under his robe and pulled out a thin chain, on which a coin hung as a medallion. He took it off and handed it to me.

I recognized it at once. We had some just like it: the currency of Mahnoma, with Crazy Jerry's profile on it.

That wasn't necessarily a clue, of course. Gold from anywhere worked pretty much everywhere. If it didn't, it could be melted down and recast with ease. But it was a big coincidence.

And finally, at long last, I also recalled the glowing glass Opulora the sorceress used. These were direct ties to Mahnoma; even more, direct ties to the royal household. Yet even if Isadora was somehow the illegitimate offspring of Crazy Jerry, sent away all those years ago, it wouldn't matter. A bastard son might ascend to the throne, but not a daughter, not in this part of the world. She was less than a threat; she was a nonentity, politically speaking.

So if she was the secret love child of Crazy Jerry and someone else, it explained why she was sent away. It did *not* explain why anyone wanted to kill her badly enough to send troops after her back then, and just forget about her ever since.

I handed it back to him. "Thanks."

"Did it tell you anything useful?"

"That I gave up a fortune?"

"It wasn't a 'fortune.' But it did get all this started." He put the medallion back around his neck and tucked it under his robe. "Will there be anything else?"

"Just a question. In all this time, has anyone else come around looking for her?"

"People show up every so often claiming to be her father. They usually have some elaborate story about how they met Beatrice one night and had a tryst with her while they were both drunk. They clearly don't know Beatrice. We send them packing."

"You said usually."

"I beg your pardon?"

"You said that usually they have some elaborate story. That implies that sometimes they don't."

He thought again, although this time he seemed to be lining up his facts before revealing them. "About five years after Isadora came to us, a man visited in the middle of winter. I didn't actually meet him, because when the snows come, no one leaves home if they can help it. But I heard that he seemed to be military, and Audrey—she used to run the Head Boar— said he was asking about a baby found hereabouts. Most men ask for Beatrice, and try to convince her that she knew them way back when. But this one didn't, like he didn't know about her. Audrey sent him on his way, but for a while I expected him to come back with more troops. You can waste a lot of your life watching the horizon for bad things, you know. But it never happened."

There was a pattern here, all right, and although I didn't know the specifics yet, I was seeing the outline. "Thanks, Mr. Glendower. I've got a lot to mull over now."

He left, and I picked up one of the apples. I turned it in my hand, examining the entire surface for any telltale signs of manipulation: a disguised puncture where something had been injected into it, or the kind of shimmer that came from an unnatural coating. Then I carefully sniffed every bit of it. When I looked up, Liz stared at me as if I'd lost my mind.

"I saw somebody poisoned with an apple once," I said. "He spit up black foam and his body swelled so much, he nearly popped the seams on his armor."

"I know. You told me that story. That was a long way from here, and a long time ago."

"You think I'm being too cautious?"

She just grinned and shook her head. "You tickle me sometimes, Eddie."

I took one bite, made myself chew it thoroughly, then swallowed. I waited for my stomach to roil, but nothing happened. If anything, it began to settle.

"Is it working?" Liz asked.

"It is," I said, and took another bite.

She began undressing.

I said, "I don't know if it's working *that* well."

"Ha. You wish. No, I'm going to try on this dress and make sure it fits."

More clothes hit the floor as the apples nullified the Devil's Dew. I stood, and my head did not wobble. She reached for the dress, but I grabbed her wrist.

She looked at me. "Are you sure about this?"

"Check for yourself."

"Oh, you *are* sure." She slid into my arms. "But is it a good idea?"

"It's best idea I've had all day."

"I'll grant you that."

"Besides, don't you want to show me how jealous you are? Make sure I know what I'd be giving up?"

"If I did that, you might not leave this room alive."

"If I've got to go, that's how I want to do it."

And then more clothes hit the floor, this time mine. She ran and bolted the door, drew the drapes, and then very emphatically showed me what I'd be missing.

SIXTEEN

I t wasn't a marathon battle, and I did little but lie back and enjoy it, but it certainly helped me shake off the last of the hangover. And as Liz rose back into my field of vision, hair tousled and with a knowing half smile, I felt the kind of assurance in her affection that allowed me to relax and think about my erstwhile case.

"You're already working again, aren't you?" she said.

"It's no reflection on you, I promise. Two minutes ago, you had my full attention."

"Uh-huh. Any ideas?"

"Not yet. Still mulling."

She climbed off the bed. "Well, I'm going to get ready while you mull. It takes a lady longer to get beautiful than it does a man to get dashing." She opened the curtain, and what I saw revealed in the late-afternoon light completely refuted her argument.

I tried to focus on the case, on Isadora's mysterious origin, but my brain wouldn't cooperate. Instead, for whatever reason—

maybe it was seeing Beatrice's ferocious maternal loyalty, or lying in a bed so reminiscent of those in my own childhood home—I thought about my mom, Lady Caroline, the Baroness LaCrosse.

Like Beatrice, she'd been the oldest daughter of a rich Arentian, and thus knew both the value of money, and its ultimate worthlessness. She never worried about what things cost, but she did insist on value for the gold, and woe to anyone, merchant or noble, who tried to cheat or shortchange her. As her only child, I absorbed a lot of her attitudes toward things, and even the rigorous training my father insisted on was unable to change what had become my core values. As I approached middle age, I became more and more thankful for that.

She was the steady wind to my dad's raging gales, and the one person he never tried to bully or impress. Tall, spare, elegant, and very intelligent, she ran the day-to-day workings of our estate with an ease that belied its complexity.

She had dark brown hair that, as soon as she could each day, came out of its elaborate public coif and fell in brushed waves around her shoulders. When she saw me, her face would light up, even if I was being dragged by the ear after doing something ill-advised. Old Wentrobe, the king's chamberlain and principal bane of my existence back then, considered me a lost cause before I'd gotten out of diapers. He bemoaned my influence on my best friend, the crown prince Philip, and when I got older made no secret of his disapproval after I started courting Phil's sister Janet.

When Mom learned about the relationship, she took me aside for a walk in the family orchards. It was a beautiful spring day, and the white blossoms glowed in the sunlight. Backlit bees swarmed the flowers, but they seemed to know better than to pester Mom.

"So you have a girlfriend," she said.

"Uh . . ."

"It's okay, son, you don't have to pretend. You're fourteen, it's normal to start liking girls at this age. Certainly I can't fault your taste; Princess Janet is a beautiful and intelligent girl."

My faced burned with the shame only a teen boy can feel in such a situation. I was terrified she'd try to tell me about sex. "Yeah, she is," I muttered.

"'Yes,' not 'yeah.' We're not in the stables."

"*Yes,* she is."

"She's not heir to the throne, so that simplifies some things. But socially she *is* above your station. Have you thought about that?"

"She's not *that* far above. I'm not a commoner." I scuffed the dirt with my boot.

"No, you're not. You will be the Baron LaCrosse one day, but she will never be the Baroness. She will always be Princess Janet."

"Gee, Mom, I'm not gonna marry her," I said petulantly.

"''Going to,' son, not 'gonna.'"

"I'm not going to marry her," I repeated with even more petulance.

"Not if you don't learn to speak correctly."

"So are you telling me you want me to break up with her?"

"What? No, not at all. I like Janet, and I think she's a good match for you. I just want you to be sure you're dating her for the right reasons, and not because she's a princess."

"I don't care if she's a princess," I said with the kind of righteous anger you stop feeling at about age twenty.

She smiled and tousled my hair. I usually hated that, but not this time. "That's my boy," she said, and kissed me on the cheek.

A year later, after my mother's death, I told Janet about this conversation. We were in one of the castle's lavish guest rooms where we usually met, reclined on the bed but still fully dressed. She said, "I'm glad she liked me. I don't think your father does."

"He doesn't like anybody. What does your mom think about me?"

"That you're after just one thing, like all boys."

Despite my sadness, or maybe because of it, I said, "Not *just*. But it's on the list."

"I'm glad to hear it. Baronness Rossington sent her son Vincent to court me, but his heart definitely wasn't in it. Nor any other body parts."

"Really? When was this?"

"Not too long ago. Jealous?"

"Not of Vinnie Rossington. So your mom doesn't like me?"

"I'm teasing. She likes you fine. She thinks you're very handsome, and have the makings of a fine nobleman."

I felt strangely comforted by that. I kissed her, and it led into something more heated without any effort. She looked into my eyes and said, "Okay."

"Really?"

"Yes."

"It isn't because my mom died, is it? Because if—"

"No, you moron, it's because I want to. I've wanted to for months."

"Have you ever—?"

"If you complete that sentence, I'm leaving."

"No, I just meant . . . neither have I."

"Really? The way you talked—"

"I know, it was just . . . I wanted you to think I was more experienced than I was. Am."

She grinned and kissed me. "You're adorable."

"I love you."

"You better. Okay, so we're a couple of virgins alone in a big comfy bed. Think we can figure out what happens next?"

"We're reasonably intelligent people, we should be able to."

"That's exactly what I thought." And she began unlacing her gown.

I snapped back to the moment before the recollection got any more vivid. It should have been a beautiful memory, and it was, but the events of a year later—the things that drove me from home, from my castle, from Arentia itself—overshadowed it. And always would.

LIZ looked positively magnificent in her borrowed finery. I washed up and changed into my clothes, which would have been stylish five years earlier; in most courts, the ruffles and bits of lace that stuck out at the sleeves and collar had since been replaced by severe cuffs and elaborate links. But I doubted anyone here would know that. The simple jacket and trousers made it bad form to carry my sword, and the dress slippers had nowhere to hide my boot knife. I'd have to approach dinner unarmed except for the tableware.

Liz checked the ruffles at my collar and brushed lint from my lapels. I didn't have to do anything to her; she was perfect. The gown's slit revealed the straight red scar of a knife cut across her thigh, inflicted by a vicious man who ultimately became the last person to be killed by a real fire-breathing dragon. She had no self-consciousness about it at all. "How's your head?" she asked as we prepared to leave the room.

"Almost back to normal," I said. "I'm getting rather hungry, too."

She kissed me. "Good. I was a little worried. What do you think is going to happen tonight?"

"Well, if the crown prince announces his betrothal to a commoner, I imagine there'll be lots of gossip."

"And what about figuring out where Isadora really came from?"

"If she goes from shepherdess to future queen, it's kind of pointless. That's both ends of the spectrum. And I'm pretty sure Prince Jack couldn't care less." I offered my arm. "Shall we mingle?"

"You look very handsome," she said.

"And you look beautiful."

She grinned. "Let's dazzle the fuckers, then."

WE found the courtyard and foyer packed with people in various shades of finery. Most of it was as outdated as my suit, and a few extreme cases seemed to have come from some fever dream involving brightly colored birds and piles of jewelry. The kids looked especially uncomfortable in clothes either too little or big for them, heirloom outfits passed down from older to younger siblings and worn only once a year, if they were lucky. The adults were no more comfortable, but at least they could drink.

As before, the main topic seemed to be sheep. At one level I felt like I'd dodged a spear by not giving in to Beatrice all those years ago, because really, how many sheep jokes can you hear before you want to jump onto the business end of a pitchfork?

I looked around for a familiar face, but didn't see any. I guess the Glendowers were all busy preparing for the feast itself. I glanced toward the door, though, and happened to catch a glimpse of Billy Cudgel's bulk as he quickly ducked into the house.

"Excuse me," I said to Liz, who also saw him.

She grabbed my arm. "This isn't the place."

"This is exactly the place."

"What are you going to do?"

"I'm only going to talk to him. I'm not even armed."

"Remember we're guests."

"I promise."

I sidled through the garden crowd and into the house. The foyer was hot with the press of bodies, but I saw no sign of Cudgel. His bulk should have left a wake like a ship. I snagged one of the twins and said, "Mopsa, I need your help."

She smiled in surprise. "You guessed right."

"Not a guess. You have an eyebrow that arches differently from your sister."

"And you noticed that? No one notices that. What can I do for you, sir?" Then she added, "if it doesn't take me away from my duties here, of course."

"I'm looking for a big guy named Billy Cudgel. Have you seen him?"

"Aye, I've got a bruise on my bottom from a pinch of his."

"That's him, all right."

"He scurried into the dining room a moment ago. Looked as if someone was after him."

"And he'd be right."

"Oho. Will there be a duel, then? He's always talking about his duels."

"I wouldn't believe a word he said, even if he told you the sun rose in the east. But no, there won't be a duel. I just want to talk to him. Thanks."

"My pleasure, sir," she said with a curtsy. *So far,* I observed professionally, *all the Mummerset women have great legs.*

I made my way into the dining hall. Under a high ceiling, an immensely long table stretched the length of the room. At least fifty place settings were arranged along it. Men and women milled about, drinking and chatting. I put one foot on the bench that ran along the table and hefted myself above the crowd. I spotted Cudgel nestled into a corner, with three young ladies hanging on his every word.

I approached him along the wall, where theoretically he couldn't see me. I intended to surprise the fat bastard, but he somehow sensed me coming and turned to meet me just as I reached him. "Mr. LaCrosse," he said genially. "I believe I owe you an apology."

"I believe I owe you an ass-kicking," I shot back. To the girls I said, "Ladies, leave."

They looked at Cudgel for confirmation. "It's all right, this won't take long."

"And then you'll tell us how you defeated that whole brigade single-handedly?" one of them said with hero worship in her eyes.

"I shall indeed."

When the girls were gone from earshot, I said, "You tried to poison me."

"I tried to incapacitate you," he corrected. "If I'd wanted you dead—"

"—don't say 'then you'd be dead,' because then I'll just have to punch you for being smug."

"Well, I do apologize. Sincerely. I regret my conduct, and any discomfort it caused." He bowed as much as his bulk allowed. "I hope you'll keep it to yourself and not tell King Gerald."

He could've brought up my father's name and not taken me so off guard. "King Gerald? What's he got to do with anything?"

"Oh, come now, my friend. He hired you to do a job, and he hired me to watch you do it and report back to him."

If I'd been better rested, or the dregs of the hangover hadn't hung stubbornly on to fuzz up my brain, I might've tried to bluff him. As it was, I knew I didn't stand a chance of mentally outmaneuvering him at that moment. "Look, I don't know what the hell you're talking about. We saw Gerald, yeah. But he didn't hire me."

Cudgel smiled and patted my cheek. "That's cute."

"Touch my face again, fat man, and you won't be eating corn on the cob for months," I said. "What exactly did Gerald hire you for?"

"As I said, to watch over you."

"And what did he tell you he'd hired me for?"

Cudgel's eyes narrowed. "By heavens, you *don't* know, do you?"

"I'm going to, or I'm going to have your blood on my clothes, but not my conscience."

"You threaten when you should cajole, my friend. I'm easily persuaded to share my knowledge." He rubbed his fingers together to indicate the sort of persuasion he meant.

I put a coin in his hand. "Talk."

"I was told by the Lady Opulora, on behalf of King Gerald, that you were a sword jockey and had been hired to find someone. Since your ilk are not known as the most reliable or trustworthy of employees, they hired me to follow you, and alert them when you had accomplished your job. I was under the impression they believed you would keep the information to yourself, to negotiate a higher fee."

"But you didn't follow me." I'd certainly seen no sign of it before we got to Mummerset.

He threw back his head and laughed so deep and loud that everyone in the room turned to look at us. "Oh, you poor fool, you never even saw me, did you? I watched you play that ridiculous battle game in Mahnoma, you know. I've been behind you the whole way. Luckily, I was far enough behind that I was able to also befriend Prince Jack when I encountered him on the road to Mummerset." He shook his huge, shaggy head. "For a sword jockey, my friend, you miss an awful lot."

"You're not the first to say so," I agreed. All this new information threatened to make my skull shatter, but I had one more question to ask. I knew the answer; I just needed it confirmed. "Whom did they tell you I was looking for?"

He rubbed his fingers together again. I gave him another coin.

"A young lady of sixteen summers," he said. "She'd have dark hair, and probably a regal disposition."

"Regal," I repeated.

"You're playing dumb again, sir."

"Believe me, I ain't playing." I patted his face now. "All right. You've got two gold pieces in your pocket that, in addition to answers, better also buy your silence."

"I have no interest in the events of Mahnoma, I assure you. I've found far more lucrative pickings here in Altura."

I knew he meant Prince Jack, but that wasn't my problem. I left him to his sycophants, who rushed back to him as soon as I stepped away.

So if Cudgel told me the truth, then I'd actually been working on a case all along, and now the two ends of it, Alturan and Mahnoman, were starting to pull together. The Lady Opulora wanted to find Isadora. I doubted very seriously if she was truly acting on the king's behalf. But she *did* act with King Gerald's authority. Something she'd seen in my palm that day convinced her I knew where the girl was. But that still left me with my two central questions unanswered: Who was Isadora? And why did someone want her dead? Because if Opulora had tried to find her, and kill her, when she was a baby, I knew of no reason why the sorceress's intent would be different now.

Then a fresh truth hit me. If Izzy was in danger again, it was because I'd brought it back into her life. That was a fun realization.

I happened to glance out through one of the huge, floor-to-ceiling windows. The sun was down, but the sky was still light, and I briefly saw three figures silhouetted as they topped a distant hill. I couldn't even tell for certain if they were approaching or departing, but two of them were on horseback and the other was on foot. This third one was huge, hunched, and reminded me instantly of Tatterhead, but it was gone before I could confirm it.

Coming on the heels of Billy Cudgel's revelations, this confused me even more. If it *was* Tatterhead, what was he doing here? Had he followed Cudgel, who followed Liz and me? Had Cudgel already sent some sort of message back to Opulora?

Doors slammed open across the dining room, bringing me back to the moment. Glendower barged into the kitchen, pushing a maid and a manservant aside. He bellowed, "Izzy!" I slipped through the crowd and stood just outside, where I could hear and mostly see what happened.

He found Isadora and her cousin Cassandra at the center of

a group of maids and boys dressed as servers. Cassandra wore a severe black gown in contrast to everyone else's colorful finery. They whispered urgently, but they weren't exchanging amusing gossip. Whatever it was, it was deadly serious.

"Isadora Bianca Glendower!" her grandfather said, using her full name the way parents always do when a child's in trouble. "What are you doing here?"

"Grandpa," she began, "Cassie has something to—"

"Cassandra needs to get out of here before I tan her hide. You're not too old for a spanking, young lady. And you," he said to Isadora, "what you need to do is get out there and execute the duties of your office. Why, when your grandmother was alive and hosted the shearing feast, she welcomed all, served everyone, danced and sang and made sure everyone else had a drink before she took one."

"But Grandpa—"

"Here you are, acting as if you were one of the guests instead of the hostess. Bloody hell, girl, you're supposed to be a goddess; Eolomea would not be hiding in the kitchen with the maids."

"She would if she—"

"Forget it, Izzy," Cassandra sighed. She was used to being ignored.

Glendower took Isadora's arm, not roughly but firmly, and pulled her away from the maids. "There's no time for argument. The guests are out in the courtyard, and the dinner should be ready. Go invite them, and not another word out of you!" He pushed her toward the door, then grabbed Cassandra's hand. To the maids and servants he said, "And you—get back to work. Now!"

The staff all looked terrified, but I couldn't imagine them being that scared of Glendower, whose bluster couldn't hide his gentle nature even when he was put out. A few of them looked back, into the depths of the kitchen itself, as if some monster dwelled there. What frightened them so badly?

Glendower saw me when he came out of the kitchen, but luckily didn't realize I'd been deliberately eavesdropping. He pushed a sour-faced Cassandra into the crowd with the admonition, "Go mingle!" Then he sighed and turned to me. "If you and your wife ever have children, Mr. LaCrosse, pray for sons. Daughters are exhausting. *Women* are exhausting."

"I'll keep that in mind," I said. Still, I wondered what Isadora and Cassandra wanted to tell him. In my experience, it was always smart to let people convey their information, even if it turned out to be nothing important; you risked missing the one time it *was*.

I looked for Liz and found her in the garden, again surrounded by three young men. She winked at me, and her disappointed suitors melted away into the crowd. I quickly told her what I'd learned, and what I'd seen through the window.

"He was following us all along?"

"Apparently."

"Do you believe what he told you?"

"Yes. I mean, he enjoyed it too much to be lying. That foolish shell hides a vicious turtle."

She winced. "Don't do metaphors."

"Sorry."

"And you think Tatterhead was coming here?"

"I couldn't tell. I mean, maybe it wasn't even him. It could've been a trick of the light."

"I can't imagine there's too many like him wandering around loose," she said.

"He wasn't loose when we saw him. He was on a pretty short leash."

"Maybe the other two are his minders. How much time do you think we have?"

"Depends on whether he was coming or going."

"Enough time to get through the banquet and get everyone out of here before the trouble starts?"

"I hope."

"Should we tell anyone, try to prepare a defense?"

I thought about it. I'd seen angry Mummerset mothers chop a vile soldier apart, but whatever Tatterhead was, mere hoes and rakes wouldn't stop him, no matter how many there were. These were farmers, not fighters. "No," I said. "If it is Tatterhead, he'd just demolish them."

"Then what do we do?"

"Keep our eyes and ears open. Hope for the best."

"And prepare for the worst?" she said wryly.

"That's how I start every day, baby."

T he foyer and garden were packed now, and I couldn't imagine who might be left in Mummerset or the surrounding hills. The combined heat from all those formally dressed bodies made everyone a little twitchy. The murmurs were just on the verge of turning into complaints, when a single loud, sharp bell note sounded and everyone grew silent.

A wave of delicious odors washed over us. My appetite, suppressed by the whole Devil's Dew incident, asserted itself like lust on a honeymoon.

Then Isadora appeared in her full Eolomea regalia. Everyone applauded, a few whistled, and somewhere in the garden a dog even barked. Isadora smiled graciously, then held up a hand for silence.

"This is the great feast that welcomes Eolomea back to the world, and with her the light, heat, and flowers of spring. We eat and drink together to renew our community and our connection to the gods, and I am especially humbled that you let my family be your hosts. Welcome, then, to our table."

She bowed, to more applause, and we followed her into the dining room. I spotted the same maids that had been talking to Isadora, standing in a line along one wall. They all looked terrified.

The main door and foyer became a total bottleneck; Liz daintily held my arm as we waited our turn. I looked around for some of the other players in this drama, and at the very back of the crowd, still out in the garden, I saw Ajax's towering form. His hair was slicked down and parted straight, the way a mother might do a child with a cowlick, and the formal attire he wore strained to contain his chest and arms; if he flexed wrong, he'd burst all the seams. If he was there, it meant King Ellis was, too, but I couldn't yet spot him.

Liz saw Ajax. "Uh-oh."

"I know," I agreed. He had a matching bruise on his forehead from my head butt. I wondered if his thumb ached as much as mine.

"Well, if Tatterhead does show up, maybe the two of them can duke it out," Liz said.

Audrey was having some difficulty moving through the crowd with her cane. Liz and I stepped to either side of her and made space while people jostled us.

"Thank you, young man," she said when we'd gotten through the door. More loudly she said, "You'd think one of these ungrateful sheep dippers would show some respect and help a crippled lady to her chair, but no, it had to be the new town drunk. That's the thanks I get for pouring drinks for you lowlifes for twenty years."

There was a small table off to the side, with chairs scaled down for children. Cassandra, certainly no child, sat all alone at it, arms crossed in a sulk. A couple of other kids took seats as far from her as they could get.

We filed around the long table, which had benches instead of chairs. I chose a spot in the middle, on the side near the inner wall so I could watch both the table and the windows.

Outside, the light had faded to a dark blue glow behind the hills. Above this, the first stars appeared.

No one sat until everyone was in position and Isadora stood at the head of the table. Two young men held her chair; once she'd been seated, they went to the foot of the table and held that seat for Owen Glendower.

Glendower sighed as he sat. His face, so recently filled with annoyance and aggravation, had turned winsome and sad. He gazed down at Isadora, no doubt imagining his late wife, Bianca, in the same place. Then he said, "If you're standing on ceremony, you're wasting boot leather. Sit down, everyone."

I helped Liz negotiate her feet over the bench, an awkward move because of her dress, but one that every other woman in the room repeated. I noticed Ajax remained out into the foyer, watching through the open door. He was hidden in the shadows, so unless you knew he was there, you'd miss him. Not a bad trick for a man his size.

Liz squirmed to get comfortable in her dress. She muttered, "If I'd known it was picnic style, I'd have worn something with fewer petticoats."

I spotted King Ellis at last, seated three spots away from Owen Glendower. I wondered if the two had ever actually met before. If this was the first time, it promised to be even more memorable than it usually was when a commoner met a king.

Oddly, I saw no sign of Billy Cudgel. He would've taken up space for three, so it wasn't like he could hide in plain sight. And I couldn't imagine him turning down free food. Had I scared him off? Or was something else afoot?

The maids went around filling our goblets. The one who served us was trembling so hard, the drink barely made it into the cup. She was also white with either fear or nausea.

"It's all right, honey," Liz said. "I won't bite you, you know."

"Y-yes, ma'am," she said, and quickly moved on.

Opposite us, at the end nearest Isadora, Beatrice grabbed the pitcher from her server and poured her own drink. She looked angry, but not at the girl; her eyes stared daggers at the kitchen door.

Directly across from us, Clancy sat next to Phoebe. Even in what I'm sure was her best finery, Phoebe looked strong enough to tip the table with one arm. She wore a medal around her neck on a gold ribbon, so I assumed she won the sheep-shearing contest. Still, Clancy's goofy grin assured me he saw her as the epitome of beauty, which is exactly how a man should see his girl.

He saw me and waved. "Hello, Mr. LaCrosse! Feeling better?"

"Back to full strength, Clancy. Sorry you had to see me like that."

"Oh, no worries, Mr. LaCrosse. Seen many a drunken man at festival time."

At the children's table, the little girls Hero and Helena sat on either side of Cassandra. I couldn't hear what they were saying, but whatever it was, they were talking animatedly to each other as if Cassandra weren't between them. The older girl looked even more miserable.

Dorcas passed behind us, and I touched her arm to stop her. Quietly I asked, "Why are all of you so scared?"

Before she could answer, a crash came from the kitchen, followed by a man yelling, "For fuck's sake! More melon? Fine, I'll get you more melon and I'll ram it right up your fucking ass! Would you like it diced or whole?"

A girl whimpered a response, and the voice replied, "For fuck's sake, one minute you're fucking that stupid goatherd and now you're trying to fuck *me* from behind!"

Something else crashed, and the voice exclaimed, "You know what you are? I'll tell you, to save time. You're an ugly, six-nippled *pig!*"

The kitchen door flew open, and a serving girl no more than eight or nine ran out, sobbing. The slight heels on her shoes tripped up her inexperienced feet, and she fell beside the table.

A man appeared in the kitchen door, clad in the white coat of a chef. And I recognized him, too: it was Gordon, the smart-ass I'd encountered on my first night here. I couldn't believe he was old enough to run a whole kitchen, but it was clearly a reign of terror.

He drew breath to yell more abuse at the little girl, then realized the whole table was silent and still, staring at him. Defiantly, he snarled, "What? You work in my kitchen, you fucking wake up, move your ass, or piss off home."

My temper began to boil, but before it bubbled over, a loud slam rang out as Isadora slapped the table. "All right, that's *it*!" She got to her feet so emphatically that her heavy chair tipped over and hit the stone floor. We all jumped at the noise. "You arrogant, narcissistic bastard, I have put up with this shit all my life, and it stops *now*!"

Her brother put his hands on his hips and, in a mock feminine voice, said, "Oh, the great beauty is offended." In his normal voice he continued, "Why don't you just get your tits out and get it over with, it's the only thing anyone wants to see, anyway."

I've never seen a plate used as a weapon before, but Isadora snatched one from the table and skimmed it like a Lindwocky throwing disk. It struck her brother right in the face with enough force to shatter. He sat on the floor, hands flying to his mouth. Blood began to flow almost at once.

"My fucking teeth!" he yelled through his fingers. He pulled one hand away and looked into the palm. "You broke my fucking teeth!"

"And yet you keep talking," Isadora said. She snatched up another plate and smashed it over his head. "Does *anything* shut you up?"

He kept staring at the teeth in his hands, blood running down his chin. "You fucking cunt—"

"That's enough!" Glendower roared. He stood looming over the table, so angry, his face was almost purple. Even incognito King Ellis looked a bit apprehensive. In the foyer, Ajax stood at full alert, ready to burst in should the family feud threaten his boss.

"Gordon, clean yourself up and get back in the kitchen," Glendower said. "Isadora's right, if I'd taken the strap to you when you were younger, you might be an actual human being by now, instead of the sheep's ass you are."

Hero and Helena jumped up from the kids' table and ran to see about their father, crying, "Daddy! Daddy!"

"He's old enough to have kids?" Liz asked me softly.

"There's someone for everyone, I guess."

One of the older maids, still a mere teenager, joined the two girls. "Daddy will be all right, girls. He hasn't lost the use of anything valuable." She faced the room. "I apologize for my husband's language. Being good at one thing has gone to his head."

"Just like that plate!" someone said. There was scattered snickering.

His wife and children helped Gordon to his feet and back into the kitchen. Isadora waited until the doorway was clear, then shut it behind him. She turned, and the serving staff all began to applaud.

Then the rest of us did as well. Smiling, still bright red from her flush of anger, Isadora swept back to her seat. Two of the maids rushed to hold it for her.

"Wonder what the *after*-dinner entertainment will be?" Liz whispered to me.

"I'm sorry for the interruption," Isadora said. "Please, enjoy your drinks. There'll be no more showstoppers, at least not before we eat. Dorcas, please serve the nuts." She caught herself. "I mean, please serve the *guests* the nuts."

There was a moment's silence; then we all burst into laughter. I don't know if Isadora misspoke on purpose, but whatever the cause, it wiped out the bad taste of Gordon's little tantrum.

Smiling, she let the humor run its course, then held up her hands for silence. "Wait, before we start, I do have an announcement. Ladies and gentlemen, my cousin Cassandra, who has been almost my twin sister, will be leaving us. She's taken the first oath toward becoming a moon pr—"

"Sorry I'm late," a new voice said loudly from the doorway.

Prince Jack stood there, dressed in the same sort of formal clothes as everyone else, but on him it looked natural. His grin could've lit the room without the aid of the chandelier and candles. Behind him stood Billy Cudgel, smug as always. Behind *him,* Ajax still hid in the shadows, where neither Jack nor Billy had seen him. Jack would, of course, recognize Ajax immediately if he had, and known what his presence meant.

This was going to be interesting.

Cassandra, half-standing, sat back down with a disgusted look on her face. The younger kids at her table snickered, and she threw her napkin at one of them.

Isadora looked both terrified and ecstatic. Beside her, Beatrice reached over and took her daughter's hand. I couldn't tell if it was to reassure her, or hold her down.

"I apologize for interrupting your dinner," Jack said as he swept into the room, "but I have an announcement, one that I'm sure some of you saw coming. But I bet I can still surprise you. Isadora?"

She pulled her hand from her mother's grasp. Maids slid back the chair, and she joined Jack. King Ellis deliberately hunched down at his seat and peeked around the person beside him. He did not look happy. Not at all.

Jack knelt before Isadora, took her hand, and gazed up into her eyes. No one who saw this could doubt the way these two felt about each other. I'd seen love conquer a lot of things, so I knew its incredible power, but I'd never seen it expressed with this kind of purity.

"Isadora Glendower," he said, "I've loved you since the first time I saw you. I bless the day my falcon made her flight across your father's land. I would be truly honored if you would consent to be my wife."

A sharp gasp came, not from King Ellis where I expected it, but from Clancy Glendower. Tears ran down his cheeks. Phoebe, dry-eyed, patted his hand reassuringly.

I glanced at Beatrice. She wasn't crying, but the loss was as visible as if something had been cut away from her. Her lower lip trembled as she tried, for Isadora's sake, to manage a smile.

Isadora began to cry with happiness, but she said formally, "Sir, I must have my grandfather's permission."

Glendower stood and indicated that Jack should also stand. Around me I heard more sniffling, including from Liz. He joined the young couple, his boots clacking against the stone floor.

"You know she is not of my blood," Glendower said formally. "Yet she is of my heart, as surely as are my own blood children." He put Isadora's hand inside Jack's. "Take hands, children, and we shall seal this bargain." He turned to the rest of us. "And, friends, hear this: I give my daughter to him, along with a dowry that shall equal his portion in life."

Now all the women and some of the men were openly sobbing, and we applauded with real enthusiasm.

Jack laughed. "The virtue of your daughter is all the dowry I ask, Mr. Glendower." He kissed the old man on the cheek. "Now come on, mark our contract so we can get this party started."

"Mark your divorce!" King Ellis roared as he jumped to his feet. His fury was enough to silence the room.

"Oh, fuck," Jack gasped.

Billy Cudgel slid out of sight into the foyer, past Ajax, who had stepped into the open.

"And just who are you?" Glendower said.

"He's my father," Jack said, the way a condemned man might note the executioner's approach.

"Oh, really?" Ellis yelled, and shoved past Glendower to confront his son. "*Now* I'm your father? You didn't have the nerve to tell me about this—" He glared at Isadora. "—little piece of witchcraft you've been dallying with!"

Now Beatrice jumped up. "You will not talk that way about my daughter in my house, whoever you are."

Clancy stood as well. "Or about my cousin!" he said. "Who is, you know, like . . . the same person as her daughter."

Ajax stepped discreetly into the dining room now, ready to intercede should anyone physically threaten Ellis. With equal discretion, I lifted one foot over the bench so I was straddling it, the better to jump to *my* feet if I had to. But at the moment, I wasn't sure what I could, or even should, do.

Ellis glared at the room, unintimidated as only a man certain of his power could be. "Silence, all of you!" He turned to Jack. "And you would take a woman from this rabble and make her a queen?"

"A queen?" Glendower repeated, puzzled.

"I'm King Ellis, you idiot! *Your* king! This is Prince John!"

The rest of us stood, as you do in the presence of royalty. I used the opportunity to step over the bench with my other foot.

Ellis yelled, "Oh, sit down, you imbeciles! We're not in bloody court!"

A few did. The rest, frozen by fear and uncertainty, didn't move. I hid among them.

Isadora looked like a hare trapped by foxes. She clung to Jack's arm, and it might have been all that held her up. This was her worst fear, her greatest terror, and now it was happening and she could do nothing to stop it. Beatrice, also still standing, held one of the serving knives low beside her leg. I knew if she made a move toward Ellis, Ajax would skewer her without a thought. I couldn't let that happen, even if it meant taking on Ajax cold sober and unarmed.

Ellis turned his attention back to Jack. "I'm trying very hard not to lose my temper and order the execution of this entire sheepherding family, when really the one I want to see hanging is *you*." He poked his son in the chest for emphasis. "How dare you pick a commoner princess behind my back? Your decision affects everyone in Altura!"

Jack slapped the hand away. People gasped. He said, "I may be heir to your throne, but I'm also heir to my own heart. Those insipid, pampered whores you've paraded before me—"

"*Whores?* They're the crown princesses of our allies!"

"They're using their femininity for gain and position, Dad, that makes them whores! And I'm not interested in advancing some political agenda, yours or anyone else's. If I marry, it'll be for love, and *this* is who I love!"

Ellis turned to Isadora. I expected her to wilt before his glare the same way her father had, but instead she stood tall, trembling chin up, and met his gaze with her own.

"And you think this . . . this *shepherdess* isn't trying to advance her position? You think she's not whoring herself to become a princess, then a queen?"

Beatrice turned white with anger, but thankfully stayed still and silent.

Isadora said, with great dignity, "Your Majesty, although it is none of your business, I shall tell you anyway. I am a virgin. I have tried with all my ways and wiles to convince Jack of the very same thing as you: that a commoner such as myself is not the right match for a crown prince. He has remained steadfast and honest in his dealings with me, a son of which you should be proud. The fact that you are *not* proud does him no dishonor. Only you."

A few people gasped. I heard a whispered, "Fuck me." A commoner just didn't talk that way to a king, even in her own home.

"Traitors," Ellis hissed, so angry, he could barely choke out the word. "I'll hang you all for treason. Every last sheepherding one of you!"

Despite the tension, despite the threat of violence and possible capital punishment, Ellis's tone brought back a vivid memory: the rage my own father showered on me as I lay recovering from the sword wound that should have killed me. "I have to face the king," he'd roared in the exact same way, "and take the blame for your conduct!" His eyes had narrowed with what, at sixteen, I could only see as hatred and shame.

"I'm sorry, Dad," I'd said. I was so weak, I wasn't sure it was audible. Certainly he didn't act like he heard it, or if he did, that it mattered.

"You failed to protect the goddamn princess of the goddamn country! If you'd died, too, then maybe we'd have some dignity left, but you couldn't even do that right!"

He never said he was sorry I'd lost Janet, the first girl I'd loved. He never said he was worried about my own injuries. He was only angry about what I'd done to the family honor. He and I never had a chance to hash that out, and if someone didn't intercede, Jack and Ellis might not, either.

I said, loudly and I hoped calmly, "I think everyone, commoner *and* noble, needs to take a deep breath."

Everyone turned to look at me now. Ellis snarled, "Are you drunk again, sir? Because your prior conduct certainly doesn't speak well of your insights."

"Fair enough," I said. "But your rage isn't doing you any credit, either. Your son is more clever and insightful than you give him credit for, I think."

"My son," Ellis seethed, "is my business. Certainly no concern of some drunken foreigner."

"Dad," Jack said.

"Quiet!" Ellis faced the room. "I am leaving. If this worthless offspring of mine is back at court tomorrow, alone, we'll forget this whole thing. If, however, he chooses not to return, I'll personally lead a division of armored troops back here and burn this house, every cottage in the area, and the whole town of Mummerset to the ground. Mark my words." He turned to leave. "Come along, Ajax."

Ellis stomped from the dining hall, past Ajax and into the night. His bodyguard backed out slowly, watching the room, and closed the doors after them.

The room let out a collective sigh. Then they began to jabber at each other.

I went to Jack and Isadora. She wiped the tears that, moments ago, she'd shed out of joy. "I knew it," she said. "I knew as soon as he found out, this would happen. And you knew it, too, Jack."

He took her hand and squeezed it reassuringly. "Don't give me that look," he said lightly. "Nothing has changed. I love you, and if I have to give up the kingdom for it, well, I can learn to rule sheep, too."

She turned to me. "Thank you for trying to help, Mr. La-Crosse."

"Wish I could've done more," I said honestly.

Cassandra joined us, arms folded. "Well, no one will care about *my* announcement now. But just to make it official: Dad, I'm becoming a moon priestess. I've taken the first vow, and I'll be off to my training within a few days."

Glendower stared at her, as if she spoke another language. "You . . . you're what?"

"Forget it," Cassandra said. She turned to Jack and Isadora. "Look, you two. Nobody ever pays any attention to me, but I'm going to tell you anyway. Get out of here. Right now. Don't say anything, don't grab anything. Just go."

"Why?" Jack asked seriously.

The dog I'd heard in the garden before began to bark again, urgently this time.

"Because I have a feeling that something terrible is about to happen. I don't get this feeling very often, but when I do, it's never wrong."

"Cassie," Isadora began wearily.

Suddenly the kitchen door slammed open, and Gordon Glendower sailed through the air, landed on the table, and slid half its length, sending tableware and appetizers crashing to the floor. Through the opening came Tatterhead—so large, he had to both bend down and turn sideways to get his broad shoulders through. As big as he'd looked in Crazy Jerry's castle, he looked even larger here, as the people of Mummerset screamed and rushed to get out of his way. Behind him came two men with short swords, the kind you use when fighting indoors.

Tatterhead looked around, his big nostrils flaring as he tested the air. Then his eyes locked onto Isadora.

"Pretty," he said, and pointed a finger as big around as my forearm. "*Very* pretty."

There aren't many feelings worse than reaching for your sword and remembering you deliberately chose not to wear it. My hand closed on thin air even before the thought made it through my brain.

Not that it mattered much. In a room packed with frozen, terrified civilians, one more blade might've done more harm than good.

I dragged Liz away with the rest of the crowd, trying to blend in until I figured out what to do. The monster, because that's what he was, put one big hand on the table and leaned his weight on it so hard, the wood creaked. I half expected the other end of the table to fly into the air.

One of the soldiers, gray-haired and grizzled, said, "Stay on task, TH."

"Oh, I'm on task," he said, then sniffed the air as he'd done back in Acheron. "She's here, don't worry."

"The rest of you, just stay where you are," the other soldier said. "We're not here to hurt anyone, and we won't if we don't have to."

Tatterhead's dead-fish smell filled the room; not even the open windows mitigated it. I was reminded of something I'd once overheard: "Fish is the only food that has to spoil first to smell like what it is." His big mouth hung partially open, and I realized he was out of breath; how fast had they been moving? And why the hurry?

I needed a weapon, if only to get everyone's attention. There were a half dozen sharp knives within reach, just like the one Beatrice had grabbed earlier. Yet what good would table settings do against two professional soldiers and this vast . . . *thing* now sniffing the air and frowning?

Once he'd recovered his breath, Tatterhead lumbered over to us. Except for Owen, Isadora, and Jack, who still stood in the open, the crowd jammed back against the wall, whimpering and whispering among themselves. I fervently hoped none of them tried anything heroic.

"What is the meaning of this?" Owen bellowed. "You can't just barge into someone's home and—"

"Yeah, we can," the older of the two soldiers said. It wasn't said with arrogance, but the weariness of someone tired of having to say it. "We've got the swords and the training, we can do pretty much what we want. Now, if you'll just step aside, we'll be out of your hair as quickly as we can."

"You don't give orders in my home, young man," Glendower said.

Clancy stepped up behind him. "Uh, Dad, maybe you should listen to them. They do have a troll."

"Troll?" Tatterhead rumbled. He turned away from the crowd and looked at Clancy with narrowed eyes. "Have you ever seen a troll, boy? Have you measured your strength against his, and found your muscles wanting?" He took a step toward Clancy, which put him right in the boy's face. "Have you

smelled the brushy fur, befouled with his own droppings, as
he put his leathery fingers to your throat?"

Clancy swallowed hard. "No, sir."

Tatterhead smiled. "Neither have I."

Then he resumed his olfactory tour. He wasn't sniffing
everyone, though: only the women. Not even that, I realized.
Only the girls. Only the ones around the same age as Isadora.

He stopped in front of Beatrice.

"She's too old," the head soldier said.

"I know," Tatterhead replied. "But she's close. Very close."

"Close enough to geld you if you lay a hand on me," Beatrice said defiantly.

"I mean you no harm, dear lady," Tatterhead said.

"You could've fooled me. You burst in here, scare everyone, bring men with swords with you—"

"Ah, that's where you're wrong," he said, and raised his
chin to reveal a thick metal collar around his neck. *"They
brought *me*."

He moved to Liz, sniffed again, and smiled. His eyes closed
as he seemed to savor the aroma, the way a man might enjoy
the odor of a fresh-cooked dinner. The comparison did not
make me happy. He looked down at her and said, "I remember you. The lady with the dinner plates. Pretty."

"Always happy to get good word of mouth," she said, but
her voice shook a little.

Then he turned to me and drew in a huge, long breath. I
was the first man he'd sniffed in detail. "You've been around
her again since that day at the castle," he said softly, although
in his case "softly" meant everyone in the room could hear.
"The smell was very, very stale before. Now, it's—" He took a
long, deep snort. "—fresh."

"It's probably just the rosewater I washed up with," I said.

His mountainous hand rose and tapped my cheek. His
touch was light, his skin leathery, and his sense of power

apocalyptic. "Don't worry, I'm not here for you or your lady."

He raised his head, drew in another long breath, then slowly looked around. His head sat so low on his shoulders that he had to swivel at the waist in order to turn it. He raised one arm, almost as long as I was tall, and pointed.

Right at Isadora.

She stood behind her father and Jack, who tried to shield her from Tatterhead's view. There was no hiding from this Gargantua, though.

"Is that her, TH?" the older soldier asked.

"Oh, yes," he said with a slow, satisfied sigh.

Cassandra suddenly stepped between Tatterhead and her family. In her black dress, hands on her hips, she was the very figure of a moon priestess, even though I knew it had to be all bluff. She said, "You will not touch my cousin."

Tatterhead's head tilted, like a puzzled dog. He said, "Aw, you're afraid of the big man."

"You're not a man," Cassandra said. "You're a vile, smelly monster. And I'm *not* afraid of you."

He sighed again, this time heavy and sad. "Vile. Smelly. A monster. Yes, that's what they tell me." His voice deepened without losing any volume. "Am I truly so horrible? I can appreciate beauty as well as any man. Better than most, even. I can find a girl once I've breathed her scent, even after years. Can any of your poor farmer lads do that?"

Cassandra's expression softened. I'd seen this happen to actual moon priestesses, who had the ability to see past appearances to the soul beneath. It appeared she had, in fact, found her true calling. "But you're scaring people," she said gently.

"We're wasting time, TH," the older soldier said.

Tatterhead nodded and flicked his forefinger at Cassandra, the way I might try to dislodge a piece of lint. It struck her right between the eyes and she dropped where she stood.

I tried to make eye contact with Jack, but his attention was riveted on Tatterhead as he tried to block sight of Isadora, as if that would help. The boy was brave enough, but he didn't have the experience to understand what was happening. And when Tatterhead returned his attention to Izzy, Jack would leap to her defense, after which Altura, like their neighbor Mahnoma, might very well find itself without a royal heir.

Tatterhead stepped up to Glendower and Jack. Towering over them as he did, he had no trouble seeing Isadora. She did not move, but her eyes were wide with both fear and fury. She wouldn't let this beast do anything without a fight. But what the hell *did* he want?

Tatterhead leaned closer and sniffed again. He pushed Glendower and Jack aside like a man parting tall grass. The old man caught himself on the table, but Jack nearly went out the window. "It's you, all right," Tatterhead said to Isadora. "You are pretty. So grown up. Opulora will be so pleased."

Isadora stood her ground. "I don't know who or what you are, but—"

He raised one hand to her, and she slapped it away and warned, "Next time you'll draw back a nub, wise guy."

This was my chance. The two armed men watched Tatterhead instead of the room. If anything was going to happen, it had to be now.

So I slapped my hands to my cheeks and screamed as high as my voice would go.

Everyone turned and looked at me, including Tatterhead. I continued screaming, "Oh, God! We're all going to die! Oh, God, please, help us!" I ran around in a circle, until finally I grabbed one of the two henchmen by the shoulders and said, "What gods do they worship here? I don't know who I'm praying to!"

His eyes were wide with surprise, and he started to say something, but then I grabbed his sword away with my right hand, and gave him a solid uppercut with my left. I spun and clashed blades with the other henchman, who'd immediately come to his compatriot's defense.

We locked eyes as well, and something about him was familiar. We were roughly contemporary, so we could've met anywhere, at any battle I fought as a mercenary, or on any case I'd worked as a sword jockey. But a name came to me out of the mists of my past. *"Strato,"* I said.

I saw from his expression that I was right, but he didn't let it throw him. "That was clever," he said with no malice.

"Only if it works," I said.

I kneed him hard between the legs. His dropped where he stood. I kicked his sword under the table, where I hoped no one would grab it and try to help.

Then the crowd, as I expected, panicked.

Women screamed. Men screamed. That dog barked. People ran in every direction. And now I had to deal with Tatterhead.

Jack beat me to it, unfortunately. He launched himself at the monster, who caught him around the waist the way a child might catch a thrown doll.

The great monstrosity then raised Jack overhead and threw him at me. I dodged, and he hit the floor where I'd stood. He slid to the wall and did not move. People stepped over him in their terror.

Isadora screamed.

Unfortunately, I couldn't get anywhere near Tatterhead before he grabbed Isadora by the back of the neck and bent her over the dining table. He held her there with one hand, while his other reached for his pants.

When he saw this, old Glendower jumped on Tatterhead's broad back. "Stop it!" he yelled, trying to lock his arms into a choke hold. "Stop it *right now!*"

Tatterhead shrugged his gigantic shoulders and dislodged the man, then kicked him without looking. Glendower slid across the floor and, like Jack, didn't move.

There was no way I could just stand by and watch this. I

shoved people aside with as much viciousness as necessary and jumped up on the table. I barely avoid stepping on the unconscious Gordon Glendower. I put the edge of the sword against Tatterhead's throat, just above the metal collar where, on a human, a big artery lay just beneath the skin.

"Let her go," I said. "Now!"

He turned, caught my sword between his teeth, and tossed his head. The strength was unbelievable, and I had no time to react by doing something sensible like releasing the hilt. Instead I went with it, slung across the table so hard that my arm almost pulled from its socket.

I hit the wall, taking most of the impact on my back, which momentarily knocked the breath from me. As I winced and wheezed, I watched him remove, not his own male member, but a glass ball. As soon as it got near Isadora, it began to glow so brightly, I could barely look at it.

"Ow!" she screamed, trying to free herself. "What the hell? Let me go!"

I pushed myself upright against the wall. People knocked into me in their mad attempt to escape.

Tatterhead moved the ball closer to Isadora's bare back. The bruiselike remains of her tattoo began to smoke.

"Hey! Hey, that burns! Stop it!" Isadora demanded.

Tatterhead put the ball away, said, "That's what I needed to know," and tossed Isadora over his shoulder. He smacked her behind and said, "Keep still."

"Jack!" she yelled, still sounding more outraged than frightened. *"Mom!"*

I scooped up my sword and this time, having learned my lesson, slid it up between his legs to nestle against whatever he carried there. "Stop it. Put her down."

"Do what he says!" Isadora said, kicking and punching to no effect. "Let me down!"

"Put down your sword," Tatterhead said, "or I put her through the wall."

"No," I said. "You're here to get her. You won't hurt her."

He smiled, all yellow teeth and thick lips. "You're so sure of that."

"Yep," I lied.

"Put me down!" Isadora bellowed, and tried to kick him in the head.

"She's not going to go quietly," I observed.

"Stop it, you—," Isadora said, and then she locked up, frozen in mid-thrash, repeating, "Stop it, you—! Stop it, you—!"

Tatterhead's brow creased with worry. He forgot about me, and the knife against his balls, and instead reached back into his trousers for another of the glowing orbs. This one shone red, and when he touched it to Isadora's skin, she went limp and silent. Her eyes were still open, but they looked like a dead person's, a sight I knew very well. Had he *killed* her? Just like that?

"You just be quiet," the monster said to her, as if she were a doll. "I'll be gentle, and soon you'll be back home."

Back home? In Mahnoma, with Opulora—that was *home*?

He continued, "So come along, my—"

You'd think I'd see a fist the size of a small pig coming, but nope. I was so distracted by the mention of "home" that he blindsided me. He punched me in the side of the head so hard, I dropped right where I stood on the table, practically atop Gordon Glendower. The last thing I remember was Tatterhead's low, deep voice saying a single word, one that threw everything I thought I knew, which granted wasn't much, into chaos:

"*—sister.*"

I went into a hazy semiconscious dreamworld. At first I saw nothing except vague shapes moving through the fog in my brain; then they resolved into human forms. The first one, I thought, was Liz; then I realized it wasn't. It was her dead twin sister, Cathy, whom I'd known briefly many years earlier. The one I'd failed to save from Stan Carnahan.

"You're not going to lose this one, too?" she said, her voice similar to Liz's but softer and younger. "I mean, you let me die because you weren't smart enough. Is this girl going to die for the same reason?"

Before I could reply, another shape can out of the fog: Janet, the princess I'd watched die at the hands of the bandits. I winced at the jolt of pain that ran between the scar on my chest and the one on my back, marking the path of the sword thrust that should have killed me.

"Really, Eddie," she said, scolding and mocking at the same time. "How many young women are going to die because of you? How many are going to miss the chance to grow up, fall in love, have babies, because you just weren't sharp enough to save them?"

A third woman emerged as well: Laura Lesperitt, tortured to death by henchmen looking for the last viable dragon eggs. "You tried to save me, once, too, and failed pretty miserably. Maybe saving people just isn't your thing."

"Stop it," a new voice said. My three accusers faded back into the fog and a new form emerged. She had blond hair, kind eyes, and the knowing smile of a woman much wiser than any mere mortal. I recognized her, too: Rhiannon, current Queen of Arentia, the human incarnation of a the goddess Epona, although she'd hidden that knowledge from her human self.

She continued, "They're not real, Eddie. They're your own personal ghosts, conjured up by your conscience."

"Are you real?" I asked. My voice sounded thin and pathetic.

"I'm *more* real, at least. And yes, you failed to save each of them, but you tried. That counts for something. And remember, you *did* save Princess Veronica. And your friend Jane Argo. And Bob Kay. And most important, Liz."

"And Isadora? Will I be able to save her? You're a goddess, right? You know the future."

"You won't save her wallowing in guilt about your failures, will you?" She touched my chest, over my scar.

"Wait, how can you be here if you're also in Arentia as a human being with no memory of the fact that you're a goddess?"

She laughed. "*That's* the Eddie LaCrosse I know. It's because I *am* a goddess, Eddie. I'm more than a mortal can comprehend. Or," she added with a wink, "maybe I'm just a figment of your imagination, too. Either way, it's time to stop feeling sorry for yourself and get to work."

My eyes popped open.

I was out for only a few minutes, long enough for most of the guests to flee into the night. I awoke to Liz wiping my face with a wet cloth. She said, "Welcome back, hero."

The side of my head was numb. "Where—?"

"Gone. With his two friends. About twenty minutes ago."

"I was going to ask where *I* was."

"Flat on your back with your lights out, like all the other heroes. How many times do you think you've been knocked out in your life?"

"Too many."

"I remember the moon priestesses saying the damage could add up."

"Who are you?" I deadpanned.

She tweaked my nose. "The only person who'll always be there when you wake up, however you happened to go to sleep."

I managed a smile at that. Then I asked, "Where's Izzy?"

"Tatterhead took her. Beatrice tried to stop him, too, with just a dinner knife, so I had to . . ." She looked down.

"What?" I prompted.

"Knock her out," she said guiltily. "I haven't punched anybody I liked in a long time." Her voice grew softer. "Did he kill Izzy? She looked dead."

"I don't know," I said as I sat up. It burned me up to think that after all this time, Mahnoma had succeeded in killing the baby I once found in the woods, and right under my own damn nose, at that. And then I remembered that insane final word, and wondered what the hell freak story I'd actually stumbled into.

Beatrice lay on the table as well, along with the still-unconscious Jack and Cassandra. Phoebe attended to the prince, while Clancy held his sister's limp hand. Gordon had been placed on one of the benches. His two daughters, like grim little harpies, stood watch over him. I got the impression they'd bite off the fingers of anyone who came near. And eat them, too, probably.

"So no one's dead?" I asked.

"No," Liz said. "Just banged up a bit."

I swung my feet off the table. The two soldiers I'd incapacitated sat on the floor, gagged and tied up back-to-back. They did not struggle, but just watched with eyes that missed nothing.

"We thought you might want to question them," Liz said.

"I will, when my head stops moving on its own. But I know what we have to do next."

"We go after them," Owen Glendower said. He cradled one arm in the other. "We get back my granddaughter before something terrible happens to her."

"That's my plan, too," I said. I couldn't tell him what I'd heard, and truthfully I began to doubt my own memory. I mean . . . *sister*? He must've meant it metaphorically, maybe as a fellow Mahnoman. Right? There couldn't be any actual blood relation, could there?

"But I still don't understand the why of all this," Liz said, breaking me out of my reverie. "Why would Opulora want Izzy?"

"It isn't Opulora," a new voice said from the shadowy foyer. "At least, not directly. It all goes back to King Gerald."

I couldn't make out the face of the man speaking, but his voice was familiar. "Yeah?" I challenged. "And why would King Gerald care about a peasant girl from Altura?"

"Because," the newcomer said, "once upon a time, he drank, and saw the spider."

Part III Isidore Redux

chapter

NINETEEN

He stepped into the dining hall as casually as if he'd been entering his favorite tavern. He was my height, slender, with dark skin and close-cut, wiry black hair. He had a pack slung over his shoulder that I knew carried the tools of his trade: pens, ink, and lots and lots of vellum sheets.

It was my turn to say, "You."

"Indeed," said Harry Lockett. "Pleasure to see you again, Mr. LaCrosse. You're a long way from Neceda."

"I'm on vacation." I climbed off the table, wobbled a bit until my head cleared, then shook his hand.

He looked around at the damage and casualties. "I'm not familiar with this definition of 'vacation,' but you seem to be having a hell of a time."

"I assume you're working?" I said.

"I am. Always. We don't get vacations." He turned to Liz. "And Miss Dumont. Good to see you again as well. Your hair's longer."

"Only until I cut it," she said.

"You should keep it long. It suits you."

I first met Harry Lockett back in Neceda, where he'd appeared searching for the real story behind reports of fire-breathing dragons and the cult that worshipped them. He still didn't know the whole truth about that, but he'd helped me out when he didn't have to, which put him in the good-guy column as far as I was concerned. His appearance here was a surprise but not a shock. Scribes answered only to themselves or their Society, asked the questions no one else could ask, and generally did their bit to keep kings and other throne-holders honest.

"Who is this?" Glendower demanded of me.

"You can ask me directly," Lockett said. "I speak your language."

"Who are you, then?"

"Harry Lockett, Society of Scribes." He offered his hand, then saw Glendower's injury. "Whoops. Sorry."

"What has happened here?" King Ellis said from the foyer. He and Ajax stood there, as aghast as Harry was calm. Ajax had his sword in his hand, and flexed his fingers eagerly around the hilt. I would've loved to see Tatterhead mop the floor with him.

"You left the party too early," I said to Ellis. "A monster belonging to King Gerald's court sorceress came and stole your son's girlfriend."

"I beg your pardon?" Then he saw Harry. "A *scribe*," he said disdainfully.

Harry bowed his head, the most respect a scribe had to show anyone. "Harry Lockett. You're King Ellis, I take it."

"Yes," Ellis said, annoyed as only a king can be when presented with someone who'd note down his every word.

"What brought you back?" I asked.

"We saw . . . well, your monster, I suppose, with a girl over his shoulder, heading away from here. So I insisted we come back. And on the way—" Then he saw Jack. "Son!"

Jack blinked awake, winced at the pain, and tried to sit up. Phoebe said, "Easy, Jack. Wait till the room stops spinning."

Ellis rushed over as if to hug Jack, then caught himself and stood awkwardly until Jack registered his presence.

To Ajax I said, "You can put the sword away. The fight's over." He scowled at me, then reluctantly slid the sword back into its scabbard.

I turned to Harry. "So why are *you* here?"

Before he could answer, Jack jumped to his feet. "Where's Billy?"

"Your friend Billy Cudgel?" King Ellis said with a sarcastic sneer. He snapped his fingers. Ajax stepped out into the garden, and returned with Cudgel. The fat man's hands were tied behind his back, and a noose was around his neck like a leash. He was sweaty and clearly exhausted. One eye was swollen shut.

"As we were returning, we found him bravely scurrying away," Ellis said. "On a horse that I'm certain he stole."

Jack glared at his former friend. "What the *hell*, Billy? Did you set me up for this?"

"I assure you, friend Jack, I didn't—"

"Oh, shut up. I know better than to expect a straight answer from you." He turned to Ellis. "*You* sicced him on me, didn't you? He was your spy."

Ellis began to bluster. "I did no such thing, and—"

"What the hell does any of this have to do with rescuing my daughter?" Beatrice demanded loudly, silencing us all. She sat up and glared at us as if we were the stupidest group of people she'd ever seen. I couldn't really argue with that.

She fixed her glare on Liz. "You knocked me out."

"If I hadn't, Tatterhead would have," Liz said. "Sorry about that."

Then she turned to me. "And you let that monster take my daughter."

"I tried to stop him," I said. It sounded as pathetic as I expected it to.

Harry laughed. "Before you all start beating each other senseless, let me give you the backstory. Sit down, pour yourselves a drink, and get comfortable."

Beatrice was having none of it. "Not while my daughter is—"

"Your daughter is perfectly safe," Harry said. "Really. Tatterhead won't hurt her. Think about it: He came all this way to get her and take her back to Mahnoma. He could've ripped every single one of you into tiny pieces of meat, and he didn't. Whatever is behind this—and believe me, I want to know as much as you do—it's not about hurting your daughter. Now, Mr. LaCrosse here is the absolute best person to have on your side for this. I won't bore you with a list of his qualifications, but I will say if it was *my* daughter, there's no one I'd rather have trying to rescue her."

"He's got a point," Liz said to Beatrice. She started to snap something back, then took a deep breath and nodded.

Ellis and Jack had moved away, and were huddled together talking. Well, Ellis was talking; Jack was just looking at him, at first skeptically but with gradual softening. I assumed the king was apologizing. Harry said, "Your Highness, Your Majesty, if you'd like to join the rest of us, I think you'll want to hear this. It involves you, after all."

Jack and Ellis came over and sat on the bench facing Harry. He dug through his pack until he found the notes he wanted, then stood before us like a bard preparing to play. I knew he'd find that comparison insulting; after all, bards just made stuff up. Scribes strove for the truth.

"I'm going to tell you a story," Lockett said. "Save your questions until the end. And your applause.

"Seventeen years ago, Mahnoma and Altura were allies. The border between them might as well have not existed. And this was deliberate: the old kings had made sure their sons, Ellis and Gerald, grew up together as fast friends. They ran up and down the hills like some of Mummerset's lambs, pretending to slay dragons and topple evil warlords. They no doubt thought that things would never change, and the summer would be eternal."

"More matter," Ellis said dryly, "and less art, okay?"

Lockett frowned, then continued. "But nothing is eternal. The boys grew up, ascended to their thrones, took queens, started families. Both had sons born the same year: young Jack here, and Gerald's son Mannheim, called Manny. Affairs of state kept the two from as many visits as they'd once shared, but they did manage to find time every so often for extended stays in each other's court.

"Ellis's queen died in childbirth—sorry for bringing it up, Your Majesty—so when he went to visit Gerald, he went alone, leaving Jack behind because of his schooling. The visit was fine, everything was normal, until Ellis announced he had to leave. He missed his son, and his kingdom required his attention. Gerald asked him to stay, but Ellis politely refused. Then Gerald's queen, Sylvia, asked him, and Ellis agreed to stay another week."

Ellis's brow creased with the pain of this memory.

"It doesn't sound like much, does it?" Lockett continued. "But that was the spider, and Gerald was sure he saw it in his cup."

Clancy raised his hand as if he were in school. Lockett smiled and said, "Yes?"

"What does that mean, about the spider?"

Lockett turned to me. "Mr. LaCrosse?"

"It's a superstition," I said. "Some people believe you can poison someone by slipping a spider into their drink, but the poison only works if they actually *see* the spider."

"Exactly," Lockett said. "Gerald's spider was the fact that

his best friend since childhood had refused *his* entreaties, but given in to his wife's. That could only mean one thing: the two were having an affair."

Ellis started to protest, but Lockett held up his hand for silence. "It was absurd, to be sure," the scribe continued. "But that didn't make it any less deadly. Gerald attacked Ellis and tried to kill him, but Ellis escaped and returned to Altura, where he sealed the borders. Gerald took this as an act of war, and both kingdoms began massing armies."

And that, I thought, was when I got involved. That was the war I was looking for that day I found Isadora. The war that never happened.

"But before he could devote his attention to war, Gerald had to deal with his treacherous queen. He put her on trial before his court. His nobles, bless them, stood up to him and told him he was out of his mind. In response, Gerald sent for a sorceress, one who could ferret out the truth no matter how well it was hidden. 'For if you hide the truth, even in your hearts, there will she rake for it,' he told everyone, to scare them into cooperating. And that's how Opulora enters the story.

"She's by far the most mysterious person involved in this tale. I have it on good authority that she was once childhood friends with Queen Sylvia. I don't know if Gerald knew this, or if he just didn't care, given her reputation. She was known as an unerring truth-seeker who had toppled kingdoms before, and would no doubt do so again. And so Gerald had her visit Sylvia, use all manner of spells and sorcery to compel the queen to tell the truth, and then report it to him before his court.

"And she did. I have her exact words here: 'Sylvia is chaste; Ellis, blameless; Gerald, a jealous tyrant.' Then she made a prediction that no one, at the time, understood: 'And the king shall live without an heir, if what is hidden is not one day uncovered.'

"Now, I know what you're thinking: Gerald had an heir, Prince Mannheim. And that was true at the time of this announcement. But later, probably no more than an hour, the young prince fell to his death trying to scale the outside of the prison tower and rescue his mother. He'd been raised on tales of brave knights and noble warriors, remember. So when his father refused to accept his mother's innocence, even after Opulora pronounced it so, Manny did what one of his heroes would have done."

"He was ten years old," Ellis said sadly. "A wonderful boy."

"And his death broke Gerald out of his delusion. He saw that he'd been mistaken, and that his jealousy had led to something horrible. He forgave the queen at once. But it was too late, because seeing her son die, she killed herself, rather brutally.

"And so King Gerald, left without a queen or an heir, went mad. Opulora quickly became the public face of his rule. He's gotten better over time—for those first few years, no one saw him at all—but everyone believes he's still mad, and she's still in charge."

I thought about the way Gerald reacted when she appeared during our visit. Apparently *he* thought she was in charge, too, although he was starting to chafe from it.

"But there's still that prophecy, about something hidden being uncovered. Opulora claimed it came to her in a vision, and she didn't know what it meant, either. Certainly the king had no other legitimate children, and the Mahnoman Charter forbids bastards of either sex from ascending to the throne. And there things sat, until you and Miss Dumont showed up at the castle."

"Us?" I said in surprise.

"What did we do?" Liz added.

"I have no idea," Lockett said. "But as soon as you left, Opulora summoned Billy Cudgel, and he headed off for Altura."

We all turned to look at the bound fat man. He said nothing, only stared at the floor in defeat. Jack walked over to him and said quietly, "I thought I knew you, old man. You were the friend I always dreamed of having. But now I'm wide awake; no dreams left."

"Jack, I—"

"You will be silent," Ellis commanded, "or you will be dead. Ajax?"

The bodyguard drew his dagger and laid it against Cudgel's throat, although he'd have to do a bit of cutting to reach anything vital under those jowls. Cudgel sagged in on himself, thoroughly defeated; or, at least, doing a good job of acting it.

"That tongue of yours has done quite enough damage," Ellis finished. Then to Lockett, he said, "Please continue."

Lockett said, "I'd noticed over the years that Cudgel was always around when a certain kind of trouble broke out, so I followed him here, assuming there'd be a story at the end of it. But instead of doing what he was hired to do—follow Mr. La-Crosse and Miss Dumont—he began ingratiating himself with Prince John. He seemed to think he could talk his way out of things with Opulora, if she asked what he'd done to earn his money. Again, that's not out of character for him. And so Opulora decided on the direct approach, and sent Tatterhead."

"But what," Glendower said, "has this all got to do with my granddaughter? She's no missing princess, is she?"

"Not that I've ever heard," Lockett said. "There's a rumor that Queen Sylvia was pregnant when she died, but I haven't been able to confirm it, and even if she was, she was certainly nowhere near giving birth. Her baby died with her, if it ever existed."

"And Opulora?" I asked, remembering the glass beads in the baby blanket. "Did she have a baby around that same time?"

"Not that I've found any trace of," Lockett said.

"So we don't even know," Beatrice said with a mix of anger

and annoyance, "*why* she's gone to all this trouble to kidnap my daughter."

I realized we had an untapped resource right there in the room. I went to the bound soldiers and removed the gag from the older one. "Your name is Strato, right?"

He looked up at me and slowly nodded. "If you don't mind my asking, how in the world do you know that?"

"You were here sixteen years ago, when I first brought Isadora to town. Your commander was ordered to kill her. Right?"

"So that was you," he said.

I nodded. "Who gave him that order?"

He thought it over. He'd heard all Lockett had said, and knew if nothing else, there were too many secrets at work. He said, "King Gerald."

"Directly? Or through Opulora?"

"I don't know."

"Who was the baby?"

"Honestly, no one ever told us. We were in prison as deserters because we didn't want to fight with Altura. I mean, my wife was Alturan."

"And you came back to look for that baby five years later, didn't you?" I pressed.

He blinked in surprise. "How did you—?"

"I'm really good at my job," I said, not seeing any need to mention Glendower's earlier story. "Who sent you then?"

"Opulora. She said . . . she knew the baby hadn't been killed by the bear, and this was the closest town."

"But you didn't find out anything?"

"I didn't look that hard. I mean, I asked around, but . . . wherever that little girl was, it was better for everyone if she stayed there."

I nodded. I was seeing a pattern, which wasn't the same thing as having answers, but was better than nothing. "Now . . . how did you find us?"

"I didn't. Tatterhead did. He said he'd smelled her on you, and could follow your scent."

"He could smell her on me after sixteen years?"

"He's not a human being," Strato said with a shrug.

I looked a question at Liz. "Maybe," she said. "I suppose it's possible."

"It does explains some things," I said, not entirely willing to accept it myself. I recalled the glass beads hidden in Isadora's baby blanket, and the way they glowed like the ball Opulora used on me, and that Tatterhead used on the girl. "We did mention to Opulora that we were coming this way."

Lockett, practically bouncing with excitement, said, "So, Opulora sent Billy Cudgel here, where he buddied up with Prince Jack, having no idea that Jack's girlfriend was the very girl he was supposed to find by following you two." He turned to Cudgel. "Is that right? Was it right under your nose the whole time and you didn't even know it, you greedy old leech?"

Cudgel grumbled, "If I answer, you jarring rough-hewn clotpole, this hedge-born death token will open my windpipe."

"Oh, this is going to a great story," Lockett said with delight.

Beatrice got right in his face. "Listen to me, scribe. You may be used to considering people just notes on vellum, but that girl is more important to me than my own heart, and I'd appreciate it if you'd show a little respect."

"The more interesting question," I said, "is why King Gerald wanted her dead in the first place. Who *is* she?"

"And why does Opulora want her back now?" Liz said.

"Whatever the reasons behind this," I said, "it's still pretty clear that Tatterhead is taking Isadora to Opulora."

"Then we're going after them," Beatrice said firmly.

"Yes," I agreed. "We are."

Lockett grinned. "I can't wait to see how this ends."

I t was all I could do to keep the entire population of Mummerset from coming with us.

They took this whole thing personally, especially the idea of another nation kidnapping one of their own for hazy but probably nefarious purposes. Not to mention, it had ruined the one fancy dinner they were likely to get all year. People were pissed. And while the idea of having a band of forty or fifty men was appealing, the fact that they were basically only trained in sheep-shearing and manure shoveling dimmed my enthusiasm. I'd led amateurs into battle before, and I knew what would happen when they met up with professionals. I had no desire to see that much blood in one place, ever again.

They waited outside in the garden, milling about and getting more and more angry. A lot of them were women; in this community, no one had any illusions about how strong women could be, and after seeing them hack apart Arcite back in the day, I understood why. Much of their anger, no doubt, had its roots in their panic when Tatterhead first appeared.

Nobody likes to remember moments of cowardice. Still, they weren't up to this, and I had to make them understand that.

I went out to see them. Before I could speak, they began peppering me with questions.

"When do we go?" one demanded.

"Does Glendower have swords for us?" asked another.

"Will there be plenty of ale?" asked a third, the first sensible question.

I held up my hands for silence. "Look, Mr. Glendower appreciates your interest, but really, we need trained fighters, not eager amateurs."

The crowd grumbled.

"Okay, okay," I said, pretending to soften. "Maybe you're not so—*Boo!*"

I said it in my battlefield voice, the one that began deep and high in my throat but used all the power of my lungs so that it came out as a deep, loud bellow. The crowd leaped back as if they'd been choreographed. A few people screamed.

When they'd settled down, I said seriously, "Everyone who jumped needs to go home. Really. It's no reflection on your courage, just your experience. If you jump in a garden, you'll piss yourselves in a battle, and I don't have time to train you otherwise."

A moment of silence followed, then with lowered heads, everyone turned and left. In moments the garden was empty.

I turned and found Liz watching from the doorway, arms crossed. "I wondered how you'd handle that. Not bad."

I kissed her. "Did *you* jump?"

"I'll never tell," she said.

WE agreed to leave at first light the next morning. Barking at Tatterhead's heels seemed pointless, since we knew his destination and we were reasonably sure Isadora was safe. It would give Jack, Beatrice, and me time to rest a little and recover from our head blows. I didn't sleep much, but having a goal and a strategy to come up with was more restful than you'd think.

When Liz was asleep, sometime after midnight, I slipped out of bed and went barefoot downstairs into the dining hall. The chandelier was still lit, but the candles were almost gone. The stones were cold and damp against my feet. The debris from the fight had been cleaned up, and place settings were ready for breakfast, which someone would probably begin cooking in a couple of hours. I wondered if it would be Gordon.

I went to the window and stared out at the night; a shooting star sailed across the sky and disappeared behind the trees, in the same direction Tatterhead had gone.

"Dining on ashes?" a female voice said quietly.

I turned. Beatrice stood in the doorway. She wore a robe cinched tight against the night's chill, tight enough to let me know she wore nothing beneath it. She joined me at the window and I fought valiantly not to look below her chin.

If she noticed my discomfort, she didn't let on. She continued, "I couldn't sleep, either. I keep thinking about how scared Izzy must be right now. She's a strong girl, but she's lived a very simple life. She has no experience of anything like this."

Not many people do, I thought, but kept it to myself. I said, "If it's any consolation, if I really thought she was in life-or-death danger, I'd be halfway to Mahnoma by now."

"I know. It's not much consolation, but it'll have to do." She rubbed her jaw. "You girlfriend hit me."

"Yeah. Sorry about that. Did she leave a lump?"

"See for yourself." She took my hand and put it to her face, where I felt a small, hot bit of swelling.

While my hand touched her, she looked up into my eyes with the same look I remembered from that night so long ago. There was something unfinished between us, and while I'd had a life that thoroughly distracted me from it, she'd had a decade and a half of relative quiet to nurse it, whether she meant to or not. The promise I saw now was that of a grown woman who knew what a man liked. If I took her up on it, she'd never let on. Liz would never know.

But I would. I pulled away my hand.

"You haven't changed much," she said.

"That's the first thing you've said that's been dead wrong," I said.

She joined me in looking out the window. Another pair of shooting stars went over. "It wasn't you," she said.

"What?"

"The man who broke my heart. It wasn't you. I was pissed off at you, yes. But that's all."

"Okay."

"You're not going to ask who it was?"

"It's none of my business."

"But you're a sword jockey, aren't you? You spy on lovers for a living."

"I try not to take cases like that, actually. Neither side usually tells me the whole truth."

"He was the son of a neighboring farmer," she said, her voice turning somber. "We were betrothed. A month before the wedding, he did something stupid, then took ill and died."

"Something stupid?"

"He went out on a winter's night to meet me. On his way, he fell through the ice into a stream. He caught a fever and never recovered."

"I'm sorry."

"Don't be. It was a long time ago."

"It seems pretty fresh to you."

She turned sharply away. "Are you always so tactful?"

I could tell she was crying. "You blame yourself, don't you?"

"Are you still talking to me?" she said sharply. "A woman turns away, it means she doesn't want to talk anymore."

"Yeah. But if it matters, I know how you feel. Two people I

loved died because of me. One was my teenage girlfriend, the other a woman I knew after I left here."

Slowly she turned back, wiping her tears. "And now you have Liz."

"Yes. Because I'm very, very lucky."

"Yeah, well, I'm not."

"No, you just haven't been. Maybe you still will be."

"No, that's wrong. I've got Izzy. She's the luck of my life."

Tatterhead's half-heard word came back to me: *Sister.* I didn't know what he meant by it, so I saw no need to mention it to Beatrice. But it hovered here, like a shadow with nothing casting it. "And we'll get her back," I assured her with all the sincerity in me.

She said nothing. I put an arm across her shoulders and we stood watching the sky. No more shooting stars appeared.

ELLIS wanted to send Ajax back to his castle for reinforcements, but Jack would brook no further delay. I agreed with him; Tatterhead would move slowly and leave a pretty easy trail to follow, but I didn't want him to get too far ahead. I did believe he was supposed to bring Izzy to Mahnoma unharmed, but after what I'd seen him do to her before they left, I wasn't sure he quite got the definition of "unharmed."

Just before dawn I visited Strato, who was kept confined in a storeroom with his fellow soldier. They were also chained together by their left ankles, an efficient way to prevent them making a run for it. I closed the door behind me and said, "We're going after Tatterhead."

"You know where he's going," Strato said.

I nodded. "We could use your help. Except for the king's bodyguard and me, no one here has ever fought in a real battle."

"You can't take him on," Strato's companion said belligerently. "He'll tear you into bite-size chunks."

"Martius," Strato warned. To me he said, "It would make me a traitor."

"That depends. If your orders came from Opulora and not the King, then you'd be a hero for helping expose her."

"There are no heroes," he said wryly. "And I can only trust that King Gerald gave the orders. It's in my job description not to ask questions."

I nodded. I wished he felt differently, but I understood his reasons. "Either way, I'll order you released in two days. By then we'll have reached Acheron, or been left as a pile of corpses somewhere between here and there."

"Thank you. I'd like to wish you luck, but that seems hypocritical under the circumstances."

I offered my hand. We shook, but his fellow soldier did not. I left them to their solitude.

"You don't stand a chance," Martius called after me. "He's not fucking *human*."

WE sworded up, saddled up, and left at first light. In addition to me and Liz, we had Jack, King Ellis, Beatrice (there was no stopping her), Clancy (Phoebe's tears notwithstanding), Owen Glendower, and Ajax. Harry Lockett was also part of our group, but as a noncombatant. Scribes never took sides. Billy Cudgel was along as well, not exactly in custody but certainly encouraged to think of himself that way. He was too dangerous to either turn loose, or trust to the naive Mummersetters.

I knew Liz, Ellis, Jack, and Ajax could handle the weapons they carried. I was less certain about Glendower, who brought along a dusty heirloom sword no doubt snatched from a wall somewhere in his house, and Clancy, who carried a staff sharpened to a point. I had the dire premonition that before this little adventure was over, he'd end up impaled on it. Beatrice had two knives on her belt and another two on her saddle, and just the set of her jaw alone convinced me I shouldn't question her ability with them.

The nine of us made good time, because as I suspected the trail was really easy to follow, especially once we hit the woods downslope from the town.

At the forest's edge, two trees as big around as me were pushed aside, their root balls partially uncovered. Tatterhead was making a beeline for Acheron. His mission was so urgent that he couldn't even bother to take roads.

"Good gods," Glendower said softly. "What manner of being *is* this creature?"

"Don't be scared," I said so only he could hear. "Your son and daughter are watching."

He swallowed hard and nodded.

Ajax dismounted, walked to one of the partially toppled trees, and pushed against the trunk, lightly at first and then harder. It did not move. He went to the other side and tried to push it back upright. It didn't move that way, either. A crow sitting atop the tree cackled his amusement before flying off.

"How big was he?" Ajax asked.

"Seven feet," Beatrice said.

"Tall?"

"No, across the shoulders," she said wryly.

Ajax didn't look frightened, but a lot of the cockiness drained away as he got back on his horse.

"If you've got second thoughts," I announced, "this is the place to turn back."

"No one's turning back," Jack said. "And we're wasting time talking about it."

He nudged his horse forward between the trees and along the newly cleared path that led straight ahead through the woods.

"Tatterhead's like a homing pigeon," I said quietly to Liz. "The straightest line between here and there."

"My God," Liz said as she surveyed the destruction. "How strong *is* he?"

"Strong enough that I hope we don't catch up to him until we reach Gerald's castle. He'll massacre this bunch."

"Including you?" she teased.

"Yes," I said seriously, "because I'd have to fight for all of them. Except maybe Ajax."

"Jack looks pretty tough, and I assume he's well trained in combat arts."

"Doesn't matter. He's young, and he's pissed off. Tatterhead stole his girl, and that insults his masculinity. You know what young men are like; he wouldn't last five minutes."

"Are we talking about the same thing?" she said with a wink. Then she asked, "So what do we do?"

"Follow slowly enough that he gets to the castle first, and then we can deal with Opulora, not Tatterhead."

"What if she sics Tatterhead on us?"

"We'll deal with that if it happens."

The trail left by the monster was easy to follow, although we could only ride single file. Anything in his path had been removed, including trees and boulders as well as smaller things like bushes and logs. Eventually this new path met an existing trail that was broad enough for wagons, and we made better time.

Heavy dark moss hung from the trees and gave them the look of solemn old men who passed judgment on those who passed by. I got the feeling not many earned their approval.

Around midmorning, I let my horse drift back until I was beside Harry Lockett. He was writing something as he rode, the reins clamped in his teeth. His horse seemed used to this.

"Got a minute?" I asked quietly.

He put away the vellum and stylus. "Sure."

"What exactly are we up against?"

"With Tatterhead?"

I nodded. "I mean, I've seen him up close. He's not human. And you seem to know a lot about this situation."

Lockett grinned. "The last time I saw you, you were chasing dragons. Now you're after monsters?"

"I don't know what I'm after, that's why I'm asking. What *is* he?"

Lockett squinted into the distance as he organized his thoughts. "There are two schools of thought on that. One is that he's simply a freak, a man who grew up different and, most would say, wrong. Who kept growing when other men stopped."

"And the other school?"

"Agrees with you. That he's not human at all. There's all sorts of stories about him, mind you. Most say he was found by Opulora, who trained him to be her monster on call. Some say he's actually Opulora's son. And some say Opulora actually made him."

"As opposed to giving birth to him?"

"Exactly. They say she grew the different parts in her chambers in the castle, then stitched him together and brought him to life. He's made up of parts taken from other creatures, such as bears, wolves, and vipers, all the dangerous and powerful things of the world, and then changed and strengthened by the sorceress's skills."

"That sounds like a children's story."

"So do dragons," he said with a grin. "Did you find any, by the way?"

"There's no such thing," I said, then urged my horse back to the front of our little band. Lockett laughed knowingly behind me.

The trail of destruction began again as Tatterhead left the road and continued on his straight-ahead path. Once again we rode single file, with Jack in the lead, me right behind him. It made conversation impossible, so I was left alone with my thoughts until Jack's horse suddenly balked, neighing and refusing to continue.

"Whoa, girl," Jack said calmingly, not trying to force her forward. "What is it? What—?"

He stopped, then quickly dismounted and knelt to look at something on the ground. I turned to the others. "Everyone stay here." Then I dismounted as well and cautiously walked toward Jack, checking the surrounding woods for any sign of movement.

"What is it?" I asked when I stood over him.

He held up a hand, stained bright red. "Blood," he said, his voice trembling a bit. Before him was a small pool of it, and beyond, a trail of dark droplets spattered on the ground and some low-hanging leaves. It was enough to convince me that whatever bled it out was likely no longer among the living.

"Don't panic," I said quietly. "It doesn't make sense that he'd kill her here, on a whim."

He wiped his hand on the ground. "Maybe she pissed him off. She could be touchy."

"No. It doesn't feel right. Whoever or whatever died here, it wasn't Isadora."

He didn't protest, but we continued on foot. The blood trail preceded us along Tatterhead's path of destruction.

This was old forest, untraveled and thick. On either side, beyond Tatterhead's recent damage, huge fallen trunks covered the ground. Many were already rotted, and those were covered with multicolored fungi, wan gray lichen, and green moss. Seedlings also rose from the remains of their ancestors, reaching for the sunlight that only rarely made it through the tree canopy.

Suddenly Jack stopped, wiped his cheek, and stared at his hand. "What the hell?" Blood smeared his face from one ear to the corner of his mouth, but there was no sign of a wound.

He looked back. A low leaf had brushed his face. Blood still dripped from it.

No birds sang around us, and even the insect buzzing was suddenly absent. "Quiet!" I whispered, and drew my sword. "Stay here."

"Not a chance," Jack whispered.

"All right, but just don't do anything unless I tell you. Understand?"

He nodded. He meant it, too, I could tell. But if we found something horrible, he might not be able to control himself.

We crept forward. The ground rose before us, and we ended up crawling up to the top of the hill. We peered down into a wide gully with a trickling stream in the center. It was beautiful and bucolic, except for the blood splattered on a wide swath of ground. Across the stream, Tatterhead's trail continued.

"Izzy," Jack said, and swallowed hard. He pointed. A strip of cloth from the banquet gown she'd been wearing was tangled in a briar patch across the stream.

He started to rush forward, but I grabbed his arm. "Wait," I said. "Look around. The blood's all on this side of the stream. If he'd murdered her this brutally, that cloth would be dripping red, but it's not."

"Then where did all the blood come from?" he demanded, his eyes wet despite his attempts at control.

"I don't know. But get a hold of yourself. You go off half-cocked, you're not doing Izzy or yourself any good."

I walked down into the gully, watching in all directions. The eerie silence worried me more than anything, because animals always know when something unnatural is around, and few things were more unnatural than Tatterhead.

Jack followed, mimicking my slight crouch. It was funny, sort of, but it also showed that he had sense enough to recognize when someone else was better informed. Many a prince would ignore my advice just because it came from a commoner.

I stopped just this side of the stream, at the biggest splotch of blood. Part of it drained into the water, making a red ribbon that faded as it drifted downstream. If all this liquid came from one person, there's no way they were still alive.

When he reached me, Jack whispered, "Why is it so quiet?"

This kid *was* smart. But before I could answer, something snapped overhead. We looked up as a huge, dark form dived down through the branches straight at us.

I shoved him hard one direction and leaped the opposite way. The form hit the spot we'd been standing with a wet *splat*, jiggled a bit, then didn't move.

Jack's eyes were as wide as one of Crazy Jerry's dinner plates. "What the hell is that?" he almost shrieked.

It took a moment for the shape to resolve itself. "A bear. A *dead* bear."

I held my breath as I poked the bear with my sword. It was a big, full-grown monster, much like the one I'd killed sixteen years ago in these very woods. But there was one crucial difference. I hadn't beaten it to death with my bare hands and thrown it twenty feet up into a tree. Tatterhead did.

"Holy shit," Jack said as he realized what had happened.

"Not exactly princely language," I said wryly.

"Not exactly a princely situation. Do you still think Izzy is all right?"

"I'd bet on it. His whole job is to get her back to Acheron safely."

"Good god, what is that?" Glendower called from the rise behind us.

"A dead bear," I said. "There's nothing to be afraid of. Come on down, we can water our horses."

"We need to keep going," Jack said.

"Hard to ride a dead horse," I said. "While they rest, let's go check out that ribbon."

We crossed the stream and reached the bush where the strip of cloth hung. Jack reached for it, but I stopped him. "Don't touch it yet. We need to see what it can tell us."

"It tells us Izzy came this way," he said impatiently. "What else do you need to know?"

I understood his impatience, but it was starting to bug me. "You really need to calm the fuck down," I said firmly. "We don't even know for certain who the bad guy is in this situation."

"I'd say the woman who sends a monster after my girlfriend would fill the bill," he fired back.

"Really? What if King Gerald sent him?"

"Well, then—"

"What if Opulora sent him, but wanted everyone to think King Gerald did it? Or what if—?"

"You're making this too complicated!" he said, sounding for a moment like a spoiled little boy.

"It *is* complicated. And the only way to uncomplicate it is to look at the clues. Now . . . this does tell us that Isadora came this way. What else does it tell us?"

He bent close and looked at the cloth. It was torn from the hem of her gown, as if it had snagged as they passed and ripped free. There was no blood on it, which told me that Tatterhead probably put her safely aside while he dispatched the bear. On the ground, I saw deep impressions from his feet, including one clear mark in the mud. There were no matching prints for Isadora, so he was likely still carrying her. Was she still unconscious, then, from the effects of that last glass ball?

"I don't see any blood," Jack said. "So it must mean she's okay."

I started to indicate all the other things he'd missed, but didn't; he'd discerned the most important fact, and that was enough. "Right. So that's one worry we don't have."

Clancy looked over the destruction and let out a long whistle. "The monster beat up a *bear*?"

"Looks like it," I said.

"I'd purely love to have seen that fight."

We let our horses rest and drink for a while, then continued on, following the trail of a monster and a girl who'd been saved from a bear for the second time in her life.

THE terrain grew rougher for the horses, which slowed us down. As the sun set, we were still half a day from the Mahnoman border, and probably wouldn't reach Acheron before nightfall the next evening. There was nothing for it but to find an open spot and pitch camp.

"We could keep going," Jack said. "It'd be slow, but we could do it."

"Do you want to be exhausted and sleep-deprived when we finally catch up to Tatterhead?" I pointed out.

"I'm already exhausted," he said, "and I doubt I'll be sleeping much tonight." But in fact he was out ten minutes after wrapping up in his blanket on the ground.

Liz and I sat beside the fire, Beatrice and Harry across from us. Ajax stood guard, watching the trail ahead in case Tatterhead saw our fire and doubled back. Ellis sat beside his son, watching the boy sleep. Glendower, having cooked us dinner, washed his utensils in the nearby stream. Clancy was also asleep, snoring so loudly that occasionally Beatrice poked him with a stick to make him change positions.

Billy Cudgel sat with his hands tied behind his back, around a tree. Well, the rope went around the tree, although his hands didn't. So far as I knew, he'd said nothing since we left Mummerset. To anyone, even the inquisitive Harry Lockett. I worried that he'd died a couple of times, but I could see his breath in the chill night air. He stared down at the dirt, his thoughts apparently far away. He shook his head when he was offered food, a sure sign that something fundamental was wrong with him. Still, I wasn't about to take pity on him.

The wood crackled and smoked. Liz said to Beatrice, "How are you holding up?"

"Okay, I guess," she said.

"I'm sorry if I seemed callous back at your home," Harry said. "My job requires me to keep a distance, you know? It doesn't give me an excuse to be rude, though."

"Thank you," Beatrice said. "You never think your own family will make the news, I guess."

Ajax suddenly strode into the clearing, holding someone by the collar. This newcomer kicked and punched, but might as well have been smacking a tree for all the effect it had. "Look what I found sniffing around," he said gruffly.

"Let me go!" the newcomer said.

He tossed the boy into the dirt. The kid got up, arranged his clothes, and said, "That's a mark against you in my book, mate." He wrapped his arms around his spindly body and shivered.

"When you get ready to settle accounts, make an appointment," Ajax shot back. "I found this little gopher trying to sneak up on the camp."

"I just wanted to see if—" He stopped, reconsidered, and said, "I mean, 'Fuck you.'"

The words were so ludicrous coming from such a youngster—he couldn't have been more than ten or eleven—that I laughed. I said, "Son, you're starting off on the wrong foot here. Come up to the fire and get warm."

Liz whispered to me, "That's a girl."

I looked more closely. "Really?"

"Yes. That disguise wouldn't fool anybody."

"I'm not a stupid girl," the newcomer said. "I'm a boy, a son, I'm strong and I'm tough!"

"The toughest people I know are women," I said. "What's your name?"

"Uhm . . . Pat. Yeah, that's it. Pat."

"Okay, Patricia—"

"Patrick!"

"Okay, *Patrick*. Why are you sneaking up on us?"

"To see if you were another monster. I saw one today, but nobody believed me."

"What sort of monster?" Harry asked, pen and vellum ready.

"He was huge! Twice, no *three* times as tall as me. He smelled like dead fish. And he was carrying a girl on his shoulder."

"Was she hurt?" Beatrice asked.

"I don't think so. She looked like she was asleep."

"Where were they going?" I asked.

"I don't know," Pat said. "Toward the Mahnoman border, that's all I could tell."

"Are you hungry?" Liz asked. "We have a few leftover biscuits."

"I wouldn't spit at 'em," Pat said.

"But you have to be honest," Liz said as she put the bread on a plate. "What's your real name? Patricia?"

After a long moment, she said petulantly, "Viola."

"And why are you disguised as a boy?" Harry asked.

"I'm running away. My father wants me to marry some old guy. He's nearly *thirty*."

I managed a smile, since I was a few years past that age myself. But I didn't approve of forced marriages, so I said, "Are you telling us the truth, Viola? Because you haven't got a lot of credibility at this point."

"Credi-what?"

"It means you've lied to us already," Liz paraphrased.

"Why would I lie about this?"

"To get away from home," I said. "I don't have a problem letting you come with us, but I need to know you're not yanking my chain."

She looked me up and down. "I don't see a chain. Are you a slave?"

"I can't wait to hear her talk to Clancy," Liz said softly.

"It's an expression, Viola. It means you're telling us lies to get us to do what you want."

She turned her back to me and raised her tunic. Her skin was crisscrossed with welts, some recent, some old enough to become scars. Her feminine form was also more obvious without the baggy clothes to hide it. It confirmed that wherever she came from, it was no place for a child to return to. She said, "If I drop my pants, you can see more."

"That's plenty," I said gently.

Beatrice said, "I've got some ointment in my bag that might help." She took the girl by the hand and led her off into the dark.

Liz turned to me. *"Thirty,"* she said, in the exact same tone of voice. We both laughed.

★   ★   ★

LATER, Ajax returned to camp and filled his canteen from the stream. I was the only one still awake, and he sat down across the fire from me. At last I said, "Do you and I have a problem?"

"We're on the same side," he said flatly.

"Yeah, but that whole head-butt thing back in Mummerset—"

"Forget it. You were drunk."

He was right, and even though the words "but it wasn't my fault" desperately wanted to come out, I choked them down. There was no way to say that without it sounding like a whine. Instead I said, "There's some bread. You hungry?"

He shook his head, then indicated my sword. "Is that a real Cillian Skirmisher?"

"The hilt is," I said, and slowly drew it. "The blade's from a Kingkiller Mark Four."

"Really? I've never seen one, only the Mark Three. Even a king's bodyguard can't afford the Mark Four."

I handed it to him across the fire, hilt first. "See what you think."

Ajax took it and felt the balance. "Nice. But why'd you combine them? If I had a Mark Four, I'd be showing it off."

"What's the worst thing about a Skirmisher?"

"The way the blade snaps if it's parried by anything heavier." Then he grinned. "And when they see that hilt—."

"Makes people overconfident," I said. "I like it when my opponents are that way."

He handed back the sword. "There's only one thing more beautiful than a good sword: a bottle of Teska or a woman from anywhere." He winked at me. "You ever had a good . . . bottle of Teska?"

I laughed. Despite our matching forehead bruises, I was glad we'd found something mutual to ease the tension.

★ ★ ★

BY noon the next day, the trail merged with another road. It was a real one, as the deep wagon ruts made plain.

"We're across the border in Mahnoma," Jack said.

"How do you know?" Liz asked.

"We don't do our roads this way, with the ditch on either side. We have a ditch down the middle."

I said, "Okay, that means our quarry took the road the rest of the way. Remember, we're essentially enemy troops in a foreign country, and we have a king with us. So let's try not to draw any more attention than we have to. And for god's sake, don't pick any fights."

I turned to Jack. "You have a special job. Watch him." I indicated Billy Cudgel.

"But you need me up front," Jack protested.

"No. I'll take the point. Whatever we do now, we need experience and stealth more than your stout heart and sword arm."

Jack started to protest.

"Look, you know Cudgel better than any of us," I said. "You know what he's capable of, and how good he is at getting other people to do his dirty work. Don't let him talk to anyone, don't let him out of your sight, and there's no one here who will mourn him if you feel the need to lop off his head." I glared at Cudgel. "Are we clear on that?"

"I assure you, I have no plans to attempt anything," Cudgel said.

"Which means he's got half a dozen, and he's trying to decide which one to use," Jack said.

"Sir, you dishonor me and yourself with your suspicions."

"I can live with that," he said. "I trusted you. I wanted your help, preparing to be a better king."

"The throne's not empty yet," Ellis said dryly from behind us. "You have plenty of time. But we'll talk about it later. Perhaps I've been too hasty in accepting the general opinion of your conduct."

That made me smile. A man who could acknowledge his own errors, whether as king or father, was a good man. Perhaps all Ellis and Jack needed all along was a common cause.

The day was sunny, with a nice breeze rattling the leaves around us. Here and there, Tatterhead's foot had left its broad mark on the hard-packed road. It confirmed we were still on his trail.

"Fuck me," Viola said when she saw them. She rode doubled up with Beatrice, her arms around the woman's waist. "He really *is* a monster. I thought I'd just fucking imagined how fucking big he was."

Liz said, "You're new to cursing, aren't you?"

"Yeah, but I've been practicing," she said, missing the irony. In daylight, she looked just a little younger than Isadora. But where Isadora had already bloomed into womanhood, Viola was still half-child.

Suddenly Viola pointed. "There's a town ahead. Illyria. We take produce there to sell sometimes."

"Friendly place?" I asked.

"Yeah, I guess," she said with a shrug.

The road curved wide to the right and when we came around it, we saw a tiny village, one even smaller than Mummerset. It had a tavern and a blacksmith shop on one side of the road, and a covered shed on the other, with tables where produce would be sold at harvest time. The tavern, named the Three Tunns, looked deserted.

Three men quit whatever they were doing in the farrier's shop and watched us.

I stopped, and everyone behind me did as well. All the mental alarms that I'd honed in battle were going off, despite the outward peacefulness. "Hi," I said. "Good morning."

"It's morning," one of the men agreed. "Where you headed?"

"Acheron," I said. "Visiting some friends."

"Looks like you got plenty of friends with you," the blacksmith said, and made an odd motion with his eyes toward the tavern.

I shifted in my saddle and made sure my sword hand was near my weapon's hilt. "It's always a party with me," I said. "Any chance for a drink at the bar?"

"Not open," the blacksmith said too quickly. "If I was you, I'd just keep riding." I noticed sweat that had nothing to do with the fire under his forge.

One of the other men shot the blacksmith a deep-eyed, hateful look. I got it then: Two of them were not natives, and they were forcing the blacksmith to go along with something. The most likely thing was, of course, a trap for us.

"No, the tavern's open," the third man said. "Nothing like a full tankard to start the day, right?"

"I'm more of a tea-drinker in the mornings myself," I said. I couldn't risk looking around to see if anyone else had spotted the danger. If they hadn't, I could only hope they'd go along with whatever I did.

"Hey, Mr. Klinger," Viola said to the blacksmith, "where's Ken?"

"He's upstairs, sick," Klinger said. He laughed, nervous and choked. "Lucky bastard, huh? Missing out on the work. I'll tell him you asked about him."

"I could use a drink," one of the other men said. "And I've just come into some gold, so the first round's on me. Come on, everyone."

He crossed the street, stopped at the tavern door, and looked back at us. None of us had moved to dismount.

He laughed. "Come on, I know it's early, but you can't turn down free ale, can you?" He nodded at Billy Cudgel. "That man sure looks thirsty. And hungry."

A familiar rank smell reached us, faint but definite. Ajax, who hadn't yet encountered Tatterhead, looked accusingly at Billy Cudgel. "Come *on*, man, really."

"I assure you, you canker blossom, it's not me," Cudgel said with outraged dignity.

"He who denied it, supplied it," Viola said. Then, her lips barely moving, she said quietly to me, "Something's weird. I don't know those two guys, and I know everyone in Illyria."

"We'll be on our way," I said evenly.

"Yeah, that's the best idea I've heard all day," the blacksmith said before I'd hardly finished speaking. "Go back the way you—"

Tatterhead burst from the tavern. And I mean *burst,* taking out both the front door and most of the wall around it. The man at the door was crushed under it, his last cry a wet-sounding "Ugh!" I wondered how the monster had ever gotten *in* there. But I didn't wonder long, because there he was right in front of me, as tall as I was in my saddle. I drew my sword, but it looked like a sewing needle next to this creature.

"The monster!" Viola shrieked, pointing from behind Beatrice. *"The fucking monster!"*

My horse reared in surprise and I let her, hoping the slicing hooves might do some damage. With an impatient grunt, Tatterhead slapped both me and the horse aside. I released my sword as I flew from the saddle, not wanting to impale myself on it. I hit the ground and managed to roll with the impact, so I wasn't hurt.

Then Ajax strode through the chaos, sword in hand, eyes fixed on Tatterhead. He saw this as a personal challenge, and despite what he'd seen done to the trees and the bear, he was going to take it on.

"Ajax!" I yelled as I got to my feet. "Don't be an idiot!"

He pointed his sword at Tatterhead. "Release those civilians, you overgrown two-legged warthog! A warrior calls you out."

Tatterhead turned, frowned in puzzlement, and flicked one prodigious hand at Ajax. The bodyguard barely dodged it, swung back hard at the monster, but his blow glanced off the metal manacle on Tatterhead's wrist.

I looked around for my sword, but didn't see it, and had no time to search. Tatterhead knocked Ajax aside with the same ease, then grabbed Prince Jack in one hand around the boy's waist. His other fist struck indiscriminately at the rest of our band. Liz ducked one blow and tried to turn her horse, but the animal was too panicked and confused. The next backhand caught her and knocked her aside.

With almost its whole front torn away, the tavern building looked like one of those open-front dollhouses. What must have been Illyria's entire population cowered in a back corner. One man guarded them, sword drawn, although he, like them, watched the conflict openmouthed.

I ran and jumped as high as I could onto Tatterhead's back. The dead-fish smell was nauseating. I climbed up his greasy tunic and put my arms around his neck, intending to bend back his head and maybe snap his spine. I was not up to the task; it was like trying to twist a chimney.

"Everyone get back!" I yelled. "I mean it!" Ajax was about to charge forward, but Ellis, ever sensible, put a hand on his shoulder.

"Hey," Tatterhead said, annoyed. This close, in physical contact with him, his voice was so deep, it made my whole body vibrate. He tossed Jack aside like a doll. "Get off me."

He reached back and grabbed a handful of my clothes, just as I got the knife from my boot. As he started to pull, I slipped the knife in one of his nostrils, and when he yanked me free, the blade slashed through it.

He dropped me and yelled, *"Ow!"* He put his hand to his nose, and when he saw the smear of blood on his palm, rumbled, "That really hurt. You did that on purpose."

A rope dropped around his massive shoulders and yanked tight when it got to his forearms, pinning them to his sides. It came from Beatrice, who quickly tied it to her saddle. Viola, still riding behind her, held on for wide-eyed dear life. Liz, back on her horse and apparently uninjured, caught a rope thrown by Clancy. They lashed it to their saddles so that it stretched horizontally, then ran their horses forward and clothes-lined the monster across the chest. This caught him off balance, so he went down on his back with a thud that I felt through the ground. I swear the leaves rattled around us.

I jumped on his chest and raised my knife overhead, ready to drive it into his heart. Both colossal hands were pressed to his bleeding nose; he looked at me over fingertips as big as my elbows. He had the largest face I'd ever seen; this close, his eyes were too far apart for me to hold the gaze of both at the same time. He couldn't *possibly* be human, yet he could think, talk, and appreciate humor. What was he?

He looked at me with outrage but no malice. "You cut off my nose!"

"No, I didn't, but I'll cut a hole in your heart if you don't lie still. Where's Isadora?"

Again he examined the blood on his hand. "I've never seen my own blood before. It's red like people's, isn't it?"

"Yes. Now answer my question."

Yells and screams made me look up. The crowd inside the tavern had overpowered their distracted minder. The remaining bad guy leaped onto his horse and took off down the road further into Mahnoma. I didn't want him to get away and sound the alarm, so I said, "Jack, Clancy, go get him." The two young men rushed to pursue.

I turned my attention back to Tatterhead. "You were saying?"

He waved one hand at the tavern. "She's in there."

Beatrice slid off her horse so fast, Viola barely had time to release her hold. She ran toward the tavern and disappeared inside. Owen Glendower and King Ellis followed.

Ajax appeared beside me, a little out of breath. He put his sword tip against Tatterhead's chest. "I've got him now," he said. "You go see about her."

I climbed off and made eye contact with Liz. She nodded; she was okay.

I went into the tavern. Isadora lay on a table, covered with an old patched blanket. Her mother, grandfather, and potential father-in-law surrounded her.

"How is she?" I asked.

"I don't know," Beatrice said, her eyes wet and her voice shaking. "She's not waking up. Izzy, honey, please, it's Mom. You're scaring me, baby."

Her eyes were closed, and at first I didn't think she was breathing. But her skin was warm when I touched her cheek, and her arm moved without the rigidity of death.

I gently lifted one eyelid. Her eye stared straight ahead, and the pupil didn't react to the light. I'd seen the same thing in men with head wounds; their bodies might live, but their minds were gone. I sincerely hoped this wasn't the case.

"Are you a doctor, too?" Ellis asked.

"I've seen a lot of injuries," I said. "But I don't know what's wrong with her."

One of the captive Illyrians, a heavyset woman with jet-black hair, said, "She was like that when they brought her in. Limp, unconscious, nothing. We thought she was dead at first."

"She's *not* dead," Beatrice insisted fiercely.

"No, she's not," I agreed. "But we need more answers again, and we only have one source."

"You're going to question that monster?" Owen said.

"I don't know if he's a monster or not," I said. "But yeah, he's the only one here who might know what's going on." Once again Tatterhead's voice rose in my mind, speaking that lone, impossible word: *sister.*

I went back outside. Tatterhead still lay on the ground, hands to his nose, Ajax's sword tip over his heart. Harry stood nearby, sketching on one of his pads.

I said firmly, "All right, Tatterhead. I want answers."

"You cut off my nose," he protested.

"You knocked my girlfriend off her horse, so we'll call it even. Now, what did you do to Isadora?"

"I put her out," he said, the words muffled by his hands.

"Put her out?"

"Yes. She was almost empty. If I hadn't put her out, she wouldn't have made it."

"Empty of what?" I asked.

"Life," he said simply.

Harry stopped sketching and looked up. "What do you mean by that?"

Tatterhead looked at him. "Were you drawing my picture?"

"Yes."

"Can I see it?"

"Answer his question first," Ajax said, and poked him in the chest with the sword.

"Ow! You don't have to be mean, you know."

I couldn't get this being's personality straight in my head. He was capable of great brutality, yet there was something undeniably childlike, if not exactly innocent, about him. I said, "I'm sorry, Tatterhead. You're right, we don't have to be mean." I nodded at Ajax, and although he looked at me as if I were drunk on Devils' Dew again, he pulled his sword away. I said, "Now, what did you mean, she was almost empty of life?"

"Opulora said I had to find her before midnight yesterday, or she'd run out of life. It was a close thing. I mean, I smelled her on you—" He indicated me. "—but the fat man who was supposed to follow you and let us know where you were never sent word."

I looked around to see Billy Cudgel's reaction, but he was gone. He'd taken advantage of the confusion to make his escape.

"Goddammit," Jack said. "That fat son of a—"

"It doesn't matter," I said. "Wherever he's gone, good riddance." I turned back to Tatterhead. "If he didn't contact you, then how did you find us?"

"I didn't. Opulora did. She said she got some kind of signal."

The screaming bead, I thought. *That let her know where we were. Damn it, it* was *all my fault.* "And so what were you supposed to do with her?"

"Bring her back by midnight tonight. After that, not even one of Opulora's spells can save her."

"Save her from what?"

"From losing all her life," he said simply.

"You mean she'll die," Harry said.

He shrugged, raising a puff of dust from the ground beneath him. "Not die like you. But yes."

"And if you get her back by midnight tonight?" I asked.

"Opulora can fill her back up."

"With life?"

"Yeah."

I couldn't decide if he was telling the truth, or if this was some nonsense story Opulora had fed him. I looked up at the sun; it wasn't quite noon. A fast rider could make it to Acheron by midnight, but I doubted our whole caravan could. Then something occurred to me. "If it was so important that you get her there by midnight, why did you stop here?"

"I knew you were following us. I could smell you. The soldiers who met me insisted we wait for you and finish you off. They didn't think it would be a big deal." He chuckled, and the deep rumble tickled the inside of my ears. "They were surprised, weren't they?"

"Yeah," I agreed. "So if we let you up, do you promise to stop fighting us?"

"I'm supposed to keep doing it," he said.

"Why?"

"Because if I don't, Opulora will punish me."

"But you've already failed. We have Isadora, and we have you. If she could punish you at this distance, don't you think she would have? She has to know you failed, right?"

He Drank, and Saw the Spider

"Right . . . ," he said slowly, turning the thought over in his head.

"I think you're safe, Tatterhead. I don't think even her reach extends this far."

"Safe," he repeated. "Safe. So . . . if I try to keep fighting, you'll kill me?"

"You bet your gigantic fucking ass we will," Beatrice said as she strode from the tavern. I was afraid she'd kick him, but she just stood over him, fists on her hips, and demanded, "What did you do to my daughter?"

"So am I afraid of you?" Tatterhead asked me with genuine confusion.

"You should definitely respect us, at least," I said before Beatrice could threaten him again. He didn't seem angry at all, just perplexed and a little put out, like someone caught in the rain without shelter. "Have you been afraid before?"

"Only of Opulora. She can pinch me like a swarm of bees stinging me, without even touching me. She can make my whole body cramp and my bones ache, no matter where I am. Except—" He shook his head in wonder. "—now she can't."

I desperately wanted to ask him about the "sister" comment, but not when everyone else was around. "Look, Tatterhead, we don't want to hurt you, really. We're just trying to rescue Isadora."

"Then you have to get her to Opulora by midnight," the big man said.

"Midnight?" Beatrice repeated. "What happens at midnight?"

"Apparently she dies," Harry said. Then he winced. "Sorry. No social skills, what can I say?"

Beatrice looked down at Tatterhead. "Is that true?" she demanded, her voice shaking with both rage and fear.

Before Tatterhead could answer, Jack and Clancy returned. Jack's right arm was in a makeshift sling, and Clancy had a bloody gash across one cheek. "We got him," Jack said, and indicated the body slung across the back of his horse. "But he was tough. We couldn't take him alive."

Ellis came from the tavern and helped his injured son from his horse. Clancy said, "We didn't get a chance to ask them where they'd taken Izzy."

"We know where she is," I said. "In the tavern."

"What?" Jack said, and started to push past his father.

"Wait, son," Ellis said gently. "She's still unconscious."

Jack twisted away and ran inside the tavern.

"What are we going to do?" Liz asked me quietly.

"Tell me if I've got this right, Tatterhead," I said. "If Isadora doesn't get to Acheron, to Opulora, by midnight tonight, she's dead."

He nodded.

"We'll never all get there on time," Liz said. "We need one rider, on our fastest horse, carrying her."

"I'll take her," I said. There was no question about it in my mind. I had the most experience with what I was likely to encounter. "Who has the fastest horse?"

"I do," Ellis said.

"Wait, why you?" Beatrice challenged.

"Because it's what he does," Liz said before I could answer. "I don't know anyone who'll try harder to save your daughter's life."

"Me," she said with certainty. "And I bet I'm at least as good a rider as you. And she's my daughter."

"But you can't also fight your way through guards, and then talk your way past kings," Liz said. "Eddie can."

"You're that good, huh?" she said dryly.

"Yeah," I said. "At this, I am." Ellis's horse would need water, grain, and rest before running like I intended to run him. "Let's get everything ready. I'll leave in an hour."

Beatrice started to snap something back, her fists clenched in rage and fury. Then she turned and stalked off.

"She'd be a handful," Harry said, but there was admiration

in his voice. I realized I didn't know if scribes, like moon priestesses, were unable to marry. I'd have to find that out someday.

"What do we do with him?" Ajax asked, nodding at Tatterhead.

I said, "Tatterhead, if we let you go, do you promise not to hurt any of us and not to try to stop us?"

"I do," he said.

"You're going to *trust* him?" Viola said, peeking from behind a tree. "He's a monster!"

"He's a monster who's never lied to us," I pointed out. I nodded at Ajax. He cut the rope around Tatterhead's arms and torso.

Tatterhead sat up. Sitting, he was as tall as most of us standing.

Beatrice returned. Her face was still set and hard, but she took his huge chin gently in her hands and turned his face to examine his cut nose. She said, "Isadora's my daughter. I'm very angry that you kidnapped her."

"I know," he said. "I'm sorry I had to."

"If you'll sit still and not cry like a baby, I'll clean that cut and bandage it for you."

"She's really good at it," Viola said.

"Pretty," Tatterhead said with a smile.

I waited for the explosion, but Beatrice just said dryly, "I bet you say that to all the girls."

"That's because you're all so beautiful. I know how ugly I am. Everyone is beautiful compared to me."

Beatrice smiled so slightly that only my trained observational skills caught it.

A few minutes later, Tatterhead sat under a tree, his nose bandaged. Ajax and Clancy stood guard, swords drawn and ready. Everyone else, including Liz, was in the tavern. If I was going to press this whole "sister" issue before I left, this was my chance. I said, "Gentlemen, I need a word with our guest. In private."

Ajax said suspiciously, "About what?"

"About something private," I said.

The bodyguard started to protest, then thought better of it and strode away. Clancy followed.

"Are you all right?" I asked Tatterhead.

"My nose feels funny," he said. His deep voice was now very nasal as well.

"I have to ask you a question. Back at the Glendower's manor, when you first kidnapped Isadora, you called her your 'sister.' What did you mean by that?"

Tatterhead looked everywhere but at me. "I can't say."

"Because of Opulora?"

He nodded.

"*Is* the girl your sister?"

He raised one hand and shook it, the widely acknowledged sign for "sort of."

"Is this something I need to know to save her life?" I pressed.

"Opulora can explain it better than I can," he said. "And if you don't reach her in time, the answer won't matter."

"So what do we do with you, then?"

"Are you going to kill me?" he asked simply.

"I don't want to. But it depends on you. Ideally, you'd stay here until tomorrow, and then leave without hurting anyone else. Can you give me your word on that?"

"Why would I want to hurt anyone else? *You're* the one who cut me."

That sounded enough like a threat that the hair on my neck stood up, but I tried to act like it hadn't fazed me. Perhaps he wasn't as innocent as I thought. "Are you threatening me?"

His brows lowered. His confusion sounded genuine. "No. Did that sound like a threat?"

"Yeah. That's why I'm worried you might get angry and hurt someone if we leave you."

Again, the huge brows wrinkled. At last he said, "I don't think I've ever been angry."

"Really," I said doubtfully.

"I get annoyed. But not mad. I wonder why?"

"I think it's probably better for everyone that you don't."

"Yeah, but you'd think I would, wouldn't you? I'm essentially a slave. I don't get to make my own decisions. I have to do what I'm told, or I'll be hurt. That should make me mad, shouldn't it?"

"I'd think so."

"You cut my nose. I should be mad at *you*."

"I'd prefer you not be. But I'd understand it if you were."

He continued to frown, then shook his skull. His plaited hair slapped together. "No. Isn't happening."

"What's your name?" Viola asked suddenly. I hadn't heard her slip up behind me, and now she peeked around me to look at the giant.

He smiled at her. "Tatterhead."

"Really?"

"Yes."

"Do you like being called Tatterhead?" she asked.

"All I've ever been called."

"But do you like it?"

"Not really. Everyone says it like an insult."

"What would you like to be called, then?"

He thought it over. "Mortimer."

"That's a much nicer name," Viola agreed.

HALF an hour later, I was astride King Ellis's magnificent stallion, with Isadora's limp form on the saddle in front of me. I'd tied her to my chest so I'd have my hands free. She was still unconscious and totally nonresponsive.

"Be careful with her," Beatrice said, holding her daughter's limp hand. "Please."

"I will," I assured her.

"I'll get the rest of us there as fast as possible," Liz said.

"Be careful," I said to her.

She winked, but didn't smile.

I glanced over at the tree, where Viola still stood talking with Tatterhead. It was too bad I'd never see how that friendship worked out.

Ellis stepped close and pressed his signet ring in my hand. "I don't know if it will help, but feel free to use my name in dealing with Gerald. He and I were once like brothers."

"Thanks," I said. I firmly nudged the horse in the ribs and he shot forward down the road, the limp girl bouncing against me.

uch like swords, with horses, you get what you pay for. Ellis's horse was like a well-oiled, single-purpose machine, galloping with the kind of smooth gait that told me he'd been born for this. If carrying two people threw him off or slowed him down, he didn't let it show. We moved along the mostly empty road like water through a streambed.

I was able to hold the reins with one hand and cradle Isadora's head against me with the other. She remained totally limp, completely unaware and, for all intents and purposes, brain-dead. Her hands flopped with every stride as if she clapped out the galloping sound herself. Even when we passed through a cloud of gnats that made me spit and gag, she did not react.

We dodged past wagons and other people on horseback, all of them in considerably less hurry than us. They all stared at me, no doubt wondering if I'd kidnapped the girl from some outlying farm. I only hoped none of them tried to be a hero and rescue her. I kept watch on the sun as it crossed into the afternoon sky and began its slow descent toward the horizon. We seemed to have plenty of time, but I knew better than to trust it. A lot could happen between now and midnight.

By sundown we were close to Acheron, whose spires I now spotted through the trees covering the road. Traffic got thicker, and I had to slow to a trot for safety, weaving around those who were blocking my way. I'd made good time, excellent time, actually, and now all I had to do was get to the castle and contact Opulora. They were expecting Isadora, at least; they should be ready for me. Of course, I'd have to explain what happened to their pet troll.

I was used to the saddle, but riding hard for an extended period still took its toll, especially once the sun went down and the night's chill crept over me. My back and butt were killing me as I let the horse set the pace up to the city just past full nightfall.

The gates, previously wide open and guarded by opportunistic thugs, were now set up with an armed checkpoint. Three tough-looking uniformed men checked papers on everyone trying to enter the city. There were only a couple of riders ahead of us, but the line behind me quickly grew long and impatient. I saw no graceful way to run off without being noticed, and probably pursued. So there'd be no sneaking in by an alternate route. I'd have to figure out a way through.

The other people in line began to notice Isadora, flop-limbed and slack-mouthed. Whispers spread out around me. The second rider ahead got through, which meant I only had a few more moments to come up with something brilliant.

Then a new voice said, "I'll handle this, good sir."

If it had been Crazy Jerry himself, I doubt I could've been more surprised. Billy Cudgel sat on his horse beside me, as nonchalant as if he'd been riding with me all along. "Where did you come from?" I managed to gasp.

"Out of Lady Cudgel, by Lord John Cudgel," he said with a satisfied grin. "I assure you, my family is quite distinguished."

"You're the black sheep?"

"Merely misunderstood in my time."

Now it was our turn, and two guards crossed their spears to block the way. "Not so fast," the third one said. "Let's see some papers."

"Do you know who I am?" Cudgel said in high dudgeon.

"I will when you show me some identification. Don't be a smart-ass, old man, I've been doing this all day and I'm tired."

"I am Sir William Cudgel, late of his majesty King Gerald's employ, may the gods protect him. And known and treasured by the lady Opulora. My friends and I are traveling on the king's very business."

"Is that a fact?"

"It is indeed, sir."

"Well, since the king himself closed down the gates, you won't mind proving that."

Cudgel slapped the man across the face with his reins. All conversation in the line behind us ceased.

"You dare ask me for identification? I shall have you taken in irons before the king, and then delivered to the tender mercies of the lady Opulora. Do you know what she is capable of? There are monkeys afoot in the castle that used to be men, men such as yourselves with rude tongues. And you—" He pointed to one of the other guards. "Perhaps you favor being turned to stone? It can all be done, you know. There's a whole garden filled with statues that were formerly insolent civilians. And you will join them, if you do not step aside and allow me and my friends entrance to the city."

He was good at this: his voice had the authority of someone used to being obeyed, and the guards crumbled under it. They stepped aside, all apologies, and we went through quickly.

"There, you see?" Cudgel said calmly. "It's all in your attitude. Act as if you have the power, and others will assume you do."

As we passed the guards, I saw only two of them: the one

Billy had slapped, holding his injured cheek, and another who glared like an angry child. There had been three; had the third one gone ahead to warn someone?

The streets were busy, and lamps lit all the taverns, boarding-houses, and other establishments that made their gold after dark. Carts and wagons headed out of town, their business done for the day, while pedestrians and carriages took their places.

"Okay, so why are you here?" I said.

Very theatrically, he said. "I found myself a bit despondent over my own behavior," he said at last. "I genuinely like that young prince. And not in one of your seedy ways, I know what you're thinking. No, I'm quite serious, and quite sincere. When I realized he was disappointed in me . . . I realized I was disappointed in myself."

"I'd say he was a bit more than disappointed in you."

"Indeed. And now, perhaps, I have a way to regain his good graces. By helping restore this young lady to his embrace."

He reached out to touch Isadora's face, but I slapped his hand away. "Hands off, fat man. How the hell did you manage to arrive at the gate at the exact same time I did?"

"Why, I followed you, my friend."

"You left that little town before I did."

"And I simply waited until you passed."

He was innocence personified, but the only reason I believed him was because he'd done it once before, when he followed us from Acheron to Mummerset. And truthfully, I had not worried about pursuit, assuming all my difficulties would be ahead. "I still don't trust you."

"And you'd be wise not to, in most situations. But I truly wish to help. I believe you have a deadline to get your charge to the castle? Allow me to be your guide." He nudged his horse forward, and I dropped in behind him. The moon had risen, and I knew we were getting close. I hoped "deadline," in this case, was merely a word.

★ ★ ★

WE rode up to the castle courtyard's main entrance, where two guards kept ceremonial watch on the drawbridge. They did not respond until Billy said, "I am Sir William Cudgel, and I must see the lady Opulora. She has left standing orders to admit me."

The guards exchanged a look, then stepped aside. We entered the courtyard, and two pages ran forward to take our reins. Torches lit the area, all the way up the stairs to the main hall's doors.

I untied Isadora and dismounted with her tossed over my shoulder. Once on the ground, I shifted her to a more dignified position, but she was still heavier than I expected, a total deadweight. Again, I hoped it was just a term.

The pages led our horses off into the darkness, and Billy started the climb toward the main hall doors. I put my foot on the bottom step, then paused. "Hey," I said quietly.

He looked back, breathing heavily from the exertion. "Yes?"

"This is the inner courtyard. Don't you think there should be more—?"

A dozen men, swords drawn and shields ready, came out of the shadows and, within moments, surrounded us. Except for the creak of their armor, they were silent, their faces set and determined behind their helmet grilles. Total pros, on the job.

"Guards," I finished belatedly.

The great doors at the top of the stairs opened, and the same retinue we'd seen in the warehouse came down the steps toward us. They stopped just above Billy, then parted to reveal King Gerald.

Billy dropped to one knee, or at least as close as a man of his bulk could get on these steep stairs. "Your Majesty, I—"

"Lock him up," Gerald said, "somewhere dark and uncomfortable."

Two of the men surrounding us sheathed their swords and grabbed Billy's arms. They muscled him back down the stairs, past me and off into the shadows. He protested the whole way, but his words were useless, and after a door clanged shut, the courtyard was silent again.

Gerald slowly descended toward me, and the guards stayed close. I couldn't do much fighting with Isadora in my arms, and wouldn't try to fight anyway. He stopped a few steps above me and said, "LaCrosse."

"Your Majesty," I acknowledged. "I apologize for not kneeling, but I've got my hands full."

"Is this the girl?"

"I'm not sure what you mean by that, Your Majesty," I said honestly. I didn't have a clue what he knew.

The shadows were too dark for me to see his eyes clearly, even with the flames flickering around us, so I wasn't sure if he was in crazy mode or not. His breath came out in raspy puffs, the steam backlit by the torches. Through clenched teeth, he said, "Is this . . . the girl . . . that Opulora wanted?"

"Yes, Your Majesty," I said.

"Where is the monster?"

"He's indisposed."

His voice dropped to a whisper. "Did you *kill* him?"

"No. But I don't think you'll be seeing him anymore. He's off the payroll."

The king snorted. "So is his damned creator. I've had enough of Opulora and her machinations. This is my kingdom, I sit on the throne of my fathers, and she has interfered with my rule for the last time."

I chill ran up my back. "Is she dead?"

"She should be. She's locked away. My interrogators are with her. Soon I'll know the answer."

"Answer to what?" I asked, dreading the response.

He pointed at Isadora. "Who that damned girl really is." Her condition finally registered on him. "What's wrong with her, anyway?"

"I don't know. Tatterhead was bringing her to Opulora. He said only she can save her."

Gerald *hmph*ed in response. "All right, bring her in."

"Ah . . ."

His demeanor darkened again. "What?" he snarled.

"I was told there's a deadline. If she doesn't reach Opulora by midnight—"

"Then what?" Gerald bellowed. "She turns into a pumpkin? Her magic carpet becomes a rug? Don't give me any of that storybook mumbo jumbo. I've already had a bellyful from Opulora. I'm extending the hospitality of my palace to her, that damn well better be enough. She's not even Mahnoman, she's some foreign peasant."

I remembered Ellis's ring, but this didn't seem the time to play that card. I followed Gerald up the stairs into the main hall. I had at least two hours until midnight—two hours to convince an unstable king to free an imprisoned sorceress, and to hope I was able to do again what I'd done once before: save Isadora.

chapter

TWENTY-FOUR

A pair of bulky, sour-faced matrons took Isadora from me. I started to resist, but the guards surrounding me forced me to reconsider. As soon as Isadora was out of my arms, one of them pulled my sword from its scabbard. Then another pushed me, reasonably gently, against the wall face-first and patted me down. He missed my boot knife, which lay hidden along a seam, but against a bunch of professional guards, I was essentially weaponless. Well, except for my charm.

Then I was ushered into the throne room. It was a standard setup, with a long open floor where banquet tables could be placed. At the far end was a raised dais with three steps leading up to the actual seat of power, now occupied by an impatient-looking King Gerald. The only thing missing were courtiers and servants; except for the guards, Gerald and I were alone.

As soon as I got close enough, he said, "So tell me more about this girl. Where is she from?"

This time I knelt, bowed my head and said, "She's been

raised by a shepherd family in Altura. She was found as a baby in the nearby woods."

"Is that their story?" he said sarcastically. He gestured that I could stand.

"It's the truth." I figured I had little to lose by taking the initiative, so I said, "May I speak with Opulora?"

"Why? I've had my best interrogators working on her, and they've gotten nothing."

That sent a chill through me. No one got interrogated if they were still on the king's good side, so apparently things had changed. And what professional interrogators left behind often no longer counted as human. Still, I had to try. "Interrogators try to make people talk. I try to make people *want* to talk."

He regarded me skeptically. "Are you that good?"

"I get twenty-five gold pieces a day plus expenses."

"You're a foreign national coming into my court in the company of that known criminal, Billy Cudgel. Why should I trust you?"

"Because your interrogators have failed, and I might not. What have you got to lose?"

"You seem very eager."

"I am. I need to know what's wrong with the girl, and Opulora's the only one who can tell me."

"You say."

"I say."

"She's a lying, conniving bitch, that one. You wouldn't believe what she told *me* about that girl."

"What was it?"

He snorted contemptuously. "Like I said, you wouldn't believe it. Let's see if she tells you the same bullshit story. Hector, take him to the dungeon."

One of the guards stepped forward and took my arm, firmly but not obnoxiously. I recognized him as the same one who'd been in disguise as the king when Liz and I delivered the dishes. "Yes, Your Majesty," he said.

"Lock him in with her, though," Gerald continued. "I don't want an open door anywhere between her and me. Let him out when he finishes, and bring him straight here."

I said, "Will Isadora—?"

"Your damn shepherd girl will be fine, whoever she is. But if this is some trick to try to break that bitch out of her cell, you'll find Mahnoman hospitality to be very, very painful."

HECTOR led me mostly down. Steps spiraled at least three floors into the earth like a corkscrew digging a post hole. We saw no one else, no other guards or prisoners, and the air grew heavy, still and cool. Our boots echoed off the stone around us. There weren't even lamps; only his torch lit the way. We paused often so he could unlock thick, old doors.

We emerged at last into a dungeon hallway. Cells lined each side, but they were all empty, and the dust told me how long it had been since they'd been used. That surprised me; I'd expected them to be filled with enemies of the king and/or Opulora.

Hector read my thoughts. "Yeah, you'd expect lots of political prisoners, what with the whole 'Crazy Jerry' reputation. But really, there's not much unrest, because everything is peaceful, everyone has enough food and shelter, and no one wants to see that end. You've got the religious nuts who claim their gods told them to depose the king, but if they make too much noise, we just exile 'em."

"What about Opulora? Doesn't she have enemies?"

He shrugged. "She's just a name to most people. She never leaves the castle, and hardly ever leaves her own chambers. Hell, I've only seen her in person a dozen times."

"Why did she lose favor with the king?"

"I don't know. She tried to tell him something. Whatever it was, it made him furious, and he started slapping her. I've seen him mad before—angry, I mean, not crazy—but never like that. We finally had to pull him off her to stop him from killing her."

"And you have no idea what they were talking about?"

He shook his head. "And I wouldn't ask him about it, either. I thought Crazy Jerry was long gone, but he's always been there, right under the surface. It just takes the right, tiny little thing to set him off. I think it's time for me to look for another job."

I filed this away. Opulora knew Izzy was returning, although of course she expected Tatterhead to be bringing her in, not me. So she'd tried to prepare Gerald for whatever revelation the girl represented. And it had not gone well at all.

After we'd reached another door and started down another spiral staircase, his voice dropped to almost a whisper. "Was it true what you said? About Tatterhead?"

"Yeah. He's off on his own now. I don't think you'll hear from him again."

"Between you and me, that's the scariest son of a bitch I've ever seen. When I was a baby, my mom used to tell me bedtime stories about trolls and goblins that would snatch up kids who didn't behave. If I'd known those things were real, I'd have eaten my damn vegetables more often."

"Did you ever talk to him?"

"Tatterhead? No. I hated it when I even had to see him. His smell made my eyes water and he tended to break things without meaning to. Including people, a couple of times." He shook his head. "Opulora won't be happy to hear that he's gone, though. I think a lot of her influence came from controlling him. Then again, it's the least of her worries right now."

In addition to the increasing chill as we descended, there was also a gradually strengthening odor. I'd been in working dungeons before and knew that smell: technically it was body odor, but it always came to represent the scent of despair, if such feelings had smells. It wasn't strong, but it was definitely present. Somewhere close, someone had given up hope of ever leaving this hole.

We reached a final solid door with a tiny, barred window no bigger than my hand. A ribbon was tied to one of the bars, with a small bell on the end. Hector said, "Here's where I stop. Go through this door, down another flight of stairs, and you'll find a room with a single cell. Opulora's inside it, or at least she better be." He lit a torch in a wall sconce and handed me the one he'd carried.

We both jumped when the door suddenly swung open, and two men stepped through. They were thin and insectlike, with long fingers and big eyes. They reminded me of animals that lived in caves and never saw sunlight. One of them carried a small satchel. They were as surprised as we were, but covered it faster.

"There's been no progress," one of them said in a properly reedy voice. "She continues to resist."

I knew what they were then: the interrogators Gerald had mentioned. I said, "Is she conscious?"

He fixed those big, shimmery eyes on me. The torchlight sparkled off the abnormally large pupils. "And who are you?"

"The king sent him," Hector said.

"We will get the information," the other interrogator said defensively. "No one can resist our skills for long. The king certainly doesn't need to bring in—" He curled one lip disdainfully, revealing a set of gleaming, perfect teeth that could not possibly be natural. "—freelancers," he finished with contempt.

"That's for the king to decide," Hector said. "Go make your report. He's waiting, and hates waiting."

The interrogators scurried past us. When they skittering footsteps had faded, Hector said, "Man, those guys give me the creeps."

"Reasonable reaction," I agreed.

He held open the door for me. "I'll be waiting here. Ring this bell when you want to get out."

The door closed behind me with a finality that would've certainly prompted many a prisoner to change his mind about his silence. The torch illuminated only a few feet down the stairs ahead, leaving most of the descent in pitch blackness. The smell of old urine, fresh mold, and damp rock rose from the darkness. Except for Hector's soft, nervous humming behind me, there was no sound.

I continued down until all light through the door above faded, and nothing shone from below. I moved in a little bubble of torchlight. At last the stairs dead-ended in a room empty except for a large cage in the middle of the floor. The bars were embedded in the ground and ceiling, and there were two locks on the door, no doubt requiring two separate keys. It reminded me of a prison I'd visited in the desert outside Mosinee. At the top of a tower, with no entrance or exit, they kept their most dangerous prisoner. He was denied all human contact until he agreed to tell where he'd hidden a treasure. As far as I knew, he was still there. Certainly Opulora was still here.

She stood inside the cage, clad only in a tattered prison shift. She had no choice about standing—a leather collar around her neck was attached to a chain from the ceiling, preventing her from sitting down. She leaned against the bars with the weariness of a woman resigned to her fate.

On the wall behind the cage was yet another portrait of Sylvia and Mannheim. The artist must be fabulously wealthy by now, I thought, after making all these copies. Why was it here, though?

The sorceress did not open her eyes. It was possible to sleep standing up if you were tired enough, and it appeared she was. She looked even older than before, her short gray hair almost white and plastered with sweat to her skull. Her exposed skin was saggy and pale. I didn't know how those mantis-men tortured prisoners for information here, but it was clearly a long, slow process.

I put the torch in an empty sconce and stepped closer to the cage. There was a goblet of water on the floor, but of course she couldn't bend down to reach it—subtle torture, but effective.

I said gently, "Opulora."

Her eyes opened. They weren't guarded and in control as they'd been before, but there was the hard steel of courage in them, the kind that only real warriors possess. And I was well aware, of course, that not all real warriors carried swords and shields. Like I'd told Viola, women were some of the fiercest warriors I knew.

Her voice was cracked and dry and, combined with her appearance, made her seem especially old and fragile. "You're LaCrosse, right? The sword jockey."

"That's me. I've brought Isadora Glendower to you."

"You?"

"Me."

I expected questions about Tatterhead, but she only said, flatly and wearily, "It's too late."

"No, it's not midnight yet. There's still time."

When she didn't respond, I picked up the goblet and held it out to her. After a moment she took it and greedily drained it.

"Thank you," she said, her voice less ragged. "I was very thirsty. Licking the sweat off the bars only gets you so far."

"Why don't you do that thing where you suddenly disappear?"

She tapped the collar. "I can only do that unfettered."

"Well, even fettered, you should be able to tell me the truth about Isadora."

"Isidore," she corrected.

"She can decide which name she wants later. Who is she?"

She closed her eyes, and I was afraid she'd pass out and strangle herself. Then she said, "Oh, Mr. LaCrosse, if I hadn't already experienced your skills, I might fall for them now. But I know how good you are at getting people to talk. So I'm on my guard."

I thought for a moment. I couldn't trick her, and I doubted I could outsmart her. So I used the only weapon I had left. I said, "I have a story to tell you. A true story, about Isidore and me. When I'm done, you decide if I should know who she is."

"I'm making no promises," she said.

"I'm not asking for any."

I told her about rescuing Isidore from the bear, and placing her with the Glendowers. Then I told her how I found Isidore again, and how Tatterhead kidnapped her after following us right to her. "I don't appreciate being used that way," I finished. "I normally get paid for it, if nothing else. But this isn't about money. It's about a girl who's done nothing wrong, being treated like she was some kind of prize toy."

"She's far from that," Opulora said. She shook her head slowly. "So that's why I lost track of her. Poor Kyle. He was a good man, you know. That's why I trusted him with her safety. He deserved a better death."

"He was tough, all right," I said, recalling the way he'd hung on to life long enough to ensure I'd care for Isadora. "Tougher than I'd be after being mauled by a bear."

"And my poor Tatterhead. I thought he might rescue me when he returned, but now that will never happen. He wanted so much to be a normal person. Now perhaps he'll get his chance."

I said gently, "If Isidore's not a prize . . . what *is* she?'"

Again she closed her eyes. "She is the heir to the throne of Mahnoma."

"That's not possible," I said. "Gerald's only heir was a boy who died. He and his wife had no more children, and bastards can't succeed to the throne."

She smiled with her eyes closed again. "That's true as far as it goes. The full truth is . . . unbelievable."

"It usually is," I agreed.

"If I tell you, even you won't believe it."

I thought about some of the things I'd seen: a dragon, a sea monster, an incognito goddess, a pair of ghost children. "I'll come closer to believing it than just about anyone you're ever likely to meet."

So she told me. And she was almost right. If it hadn't explained everything, I *wouldn't* have believed her.

When she finished, she watched for my reaction. I said, "That's really possible?"

"It's really possible. If the magic is right, and the intent is true." She brushed her hair back from her face. "Mr. La-Crosse, I'm not even fifty. Why do you think I look this old?"

"It took a lot out of you, I guess."

"Years of my life. But I don't regret it, and I'd do it again."

I was silent, absorbing the story and letting it connect up to past events on its own. "I understand why you haven't told anyone. There's no proof, I take it."

"None at all. And now, with Isidore dead—"

"She's *not dead*. Stop saying that. It's not midnight, so there's still time . . . isn't there?"

"Possibly. I have everything ready. But trapped in here, I can do nothing. And I'm so weak. . . ."

My mind raced with possibilities. The sorceress was right, of course; no one would believe the story without proof, and what proof could there be?

Then the painting on the wall caught my eye. "Why is that here?"

"I tried to tell Gerald what I told you. With Tatterhead bringing Isidore back, I knew I had to come clean with him. He did not believe me. To put it mildly. He had that painting hung to remind me of the memories I'd soiled." Her eyes welled up. "Sylvia and I were like sisters. She was too trusting and she was beautiful. Those two things will surely kill you.

You can have no idea how awful it was seeing her son die, then her . . . and all for that man's baseless jealousy."

"He drank, and saw the spider," I said.

"Yes," she agreed, "he did. And no one could convince him otherwise." She wiped her eyes, smearing the dirt on her face.

I stared at the image as an idea formed and quickly took shape. It was either brilliant, or so stupid not even Liz would stay with me afterwards. "I think," I said, "I might know how to convince Gerald of the truth. But we have to get you out of here, and now. If Isadora—I mean, Isidore—dies, then it's all for nothing."

I pulled the knife from the side of my boot, reached through the bars and cut off the leather collar. She slid to the ground, rubbing her neck. "Thank you."

"Don't thank me yet." I unscrewed the pommel on my knife and withdrew a set of lockpicks hidden there. The first lock opened easily, but I worried that the second one never would. Then it clicked and the door swung open.

I helped Opulora to her feet. She weighed hardly anything.

"Swear you're not tricking me just to get out of here," I said.

"I swear."

"All right. A couple of froggy old women took Isadora from me when I got here. I don't know where they took her, but—"

"I can find her. I have quarters in the castle, secret rooms that no one can find if I don't want them to. That's where I'll be."

"Then how will *I* find you?"

"When I have everything ready . . . I'll find you."

I looked her in the eye. Behind the weariness and abuse, there was now the fire of conviction. Outside the cage she stood straight, and the prison weariness vanished. I hoped I hadn't been sucker-played. "I can trust you, right?" I asked her seriously.

She smiled slightly. "Aren't you a good judge of people?"

"Nobody's perfect."

"Yes, Mr. LaCrosse. You can trust me."

And with that she vanished: no flash, no smoke, just there one moment and gone the next, with the same lack of drama as when she'd appeared in the king's antechamber.

I hoped I was right to trust her. If not, Gerald would probably have me in that cage before long, and he'd be right to do it. Because it meant I was an idiot.

chapter

TWENTY-FIVE

hector pushed open the throne room double doors, then stepped aside so I could make a grand entrance. Gerald, back on his throne and surrounded by his guards, looked up as I approached. I knelt before him.

"Well?" he demanded. "What nonsense did she tell you?"

"The same thing she told you," I said. "Isadora's your daughter."

"And you *believe* her?"

"I believe it's possible, yeah."

He laughed without any humor at all. "By all the gods in the sky, is everyone insane but me? My wife and I had one child. *One.* A son. His bones lie with the bones of my fathers."

Sweat trickled down the back of my neck, and it wasn't because the room was hot. "What would convince you?"

"That her ridiculous story is true? Nothing. The world doesn't work that way, and whatever she calls 'magic' is nothing more than simple tricks and nonsense. It certainly doesn't extend to—"

"Then how do you explain Tatterhead?" I said.

"He's a freak of nature."

"No, she *created* him. She used the same magic, only this time she fashioned a being from scratch."

"I think you and her need to spend some time in the same cell," he said. "Guards, take this—"

I was ready to fight, and prepared to die rather than submit to the Mahnoman interrogators, but a shrill female voice cried, *"Your Majesty!"*

One of the dowdy matrons who'd taken Isadora ran the length of the great hall toward us. With her short legs and bulk, it took a while. At last she stopped, curtsied without toppling over, and gasped, "She's . . . gone!"

"The shepherd girl?"

The woman nodded, her face red and sweaty. "One moment she was there, and then . . . she wasn't!"

Gerald turned to me, furious. "What do you know about this?"

I raised my hands. "Hey, I was here with you."

"Your Majesty!" came another cry. The taller of the two interrogators emerged from a side door, minced to the dais, and dropped to one knee. "The sorceress is gone!"

"What?" Gerald snarled.

"Someone cut her free of the restraints, and opened the cell!"

Again the king looked at me. I reached into my pocket and wrapped my fingers around Ellis's ring. I took a deep breath and began, "Before you go off half-cocked here, let me—"

"Kill him," Gerald said through his teeth, pointing at me. "Kill from the ankles up, and make sure he feels everything."

The interrogator smiled. "Oh, with pleasure."

I glanced over at Hector. He shrugged; he was sympathetic, but he was also on the job. I'd get no help from him.

I backed up a step. I didn't mind going down under the swords of honest soldiers, but I wasn't about to let myself be peeled alive by these human dung beetles.

Before anyone drew blood, though, the big main doors burst open, and King Ellis strode through as if he were in his own palace back in Altura. Behind him came Liz, Beatrice, Clancy, Glendower, Jack, and Harry. Ajax brought up the rear, and behind him were a half dozen palace guards, swords drawn but clearly taken aback by Ellis's brazen confidence and Ajax's intimidating demeanor.

"Eddie!" Liz called when she saw me, and waved.

The throne room guards rushed to block off the space in front of the newcomers. Along with the trailing guards, they formed a ring around them.

"What the hell is this?" Gerald bellowed. "Can anyone just wander into the throne room now? Should we just take the doors off the hinges and move the bedroom furniture out onto the courtyard? Who are you people?"

"Friends to this crown," Ellis said loudly.

Gerald froze. "Ellis," he said in disbelief.

Ellis pushed past the ring of guards until he stood in the open. "Gerald, I share the blame for our estrangement lasting as long as it has. For the sake of our fathers, I offer my hand to seal this rift."

I moved (okay, I ran) down to stand beside Ellis. I wanted to get as far away from the interrogator as possible. I stood beside the other king (okay, behind him) as he waited for Gerald's reaction. I pressed his ring surreptitiously into his hand, saying quietly, "You might need this."

Liz slipped up beside me and whispered, "Are you okay?"

I nodded. "You guys made good time."

"Beatrice didn't let us dally. And don't worry, I'll never tell how you scurried away to hide under Ellis's skirts."

I squeezed her hand.

Before Gerald could speak, though, Beatrice pushed past the guards and demanded, "All right, where's my daughter?"

"And who are *you?*" Gerald said.

"Beatrice, please," Ellis said. "This *is* the king of—"

"I don't care if he's the king of the goddamn moon, he kidnapped my daughter and I want her back."

"Your daughter?" Gerald asked.

"Yes, my daughter, Isadora. Your monster was bringing her here."

"*Your* daughter?" he repeated, accusation in his voice. "Oho. How do you explain *that*, Mr. LaCrosse?"

I said, "Actually, I can—"

"I can explain it better," Opulora said.

Gerald did such a full-body double take that I almost laughed out loud. The billowing sleeves of his royal raiments fluttered like a man besieged by bees. But he was taken aback only for an instant. "Grab her!" he ordered his guards. "And *kill her*! *Now!*"

"Wait a minute," I said loudly. "If you want to know what's going on, she's the only one that can tell you." *And convince you,* I thought but didn't say.

Gerald's guards had their swords out and leveled at the sorceress. She was dressed formally now, and had cleaned up the prison grime, but she still looked old and tired. She said, "Gerald, if you kill me, you deserve every bad thing that has ever happened to you, and ever will."

"Is that a threat?" Gerald hissed.

"It's a curse," she shot back.

"Please, listen to us," Ellis said, walking past me and up the dais the way only another king could do. He went past the guards, none of whom tried to stop him, and touched Gerald's arm. "We have a come a long way to uncover the truth about this girl. My son loves her. I'm asking, as a personal favor, man to man, crown to crown: Let this woman speak."

Gerald stared at Ellis. Finally, in a faint and childlike voice, he asked, "Is it really you?"

"Yes, Gerald, it's me. Ellis." He laughed. "Elly Belly."

Someone choked down a laugh. I was pretty sure it was Ajax.

"The young man with his arm in a sling?" Ellis continued "That's my son, John."

Gerald's eyes grew wet. He looked at Jack for a long moment, then slowly smiled. "Your mother was most true to wedlock, Prince; you are the very image of your father." He wiped his eyes. "If I were twenty-one again, I'd call you brother as I did your father, and talk of some wild adventure we once shared."

Then Ellis and Gerald embraced. Gerald began to sob openly now, and Ellis had to hold him up.

The rest of our band joined me at the foot of the dais. Hector and Ajax eyeballed each other the way professionals always did. Liz took my hand again, and when I looked, she was misty-eyed as well.

Finally Gerald broke the embrace and said, his voice trembling, "I don't know what to do here, Ellis. I don't know whom . . . to believe. . . ."

"Then let's hear what they have to say, and decide," Ellis said calmly. He turned to Opulora. "You seem to have the floor."

Opulora said, "Gerald, I must ask you to share something with the rest of the group. How did Sylvia die?"

Gerald made a strangled sound, and I think he would've collapsed had Ellis not supported him. "What has *that* got to do with any of this?" Ellis said.

"It is crucial," Opulora said, "to proving that I'm telling the truth."

Gerald took a deep breath, blew it out, and managed to choke out, "She killed herself. After learning of our son's death."

"I know," Opulora said. "But exactly how?"

Gerald's teary eyes were scrunched closed as he said, "She . . . disemboweled herself. She cut her belly open, and when that didn't work fast enough, she stabbed herself in the heart."

Liz gasped. Ellis sighed and lowered his head. Even Beatrice turned pale. Glendower squeezed her shoulder reassuringly, and she patted his hand. Harry furiously scribbled on his pad. I'm not sure Clancy knew what "disemboweled" meant. Jack spoke for us all: "That poor woman."

"And what has that got to do with anything?" Gerald demanded, lurching upright. "Or do you just want to dredge up as many unpleasant memories as you can? You're very good at that."

"It *should* be an unpleasant memory," I said. I wasn't going to let him get out of this with a few tears, since it was all his fault, anyway. "And maybe you deserve to get it dredged up every once in a while. Have you ever seen someone gutted, Your Majesty?"

"Eddie," Liz whispered warningly.

"Other than my wife?" Gerald snapped back.

"Yeah, other than her."

"No, thank goodness."

"I have. I've done it, and I've seen it done. It might not kill you right away, but not too many people would have the strength, or the presence of mind, to stab themselves in the heart afterwards."

Gerald was thoroughly puzzled. "Why are you telling me this?"

I looked at Opulora, but she nodded for me to continue. I think she was grateful not to have to expend the energy.

I said, "You've got things backwards, Your Majesty. Your wife killed herself with that knife to her heart. The other injuries came after."

I let that settle. "Someone *cut open* my dead wife?" he cried.

"Yeah," I said.

"But she was locked up alone in a secure tower. There was no one with her when she was found."

"That's all true," I said.

He looked genuinely distraught. "But . . . but who? *Why?*"

"The 'who' should be obvious. Who could get past your security?"

It took him a moment. Then, softly, he turned and looked at his sorceress. *"You,"* he breathed.

The room fell silent.

"Don't try to blame her," I said, my own anger starting to get the better of me. *"You* brought in Opulora based on her reputation. And she did what you paid her to do: She discovered the truth. Which was that you were in the throes of a jealous hissy fit. And *you* were the one who didn't believe her."

"Stop it," Ellis said. "This is cruel."

"Cruel?" I almost shouted. "Is it as cruel as making a ten-year-old boy think he has to rescue his mother from his father? Is it as cruel as his mother having to watch him fall to his death? Tell me about cruel again, King Ellis, I'm not sure I get it."

"Stop it!" Gerald cried, and sank to his knees.

I wasn't about to stop. "When your son died, the whole jealousy thing didn't matter anymore, did it? Your whole imaginary wounded pride meant nothing. There was no spider in your cup, was there?"

Gerald looked blasted. "No," he whispered, "there wasn't."

There was nothing for it now, but to drop the big sword, and to be honest, at that moment, I relished it. "Did you know your wife was pregnant when she died?"

Now Gerald just stared, speechless. So did everyone else, for that matter.

"Yes," I continued. "Not very far along, but definitely with child. She hadn't had a chance to tell you before all the trouble started. And then she died."

He began to truly cry. No one spoke or moved. I let the moment settle. Opulora nodded at me, tears on her own cheeks. I needed my next statement to have all the impact it could, because it was the bit that no one in their right mind would believe:

"Would you like to meet your daughter, Gerald?"

Several moments passed before that got through to everyone. The first to react, surprisingly, was Clancy. He said, "No *way*."

"Yes, way," I assured him.

Beatrice stepped in front of me and actually shoved me a little. "So what are you saying? You drop all these little hints; just come out and say what you mean."

"Okay," I agreed. "Isadora Glendower is also Princess Isidore of Mahnoma."

I'd never faced so many open mouths and wide eyes in my life. It left even Harry Lockett speechless, and that was something.

"Wait, wait, *wait* a minute," Beatrice said at last. "That's . . . I mean, that's *impossible*. You can cut a baby out of its mother if it's close to term, but—"

"It *is* possible," Opulora said. "I did it for Sylvia."

"*You!*" Gerald said, and lurched to his feet. He would've grabbed Opulora by the throat if both Ellis and Hector hadn't grabbed him. "You mutilated my wife's body, and let me spend *years* thinking she'd done it to herself!"

"I did what was necessary based on your actions, Your Majesty," Opulora said, chin high. "Had Sylvia told you, you would have probably accused your friend Ellis of being the father." Then to the group she said, "Your Majesty—Majesties—I assure you, Isidore *is* your daughter, Gerald. If you will come with me, I can explain how this is possible." She gestured at the others. "All of you, please. You all deserve to hear this."

"Why should we go anywhere with you?" Gerald said. "Why should we *trust* you?"

"Because if you don't, I will be gone in a blink, and none of you will ever see Isidore again."

"Then we have no choice, do we?" Gerald said.

"Not in this," Opulora agreed. "Not today."

chapter

TWENTY-SIX

Servants and courtiers stepped quickly aside as we strode through the hallways. I tried to map our progress, but the castle's geography seemed to change and alter behind us. I assumed it was something Opulora had done to keep people from straying into her chambers. Then I berated myself for accepting magic so easily. It was probably just basic strategy, using lots of turns and double-backs to disorient us.

Of course, the big magic was to come. If, that is, Opulora told the truth.

"My head hurts from all this twisting around," Harry said. "Hard to keep track of where we are."

I nodded at his ever-present stylus and vellum. "Are you making a map?"

"Of course. Second nature by now."

I hoped he was right, and that it would work if we needed it.

At last we came to a large double door. Below the handles, instead of a typical lock, was a flat crystal in a metal frame. Opulora put her right palm against it. It glowed, the same way the weapon-detecting crystal had done. When she removed her hand, something heavy and solid moved within the door, and she easily pulled it open.

She turned to face us. "No mortal but me has passed this threshold. Not king, nor beggar, not sprite nor troll. What lies within are singularities the likes of which you can scarce imagine."

"Drama much?" Jack muttered.

"I know it sounds ridiculous," Opulora said with a patient smile, "especially to a young man unfamiliar with magic and sorcery. Those skills are rare, and kept in the shadows for good reason. That's why I felt I should warn you."

"You said Isadora was here," Beatrice said.

"I did. And she is."

"Then at least one other mortal has passed this threshold."

Opulora said nothing. She pulled open one half of the big double door, and we entered.

The room seemed impossibly huge, the ceiling almost out of sight above, and the stone walls formed a vast circle big enough for an army to stand ready within. Only the room wasn't empty: far from it. It was filled with tables, cabinets, hanging platforms, and bookshelves. Glass bottles and other containers lined the shelves, and residue dripped from them had caked on the floor. There were cages, too, filled with some animals I recognized, but many I did not. Some hissed and snapped, while others simply stared, working claws or pincers as they decided whether or not we were edible. Oddly, there was no smell of rancid chemicals or animal dung; if anything, the place smelled faintly of vanilla.

"This is my sacred circle," Opulora said, gesturing around her. "Here, working on my own, I have discovered the secrets of life and death that nature and the gods try to keep to themselves. I apply my training and knowledge to the problems that afflict mankind, in the hope of finding solutions that may free us from our mortal shackles."

No one moved very far into the room, preferring to stay near the door. Liz took my hand and said quietly, "*Those* mortal shackles look perfect for stringing people up."

I followed her gaze to the row of chains hanging from a beam, an open wrist-sized manacle at the end of each. I couldn't be certain if the stains were rust, or blood. I did note that there were enough for all of us.

"That's a fine speech," Beatrice said, half angry and half astounded, "but what exactly do you *do* in here?"

"I look for answers," Opulora said.

Suddenly Clancy gasped and put his hands over his mouth. He pointed like a child confronted with something awful.

On a table, half-covered with a sheet, was man's corpse. The skin was cut open and peeled back, and the white ribs pointed up. The removed organs were in clear containers, floating in some preservative liquid. The expression on the dead man's face was almost beatific.

"By all the gods in the sky," Gerald said, appalled. "How many men have you killed in here?"

"Your Majesty, you do me a dishonor. No one has died in here. I do not trade in experiments on living men. This was a criminal who died in prison. He's been more use to the world here than he ever was in life. Through him, and others like him, I've learned techniques to save men. A fair trade, I'd think, for the life of a man who sowed only misery and destruction when he walked the earth."

"It's an obscenity!" Glendower said. "A man's body should be treated with respect."

"Maybe you should hold off on the judgment," I said, tired and annoyed by his sanctimonious tone. "I've seen how useful this kind of work is on the battlefield. More men live now than used to, even ten years ago, because of what women like this have learned and shared."

"Then the cost is too high," he sniffed.

"Tell that to their wives and children," I fired back. "You've never fought anything more vicious than a sheep."

"A ram can be pretty ornery," Clancy offered.

"Shut up, son," Glendower said. "Don't help me."

Before I could snap off a reply, Liz warningly squeezed my hand. She was right: This was not the time. I said, "We'll just have to agree to disagree, then."

"Where's Isadora?" Jack said, getting us all back on topic.

"Oh, yes," Opulora said. "The young lady of the hour." She nodded at his injured arm. "Is that broken?"

"Probably," he said. "It really hurt for a while. Now it's numb."

"You need to have it set, then. Otherwise it won't heal properly, and might never work right again."

"My arm can wait," Jack said. "Just take us to Izzy."

"Very well. Follow me."

When we moved away from the door, it swung shut on its own and slammed with a finality that we all noticed. If this was an elaborate setup to get rid of all her enemies at once, then I carried the blame for walking us right into her clutches.

"This is spooky," Liz whispered as we moved through the huge room, past tables and devices whose purposes may have been wholly scientific, but that nonetheless seemed like they could do a lot of damage to a human being. And the strange fluids bubbling in some of the pots and cauldrons gave off odors that, while faint, were not reassuring. "Who lives like this, surrounded by death?"

"You can't understand life, Miss Dumont," Opulora said, "until you know death. Would you appreciate the light without the dark?"

We entered an open space in the middle of the room. A ten-foot-high cylinder, five feet in diameter, rested under a shroud. Pipes ran under the fabric, adding and draining fluid. Soft bubbling came from it.

Opulora gazed reverently at it. "Your answer, my friends . . . is here."

She pulled a rope that dropped the shroud to the floor.

Beatrice cried out. It wasn't quite a scream, but it was close.

Inside the clear-sided tank floated Isadora. She was still unconscious, and her face was serene and peaceful just like the dissected man. But that wasn't the strangest part.

She was clad, not in the tattered formal dress she'd worn as Eolomea at the banquet, but in an elaborate court gown that slowly billowed in the gently bubbling liquid. It was identical to the one worn by the late Queen Sylvia in the painting.

"She's dead," Clancy said in his simple, flat way.

"No, she's not," Opulora said. "The spell that once saved her life is being replaced with one that will allow her to go on living."

"Get her out," Beatrice said in a small, trembling voice. Then it rose to a shriek. "Get her out! She's drowning! *Get her out!*"

"*No,*" Opulora repeated. "She has only a short time left. Then she will be returned to you. I swear on my own life."

I watched King Gerald. It hadn't been so obvious in life, but with her face passive and immobile, and dressed as she was, the resemblance to Sylvia was unmistakable. Just as I'd hoped when I suggested something like this in the dungeon.

Opulora smiled, the first true, wide smile I'd ever seen on her face. "I like your silence, Gerald. It shows off your wonder. But tell me, Your Majesty; *why* are you silent?"

He breathed in little shallow gasps. "This . . . this girl looks like . . . like . . ."

"Your late queen, and my best friend," Opulora finished. "As she should, being her daughter, and yours."

Gerald acted as if he didn't hear. "Her eyes, and her mouth . . . all as they were when we met, when we were so young."

"Okay, if nobody is going to ask, I will," Harry Lockett said. "Exactly what are you doing to her? And what did you do back when her mother died?"

Opulora took a moment to gather her thoughts. "What I did may seem like a miracle, but I assure you, it was simply applied science and magic, though very, very difficult. Sylvia died when Isidore was barely three months along. I removed her from Sylvia's body before the effects of her mother's death reached her. I had to do it quickly, and crudely, and for that I am sorry."

"But she was locked up alone in a secure cell," Harry said. "There was no one with her when she was found."

"That's all true," she said.

Gerald looked genuinely distraught. "But . . . but . . ."

"There's no way a baby could survive at that age," Beatrice said. "Absolutely not."

"She's right," Gerald said in a mutter that might've been meant only for himself. "You're a traitor, trying to drive me mad."

"Would you prefer to execute me without trial, then," Opulora said, "or would you care to know how it was done?"

"Oh, I think we'd all like to know that," Liz said.

Through all this, Gerald continued to stare at Isadora as she floated in the tank. Only Hector and I noticed. I couldn't tell what the king was thinking, and that little glimpse of Crazy Jerry had me on edge. I wished I had more than my boot knife in case things got chaotic again.

Opulora led us to another door set into the curved wall. Again she pressed her palm to a glowing crystal, and the bolt drew somewhere on the other side. The new room beyond was dark, and the air that came out was cool and stale, as if it had been closed off for a long time.

Opulora snapped her fingers and lamps flared to life within.

"Can you teach anyone to do that?" Jack asked.

"Anyone who spends five years learning to speak the language of fire," Opulora said, and led us inside.

This room was also high-roofed, but much smaller. Far less sorcery-related stuff filled it, and what was here was neatly cleaned, dried, and put away. Most odd were the walls, whitewashed to a semblance of almost cheeriness, with framed paintings of bright flowers and friendly animals, along with a wide window that, during the day, would fill the place with light.

Before us stood a long table. Containers that once held liquids were all over it, either sitting alone or in metal racks and braces that held them at various angles. All were connected by tubes and funnels to a washboard-sized tank in the middle, raised on a platform so that braziers could be used under it. Whatever went in the tank, then, had to be kept warm, with many varied chemicals added at different times. And against the wall, neatly made up with pink blankets, pillows, and even a stuffed bear, was a baby's cradle.

I ran my finger along one table edge. Dust coated everything, not from neglect, but the light kind that only occurs over time in sealed chambers.

"Is this where you brew your own ale?" Clancy asked. "I've seen a setup like this before."

"Not exactly," Opulora said. She put a hand reverently on the central tank. "This is where I saved Isidore's life."

No one had any response to that.

"A mother's body provides everything a growing child needs," Opulora continued. "When Sylvia, in her despair at her son's death, stabbed herself in the heart, it should have also killed Isidore. But I removed the tiny baby, no bigger than my palm, and brought her here. I sacrificed some of my life to help her survive until I was able to make all this ready. This . . . mechanical womb nurtured her, and allowed her to grow until she was ready to breathe our air and take her own nourishment."

I eased to one side of the group, ostensibly to get a better look at the table. In doing so, I caught Hector's eye. I cut my own eyes toward Gerald; he nodded. He was as ready as anyone could be in the presence of someone who might be crazy, but then it occurred to me that he might not necessarily be on our side. After all, Gerald paid his salary.

Jack was a wild card, too: if he perceived danger to his girlfriend, he might also do something stupid. Youth and insanity weren't that far apart. I had a lot to keep my eyes on.

And something, some tiny detail, didn't add up. I struggled furiously to dredge it from my mind.

Opulora ran her hand reverently along the edge of the tank. "But when she was born from this, she was still in great danger. You, Gerald, were mad with grief for both your wife and son. I could not risk how you might react if I told you of Isidore. So I determined to send her to safety. I chose Kyle Antigonus, your trusted horse-master. He was a very learned man under the straw and manure; it was the secret of his skill with your horses. I sent him off with no destination, only an instruction to find a home where she would be loved until it was safe for her to return. When the time was right, I had a means to find her. But there were things I couldn't anticipate. My dear Kyle vanished, killed by a bear, as I've only recently learned. And for years, I assumed Isidore had died as well."

She closed her eyes and seemed about to pass out. She recovered before anyone else noticed.

"She lived because of the spell I'd placed on her, literally. I'd engraved the mark on the flesh of her back. But as she grew, the mark spread, and faded, and I knew that what I'd done would not last. I had to find her again, to repair and replace my initial work, if she was to live."

She looked at me. "Then Mr. LaCrosse came along and did what my magic could not do."

For a long moment no one else spoke. Then Clancy walked

up and peered into the tank. "Was Izzy really born from this?" he asked, the tank giving his words a metallic echo.

"She was," Opulora said. "I'm sorry such a hard and un-yielding womb nurtured her, but there was no other choice. I assure you, though, she was conceived in love, by her mother and father."

"*I'm* her mother," Beatrice said. "Let's not forget that, okay?"

"Wait," I said. Suddenly I knew what was wrong.

I turned to Gerald. "When we were here before, you mentioned that you'd hired sword jockeys to look for something. I thought it was Isadora, but you didn't know about her then. So what was it?"

Gerald started to speak, then thought better of it.

"So you *did* know about Isadora all along?" I pressed.

"No," he said. "I did not."

"Then what did you hire sword jockeys to find?"

"He believed," Opulora said, "that perhaps his son had merely been kidnapped and another child's body substituted in his place. He thought he could find the perpetrators." She shook her head sadly.

"No," he said with sudden venom. "That's what I told *you*, to put you off the scent. I really wanted to find out where *you* came from, and why you took over my kingdom. And I did."

He faced the rest of us, a leer of smug satisfaction. "She was born the daughter of a whore in Calamus. That's how she met Sylvia: she was a servant, a disgusting little scullery maid, but she was the same age as Sylvia, and they became friends. Then, when she came into womanhood, she was sold to a sorcerer, not as an apprentice, but as a concubine."

Opulora's haughtiness faltered. "I had no choice in the matter, Your Majesty. I was a child. I was *property*."

He ignored her. "She used the power all women have over men to learn the sorcerer's secrets, then she sealed him away in a cave, neither living nor dead. Isn't that true, Opulora?"

"Your Majesty, my past is irrelevant. I have served you faithfully—"

"So you say," he continued, clearly building toward something. "But you were run out of Sorwind, weren't you? For doing something so vile, it can still scarcely be believed. Tatterhead was no freak of nature, was he? He was *your pet project*. You created him from pieces of dead bodies, imbued him with life just as you did this unborn girl, then when he turned out to be less than what you thought, you cast him out. Am I wrong?"

"That," she said, "was many years ago. And later I sought him out, reclaimed him, and tried to civilize him. To correct my mistake. And the skills I learned creating Tatterhead were the same ones that allowed me to save your daughter."

"But Tatterhead can't be civilized, can he? He's not human. Any more than that girl floating in there!" In that instant he became, without a doubt, Crazy Jerry. His voice now shrill, he continued, "Whatever she is, she's a monster just as much as Tatterhead ever was." He pointed an accusing through the open door. "She bears the face of my late queen, and that sort of sacrilege will not stand. She, and you, are both guilty of treason and I intend to see you both hang for it." He turned and glared at the rest of us. "Along with all your accomplices. Hector, arrest them all!"

That put Hector in an uncomfortable position, since he was outnumbered, and at least two of us, Ajax and me, were pros like him. "Uhm, Your Majesty, maybe we should—"

"Then you hang, too!" Gerald said. "All of you! I charge you all with treason, and I find you all guilty!"

"Gerald," Ellis said calmly as he stepped forward, "please. There's no need for this. It's an unusual situation, to be sure, but it's nothing we can't work out. Two kings should be able to handle anything, shouldn't we?" He smiled and put a hand on his friend's shoulder.

Gerald stared for another moment; then the light of madness slowly faded. He took a deep breath, closed his eyes, and blew it slowly out. "You're right," he said with a chuckle. "A pair of kings are indeed a rare resource, and—"

The sly bastard. Once he had us off guard, he snatched a metal beaker stand from the table and ran back into the main room, right past us all. I grabbed for him, but felt only the brush of his expensive and stylish clothes as he passed.

"Stop him!" Opulora yelled. But before any of us could, he threw the beaker stand hard at the tank holding Isadora. It shattered, and the thick liquid gushed forth, carrying the girl's limp body with it.

Whatever the fluid inside the tank had been, it was slippery and tripped Gerald as he tried to run. Hector and I quickly secured the king, while Liz, Opulora, and Beatrice rushed to pick up Isadora where she had sloshed against a table.

"Kill her!" Gerald cried as we tried to hold him back. "She's a monster! *Kill her!*" I didn't know which woman he meant, the sorceress or his own miraculous daughter.

Beatrice picked up Isadora, who was as limp as she'd been on our ride here. Liz pushed the vials, beakers, and racks off the table. The noise was deafening, and echoed from the distant ceiling. "Lay her down here," Liz said.

"Carefully!" Opulora added.

Gerald began to shake, then convulse. It took all my strength, and probably most of Hector's, to hold the writhing monarch between us, especially with the floor now slippery beneath our boots. "Guards!" the king cried at the top of his voice. *"Guards!"*

Then Owen Glendower, the last person I'd expect this from,

stepped up and slapped Gerald so hard, I worried that he'd broken the king's neck. The rich shepherd's face was red with anger, and his voice trembled as he said, "I don't care who you are, or what kingdom you rule, how *dare* you attack my grand-daughter? If this is how you behave, then I thank whatever gods you care to invoke that she came to us and didn't stay with you." He turned, and sobbed when he saw the the girl's lifeless head loll to one side.

Opulora darted around the room, gathering things from other tables. "She's drowning," I said to myself; she'd missed the diagnostic forest for the trees, and no one else seemed to notice, either. I yelled, "Hey! She's drowning! Ajax, take over for me here!"

When he did, I rushed to the table, sliding the last couple of feet, and grabbed Isadora. The formal gown, soaked with the gummy fluid, made her weigh as much as me. I tossed her legs over my shoulder so that she hung facedown, and shook her until thick liquid dripped from her mouth and nose. When it stopped, I put her back down and said, "Liz!"

Liz knew what to do. She began bending Izzy's legs, push-ing them up so that it forced her lungs to contract and ex-pand. I pinched her nose shut and blew hard into her mouth. It was something I'd learned from a moon priestess on a sea-side battlefield, where injured men were as likely to drown from falling face-first into the surf as they were from their sword wounds. Unfortunately, it only worked on one man out of five, and I'd never tried it on a woman before.

With a gargling cough, Izzy spit a mouthful of liquid di-rectly into my mouth, which made me choke and fall back. My boots slid on the wet floor and I landed on my butt. Izzy gagged and sputtered some more, then winced and said raggedly, "Guys, I *really* need to pee."

After a stunned moment of silence, we all—except Gerald, of course—began to laugh. Hard. The kind of uncontrollable laughter that comes when you've narrowly avoided disaster.

Losing this girl had become such a terror to us all that our relief overwhelmed us.

Beatrice helped the girl sit up on the edge of the table. "It's okay, honey, I'm right here. You'll be all right." She hugged her daughter fiercely, unconcerned with the slimy liquid soaked into the gown.

Jack grabbed Isadora's arm with his good hand. "Will she?" he asked, his voice high and trembling, hope battling with fear.

"I need to do one more thing," Opulora said. She gently shouldered Beatrice aside and took Isadora's chin firmly in her hand. She shoved one of the glowing glass balls into the girl's mouth. Isadora gagged again, but the ball seemed to dissolve into her tongue. She spit, scrunched up her face, and said, "Man, not to be crude, but that tastes like sheep ass."

Jack laughed. "You kiss your mother with that mouth?"

"I kiss you with that mouth, smart guy. I'm a farm girl, remember?"

Opulora said, with visible relief, "She's fine. For good."

Gerald made a noise halfway between a shriek and a growl, twisted away from his minders, and snatched a dagger from Hector's belt. I tried to grab him, but from my position on the floor, my fingertips only brushed his leg.

He flung himself at Isadora; the wet slicing sound as he drove the knife into her was clear in the silent chamber.

Isadora said, softly, "Umph!"

Jack screamed, *"No!"* Beatrice just screamed.

Isadora and Gerald, with similar looks of confusion and surprise, both looked down at the blade protruding from her belly. Then Isadora slid off the table and fell to her knees on the floor.

Hector and I pulled Gerald back, and Ajax put his sword to the king's throat. No one questioned his etiquette.

Jack helped Isadora stand. The blood was vivid, and seemingly everywhere. The king had cut something vital.

"He *stabbed* me," Isadora said in disbelief, and clutched the table edge for support.

"Here, let me," Jack said, and reached for the knife.

"Don't pull it out!" Opulora cried. "She'll bleed even more. Get her back on the table, carefully."

As Jack, using his good arm, helped Beatrice lift the girl, Gerald began to shake, then convulse. "Guards!" he cried at the top of his voice. *"Guards!"* But as before, no one answered his call.

Jack glared at Gerald with all the hatred he could muster in his young, sheltered life. Even Harry had lost his professional distance, and no longer took notes.

I didn't even remember getting to my feet, but I had my boot knife at Opulora's throat. "Save her," I said, my voice faint and tight. When I looked at the girl's drawn face on the table, I saw in my mind the tiny scrunched-up countenance of the baby she'd once been: the baby who'd trusted me implicitly to keep her safe.

Opulora looked genuinely scared, but not necessarily of me. She said, "I can't—"

"No sentence I want to hear right now begins with those words," I said.

"All right," she said. "I'll save her. You're right—this is all because of me, anyway."

I put away my knife.

Opulora bent over Izzy and pushed the goopy hair from her face. "Try not to hold your breath," she said gently.

"Let me stick a knife in you and see how well you breathe," Izzy shot back.

"If she dies—," Jack said, his voice shaking.

"If she dies, it's the will of all the gods in the sky!" Gerald shrieked.

"She won't die," Opulora said calmly. She closed her eyes, and the lids fluttered as she whispered something. She put both hands flat on Isadora's stomach, the blade sandwiched between them. The gooey tank fluid, now stained red, oozed out between her fingers. "Pull out the dagger," she said sepulchrally.

I reached for the hilt.

"No," she said, her eyes still shut. "It has to be him."

"Who?" Jack demanded.

"You. It has to be the hand of love to give life."

Jack grabbed the hilt with his left hand and took a deep breath. But when Izzy hissed in agony, he couldn't do it. More blood seeped around Opulora's hands, the heavy red kind you only bleed when you're dying.

"Oh, come on, you big baby," Isadora said through her teeth. "Grow a pair, will you?"

Jack smiled wryly, took a deep breath, and with one slow, smooth motion, withdrew the blade.

Isadora doubled up and grunted, the sound somehow conveying more pain than even the loudest scream. Opulora pressed down with all her strength, and more blood squirted up between her fingers. Again she whispered something I didn't catch. Then she pulled her bloody hands away.

Through the rend made in the gown, Isadora's skin was soaked with blood as well. But the injury was entirely gone.

The girl collapsed back on the table, gasping. Jack dropped the dagger to the floor.

Gerald also went limp except for the great gulps of air that racked his body. Suddenly he wrenched free of Ajax and Hector and bolted for the back of the room, where I saw another door, this one without a crystal lock. He slid into the wall on greasy boots, then opened it and dashed through.

I reacted without thinking, because hell, thinking hadn't done me much good so far. I ran after him, calling back, "Wait here, all of you!"

chapter

TWENTY-EIGHT

The door opened into a spiral stairwell. I heard Gerald above me, his slippery boots loud and wet on the stone. I raced to catch up, my own footing uncertain.

The steps were worn and crumbled with age, and cobwebs clung to the walls. Dust stirred by Gerald's passing filled the air and made my eyes water. My legs and back protested this exertion, and I dearly wished I'd thought to grab Hector's sword.

"Gerald?" I yelled up. "You can run, but you'll just get caught tired. Gerald?"

I listened, and thought I heard distant footsteps.

"This is stupid, Your Majesty. You're the king, you can't just *hide* somewhere! If you can hear me, wait a minute before you do anything. I just want to talk to you, not drag you back."

Hinges creaked somewhere above, followed by a loud slam. I climbed as hard as I could, and found that the stairs went straight up to the ceiling, where a wooden hatch had been flung aside. Moonlight streamed through the opening. I paused long enough to catch my breath, then went through.

I emerged onto a tower roof. It was about thirty feet across and completely flat, with no battlements or railings. The only way up or down were the stairs I'd just climbed. Above me the sky was clear, and a bright moon lit the area. The night wind blew steadily, just hard enough to constantly remind you that you were far above the ground with slippery feet. And it was cold—my clothes had soaked up enough tank juice so that the breeze made my teeth chatter.

Gerald stood at the edge of the roof, looking down at the courtyard a hundred feet below. A strong gust would send him right over the edge.

I said, "Your Majesty, why don't you back up a few steps? Heights make me nervous, and your boots must be as slick as mine."

He looked over his shoulder at me. I couldn't make out his face. He said calmly, "I should've done this the day my wife and son died, and let Mahnoma start over with a clean slate. It couldn't be much worse than it is now."

"Don't be hasty," I said. I swear I felt the tower sway beneath me, and I had the urge to drop to all fours, maybe flat on my stomach. "I've seen kingdoms where that's happened. Everything usually gets burned down, and that 'clean slate' costs a lot of lives. You've got some chaos, sure, but nothing a strong royal hand can't straighten out."

"How can I face them? How can 'Crazy Jerry' command any respect now? I just tried to kill a defenseless girl."

"Yeah, you did," I agreed. "But at least she's okay. Thanks to the very sorceress you imprisoned, I should point out. You're really not a very good judge of people."

"That's truth," he said with a cold, self-mocking laugh. "I can be lied to with impunity. I can be manipulated and flattered. And I *know* it, which is the worst part. I can just . . . never see it coming."

I eased toward him. I couldn't make a grab for him unless I got him away from the edge. "Tell me something. What made you think your wife was unfaithful?"

He sobbed once, then choked it down. "You really want to know?"

Another step closer. I hoped Opulora was right about my skill in getting people to talk. "I think it's important that *you* know."

"He made her laugh. Ellis did. She never laughed for me. She never found my jokes funny. She never laughed with delight when I came into the room, the way she did with him." Then he genuinely began to cry. "I wanted to humiliate her, for the way she made me feel. I wanted to humiliate *him,* for helping her do it. I imagined the two of them laughing at how easy it was to make me jealous. See, I knew they weren't really having an affair, they were just *pretending* to, to make a fool of me! Or at least, that's what I told myself."

I was within arms' reach now, but that was also close enough to either miss, or send us both over the edge. I said, "Gerald, do you know what it means to see the spider in your cup?"

Tears and snot glimmered in the moonlight, and his face was contorted with emotional agony. "The what?"

"The spider in your cup," I said more distinctly.

"Yes, I know that the poison supposedly doesn't work unless you see the spider. But that's just a tale, isn't it? Poison doesn't really work that way."

Now that I had his attention, I discreetly slid back and spoke just softly enough that he had to lean toward me to hear. "It did with you, Gerald. You drank and saw the spider, right there in the mirror. The spider is *you.*"

He began to cry again. He wasn't one of those dignified criers, either. His whole face and body contorted with sorrow and self-pity.

"But it's not the end of the world," I continued, and felt a twinge through the scar over my heart. "Something similar happened to me once, a long time ago. I ignored it and denied it, too, until it almost chewed me up inside. But eventually I worked through it."

"How?" he sobbed, and took a step closer to me, away from the edge.

That was enough. I grabbed him by his expensive tunic and threw him to the ground, then jumped on him and wrapped my arms around him, pinning his arms to his side. I did my best to hold him there against the stone despite our mutual slipperiness.

"No!" he shrieked, kicking and screaming like a child. "No, let me go! *Let me go!*"

"Stop it!" I said.

"I don't want to go through this anymore!" he yelled. "I just want it all to *end!*"

He fought the way only a desperate man could fight, but he didn't have any stamina, so he quickly wore himself out. He finally collapsed, sobbing and beating the stone with his fists. I held him down until I was sure it wasn't another bluff, the way he'd done with Hector and Ajax.

I crawled off him and awkwardly patted him on the back. "Just get it out, Your Majesty," I said. "Just get it out."

And he did. I was embarrassed for us both, but sixteen years of repressed guilt and grief was bound to be ugly. It took a while, but eventually his sobs slackened, and he lay face-down, breathing heavily and whimpering.

"It's okay," I said. "It's all going to be all right."

"No," he said, wiping his nose like a child. "It'll never be all right. How can I look at any of them, ever again? I'd have to kill them all."

"I don't think that would send the right message."

He sat cross-legged, and I did the same, ready to tackle him again if he made for the edge. He wiped his eyes and said, "Why do *you* care about all this, anyway? It's not your kingdom. You're not part of Ellis's court, or mine. Why are you *here*?"

"Because a brave man once died saving a little baby girl, but before he did, he asked me to help her, too. And I did. You know what's funny about that, Jerry? Although I barely knew her for a day, that little baby girl claimed a place in my heart. And even though she's no longer a baby, I wasn't about to let anyone hurt her again for their own selfish reasons. Not even a king."

He wiped his face again. He looked smaller now, and more frail, as if all the nervous insanity that had built up in him had been exorcised. And maybe it had. "You know what, Jerry? You need someone to talk to. A friend, or a wife, or even a dog. I think you keep to yourself too much."

"I'm the king," he said. "Who can I talk to?"

"You used to be friends with Ellis. At least he also knows how heavy a crown can be."

He looked at me for a long moment. "You don't talk like a sword jockey. Anyone ever told you that?"

"Not once they got my bill," I assured him.

WE sat on the roof and talked about nothing in particular for a long time. Then Liz poked her head through the open hatch and said cautiously, "Hello?"

I waved. "Over here."

She came up onto the roof, then hunched down when she realized how high and exposed we were. "Are railings against the law here?"

"This is actually the execution platform for high-ranking prisoners," Gerald said. "Allowing them to jump off on their own supposedly lets them maintain their dignity. Truthfully, if the family stories are to be believed, most of them dropped dead on the climb up. Royals aren't usually in the best shape."

Liz sat down beside us, careful to stay out of Gerald's reach.

"I was elected to come see if you two were okay. It's been a while."

"No," Gerald said. "Far from it. But I won't get any more okay sitting up here in the dark, will I? And you're right, Mr. LaCrosse, it *is* cold."

He stood and offered Liz a hand up. She took it warily.

When we got back to the laboratory, it reeked of smoke. The first thing I saw was a body on the wet floor, covered with a blanket. A quick head count told me who it was: Opulora.

"She just . . . died," Beatrice said. "Almost as soon as you left. She just dropped, without a word. And then all her books burst into flame and burned themselves to ashes."

The remains on the shelves confirmed this. The secrets that created Tatterhead, and saved Isadora, were now lost.

When they saw Gerald, Hector and Ajax drew their swords and stepped in front of him. "I'm sorry, Your Majesty," said Hector, "but it's not safe for you here."

"You mean it's not safe for anyone else, having me here," Gerald corrected. There was a weary wisdom in his demeanor that I'd never seen before. "You're right, Hector. Feel free to guard me."

I knelt and pulled the cloth back from Opulora's face. She looked impassive in death, the lines of age and strain faded to the kind of serene beauty she must have possessed in youth, when she became friends with a future queen. I lowered the cloth and said, "She used up her life to save Izzy's."

"What?" Isadora said.

"You were mortally wounded. I could tell it, and I bet Hector and Ajax could, too. She gave you enough of her life to heal the wound, just like she did to keep you alive when you were unborn. But this time, it was more than she could spare."

"Oh, my God," Isadora said, and her eyes grew wet. "There was so much I wanted to say to her, to ask her—"

"That's the worst thing about this world," Gerald said.

"People can be gone in the blink of an eye. And we never get to say what we should."

Gerald and Isadora looked at each other and their eyes met for the first time. Something passed between them; I couldn't say what, or where it would ultimately lead, but there was now a connection where there hadn't been before.

Man, I was tired of these people. Not that I disliked them, but I just wanted to not have their problems on my head anymore. "Look, I don't think we have any more secrets to reveal here, do we? We're all clear on who did what, when they did it, and why, right? Right." Liz came over and put her arms around me. I wanted to go to sleep right then, with her holding me.

"So," Clancy said, "what happens now?"

Isadora wrung goop for her gown. "I want a bath."

"Someone should bury Opulora," Hector said.

"Yes," Gerald agreed. "She may not have been a citizen, but she sacrificed herself for Mahnoma. She will be interred with all honor in the Tomb of Heroes. And then, Princess Isidore will be introduced to her people. Followed, it appears, by preparations for a royal wedding that will unite Mahnoma and Altura for generations to come." He smiled at Ellis.

"Let's just wait a minute," Jack said. "You're all talking about Izzy like she's not here. Shouldn't we ask her what *she* wants to do?"

Gerald said, "You're quite right, Prince John. My dear, my . . . daughter: Would you prefer to be announced as the princess of Mahnoma, or as the future queen of Altura?"

Still wet and sticky from her time in the tank, she looked like a bedraggled doll. "So my choices," she said at last, choosing her words carefully, "are between staying here and being a princess by birth, or going back to Altura and being a princess by marriage?" She looked at me for confirmation.

"Those are two of your choices," I said.

"There's no 'choice' to your royal blood," Gerald said. "You are Princess Isidore, and this is your kingdom."

"And as either visiting princess or prospective daughter-in-law, you'll be welcome in Altura," Ellis said.

Harry Lockett stood poised to mark down her words. Even Liz and I held our breath.

"I think," she said slowly, "that until I have time to ponder all this in detail, I just want to go back to being the grand-daughter of the richest sheep farmer in Mummerset." She moved over to stand between Beatrice and Clancy. "And the daughter of his eldest child. I can't change where I came from, but I can determine where I'm going. I'm no one's property, and no one's slave. I choose for myself." She smiled. "Jack, do you still want to be a sheep farmer's boyfriend?"

"More than I want to be a prince. No offense, Dad."

Ellis said nothing; if he was bothered, he knew enough to keep it to himself at that moment.

"You will always be welcome here," Gerald said, too worn out for a new disappointment to register. "I know you may find that hard to believe, and I don't blame you for being a bit skeptical. But I hope one day I may be honored with your presence, and learn more about you . . . Isadora."

"So that settles everything," I said with genuine relief. "All the secrets are out. Everyone now knows who everyone else is, and where everyone else is going. Is there anything we haven't cleared up?"

"I plan to track down Billy Cudgel and settle accounts with him," Jack said. "I don't care what rock he hides under, I'll find him."

"He's here," I said.

"He is?"

"He showed up out of the blue and helped me get past the guards at the city gate. He got arrested."

"He totally convinced me that he was my friend. I need to look him in the eye and tell him I'm on to him. That when he gets out, I don't want him sniffing around Altura for a royal handout."

"Where would they take him?" I asked Hector.

"The city jail, most likely," he said.

Jack turned to me. "Would you come with me?"

"Me? Why?"

"Billy can be charming. Very charming. I'd like somebody there who's immune to that."

"As long as there's no Devil's Dew involved," Liz said. There was some laughter.

"And while you're doing that," Beatrice said, "we'll be washing up and getting ready to go back home. Right?"

"Right, Mom," Izzy said.

I watched Gerald closely for any sign of incipient Crazy Jerry–ness. He seemed like a beaten man, too weary to manage another outburst, but who knew how long that would last? Yet hopefully admitting the truth about himself, even to someone like me, had let off some of the pressure he'd let build for sixteen years.

"Go on with Jack and Hector," Ajax said quietly. "I'll take care of things here." He gave Gerald a significant steely-eyed warning glare.

"And I'll make sure he does," Liz said.

I nodded, then followed Hector and Jack out of Opulora's hidden laboratory. And it only took us half an hour to find another part of the castle that Hector recognized. Was that Opulora's final little joke?

HECTOR and the scruffy jailer led me and Jack through the cell block. Each cell held multiple prisoners, many of them drunks. The smell of vomit, urine, and body odor hung heavy in the air. Somewhere a drunk cried.

We reached one of the last cells, and the jailer put the key in the lock. Three other slovenly men stood aside as we entered, and Hector eyeballed each of them, alerting them to what would happen if they got cute.

Billy slept on the pile of straw in the back. He did not

awaken as we approached. The jailer nudged him with his foot. "Hey. Fat man. You've got visitors."

Billy's head lolled in an absolutely unmistakable way.

Hector and I exchanged a glance. He knew it, too. So did the jailer, who drew his long knife and backed the three prisoners into the corner. "All right, you murdering cowards, who did this? Tell me now and you'll be the one who doesn't hang for this!"

I knelt and turned Billy onto his back. His face was half purple, where the blood had settled while his corpse remained on his side. His swollen tongue also protruded slightly between his teeth.

One of the other prisoners screamed when he saw it. The scream was picked up along the cell block, mockingly and with delight. I checked Billy, but found no sign of injury.

"No one killed him," I said. "At least, not with anything obvious." I suppose there was a slight chance he might've been poisoned, but it seemed far more likely that the terror of finally facing the consequences of his actions had stopped his heart as surely as any weapon or venom. For a man used to talking his way out of things, there could be no worse fate.

"The fat lying bastard," Jack muttered. Yet he said it with such compassion that I checked to see if he was crying. He wasn't, but when he knelt and kissed the dead man on the forehead, I heard one of the other prisoners sniffle.

chapter

TWENTY-NINE

We journeyed back to Mummerset in the company of the
Glendowers and Altura's royalty, with promises to visit
Mahnoma again in the near future. Gerald also assured Ellis
he would pay an official social call to the Alturan court in the
very near future. We passed back through Illyria, but no one
knew what had become of Tatterhead, or Viola, who'd apparently accompanied him of her own free will. I hoped they
found some peace, wherever they ended up.

That first night back at Glendower's Aerie, Isadora asked
to speak with me privately. We met in the same room in which
she'd earlier pulled a crossbow on me. Once the door was shut,
she said, "I haven't properly thanked you for saving my life.
Repeatedly, it seems." She rose on her toes and kissed my
cheek. "Thank you."

"That's okay."

She was dressed simply, in a tunic and trousers, with riding
boots and her hair pulled back. I knew she'd just returned

from a no doubt chaste riding excursion with Jack. She looked fresh and beautiful and not at all like a princess. She said, "You seem like a very sophisticated man. You've experienced a lot, and not very much catches you off guard."

If only that were true, I thought, but I said, "Part of my job."

"What do *you* think I should do?"

"I can't answer that for you."

"No, but you can give me your opinion. I have no idea how to be a princess. What do they *do,* anyway?"

"They provide a face for the royal family, a promise of the future, and an heir when it's time."

Her lip curled in a slight, ironic smile. "I see. And what do they do the *other* twenty-three hours of the day?"

"Truthfully, not much. But Mahnoma could stand a little of your stability and good sense, and it would give you experience for when you become queen of Altura. The question is, why would you *want* to do it?"

"Because . . . it's my blood?"

"Blood isn't what makes families. Only love can do that. You should understand that by now."

"Then . . . because it's the right thing to do?"

"Is that a good enough reason to dedicate your life to something?"

She pursed her lips in amusement. "You're supposed to help me clarify things, not make them more complicated."

"It *is* complicated, honey."

She thought this over. "All right. I'll just have to keep thinking, then. There's no immediate crisis that requires a decision."

"That's probably the best thing. And if you need another sounding board, your mom is one of the smartest, toughest women I know."

She stepped closer. "May I ask you something personal? Why didn't you stay with her back then?"

"I wasn't the person I am now."

"Was she?"

"Yeah, pretty much." We both laughed at that.

"You could've been my father," she said.

"I know. That's crossed my mind, too. But I can't imagine how you could've turned out any better."

She smiled shyly, and her cheeks flushed at the compliment. "Your wife is a lucky woman, Mr. LaCrosse."

"I'll tell her you said that."

As I went to rejoin the others, Harry Lockett waylaid me in the hall. "What were you and the princess talking about?" he asked.

"Off the record?" I said.

"Of course not."

"Then we were talking about the price of wool."

He laughed. "You're a fascinating guy, LaCrosse. I think it might be fun to sit down with you sometime and get your life story."

"I can't think of anything more dull."

"Are you kidding? The two times I've crossed paths with you, you've had beautiful princesses underfoot, strange beasts tearing up the countryside, and elaborate plots you've had to unravel. That sort of thing is gold to someone like me."

"Maybe when I'm old and retired."

"I'll hold you to that," he said.

A week later, Liz and I drove her wagon away from Mummerset. There were hugs, hearty handshakes, and yes, tears. But Beatrice told Clancy to get a hold of himself.

When we reached the forest, she said, "Well, that vacation was exhausting. I can't wait to get back to my routine in Neceda, so I can get some rest."

"At least everyone's where they want to be now," I said.

"Except Opulora. And Billy Cudgel."

"Wow, you're really seeing the bright side of everything, aren't you?"

Sunlight that got through the leaves sparkled in her eyes. She said, "I'm sorry, I *am* being a downy clowny."

"If you ever use that term again, I'm leaving you," I said mock-gravely.

She smiled. "There's a lot of happiness back there, but it's built on a foundation of tragedy. I mean, Gerald's queen and prince are still dead. It was a long time ago, but it counts in the tally, doesn't it?"

"Interesting observation."

"I asked Izzy what she was going to do about Mahnoma. She said, 'Blood isn't all that matters.' Do you believe that's right?"

"Yes, I do," I said with certainty, secretly delighted to be paraphrased. "I *know* it's right."

"Because of people like Duncan Tew?"

The bitter teenage son of a pirate and a barmaid, both of whom abandoned him for selfish reasons, had managed to get a toehold on maturity during a particularly rugged sea voyage. I'd pointed the way, but he'd made the journey. "Partly. Partly because of myself. I drank and saw the spider, too."

"When Janet was killed?"

"Yeah. I was convinced that because she died, the world was cold, and evil, and that it was okay to take what I wanted. It took me almost as long as it did Gerald to get past it." I didn't envy him the dreams he'd have for the rest of his life, either. The nightmares were easy: they scared you, and you woke up. It was the other dreams, the ones where the people you loved were still alive, with all the emotions that entailed, and when you woke up you had to accept their loss all over again. No matter how happy you became, you never completely outran those.

"There never really is a spider, is there?" Liz said. "I mean, there's nothing to that story. Whether or not a poison works has nothing to do with seeing the source, right?"

"Right. The spider is only in their mind. Like Gerald's jealousy."

"But the web can cover a lot of ground," Liz said sadly. "And a lot of time."

"You're mixing your metaphors," I pointed out.

"Yeah, well, your royal roots are showing."

"Not royal."

"Then what?"

"I'm just a sword jockey with a big vocabulary."

"Not only a vocabulary," she said with a wink. "Want to find an inn and do some more interrogating?"

"You bet. I've got tons of secrets."

We continued on, laughing and enjoying each other's company. It was a beautiful day, and the sun shone through the trees like the bright promise of a future. It shone for Mahnoma and Altura, too: a joint future, inextricably linked, as they should have been all along. No spiders in anyone's cups anymore.